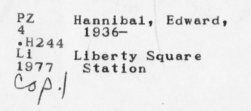

DATE			

Liberty Square Station

Liberty Square Station

EDWARD HANNIBAL

G.P. Putnam's Sons, New York

PZ
4
.H244
Li
1977
Cop. 1

SBN: 399-12058-0

Library of Congress Cataloging in Publication Data

Hannibal, Edward, 1936-
  Liberty Square Station.

  I. Title.
PZ4.H244Li   [PS3558.A477]   813'.5'4   77-21868

PRINTED IN THE UNITED STATES OF AMERICA

TO MAGGIE

*The author wishes to extend special acknowledgment
to Mary Ellen Twomey
and to Judith and Lief Hope.*

One

Angie waited until the last possible minute to deliver her stunner. Harry was flying American, Kennedy to Phoenix, on a Saturday morning in spring. She and the kids drove him there in their black Rambler Classic: their "undercover cop car." They drank coffees and sodas on snack bar stools. Constance and Jake corralled Amy, Kate and Dennis Trowbridge after Harry had kissed them all and spoke his buck-up good-byes and Angie walked with him to the opening of the long, NASA-looking corridor leading to his gate. Final call had sounded and he'd have to run. She'd take them to the observation deck to watch his jet taxi and soar away. She kissed and hugged him, then said, "Tro ... I hate my life." It was a line they'd got from Cassavetes' film *Faces*. He knew she didn't mean it literally; it was a code phrase with them meaning *serious trouble*. She said, "While you're gone, think real hard about us, will you? It's going wrong and I'm down and scared as hell."

He felt shot by a sniper using a silencer. He dropped his carry-on bag and said, "Fuck this, I'm not going."

She stiff-armed him gently away. "Go!" Her eyes were dry and clear but not cold. All he could do was pick up the bag, turn and run. The corridor was a drawn perspective, like railroad tracks, like desert highway, like the echoing entrance tube to a spaceship.

From then to the end of his job, he lived in a constant state of keen, conflicting passions, on the razor's edge of outward joy and inward pain. For weeks only work gave him relief, work that ended each day to leave him straddling the same precarious rock; he assumed that Angie at home was experiencing the same anguish, but that hardly helped. Harry sensed that he should know what had hit him, and in a nebulous way he did but found himself utterly incapable of gathering it into a specific, or, for God's sake, nailing it down and *naming* it! And if he couldn't do that, what the Christ was he supposed to *do* about it?

This job was supposed to have been Harry's long-sought "big break." It was an ad campaign for a new kind of soft drink one of the giant cola companies was planning to introduce. "Just what America's crying for, right?" he'd cracked to Angie, but in truth he was excited, and she seemed to be, too. Some figure in excess of a quarter of a million had already been spent in market research, product development, naming, and package and logo design. Now they were ready to make ads. It was still Woodstock and Flower People time, and the target audience was the Young. Prevalent strategy in the category, as with beer, was to show mythical Americans cavorting clean-cuttedly, all quenching wholeheartedly with icy Product, bottlenecks fellated as exuberantly as the bounds of decency would allow. All lushly cinematographed by back-lighting experts, and montage-edited to stirring, hummable theme music—wowgoshgollyand*good!* and never mind who and where in hell *were* those people? They were a relief to watch within the wasteland. Some smaller brands resorted to comic situations and nostalgic big-production numbers in an attempt to stand out. The idea for this new drink was different: See this

guy, this *character,* seeing the USA in, literally, a Chevrolet, a
used Chevy Nova wagon, the cult car of the Californian
surfers.

The guy was to be as carefully and significantly designed as
his car. Whole Earth, but no hippie drifter. Kerouac, but
without his friends or aims; not beat, but upbeat; he hasn't got
much, but what he's got you somehow know he worked and
saved up for. Kind of a hip Johnny Appleseed. A young Walt
Whitman, but hetero, yet no prowling cocksman. A young
Steinbeck traveling without Charley (but with Product. By the
case. His Nova's rigged inside: steering knob, bucket seats,
curtained windows, camping gear arranged, a minivan before
the van age; the case sits behind and between the bucket seats;
driving, he reaches them out one at a time, opens them up on
the old variety-store *decapper* mounted on his dashboard).
Driving byways, not highways, and well under the speed limits,
the better to get a *look* at the grand land of his and maybe, just
maybe, find and show the viewing audience what's still *good*
out there in those free states of ours. So, roughly, the ad agency
guys running the auditions sketched the X-Cola Man to Harry
and the other contenders for the part.

Casting sessions went on for five long winter weeks. Harry
never expected to return after the first, a cattle call that
crowded the agency's thirtieth-floor reception area, a hall and
two small conference rooms, not to count the tiny, hot studio
where each man was videotaped, full length and face, straight
on and in profiles. Against the male models, he felt deformed;
against the other actors, he felt eminently forgettable. He was
called back six times. At each callback, the competition was
fewer, and the number of agency and client people were
greater. Although it was a nonspeaking role, he was made to
read lines on camera and, another time, to "just sit around and
rap for a while, okay? Frankly, we're separating the real
friendly bastards from the gushers right now, dig it?" He found
it very easy not to gush and was called back yet again. (Yes,
he'd let his hair be cut a little bit.) The closer he got to the

finals, the more confident his agent, Jay Wolf, got, and the
more paranoid Harry grew. He told Angie, "I mean, yeah, I'm
excited, but it's starting to feel *insulting* not to get eliminated!"

"You going to eat another chip?"

"No, it's not that bad. No chips. I don't know what it is."
He had once auditioned for a potato chip commercial; four
greaseless guys with vests sat at a table, told him to take a chip
from the bag and to "contemplate it, method it, you know?
Take as long as you need, then give us your impressions,
freestyle." He ate it, gave them the finger, and left, with the
bag. But then Harry had long been making his work life more
complicated and grueling than maybe it had to be.

He was hustling and making a living, and a relatively decent
one, as a voice, mostly as what is called a voice-over narrator
for TV commercials. He did a little radio, a documentary now
and then, sales films, industrials, but mostly television spots.
And he'd get *in* some things, too, now and then—on camera!—a
series here and there and perhaps three or four commercials a
year. They were small parts usually, but paid full SAG and
AFTRA residuals, which were pretty fat. It wasn't much more
than being an unpretty male model, really, and Harry knew
that's all it was, but he called it acting. He thought of himself
as an actor and couldn't stop. In *Rosemary's Baby* it's a would-be
actor who sells his wife to Satan, and it isn't entirely far-
fetched. Harry was convinced he still had a chance to make it,
so he didn't answer just all the announcer calls, but every on-
camera call he could get as well. That was a lot of running,
more than most did, but Harry figured it was his only chance,
considering what a poor and late start he'd got.

In high school Harry had won parts in two plays and fallen
in love with acting. Again in college it was all he cared about.
But then he plodded on into life as if he'd majored in
economics or marketing or some such catalogued trade; he got
married, started his family, and did his Army stint, then got
jobs. He built walls between himself and what he wanted and
didn't realize until very late that he had missed the years of

summer stock and repertory, hadn't paid the ten million auditions and little-theater dues. He had sat, finally, out on the Charles River in Boston writing news for WBZ (getting to read some on the radio after a while), thinking someone was going to walk through the door and say, "Hey, wanna be in my play, my movie?" He hadn't been afraid, merely unconscious. One drug was, in those days, the late fifties, nobody from working-class Prospect, Massachusetts, *really* went out and became an actor. A college grad (and dramatics carried no credits) went out and made dollars; he was a college grad, therefore. ... When the light dawned at last, Harry and Angie bolted to New York, two kids in tow.

The time he ate the potato chip and walked, they had been momentarily in the money. This time they weren't, and getting the X-Cola job meant dollars bigger than he dared even think about. Angie said, "Well, it doesn't sound Mr. Whipple-ie, or anything like that. Are you afraid you'll look asinine, is that it?"

"No. I don't know. The guys getting rejected must be *too* something, though, right? But too *what?* *What aren't I too much of?!*"

"Secure. Financially and emotionally."

"That's it. They're looking for a jumpy bum."

"Is Jay having his doubts?" Meaning: Could it hurt his still-breathing "real acting" chances?

"God, no, just the opposite. He says if I get it, and they do it, and it runs, we're not only rich, I get a feature for sure. Or a regular in a series anyhow. Or at least that I can afford to go try some Off Broadway."

It was midnight. He was walking around their bedroom, feeding the wide-eyed Kate. Angie was folding and stacking her and Dennis'. diapers. She said, "Then maybe all you're doing is preparing yourself for getting eliminated." If she was right, his worrying was needless because, two weeks later, Harry got the job. On the phone, after gasping and whooping, she said, "So what weren't you too too of, did they tell you?"

He laughed. "Uh, not exactly. They said I look and move right, that's all. Well, they did say I don't come off too threatening."

"Ha. Let's hope they're smarter than that about the rest of it!"

It was to be a four-to-six-week shoot. Harry learned that to suggest all the country you didn't have to go all over the country; you could get it all in California and Arizona. They talked about the possibility of Angie's going with him, at least for a couple of weekends when he'd be at the more attractive places, like the Grand Canyon or San Francisco, but neither gave it much credence. She had gone on location jobs with him twice before, to Miami Beach and San Juan. Both times had been disasters; she didn't mind lounging at poolside and being waited on, but in each case the job had gone into Condition Red (anxiety-panic), and for the four hours out of forty-eight that they got to be together, he had been uptight and preoccupied, and she'd felt in the way. This time they left open the maybe of her joining him at the end somewhere, after the work was done. Even that, of course, meant preparations on her part comparable to those for the Normandy invasion. They had had a full-time, live-in Jamaican for a while but had had to let her go for lack of money. Constance was still only about ten, then; only she and Jake, eight, went to school all day. Amy went half days to a Montessori and needed both dropoff and pickup; Dennis and Kate still needed changing and naps, etc. "For what I'd have to do to get there," Angie'd frowned, "there'd have to be a helluva lot more than little cable cars at the other end!" Killing the idea, really, and leaving him then with just his guilt and distress over his leaving her to run the ship solo for such a long time.

They rationalized it nights, likening it to being back in the Army: He was going out on war games, she'd hold the fort; it was what they had to do and were supposed to do, so they'd do it, that's all. The forced, temporary separation might even do the marriage some good! Apart, each might rediscover his-her individuality! So that, reunited, they might be better able to stay off each other's backs and quit using each other as punching bags (when you can't hit the ones you hate, you hit the ones you're near) for their separate and mutual anxieties. Right on. Do your own thing for a while. What neither of them said was, in the Army Angie wouldn't have been left alone-alone; there'd be hosts of other women and children in the same boat. In New Chaumont, there'd only be Naomi and Gus Roth from across the street, and Naomi at the time was, they sensed and feared, on the verge of hugging radiators.

Never mind, it'd be all right. Angie was immigrant stock, had a backbone of steel; she'd *manage fine,* as they said in the old days and old countries, and as she said outright, several times, in their nightime huddles. The thought that she was being a shade too airy about it blew across his mind occasionally, but too swiftly and elusively for him to get a fix on it. Even if he had, he realized long after, no examination he was capable of then would have revealed what was really going on behind her face.

Out West, his workdays were long, fast, and fun. The call each morning was for six-having-had (breakfast), and they went until the light went out. It all did feel, in fact, like Army maneuvers. It was a small crew run by a funny, hyperthyroid director-cameraman who called it "shoot and scoot," just as they did in the artillery. There were only the writer and art director-producer from the agency and one client, who was a Forbes type but not entirely embalmed; he turned out to like pot, booze, the big, all-together nightly suppers, and the general little-theater camaraderie as much as the rest of them. In Fort Apache, Arizona, the Indians did live like in the cartoons, dozing drunk in the shade of mean, flat buildings. They owned it all, but whites ran it all, including the Honda Motel, where the film company stayed. The Indians owned the sawmill, too, but imported blacks to work it. Only the blacks lived lower than the redskins—in tarpaper huts. Harry wasn't alone in feeling squeamish at glorifying American soda amid such American squalor. They passed free samples out so lavishly that the client guy had to order more from LA (not the actual X-Cola, which wasn't yet in production; what Harry guzzled and dispensed on film was actually parent famous Product out of X-Cola bottles—sprayed with glycerine to look sweating-cold).

He spent his sleeplessness clawing at his back in the dark, trying to get inside Angie's head twenty-five hundred miles away. About all he learned was why he'd got the part of Jack Chesney and not the "woman" in *Charley's Aunt* back in college. Cracked falsetto, clothes, and body movements didn't even come close; the female condition was beyond him. *Good God, how could anyone be a woman!* The only way to be one was to be born one! All right, genes or something could make you the fem queer, but that was only the body part, the involuntary heating up to the male signals instead of the female. He couldn't imagine it, but he could understand it. But *being* a woman! Actually to *be* a woman! ... He guessed that he'd always just accepted the usual notion, the two overlapping circles; where they overlapped, the man and woman were alike, as humans, sharing likes and dislikes and interests and the rest in common. And where they didn't overlap, on the outer moons beyond the crosshatching, well, that was where they were not alike, where the man by nature felt and acted in one direction and the woman in another, often conflicting direction. Harry tossed and clawed. Come to think of it, *forced* to think about it ... it did seem pretty goddamn pat. And if he'd learned anything by now, it was automatically to suspect anything appearing pat.

He got up and smoked, went back and clawed. His back had never left its teens; he'd taken sun ray, X ray, pills, and ointments, and nothing made the volcanoes dry up. Being a worrier didn't help either. The best he could do for his back was leave it alone. Normally he was able to. Normally he could sleep, too. *Jesus,* what was she hating so much? All right. For himself he couldn't imagine for a second doing what she did:

conceiving, then carrying a life; bearing it; waking up morning after morning to exist in an adultless container of rooms, unable to get out into the air for very long, overwhelmed by chores. Menial labor—but wasn't *She* supposed to come equipped with some innate tolerance, even liking for it? Versus *His* natural ineptitude and incapacity for doing it (except now and then, to help, as a good mate should)? Or was that crap and a con, promulgated by Cave Guy with club in fist and *Her* hair in hand? Harry had long suspected that "The show must go on!" was never coined by any actor with a dying brother, but by some theater *owner*. Vested interests. Maybe a similar hype was at work here. But how the hell could *He* say, "Have a good day, hon," and stay home to care for house and young? Damn it, that was being ... a *mother*, wasn't it? And if there was one thing *Man* couldn't be, that was it.

And *Male* was physically stronger, right? Meaning that if it came down to it, *He* could clobber *Her*. So when *He* not only refrained from whomping *Her* but went so far toward anti-whomp as to open doors for *Her* and throw cloaks in puddles and take *Her* dancing and all such romancings, wasn't that *His* making up to *Her* for *His* inability to get pregnant? Didn't that effect a balance, didn't it make everything okeydokey? Apparently not, goddamn it.

Oh, the devil ... is a woman, some *He* wrote in the song. Harry could see *His* point now. That was one possibility—there *was* no reason or unreason for *Her* bitching and revolting and bemoaning *Her* lot out loud. Fish gotta swim, *She* hadda riot and mutiny, above or belowdecks, *forever*. Devil or not, though, did "woman's curse" mean more than menstruating? Was it part of femality to resent *Her* status, part of *Her* nature to begrudge *Him* his cock, size, role, "freedom," and the rest of it? If so, then there could be no solution possible and Harry's back was suffering in vain. His eyes stung from being open in the dark.

Women's Liberation was only beginning to make sounds of forward motion, yet already carried the diminutive tag "fem-

lib"; already the notions of Men's Liberation and the conse-
quent Human Liberation were being liquidated by lip service.
Unisex looked freaky and smelled fishy. Like most, or at least
many, men he knew, Harry had instinctively and perhaps
hastily cheered Women's or anybody's Liberation. Right on.
You've come a long way, baby, have a Tiparillo? Here again
he had to admit it, he couldn't get into the part, any more
than he could know the feeling of being a Jew, a black, a PR,
a Chicano or anyone else who could claim, "They scorned us
just for being what we are," as an earlier generation of Irish
had sung. It had never happened to him. He passed. For a
privileged person, whatever the hell that was: white, male,
educated, not old, healthy, and with a trade to ply. Nor could
he exactly wish it wasn't so. But wait—he was searching in the
wrong jungle perhaps. Angie? If Angie had ever felt the need
to march, sit in, join, go to school or work or any of it, she had
never said so. And if she'd felt it, she would've said it! He
knew *that* much, for Christ's sake. It wasn't enough to allow
sleep. Just what the hell was her problem, then? So he tossed
and turned, clawing wildly nights in the Honda Motel, all his
thoughts back in New York.

After Harry's and eleven other jets had roared up and off
into invisibility, Angie had trooped the kids back to the car
and driven home. Chatter about Daddy stopped before she
crossed the Whitestone Bridge and headed up the Hutchinson
River Parkway, and she thought: Was he really so quickly
forgotten? For herself, she was mixed, already missing him and
at the same time glad he was gone. For good or not, she felt
that a dense weight had been lifted from her spirit. The feeling
was pleasurable but followed too quickly by a trickle of guilt,
which, the second she acknowledged it, swelled to the larger
fear she'd been avoiding: *Some sendoff. What if I really screwed him
up? If he blows the job, we'll both know it was my fault.* She snapped
on the radio, lit a cigarette, and opened the butterfly window,
willing all such qualms—in fact, any and all such *thinking*—to

be sucked out the hole like her smoke. *I can't help it. I'm telling him the truth. Let it be his problem for a while.*

Constance said, "Can we go to the water without Dad?" The water was Glenn Miller Island, a park in the Sound off the shore of their town, New Chaumont. At least once a weekend they went there to cook out, walk the rocks, see the boats, get ice cream.

"Not today. We'll see tomorrow," Angie answered and prayed for rain. Next week would be soon enough to resume Harry things without Harry. Home, she dished out tuna and peanut butter sandwiches, put the two smalls to bed for "quiet time," and let the others go out to play. In the cellar washroom she moved done laundry from washer to dryer, then heaped a new load from basket to washer. Up, she stepped outside and walked to the end of their long side porch and stood there, smoking and wondering how soon the bulging dogwood buds would blossom and how soon the small, glittering lake below would vanish altogether behind the coming greenery.

Although she heard no sound, she was tense enough to immediately sense the sudden, new presence behind her and whirled to see Naomi Roth standing at the other end of the porch, silent and frightened-eyed. She was again wearing the damned, drab dungarees and dark-blue sweat shirt, and her hair was dirty. Naomi was Angie's age, lived across the pretty street, had two girls Constance played with, and was the best friend Angie had made in the four years there. Now, as if chased, she opened the screen door and fled into Angie's house. Angie followed and found her in her usual chair at the kitchen table, body taut. "Nome? Are you okay?"

Naomi only looked up at her, forlornly.

"Want some tea?"

Naomi nodded yes, and Angie set the kettle to boil. She reached down cups and saucers, her adrenaline and fear felt to be rising at the same swift speed in her. She served the tea and sat in the closest chair, not knowing whether to act at once or wait; maybe it wasn't anything truly serious this time and would pass. She chose to wait, for a little while anyhow, and waiting, she sipped her tea and tried to place in time exactly when this had started with Naomi; she had seemed so different in the beginning.

The Trowbridges had first seen the Birchwood Lake Area of New Chaumont on public TV one night when they were still in Greenwich Village. It was not Scarsdale, not Englewood, not the Island, not Connecticut. It was Westchester, yes, but with a kink that engaged them, a kink that just might, possibly, make it bearable for them. They still loved the City, but by then the conception of child number four had fixed their need to flee as fact—but *really?* Them? Out with the stiffs, out in the cartoons? Dick Van Dyke and Mary Tyler Moore didn't *actually* live out in that house in New Rochelle, it was shot in California! They could bring themselves to talk about it only with pain. They both knew the fact had not only to be faced but acted upon, and soon; but the increasing urgency itself seemed to bring with it thick, paralyzing dread.

Angie once confessed to him, "Sometimes I have this, like, wicked and delicious *curiosity* about it—what *will* happen? How'll it *feel* to just sit and wait and let the worst that can happen happen? It's spooky—do you think it's possible for something to go wrong with your survival instinct?

Harry said, "No," and when Birchtree Lake appeared, they jumped at it. They were still in their twenties; it wasn't quite yet the mid-sixties; little did they know. Even after they had accomplished the actual move, with all the subleasing and packing and shipping and unpacking and cleaning and eating of Chinese food and dressing out of crates, even then they never clearly connected the *making* of their children with the changes that fast followed. It took number five's arrival, plus all the rest that happened in those times, to force them finally to unblur their picture of the new world around them.

For all the Future Shock media barraging of them, there seemed to have been a time lag between the latest news and them. The sun of swashbuckle had already set. What Harry and Angie had been cakewalking in was merely afterglow: warm and shiny still, but chilling and darkening so swiftly that suddenly all was dark and cold, and they had to run inside and shut their child-making doors behind them. Just in time, and with some real relief—but rather reluctantly and rather sadly, too. Against the ideal, the shaggy human leaves a lot to be desired.

Which they learned in part the Friday night of their very first week in the New Chaumont house. It was about midnight, and they were in bed, not quite gone asleep. The three kids had been sound for hours. The fourth, eventually Dennis, the final trigger pull of their shot from the Village apartment to the suburban house, was still inside Angie. The house perched on the brink of a long, steep slope. Below the bottom hedge of their lot, three streets intersected, and below that lay small Birchtree Lake, for which the area was named. A narrow paved lane passed very close to the side of the house that was anchored in level ground. The thin strip of earth between the sidewalk and that side of the house got no sun and was always bare. Some pachysandra finally took, a couple of years later.

Sshclatash! The awful sound screamed *Insane Men Through Front Door!* Harry, half-naked, was down the dark stairs, across the living room, and at the locked, solid front door with the fireplace poker in his hand before Angie was believing it was happening. He found it in the dining room: Someone had taken one of the full, metal trash barrels off its bricks in the back, carried it around the corner, and hurled it through the nearest first-floor window.

By the time she got down Harry had snapped on the light, and, stepping carefully through the mixture of swill and glass on their just-sanded and Fabuloned bare wood floor, was pulling the drapes closed. The cold night wind poked sticks in from the outside immediately. The dancing heavy cloth seemed alive and frightening. The trash barrel was lodged between a chair top and the veneered walnut table, which now showed big cuts, white. Cradling her full womb, Angie saw and felt sick. "Oh, my God, Tro."

"Nice, huh?" He was shaking now, too.

"Well, just thank God it—"

"It could've been a kid's bed! Or a crib! *They* didn't know it was a fucking dining room!"

"Oh, who would ever?"

"Go ahead up. Lemme clean this mess up and block that window with something, it's sucking all the heat out." He started scooping guck back into the barrel.

She stayed but could only watch. She remembered a story she'd read in *The New Yorker* once about a couple who had had the same apartment for a long time and loved it very much and then it got broken into and burglarized one night when they were out and after that it wasn't the same anymore; even after they had replaced the stolen things, a terrible sense of something-lost pervaded the place, and finally they moved. She prayed this wouldn't mean that for them.

Taping cardboard over where glass had been, Harry, calmed, said he figured it had probably been "just some kids on their way home from the basketball game at the high school."

She agreed quickly, "Yeah. They probably feel lousy and ashamed already. They might even come back in the morning and apologize and offer to pay, or something," thinking, the *Birchtree Lake Area* of New Chaumont or not, this *was* Westchester, after all, where people were supposed to be decent.

"Bullshit. It could have been a crib with a baby in it. Get my hands on one of the pricks, I'll fucking kill him!" He doused the lights, replaced the poker, and they went to bed again. He said, "Beautiful—three years in the filthy, rotten old city and nothing. Well, the typewriter that one time, but I'm still sure it was that driver from the Jane Street place, delivering the desk. Now! Not seven days in this wonderful American-Way *home*-house, and here I am smelling *bacon fat* off my hands!" He got up and washed in the dark, in the private bath off their master bedroom. She was afraid he'd never forgive the house for that night.

There was a Birchtree Lake Area Association, good souls and

neighbors organized to keep that section of the residential city
... balanced. That was the kink about Birchtree: It was
integrated. And it was *working!* It and only one or two other
places in the country at the time: mixed, fifty-fifty and side by
side, yet with real estate values going up instead of down. All
houses were registered with the Association. You bought and
sold through them. If a black slot on their chart was vacant
and you weren't black, sorry, and vice versa. There were some
mutterings about segregation in reverse and civil liberties and
so on, but in general, the consensus was in favor of the ends
justifying the means in this special instance. It appealed to the
young Trowbridges. It let them feel they weren't just moving
to the subs like any other Puritan robots; they were entering
upon a modern, moral experiment in living.

Promptly came their first invitation to dinner from black
neighbors. Both were gorgeous. He was goateed and in commercial art; she had a luscious face and body and was active in
the local school. They owned a mock-French farmhouse, with
trikes in the drive and slate floors indoors. Despite their
affected worldliness, Harry and Angie were thrilled by the
prospect. Now this was how life was supposed to go; we're all
people, not skins!

"I just hope they're not too, you know," Angie had said.

"Uppity?"

"Shut up. You know, too ... *preoccupied* with the rights
movement and all. I can't stand speeches."

"Nah, they look hipper than that."

"I hope we *dance!* And no dumb cracks, either, Tro, okay? I
hate that whole we're-so-liberal-we-can-make-jokes-to-your-face
routine."

"Give me a little credit, huh? Listen, I want to *learn.* They
having anyone else?"

"Just us, I think."

"Terrific. Geez, though, now I wish we asked them first."

"*We're* the newcomers. I wonder what *food.*"

James Beard veal. They were home before eleven-thirty, cold
sober, skulls aching. No booze. Mateus rosé with dinner. New

math. Lady Bird. Mortgage rates. James Reston. Low AM
radio Mantovani. Wallpaper. Seventh-day Adventists! Whiter
than Harry or Angie would ever be. "Damn!" Angie said.

In all their years in Birchtree, in fact, the lone, Georgia-born
broad-backed, big-grinned, Continental-driving, U.S. Grade A
black they met was Bert next door. Bert and Louise. "The
mixed marriage." She, also black, had a master's in economics
and worked for General Foods in White Plains. He slipped the
Continental away each morning at five-thirty to a lathe in the
Bronx. Bert said "sheeit" and called his boss Bo and every
Saturday put on his rivet-studded black leather jacket that said
"Dirty Berty" across the black in chrome buttons, kick-started
his giant Harley, and blasted off to unimaginable adventures
with his son Bobby, twelve, arm-strapped to his back. Jake
Trowbridge, then five or so, watched, wet-eyed and waving.
He thought Bert the most splendid man he had ever seen in
real life, and not even Harry ever denied or qualified the
estimation. They had a hundred· miles of sidewalk bordering
their hilly corner lot, and Harry rarely got home from Manhattan before seven. Bert was home at four, had two feet of
walk, but he was the one who came by with a snow-blower.
Every snowfall Harry came home to sidewalk cleaned to the
bone. Never a word passed about it. Bert knew they needed the
hand; they knew Bert loved to run the machine.

Bert had his friends in to the basement playroom he'd
finished off himself. Louise entertained hers upstairs. Never on
the same nights. Louise invited Angie and Harry a few times.
Bert never did. One March Sunday, though, Harry heard tires
whining outside and went out. There'd been a thaw, a heavy
rain, then a sudden freeze. Bert was pushing a departing pal's
car to help it grab traction. Harry helped, then said sure and
followed Bert down to his basement. It was about four.
Monday morning Angie told him it had been "the stroke of
midnight, you jerk! With *these!* For the *kids!*"

Harry examined the cardboard party hats. Two derbies and
a cowboy Stetson, all laminated glossy, and not plain cardboard: pictures of naked women. "I've never seen these before

in my life. You lie." He laughed. But stopped fast. "Oh, Jesus. Angie? Take the hatchet out of my forehead, and I'll try to make the nine nineteen. *Holy mackerel, Sapphire!*"

She grinned. "Must've been boring, huh?"

Louise never invited them again after that. A couple years later Bert and Louise split. Harry and Angie weren't surprised; the only sad part to them was that she got Bobby. Bert had headed south, alone, on the Harley. Angie said, "The Divorce Angel's getting busy on this street, isn't it?"

"Yeah. Well, better them than us."

Silence.

He looked up from his script. *"I said better them than us, Ange!"*

"I'm thinking, I'm thinking!"

"Ha-ha, Mrs. Benny."

The Roths and kids had been at their doorstep the morning they moved in, with broad grins and an invitation to supper that night. They hit it off right away. Harry's Prospect, Massachusetts, and Gus' Brooklyn, New York, boyhoods matched as nearly perfectly as their unfashionably enduring Catholic and Jewish faiths matched. (Gus and Naomi, but it was really Gus, still kept a kosher house and went, sometimes, to Temple.) Balding, stooped, and scowling, Gus looked like a pain in the ass but turned out to be wry, romantic, and game for anything, the zanier the better. He drank goy gin martinis with Harry "as a personal sacrifice. It isn't for me, it's for the souls of all the Irish Pioneers wallowing in teetotaling!" They'd both been city Boy Scouts. Gus was an architect and worked out of his house. Naomi then was original earth mother, with breasts like Sophia Loren's in *Two Women* and a voice soft as rain on grass. A Juilliard dropout, she'd given up the piano for the flute, the flute for the guitar, and was now eyeing the cello longingly. She collected rocks and still read Schopenhauer and Gibran. In the kitchen the day of Harry's departure, Angie realized that the change in Naomi, her downturn, had happened so gradually that maybe it hadn't been a change at all. "Nomie," she finally whispered, "can you hear me?"

Naomi hadn't touched her tea, had only stayed staring

blankly out the window beside her—at the dogwood buds? Only the week before, she'd come over to tell Angie that she just "couldn't do it."

"Couldn't do what, lady?"

"The wash. I . . . can open the hamper, but then I . . . I just *can't*, Ange!"

"The hell with it, take it to the laundromat."

"No! Gus' shirts! He needs them! And the girls' things! They. . . ."

That time Angie had phoned Gus, who came across and took her home. This time she called Manhattan Information and found Lorenzo Carcaterra, a friend of Gus' from Flatbush stickball days and a shrink. He told her to get her to Parkchester Hospital immediately, he'd get there as fast as he could, and he'd phone ahead. Angie then dialed Gus, but there was no answer; she yelled Jake up from his cave under the forsythia bushes and sent him across to see if Mr. Roth was maybe asleep. The boy came back and said only the girls were there. She said, "Okay, now I know you hate to, but go back over there and stay with Constance until Mr. Roth gets home or I come for you." Then she woke Dennis and Kate and packed them and Naomi into the Rambler and took off for the hospital. In the car Naomi spoke at last, but all she said, over and over, was: "I'm sorry, I'm sorry," to nobody in particular.

Harry, the X-Cola Man, still had only the daywork to relieve his anguish over Angie and their life. Between the weather they were running into and the travel time they'd underestimated, it now looked certain that the shoot would take closer to six weeks than the hoped-for four. When he called home the first night and got the baby-sitter, he felt outrage; when she said Angie had gone to the hospital, it turned to panic until the kid added that it was the lady from across the street. That night, and every other time he called after that, speaking to his children long-distance was less than fulfilling or reassuring:

"And Dad?"

"Yeah?"

"Um . . . you coming home?"

"Yeah, but not for a while yet."

"You gonna bring us something?"

"Oh, yeah—I already got you some stuff."

"What?"

"Oh, no, I'm not going to tell you."

"Oh, shit."

"What did you say?"

"Here's Mommy now." Kalunk.

Nor were Angie's conversations much more productive. She was so preoccupied with poor Naomi, she said, she really had no mind left to think about anything else, let alone talk to him about it. They both were terrible phone people anyhow, but her going on and on about Naomi, as bad as he felt for her and Gus, only made Angie sound more like a stranger and farther away than the damned phone itself did anyhow. Naomi had been put at once into shock treatment. "And, oh, Tro, know what they *call* it?"

"No, what?"

"Zapping! Can you imagine? Isn't that sick?"

"How's Gus under it all?"

"Incredible. He's a fantastic guy, he really is."

"Good. Well, listen"—since she hadn't asked, he'd tell her anyhow—"we're going twenty-eight hours a day out here, and I'm not sure if and when I'll be able to call you next, okay?" which was only half a lie. Angie said sure, that was okay.

They shot him shooting rapids, working with lumberjacks, frying eggs on a mountaintop; they shot him driving the Nova, swigging the stuff, sharing a clan family's barn-party reunion, fixing a flat, watching a lonesome sunset; they shot him playing shirts-and-skins with city kids, playing cards with cowboys, trout fishing with hill people, hunting with a club of good old boys, which was the one and only time he gave the director, Stone, any problems. "Cut! Hey, Trobe, will you eighty-six that asshole *grin?* What's that about, man? This is the third time!"

Harry went over close and whispered, "I can't help it, Kurt. I keep seeing them all as Elmer Fudd, and it breaks me up."

"Elmer Fudd! ... Ha, I see what you mean. Dwat that wabbit!"

"Yeah, but I'd rather be the wabbit."

"Gun laws and all that? You anti ... ?"

"No, I don't know, it's more ... well, like in the cartoons, I could never figure what Fudd or Porky Pig or even Mickey Mouse *did,* you know? I mean, where'd they get the house and car and clothes and gun and the fucking time to go hunting all the time, you know?"

Stone was hip and quick. He said, "I know, and I'll tell you. The guy that wrote the sketch and the guy who drew the pictures—*they* gave them all that shit and put them anywhere they felt like. Just so the jokes and gags could happen. *They* were real. The pictures weren't. Now go jump back into *my* pictures, okay, man? *Sans* grin!"

Harry laughed. "Okay, nobody ever explained it before."

"That's my man. Also, because it's on their fucking story-board and also because I'm already three days behind. Hang in there, kid."

Between work and "home," Harry was getting pretty punchy by then, which was midway in their third week. Stone knew it as well as he did and kept reminding him of the three-day break coming up. Harry looked forward to it and dreaded it equally. A film shoot being like an Army maneuver also in the long, rushed rides ending only in long, slow waits, he was getting too much brood time as it was. Being Catholic, he was, of course, good and thorough about it, and, my God, what depths would three whole *days* let him reach? He couldn't tell which depressed him more, the news of Naomi or Angie's relentless silence. He carried *I hate my life* around in him like an impacted tooth and, without any further clues from her, began to wonder just how literally and how symbolically she'd meant it, after all. She hadn't accused him personally of anything specific, granted, but if it wasn't *him* she was fingering, then why was it *him* she'd dropped it on, with one foot on a goddamn plane and right on the brink of maybe the breakthrough of his life? Did she *want* him to fuck up? Maybe. He couldn't imagine why, but yeah, just maybe she did! This labyrinth opened into a cave of anger, where he felt like some kid under a back porch pretending to have run away; *You'll be sorry! You're playing with fire, baby, because from where I sit* (over coffee in the honey wagon, at the time) *a dose of the outside, make-a-living world might help you like your pretty snug, busy little life more!*

Then, on the eve of the break, tearing at his back in the dark of his room in the swank lodge high over the Pacific near Big Sur:

Ah, that's it! You meant GET OUT, *didn't you! The subby wives and the magazines got to you, and it's stay away, just send money, right? Well, what happened to till death do us part, huh? Who died? Me? You? It? If there was a death, I missed it! And stand by for a news flash: They're my kids as well as yours, and where's it say* I'm *the one what gets to do the getting out? I'm, by God, and I can't believe you don't know this by now, not so easily gotten rid of! Have you possibly forgotten who the fuck you're dealing with?*

His veins hot with too many after-dinner Black Russians, there was no stopping it: *And you're screwing Gus! I can sense it!*

It was true then; he'd lost her. And he'd lost his friend, too. But why, when, where, how? He'd *worked* a lot, that's all. Christ! What else were you supposed to do?

That was where Harry was when his backclawing was interrupted by a light but not furtive knocking on his door. He put on his robe and answered it, and it was Anne, with a bottle of iced akvavit and a fat joint of yellow paper. She was the script girl: tall, red-haired, nineteen going on nine and eighty, and from Copenhagen, for God's sake! She'd said it before, and now she said it again, "I do luv you, you know, Troby. Doing anything?" She filled his three-day break with an unreality that didn't feel bad, compared to where he'd been on his own. Upon his first naked, entwined wake-up with her, he was surprised by what he felt: It was neither guilt nor remorse; it was rather a strange sense of sadness, as if he'd lost something, as if something had ended. They climbed the coastal rocks together, trying to discover if that was really Kim Novak's house, and they walked in the woods. She taught him how experienced he was. At the least, she helped him sleep.

He figured out that he'd already been in the eighth grade when she was born. Blithe, modern, making the most of her days and nights, Anne would sing, *You're just too good to be true* ... and he'd answer, *Young girl, get out of my mind.*

"My God, why do you think that way?"

"I don't know, I just do, that's all."

He asked her once if Stone had sent her to him, and she wept, making him feel truly mental, as well as a cad. She asked him no questions, but by the third day he had her story and had seen her cheekbones in a photo of her mother and was worrying about her chances of getting an education in the States. He ended it on the second night after work had resumed; he didn't tell her about Angie, his kids or problems; he only told her the truth: "I can't handle it." A philosopher, Anne simply sighed and said, "About all I can say for American men is that you're better than British men and older than American boys!" All Harry could think to reply was: "It'll probably be different when you get to LA."

Dailies or rushes were raw film, just as it was shot and developed, without color correcting or editing. From the start, Stone and the agency guys had been viewing dailies on a portable Movieola head, as they arrived on location from the Los Angeles lab. Stone had spent most nonshooting time flying to LA to do preliminary selecting and cutting with an editor there. Usually he came back satisfied and encouraged. They completed the final sequence and wrapped the job in the Sierras east of San Francisco. To celebrate, the crew pooled money and rented the job's old DC-6 to fly them over the mountains to Lake Tahoe in Nevada for a night's wassail and gambling. Stone flew to LA to finish the first prototype spot of the campaign.

Harry went with the boys to Harrah's Club. It felt very much like his old Army outfit hitting Nürnberg after a month in the boondocks. They ate, drank, played the tables, and saw Buddy Greco sing. In the morning the pilot dropped Frank "The Trucker" Tucker off to pick up his rig, then flew the rest of them, hung-over and snoring, to Los Angeles. Stone met Harry at the Beverly Hills Hotel and invited him to the Test. It meant postponing his return to New York a day, but Harry was too curious to miss seeing the whole he'd been a part of and viewers' reactions to it.

A Pink Panther cartoon was the "control piece," followed by an hour-long pilot for a TV series, interspersed with commercials to be tested, including the X-Cola spot. Harry's group observed from a booth high above the packed theater. Their guide and host, a Swedish woman called Doctor something, explained: The audience was Californian, hence mostly from someplace else, hence as representative of the whole country as you could get. Half would provide Voluntary Response, half Involuntary. The Voluntaries held little boxes in their laps. When they liked something, they turned their knobs to the right, to the left when they didn't like, all turns fed directly to computers, which instantly recorded and translated. The Involuntaries were wired, gauges taped to their skin. Other computers churned this information into intelligence. Complete, written analysis would take weeks, but "top-line" readings could be made this night. As Harry watched, his heart sagged, to the left, involuntarily. To him, the audience looked like game-show contestants. He asked, "What do they get, cake knives?" Nobody answered.

Like the others, his was a thirty-second commercial, complete with dissolves, music, and a voice-over, not his. He whispered, "Hey, Stony! I do voices, too, you know!"

Stone grinned. "Greedy fucker—some symbol!"

Like the others, their spot went by in what seemed like five seconds, and Harry could only barely recognize himself. It had felt like little movies; it came out like four or five transparencies. On the one clear shot of his face he searched for any signs

of the anguish he remembered, found none, and thought: No
wonder nobody ever knows anybody else. That goon looks as
carefree and sure as ... Elmer Fudd.

X-Cola was paying for more than the wires and boxes.
Doctor lady next led them downstairs to a plush lounge.
Drinks and canapés sat on teak; the men sat in leather that
whooshed. Peons served refreshments and, when it was time,
turned on and tuned the huge color screen behind the sliding
wall panel. Here now were company men Harry had never
seen before and agency men he hadn't seen since the auditions.
They got closer seats than the ones who'd done the shoot and
bent forward when the picture spread clear: a T-shaped table
in a room, elsewhere in the building, lined with ... college-age
kids. The "moderator" was a young, charismatic, articulate
black guy who knew what the kids didn't: that people outside
the room were watching and listening to them ... and that
they were not there to "rap" about the pilot film and television
in general at all, but to critique the X-Cola spot.

Cool, grad-schoolie Mr. Black ("Call me Joe") deftly worked
them through the ruse and down to the reality in eleven
minutes. At first, the men in the remote room seemed to have
something to unclench and grin about: The kids not only liked
it, but played back copy points right and left! Second drinks
were signaled for and received. *Unusual ... not stoogie ...
contemporary ... where it's at ... like it is ... far out ... groovy ...
like hip, you know?* ... Then up spoke Leola. Not a beach girl,
no groupie, more a latter-day Jane Fonda, without the looks,
but what a mouth. Harry's ego joined the others in despising
her; his head and heart sent her love. In a low, sweet, demure
voice as flat and straight as her hair and burlappy dress, Leola
said, "You're really all assholes. We're being ripped off, and
you don't even know it. These fuckers are having us! ..."
which, immediately, became what the others in the focus
group had *really* been thinking all along. *Right on ... as fake as
everything else ... just more fucking adult lies ... "Plastics!" ... mind
pollution. ...*

Stone flicked his head from the door, and Harry followed. "No place for you and me there now, Tro; here's where us outside suppliers *split!*"

In the car going west on Sunset, Harry said, "Remember when kids were the leaders of the future? Christ, those babies are the leaders of *now!*"

"Fuck 'em. That didn't necessarily mean anything back there."

"No?"

Beat, Stone went straight to his cottage. Keyed up and confused, Harry went right in the lobby and walked to the bar, to find it just closed. The bartender was doing his receipts. "Sorry, sir."

"Come on, man, one pop, huh? Save a life."

"Sorry, sir."

"Poco, you fucker, give the guy his goddamn drink!" came a voice. Poco shrugged. "What'll you have, sir?"

"Chivas rocks. Double." Harry peered behind him into the gloom of the darkened room and saw his benefactor, a bearded guy slouched in a booth beside a woman Harry couldn't see as clearly. The guy lurched up and through the shadows and threw a heavy arm around Harry's neck. "From New York, right?" He was a bit in the bag but not drunk. "Good *Christ*, it's good to hear you talk! One more for me and Loretta, too, Poco *amigo!* Ah, my friend, you don't know. You just don't *know!* This fuckin' *town!* I'm *dyin'* here. *Say* something to me! Talk to me from *home*, man!"

Harry, astonished and glad, said, "You're Val Avery." After Rip Torn and Stacy Keach, the gravel-faced man embracing him was Harry's favorite actor alive.

The recognition snapped Avery clear-eyed, and he let go of Harry's shoulder. "Son of a *bitch*, now I *know* you're out from the Apple! *No*body knows me. Without this pissant *beard* even, nobody knows me. I'm in more pictures than anybody in the *world*, and nobody fuckin' knows me!"

"I know you, and I think you're great."

"What's your name?"

"Harry Trowbridge."

"Harry, you're pullin' my chain. Name a picture."

"The Brotherhood, with Douglas. But fuck that—*Faces!* Man, when you're alone with Gena Rowlands and all you do is talk about your ... marriage ... and *kid,* I. ..."

"Oh, my God, Harry, ya been sent to me *this* pisspoor night, let me tell ya!"

Loretta joined them at the bar. Avery introduced her as Helen something. They drank, and then the woman, obviously glad to see her grizzly animated and electric again, drove them to a doughnut place. The three of them ate eggs and drank coffee and smoked cigarettes until five in the morning. Avery said he'd just that day walked off a big picture because the director was "a fucking Nazi. I knew it before. I shouldn't have taken it. But I needed the work, man. You know what that is. I figured I could eat it and make it through. Work's work, right? But I couldn't. He's a fucking Nazi gas-oven pig, and I told him!" One of the score of stories the ugly, beautiful actor poured out to New York. Harry felt drunker than he'd ever felt from liquor: *Faces. Angie. The blur of his own wispy flick of a "film" loathed by kids. This real, working, great, sorrowful actor's actor saying "You gotta come out here, don't ever come out here!"* ... and just who was sent to whom, this pisspoor night?

Angie's letter was standing slanted in his room slot at the front desk that noon. He tore it open. Gregory Peck walked by in a gray flannel suit, carrying an attaché case. Harry saw only her scrawled words. He forced himself to read them slowly, shutting his lids when his eyes would start racing. He wanted it one word at a time, one syllable, one *letter* at a time. He read it through there in the lobby, read it again in the cab, read it again four times in the plane to New York.

Oh, Tro, Naomi up that god-awful hellhole scared me to death. ... You may be the star of the seventies, we may be doing everything right, all we can do, all the necessary, moral and brave things put us to do, but I don't care. Something's terribly wrong, going on here. We have to somehow stop and change, babe. I don't know what else, but something. Something different and better, and I know we can do it, whatever the hell it is . . . assuming you're coming back to us. I know that may not even be true anymore. But I want you to, Tro. I do. I miss you and love you and . . .

She'd started going to a shrink, a woman psychologist in Pelham recommended by Carcaterra.

It was a long letter. Harry had had no idea she could write so lucidly, her thoughts and observations belying her anti-Palmer-Method, girlish scrawl. It felt like reading a letter from someone complex he didn't yet know very well. She wrote:

I know this'll probably read fragmented and disjointed, but that's because I've written it like a diary or journal, a bit each night starting the day you left. I swear Naomi happening now is a sign to us. I know there must be all kinds of personal, psychic things with her, but I also think she's reacting to real, outside causes, the same ones confusing us.

As she'd told him by phone, Naomi was making progress. Gus went up every afternoon, and evenings Angie went with him. The zappings left Naomi at varying stages of memory loss: Sometimes she knew their names; other times they'd have to remind her. A definite change had come over Gus. With Naomi down, he was suddenly the essence of can-do and energy, running his house and children from meals to laundry.

It's scary—did she have to drop before he could wake up? If she makes it back, will he go back into his old slump? The answer, my friend Tro, is, I think, literally blowin' in the wind. My friend. That's something, isn't it? We. . . .

Flying East, reading her again and again, it occurred to Harry that if all this amounted to that "rediscovering of his/her individualities" they had talked about so vaguely, then,

Jesus, it sure came hard, didn't it—and was it really as worth it as the current vogue claimed it to be? Like his first, blurry adultery, it right now felt more like a loss of something than a gain. And he wished he knew even a splinter of what the hell he was going home to. About all he sensed for sure was that his career as an actor, or his illusion of that career, was lying dying somewhere west of him, on the table of a doughnut shop and in a room containing hidden microphones and a concealed camera.

Coming into the terminal out of the tube, he saw her face there small and bright in the crowd, and didn't see it; it couldn't be her, so it wasn't. But when he looked and found it again, of course, it was her, and his heart jumped. He smiled, and then she did. They met in the mob and embraced tightly.

"How'd you know what time?"

"I called the computer."

"Who's with the kids?"

"The Service, who else?"

"Another drunken mammy?"

"I didn't even notice. Oh, Tro."

"Yeah." He scooped up the bag he'd dropped, and they walked in the throng following baggage claim signs. The unfamiliar feeling of her new raincoat made him finally blurt, "What the hell did you *do,* Ange? I mean, I love it! You look fabulous!"

"You sure? You mind the hair?"

"No! Well, er, uh, I'll probably miss it in bed, but no, it's like years ago, huh? I like it short."

"Good. I hope it's chic-er than back then, though. It cost chic, I'll tell you."

"It does, it does—and a new coat, too, huh?"

They each talked straight ahead to the bobbing backs of heads or down to the gray floor rolling beneath their feet. Angie said, "You ain't seen nothing yet; there's a dress. Even new underwear. I wanted to look all new, Tro."

"You do."

"You do, too, you know it? And I *know* they're the same old duds. You got a lot of tan, though, and lost some weight."

"Oh, my God, I'm glad you came!"

"Lucky you came off alone, I'll tell you."

"We separated on the plane."

"Hmph."

"In the john."

They stopped at the luggage carousel, spinning empty. She grinned up at his face. "How bad do you need to see your gang?"

"Hmmm ... why?"

"Because I have reservations at the Motel on the Mountain for tonight and tomorrow night." Her voice thinned out at the end.

Harry said, "Hey, what's the matter? That's the best thing I've heard in a hundred years." He kissed her on the mouth.

The first suitcases started to slide down the chute, and people pushed past them to get near the conveyor belt. She said, "I guess I wasn't all that sure how you'd react."

"Oh, hey."

"Well, it was a long time. It felt long, anyhow."

"It felt forever." He laughed. "If I reacted the way I want to, first we'd get trampled, then we'd get arrested!"

She laughed, too, and this time started the kiss. In it he thought how he'd always wanted to be part of the couple doing *that* in the airport, and now he was, and it felt exciting and sweet inside.

All the way to the place their bodies did most of the talking, feeling each other's fronts and legs and groins, both giggling like teenagers and Angie riding close beside him, forehead and new hair in his rearview mirror, something she never did. In their room at the high, clear-aired motel he celebrated every article of her newness down to her scant bikinis, which he stuffed into his mouth and tried to eat, and they made love in the moonlight so consumingly it felt illicit. In early daylight they ate huge breakfasts on the terrace outside their room, then walked through the delicate Japanese garden in the back. He said, "It feels like California here."

"What's the story on out there anyhow?"

"Nuts. It is outdoor living, I guess, but I think your brain turns to farina in about six months."

Later she asked thinly, "Did you have anyone else, Tro?"

"No. Did you?"

"No. Almost, though, once."

"Well. Oh, Christ, what do we do to ourselves anyhow?"

"What nobody else can, I guess. What should we do now is the question, though, I think. Any ideas?"

"My mind boggles. My instincts say sell the house and get out."

"Where, though? New York is still—"

"I met a real actor out there," and told her the Val Avery night.

She told him more Naomi details, then: "But it can't be the *place*, can it? I think the *Times* can squash you, but a place, unless it's crummy or a slum or something, I don't think you can blame a place for anything."

"Nah. Birchtree's okay. I mean, as much as I bitch about the house being out to get me, we've had great times there. But . . . I don't know, maybe it's *us* in the place, you know? Maybe *we're* wrong for *it?*"

"Beats me. Something's got to give, though. Not right away, necessarily, but—"

"Yeah. Maybe now that we know we're looking for something, something will come to us, sooner or later."

They had read somewhere that '68 had been the big life-change year for Americans, the breakout time for couples to split, singles to couple, jobs to be quit. (Meaning, if they were actually going to move to change things, they were already a year late. This wouldn't bother Harry; since he had hit twenty-eight or so, he always figured he was *ten* years behind in everything anyhow, a handicap he took as compensation for what he considered his economically and culturally deprived childhood.) The New Kids were dropping out and turning on or turning *to*, depending on their particular bents, the streets, the sit-ins, the desert pueblos and rural farms, the cults, the Peace Corps, VISTA, Canada, Sweden. In the Trowbridges' sector of society, guys quit corporations or Wall Street to become filmmakers or potters. Some even went to the war: newspeople after the action, or just souls posing as newspeople after the action they weren't finding in their lives or away from action in their lives that they couldn't stand anymore. None of that was viable for Harry and Angie, although once, not long after they were married, they had briefly but seriously considered going to South America for a year to work for some Catholic missionary outfit; they didn't go, but the impulse never entirely left them.

Nevertheless, as surely as they had had to quit the city, they now had to do something toward saving their life. This pressure was in their very air now, constant and mounting. In their thirties, born in the thirties, and with five children, a steady paycheck wasn't fun money you wrote Aunt Edna to stop sending or dividends to be written over to the Civil Liberties Union or the Democratic Party. Yet, to Stay Put, to hang in the house in the subs, "Integrated" or not, commuting to Big Business and back every day, going out Fridays, having people in Saturday—*being average*—felt more and more like Consenting. Consenting to something they felt was all wrong, a sin of omission, a fraud, and perhaps even an act of cowardice. To stay and Continue On was to vote yes in the blocks beside Richard M. Nixon; taxes for nukes and spooks; the imprisonment of children for locoweed; and all the rest of what they had been taught by the nuns was evil. The wrong generation or something to be able to believe and act upon their instincts at once, they had had to wait until the prevalent evil touched their lives personally, but whatever they were or weren't, they weren't cowards.

Harry couldn't help it; he couldn't just go to Angie's shrink and be done with it, he had to call the Archdiocese of New York for a referral. He'd long ago vowed never to do three things: commit adultery, borrow money from anybody other than a bank, and see a shrink. She laughed. "Typical!"

"Well, I don't want to waste time and money trying to explain the basic Catholic condition!"

The Archdiocese gave him Catholic Charities, a "Mrs. deJesus."

"You're kidding me! Right to the top, huh?"

"That's all right, sir; do you want a male or a female?"

Harry found as much humor in the psychiatrist, a silent, green-skinned undertaker he met in a fourth-floor cell of a room in a neighborhood house in the East Sixties. No couch; just a clear, metal desk and two office chairs in a room without pictures. Entering, Harry grinned. "Ha, call the church, get a clinic."

Straight: "This isn't a clinic."

"And I suppose this isn't a rabbit on my head either!" Harry said, turned, and walked out. He couldn't do it; in the worst times of his life, he'd never been made go to a clinic for anything, not even dental work. He told this story to Dr. Rose Nolan Shultz in Pelham; she roared, and he liked her. Her office was in the sun porch of her home, with white wicker furniture, ferns, ivies, and flowers, and birds twittering outside. The more he went, the more clearly he realized: This was the new society's priest, its new rabbi; there was still some hope left.

An amazing truth surfaced fairly quickly: There *was* something else in his life that Harry had always loved almost as much as acting. It was working in gas stations, the only jobs he'd ever taken from when he was twelve years old on. He didn't love engines or cars that much; it was more just the place itself, and all the people trooping through it all the time—he'd loved just being there and getting paid for it. He also found himself telling Rose that, especially at this critical juncture of his life, he badly wanted to *own* and *run* something for a change, something with his and nobody else's name on it. The unearthing of these two simple truths excited him and intrigued Angie but didn't clinch anything; what clinched it was the call, not a week later, from his father, Big Jake. (This was before Big Jake "went away" himself.) Big Jake just mentioned, thought Harry might think it was funny or something, that Old Man Coogan had "finally put his Shell up for sale! 'Magine that?"

Coogan and sons had had it for two hundred years; Harry had put himself through college in it. Big Jake laughed. "Demented old bastard, and still as cheap as a ... but it's still a great—well, hell, you know the station well as I do, huh, bud?"

"The Queen of Liberty Square."

"Ha, that's right, too, you always usta call it that. Remember? Six in the mornin's, snow up to your ahse, you'd hike up and over the hill from Tower to Liberty, a bloody mount'in but what the hell'd you care, huh?"

That did it for Harry. It struck him like God's voice in a dream.

The rich, French-speaking UN Nigerian who hid not his lust for blond Angie of the North Atlantic winter blue eyes didn't count as a Bert next-door black with Harry either, but he did meet their asking price for the house. He didn't care. For all that Angie liked it, and for all the good times they'd had in it, that New Chaumont house had fought Harry every inch of the way for the four years; it wasn't thirty years old, yet its pipes froze and cracked, its cellar regularly gurgled and filled with gray water bearing thick silt of paper shreds and not-quite-liquefied shit, its front steps spit bricks onto the walk like decayed teeth, and its furnace died on freezing nights. Still, he had to give it to her; they could never knock that house as long as they lived, if for no other reason than the Nigerian, high in the Chase Manhattan building downtown, paid them twenty thousand dollars more than it had cost them.

Bitch to him or not, it was that house that grubstaked their

great blind move back to, for them, the brave new world of
Boston, getting them, eventually, the beloved second house
with its gables and rooms and sun porch near Harvard Square,
Cambridge, plus (How did he know the energy crisis was
coming?) Harry's, the gas station on that sweet corner down
Liberty Square, Prospect.

They were once again filling Mayflower barrels when Harry
received from an irate Jay Wolf the news that he could indeed
forget about collecting residuals from the X-Cola campaign.
The commercials, good or bad, were irrelevant; the company
had decided not to make or market the Product after all. They
were thinking now of coming up instead with an entry in the
diet soft-drink area, which readings of future trends indicated
to be a far more promising new-product opportunity. Harry
said, "Oh, shit," but by then the news meant a loss to him
only of money.

Two

At first they rented a house, in another part of Cambridge, near Angie's parents, the Duffys. This was a bit tricky. As intoxicating as their New Start was, they hadn't learned nothing over the years and were leery of leaping into the frying pan-fire trap. Having only Big Jake, Harry felt he could enter Boston as if it were San Francisco or London or anyplace else he'd never lived; when he'd left it years before, he did have a certain fear of its holding him down, sucking him back in, suffocating him and all that, but his succeeding solo in New York for so long had immunized him against any such fears. Angie, however, had both her parents and many siblings, mostly still close around, one of the last big, blood-tight Irish families, and well before they made the big decision, Harry had made sure Angie wasn't just saying, "Don't sweat it at all; they'll read the new signals fast enough."

So, of all the reasons they knew they wanted Cambridge and nowhere else, the Duffys' being there didn't count. It wasn't a suburb. It was a city one could live in decently, only a twenty-minute ride by public transportation to the Big City, only a ten-minute run by car to Liberty Square, and only a walk from the area they intended to hold out for to Harvard Square itself, ever teeming with the young and the hip and the tuned-in people from all over the country and the world. And the first few months seemed to prove Angie true on her family, at least as far as her parents were concerned. After the inevitable reunion cookouts, dinners, and visits, all went back about their business. The mother had long ago learned that Angie was no phone-chatterer, long-distance or local, and herself was no dropper-inner. Once or twice a week, the father would stop and have tea in Angie's kitchen instead of his own, but this was something she in fact enjoyed and came to look forward to. Indeed, all events and omens seemed as auspicious as could be.

The routine of the gas station hadn't changed much in the ten or more years since Harry had been on the sell side of the pump. He breezed through the company's Army-like indoc-trination course, and Coogan left him a mechanic son for a while to break him in and to handle the repair business until Harry got a guy of his own. Which took him only three days: Harry hired Cyrus Wilson on the spot, without looking at any others, better-certified or not, because the man reminded him so much of Bert next door in New Chaumont and because of how he came on. He sauntered up one noontime with Harry's want ad in his hand. "I'm working at the Volkswagen over Lechmere for two years, and they don't let me near an engine, just interior shit and tires and sweep up, and I'm better than any of them. I hear you're from New York City."

"I am, and you got it. I'll know in a month, right?"

"Say what?"

"If I made a mistake or not. Then I'll fire you."

"Sheet," Cyrus giggled, "you'll know in a day, man."

Cyrus was all he claimed and more and they even became friends. With the inside, moneymaking part of business thus covered, Harry was then free to enjoy totally this new enterprise that he owned and had his name on. The country ran on cars, cars ran on gas and oil and parts that broke down: what's not to like about it? At first, then, and for quite a good while, the only aspect of his station that Harry didn't enjoy was seeing it when it was closed, looking dead and abandoned. Arriving mornings, he activated it fast, unlocking the office door and running inside quickly to kill the alarm bells, clicking the switches in his lights box, feeding the cat, opening his books, throwing a wink at Coogan's montage of *Playboy* and *Penthouse* centerspreads (women and kids or not, what was a gas station without *them* on a wall?). In dry weather he liked sweeping it clean to the curbs. He liked the way rain turned the tar into black mirrors agleam with its lights. And he especially came to like plowing it out from under heavy snows; even when Cyrus showed up early, Harry always did the plowing himself. He'd slam up into his tow-plow truck, choke it, pump the gas pedal four times, floor it to start it, then back it out of its bay, lower the blade and go zipping and darting around like a Dodgem car, back and forth between his two islands, building his white-walled castle.

Winter snows meant extra income from both ends of his tow-plow. He had a list of clients with driveways and curbs to be cleared. In the good times he put on a high school or college kid for it; later he'd have to go out himself. Again like Bert next door, Cyrus was always dying to go on the plowing runs, but since he was the one who did the real repair work, Harry rarely let him go, much as they both would have preferred it. The fact was that Harry would rather stay at the station than leave it, in any weather. As Pavlovian as he knew it seemed, he felt comfortable being at the beck and call of a bell all day long. *Ding!* meant wheel-over-yardline meant, usually, gas sale and perhaps oil, antifreeze, additive sale, or an appointment for repair work, hence money. But more important it meant something constant for Harry to *do*.

In New York, even when a long day's running netted him nothing, or at most a callback, he could usually take some comfort nightly in the knowledge that he had done all he could; he'd done his part, met it halfway or more. The station was better. It was benign forced labor for him, every *ding!* moving him outside, away from his thoughts or other chores, to confront a human, crank a pump, insert a nozzle into tank, lift a hood, read a dipstick for somebody. He didn't imitate people's speech exactly, but he tended to play them back to themselves; it had been an automatic reflex with him since childhood. Strangers and Square people alike said at least once how he "seemed so familiar" to them "somehow." That amused him, too, as did most things when he'd let them. When they at last found *their* house in *the* area and moved into it from the rental, it indeed seemed to them that all had been worth it; they'd found their port in the storm. With the station perking steadily, their house noisy with good sounds, Harry was feeling uncomplicated and Angie was finding relief in Harry feeling uncomplicated and in having only Kate still home, with Dennis, Amy, Jake, and Constance all in school full days. Beginning with Jack Kennedy in Dallas in '63, life seemed to follow a simple, grim formula: The older you got, the worse it got. Now, just as they were starting to think that the times they were a-changin' at last, they got hit by a strafing plane called the Federal Government, which was not known to miss very often and didn't.

They had known the law, all right (when you sell a house, you have twelve months to buy another for at least the amount you got for the first; otherwise, you're liable for capital gains tax) and had honestly and earnestly tried to comply with it. But there had been snags. For one, the lion's share of their Birchtree Lake grubstake had gone into the purchase of the Liberty Square station, plus the rental of the halfway house near the Duffys in West Cambridge, plus moving expenses, plus living money to carry their sizable family operation until the station started paying. For another, they simply couldn't find, in the year, a house even near where they wanted that was either big enough or affordable.

And they did look. They used not only the three largest realty brokers in the city, but Martin Duffy. He was now retired from the city after some thirty years (and working at a *second* career, in the boiler room of a small hospital for nuns out near Woburn, which he had started, at God knew what age, the Monday morning after the Gold Watch Friday). But he still knew Cambridge and everyone in it. He had a direct line to Tip O'Neill himself, but it went without saying that housing for a daughter, hardly destitute and a returned prodigal fresh on probation at that, wasn't cause for the red phone. The father was of help later in getting the disinterested bank to come across with a mortgage, but even he couldn't flush out an eligible house for them by the deadline. Meaning one didn't exist. When the first bill arrived for the capital gains, some four grand, Harry acted reasonably. He got letters from all the brokers and sent Xeroxes of them with his explanation to Andover. When the second bill came, including a penalty fee, he sent copies of the entire first package with another explanation, this one more detailed, as well as a bit more ... American, referring to free enterprise, the pioneer spirit, etc. The third bill, now for close to six big ones, hit gunpowder. "I've been sending essays to a *furnace!* Not one human ever even saw any of my letters! Fuck'em!"

He was hustling merrily about his station with Cyrus the rainy fall afternoon that Angie called to say, "I got a revenooer in my kitchen, Snuffy." Harry said to send him down to the station, but the man said he'd have to see their returns and letters and the papers on the New Chaumont house, so Harry had to run home. On the car radio the Beatles were singing "... one for you, nineteen for me," which didn't calm him. His taxman was standing in the kitchen, hat literally in hand, a short, natty, crew-cut priss called Brian Hayes, wearing a sawed-off raincoat. Harry was immediately all forefinger and Richard Widmark. When he went up to get the files from his attic office, the taxman told Angie, "I hate guys like this."

"Why? Like *what?*"

"They make it too personal."

But then the agent himself made it too personal. By the time Harry came back down he was cool and friendly. He'd realized it wasn't the *guy's* fault. He spread his evidence over the table and began telling the story from the beginning, when the man's face melted into a flush and grin. He snapped his fingers and beamed. *"Now* I know where I've seen you from! *N.Y.P.D.,* right?"

Harry stopped. "Good God."

"Right?"

"Well, yeah, I made one, but it was—"

"And, and, oh, lemme think, wait a sec, right! That commercial! The one fa, ah, what the heck *was* it now? You were, you were—"

"Geez, it's been over a—"

"A truckdriver! Havin' coffee in a diner, right? Real greasy spoon, and the other guy comes over an'—"

"Yeah, yeah, that was me. Christ, you really—"

"I never forget a face! Never!"

"Names, maybe," Angie slid in.

"Right. Names? Forget it. But faces? Hey, wow, isn't this somethin'. And you were in *Naked City* a lot, too, no?"

"Once. But only—"

"A cop, right?"

"No, a psychopathic killer actually," Harry lied.

"That's right, too, I guess. Gee, though." The man pulled a chair back and sat down. "Tell me—why don't they make shows like that anymore anyhow?"

"It all moved to the Coast, to California. One reason I'm here now in a way."

"A movie, too, right? Guys playing football?"

"No."

He flopped his hat onto the floor and began sifting the papers. "Well, let's see what we've got here now. I see." He glanced up now and again as Harry stated the case for defense, and each look told Harry the recognition had hardly made

him an ally. The guy turned to cement. His black eyes burned.
He sighed once and said, "Bigger they come, I guess." Harry,
at the moment, was still speaking. The guy finished with the
papers before Harry ended his story and sat waiting, glaring
naked hatred and shaking his head, No, slowly. Then he stood,
put on his hat and said, "You have to pay this, sir. Maybe the
penalties can be—"

"You didn't *hear* me, did you? I wrote those letters! Nobody
answered! I've got good *reasons*—"

The agent nodded toward Angie and moved to the door.
"Look. You can take it to tax court. But I can tell you right
now what they'll say. The law's very clear. If you'd a built a
house or had to restore one like this, they'd give you the
eighteen months. But this is—"

"We looked! We tried! There wasn't a goddamn house in
the whole—"

"Tro, take—"

"—fucking city! Didn't you read those real estate letters? I
had them goddamn notarized, for—"

"Don't give me your grief, Mr. Trowbridge. I'm just—"

It wasn't the words; it was the cold flame in the eyes. Harry
pounced, dug one hand into the taxman's shoulder and with
the other grabbed a fistful of raincoat, trouser, and presumably
underwear at the man's fat ass. "You're just getting the fuck
outta here is what you're—!"

"Tro!"

"Open the door!"

She did, and Harry ran the spluttering agent through it and
halfway across the backyard before he let him go. He walked
swiftly to his car without looking back. Inside, Angie said,
"You idiot, they'll arrest you!"

"It was worth it."

"My God, what will they do?"

They went to Cambridge Savings and took the money out of
Harry and Angie's account, is what they did. Leaving a
balance of a hundred and twenty-three dollars and seventy-five

cents. This was a week later. Harry did Wolfman in the kitchen, dining, and TV rooms, petrifying kids, dog, and cats. Spent, hair dissolved from face, he whispered, "At least they lifted the penalties. What if they didn't? What would they do, take a kid?"

"They'd take it out of the refund we'll have coming on the income taxes. According to my father."

"Oh."

"He said something else."

"What?"

"He said, 'Tell Tro ta nivver wash the hand that did the ahse!' "

Harry laughed. But while the palms and fingers of his hands did practically tingle, sometimes, when he thought of his one-man confrontation with the Feds, personal satisfaction can't be spent or banked. The station had begun making some money, but without any cushion they were reduced to counting every dime and quarter. They had expected to live more simply but hadn't meant that to include scrimping and worrying. It was the constant worry that burned into them most. Especially Harry. For all his other frustrations, he always prided himself on being a good money-maker. "Jesus!" he'd curse when he got down. "All I ever want is just enough money so I don't have to *think* about money ever."

Angie added, "I hate money when we don't have enough."

Their kids aged faster than they did, of course, and in doing so contributed a surprise element that helped reinforce them in their private, small war with the world. The older kids grew more interesting and interested and capable. Talk, real talk, so long confined to each other, suddenly expanded to include Constance and Jake. Touch football, street hockey, or catch could now *really* be played, unboringly. Their part in raking leaves or cutting wood or grass was now actual, measurable help. And the younger children reminded them that levels of life existed where money, except for gum and junk, had no meaning whatsoever.

"Are we poor?"

"No."

"Good. Are we rich?"

"No."

"Oh."

It took them a good year to climb to their feet financially again. Certainly not to where they could *save* a cent, but at least to where the ghost of going into the deep red no longer hovered. And where they could go out to eat Italian and see a movie without taking it away from something else. Perhaps it was good that their sky went suddenly dark with enemy planes again almost immediately after they had made their comeback. If the infamous energy crisis had waited until they let themselves truly relax and drop their weapons. . . . As it was, Harry soon began referring to the Queen of Liberty Square as his "goddamn Edsel dealership!" And Angie would laugh, but always with eyes that said, *It would be funny, almost, if it weren't so frightening.*

The life of his work sidekick, Cyrus, gave Harry a new respect for irony. When he first signed on, Cyrus' life problems, aside from skin in Irish-Italian territory, were hardly exotic: sex, rage, booze, and asthma, only the last ever making him miss work. If a fox called his wife, he'd piss and moan and be down for a day but never slack, and he'd never lay too many details on Harry. The fury and drink were something else and eventually did get Harry more involved, but overall, listening to Cyrus' stories (like, increasingly, Jake's and Constance's) let Harry see how life could go for people different from himself. He came to realize what cover he unwittingly enjoyed: Being neither black nor literally young, he could pass through most areas of his local worlds unsuspected, unlikely to be challenged by authority. He and Angie, for instance, often walked down Brattle Street nights to the movies or bars in Harvard Square openly sharing a joint, their only precaution being to roll them fat and round in a Tops machine, with a half filter snipped from a Lark.

Whereas Cyrus could be hassled twice just walking from his house to the store for cigarettes. Before he moved out of Roxbury, his job with Harry was the safest part of his life; his rage for the world would fester and burn until it had to get outside from inside, and its ticket out was gin, and when ginned, Cyrus, built like Joe Frazier and only twenty-eight, took abuse from nobody, especially no cop, and since it was usually a cop dealing it out, it was usually a cop's face that ended up getting hammered. Three times in two years, then once with a pool cue: six months in Concord State Reformatory. Harry visited and missed him; he went through two wrench bums and lost business. He told sorrowful Cyrus, "You know, there's an old saying I just made up, babe—you can't help being a nigger, but you don't have to be a dumb nigger!"

Befriending Cyrus made Harry see his own past as privileged by comparison. Day-hopping to school, and working, and comprehending no more than a third of it (not counting the acting), he had at least been let get some kind of higher education, plus a degree for the records. Cyrus had been let get his body out of South Carolina to Vietnam, period. Later, however, it seemed to be Cyrus' fortunes that were getting the upturn, smack in the middle of Harry's agonies, yet *through* Harry, and Angie's oldest brother, Father Thomas. The first morning Cyrus was back from the slammer, Harry and he walked up the Square to try out a just-opened coffee shop. Counterpointing all the surrounding hygiene, the proprietor looked like Cookie in *Beetle Bailey,* down to the rancid T-shirt and the four-inch cigarette ash clamming from his lips. When Cyrus ordered toast, the slob leered, "You want that toast light, dark, or *real dark?*"

Harry tensed but relaxed when Cyrus grinned. "Nigger toast. Ah wants nigger toast, gimme somea thet nigger toast, heah? Feets, do yo stuff, sho nuff." Cookie loved it, laughed till he coughed and gave Cyrus better eggs than Harry got.

Outside, Harry said, "See? You turned that bastard completely around. Way to go."

"Well, Tro, I've figured it out—necks get red from working hard out in the sun or over heavy heat. They gotta hit somebody but don't mean it personal."

"Oh, Christ, talk about heavy heat. Spell chrysanthemum, old philosopher. But hey, listen, I got something for you."

What Harry had was what Father Thomas at his request had researched while Cyrus was away. Cyrus leaped at it and within a year, with a bit of books juggling in the station, and a lot of form filling and hump busting on his own, he had exchanged his two-hundred-and-sixty-dollar-a-month slum flat for a small house of his own out near Billerica, with monthly payments of around ninety dollars—via the Federal Government and via a vow to Harry that when the rage blew he would confine his ginning to the inside of his own new home. Cyrus even installed a punching bag in his basement. In no way begrudging the man his pilgrim's progress, still Harry had to resent the system that worked to support only those at the very top or the very bottom and fucked everybody else in the middle.

Of course, by now it had become much more personal and private for Harry than all that: Cyrus had more than a mortgage rate for Harry to envy; he still had his total and outright love and contentment with working in the Liberty Square station. And Harry no longer did. Whether the hard times of the energy crisis had hastened it or not, the novelty, excitement and adventure of his move had worn off, and fear and dissatisfaction had set in. With Cyrus back, Harry now had to conceal it from his mechanic as well as from his wife, a day-and-night job that didn't lessen the pressure any. Just as the station had underground tanks, so did Harry, and like it or not, understand why or not, his tanks had started going dry even before the station's did.

He hated this truth because it scared him, but his noble experiment had worked for just so long, about three years, before he once again began feeling blocked, out of place, discontent, all of it. He so hated this fact that he kept denying it, wouldn't look at it. He'd cross the street if he saw it coming, pretend to study something in a window. When it jumped out at him from around a corner, he'd walk through it. It wasn't solid. He hated and denied and avoided it because it looked like failure again. At times he saw the station's increasing jeopardy as a sign to quit lying and postponing, hence worsening, the inevitable; but he denied that, too. He couldn't believe God would whip a whole industry just to prod Harry Trowbridge, 1970's, into either plugging or abandoning his sinking little ship.

The idea of going to see a head doctor again lit in his mind, but only as lightly as a bird, flying away just as fast. It seemed as much a part of his world now as fifteen-dollar haircuts or martinis at lunch, and the money involved had nothing to do with it. It was simply something he would no longer consider doing. He'd been amused one day by Tony Cangiolosi, in with his toolbox-sided pickup. Tony was a builder. Friendly, he said, "Hey, Harry, gotta guy like you on the job with us now! Just started."

"Looks like Robert Redford?"

"Your face his ass! Nah! Another big city slicker from New York. Way up on some company does the TV. Pullin' down the big bucks. Has the nervous breakdown."

"Raises bees in a cigar box."

"Nah! Says that's it! Gets a saw and hammer. Oughta see him runnin' around with us. Happy as a pig in shit. Pretty good on the roofs, too. Name's Pressfield, know 'im?"

"Oh, yeah. Seventy-second street."

"No shit?"

"Sure. Real stupid."

"Whaddaya mean? I told you he—

"Well, he's working for you, ain't he, Tone?"

"Ah, mafungool."

Harry let most people think what they wanted and never told stories or gave reasons, true or otherwise. "Nervous breakdown" was never entirely untrue no matter who said it, he figured, and if that was the number running on him, fine. He had no trouble realizing what *wasn't* wrong with his life.

But that quicksilver, underground emptiness he'd begun to feel and to fret about stayed on, murkily elusive and unidentifiable. For relief, he'd frequently pretend it *was*, after all, only the aggravation from his money problems. He'd feel better, but never for long. He knew otherwise. His dead mother's voice would sometimes come ringing out of the past: "Nothing ever satisfies you, does it?" He, the kid, would ignore or contradict her, but now he wasn't so sure. He hated to believe that that could be all it was, some unfillable, blind desire in him that he'd have to endure all his life. Making him just another sourball at heart, only disguised as an upbeat scrapper, to suck in innocent victims. Sometimes, during long lulls between bells, when he'd be wirebrushing somebody's spark plugs or changing a tire or doing some such handwork, he'd get a bit spacy and have the urge to go through Liberty Square, taking a poll. If everybody or at least a sizable majority of people admitted that they too carried this constant blank (fear? discontent? sorrow?) buried inside them practically all the time, then maybe he could lay it to the human condition or the temper of the times or some similar universal and just try to learn how to live with it better. He never took the poll, of course. All he did was continue chewing it like some acrid cud, all the while hiding it from Angie.

The first time this poison circulating through Harry's system finally erupted through the crust was on a freezing November Friday night in '74. It burst without warning. It was Cyrus' night off. After eight or so, the business died down to nothing. It was, as they say, a good night for staying home. Harry tried to do his books, a chore he dreaded more with each passing month. He was really getting hit hard; he was, he now knew, one of the ones the company wanted to see close. It was getting harder and harder to pay Cyrus, but without Cyrus he'd be a filling station and have to stock one of his bays with discount

soft drinks or something to get by, like Sunoco on the other
end of the Square. He was ready to shut down, just before
midnight, when Steve Miller pulled in on his way home from
the Lions. Steve was one of Harry's regulars, but somewhat
special to him. Steve also had come back to Liberty Square
from someplace else and was also wondering if maybe he'd
been crazy to do so.

Steve was about ten years older than Harry. His big time
had been IBM in Poughkeepsie in upstate New York. Nine
years of up, up, up to 1968, when he and his wife upped and
said enough, quit, and came back to Boston. He'd been
making good money, had even been saving some. "I don't
know, Tro, we just reached the point where we woke and said,
'Shit, not one thing has changed for five years.' And from the
way it looked then, nothing was *gonna* change much for the *next*
five! We were getting older and never having any fun at all.
Just new golf shoes every year." Harry never had had that
kind of security and guaranteed annual gain, but their experi-
ences were like enough to make a link and let them talk about
more than sports. Steve was an engineer for the county now.
He drove in this night in his new little Gremlin—*the shoe*, was
their joke. "Hey, Steveo, whaddaya want, soles and heels?" He
owned it jointly with the oldest two of his four kids. His wife,
Boots, needed the Volvo to get to and from Prospect City
Hospital, where she was a nurse, nights, full time. Seeing
Harry was closing, Steve said, "You want to go have one, or
you going home?" Harry said sure, and they walked across the
avenue to Shea's Lounge. It was all normal.

There were four different drinking places around Liberty
Square. A tavern, a gin mill, a barroom, and Shea's, the beer
joint. For business' sake, Harry made his appearances in them
all fairly equally, but Shea's was his favorite because it was the
closest and because he knew the owner was totally unaware of
the joke in his establishment's name. The paynight crowd was
still having at it. Steve and Harry stood at the bar and got
their scotch and waters without singing more than "Hiya,
Paul." It was normal. Steve told a gag, Harry told one, and

the drift took its normal course. The appealing thing about Steve was, he was a complainer but didn't sound it. He was pink and rotund, his glasses sat on his nose, he was balding, and his sideburns puffed almost white over his ears. He reminded Harry of Smitty's boss in the comics, and his look seemed to take any whine out of his lamenting. Steve stuck mostly to his own viewpoint, which boiled down to: There's no getting out from under, ever. For example, he'd always wanted to get a boat. It'd be for them all, but he'd always seen himself and his oldest boy out on it. He still didn't have it. The kid was starting college next fall. So even if he *got* the goddamned boat now, it wouldn't be the same boat; it wouldn't be *how* he'd always wanted it. Harry liked the quality of the guy's bitching. Of course, having done something to his life, having made a move, Harry had to like Steve anyhow.

Harry couldn't remember feeling any Call of the Wild coming that November night. He still couldn't remember exactly what happened. He'd said yes, he'd stop by Steve's house for a quickie. That wasn't entirely abnormal; he'd been there before, Miller had been to his house, but he couldn't recall why he would have wanted to go that night, other than it seemed like a good idea at the time. He'd called Angie from Steve's kitchen so she wouldn't worry; then he and Steve had apparently gone at it. That wasn't normal at all. Harry's idea of a toot was shots and beers in front of two late movies on the tube maybe twice a year and an occasional blast with one or more of Angie's brothers when he didn't have to get up in the morning and had Angie there to drive.

Harry had learned to drink as a gentleman and officer of the United States Army, by an act of Congress, and he was still proud of it. The night with Steve was insane. He'd worked fourteen hours; snow was still banked on curbs; there had been a rain and a freeze. Steve lived high on Tower Hill, two streets down from the top, and the hill was seven cross streets high, by Harry's own actual, walking, teenage count. A rather "grand" area. Working class lived down in the flat lowlands in two- and three-deckers, along with, more and more, students and others somehow associated with Harvard. Up here lived doctors, lawyers, senior firemen, teachers, and professionals like Steve. He remembered Steve's trying to make him stay, trying even to take the keys away from him.

Harry also recalled talking himself, but what about? The energy crisis, the gas "shortage"? He doubted it. Hell, that was still all over the papers every other day, pictures of sheikhs at coffee tables laughing their asses off, Ultra-Brite teeth under dark sunglasses. Steve never normally depressed him; he never matched Steve with woes of his own. Harry still didn't know, could never bring himself to ask Steve—what did he *tell* him that night? He couldn't remember Steve's street or going down Arsenault, either.

Just the hitting of Tower Square at the bottom. And the bleary, almost giddy, fluid, too-late realization that he had not stopped. Though he had fully intended to. And *still* had not stopped, was still . . . technically, the Toyota carrying the two ancient, blue-haired porcelain ladies had smashed into Harry, not the way the fake-brogued mick barrister had made it sound in court. Not that the difference mattered at all ever, even to Harry. He had only felt them, not seen them. And still thanked God for not killing them. He didn't remember being booked, or calling Angie's older brother Albie, or being thrown in the tank. And all he could remember about the tank was the next morning, waiting to be let out of it, fur-mouthed and consumed by shame. There had been other hulks there in the large hot cellar room, but the only one who pierced through Harry's remorseful gloom was the urine-aired, one-eyed winobum who kept constantly muttering, like Bill Bendix, "What a revoltin' development this is!"

He lost his license for a year.

No stuff for the Future Kid Talk he often fantasized having, wherein he would discuss all the ins and outs of Life with his brood, straight from the shoulder and eye to eye, over drinks or smokes.

Nor did he mention it to even Martin Duffy, who might or

might not have been able to pull some strings but would surely have wanted to try. Harry wasn't afraid of being scorned or losing any "face" with Angie's family. He just didn't want ever to be in anyone's debt. Only Angie and Albie knew then, and luckily, if there was a Duffy who could keep his mouth shut, Albie was the one. Even so, that was two too many for Harry's liking.

That was the bad part. The good part was, Harry had plummeted his Fury III wagon down into Tower Square, not Liberty. So it had not been his own cops who had nailed him. At the time he intended to abide by the suspension, but another of Harry's cement principles was: Never let Authority know where you're vulnerable. He'd lapsed on it only once, in the capital-gains affair.

Not that it helped much, but the next time whatever *It* was burst, Harry sensed it coming first. It was another Friday night, late in the next April. It was Cyrus' night on at the station. Harry and Angie were alone in their living room. Amy, Dennis, and Kate had gone to bed at nine-thirty. Constance and Jake were out. The house was quiet. Angie was reading *Fear of Flying*. Harry wasn't.

Angie finally one-eyed him over the top of the paperback and caught him staring at the fireplace. There was no fire going in the grate, only cold ashes. She said, "What are you thinking about?"

His eyes snapped clear. He grinned. "Superman."

"What about him?"

"He killed himself."

She let him see her worry but said, "Oh. How do you feel otherwise?"

"But he did—*Superman killed himself!* Sounds weird, doesn't it? And the kids are still watching him."

She lit a Benson and Hedges and tossed him his black throwaway lighter. "So?"

He lit a Lark. "So I don't know. It'd be kind of dicey to try to explain. If they ever found out and asked. That's all, I guess."

She was smiling, but her eyes squinted. "Come on. Really."

On the loveseat Harry leaned forward over the coffee table and studied Dennis' upside-down *Cub Scout Handbook.* "Nothing, really."

"That was a long thought about nothing."

"Thought you were *reading.* It any good?"

"Yeah, it's ... I think she's trying to tell the truth, anyhow."

"Will I like it?"

"Oh, Christ. Have a drink, will you?"

"No way."

"Come on, even private Lents end. And real Lent never lasts six months anyhow. I'll even get it for you."

"I do not drink hard liquor, nor have I ever."

Angie laughed. "I mean it, babe. I mean, you can get as antsy and uptight as you want, but you're driving me up a wall. I know a lot's bugging you but—"

"No."

"Have a scotch. It'll cheer you up. Oh, I know. You think I will if you do, don't you? Well, I won't. But you should. Really. You get too morose since you've been off it ... she's been meaning to tell him for quite a while!"

"Burst!" Constance came in, saving him. This was her way of entering a room at the time, at least when Harry was there. She was fifteen. She announced one day that she had been "literally bursting into rooms all my life," only to be ignored or shushed, so this was to be it now.

Harry grinned. "Hi, queenie," and Angie said, "You're early, you get gypped?"

Constance said, "No, they paid me to midnight."

"Why'd they come home so soon? It's only ten thirty."

"Moth-er"—playing TV daughter—"how would I know? I think they had a fight."

"The great professor bagged, was he?"

"I don't think so," Constance said, "they were pretty cool.

Ten thirty?" She glanced behind her, through the dining room, to the darkened TV room. "Where's Jake?"

"Ten minutes late," Harry said as Angie said, "Down the Square."

Constance dropped into an easy chair. "You guys doing anything? What's the movie on? They don't *have* TV. Some neat records, though. Oh, it started at nine anyhow." Sigh. Up. "I think I'll go to bed."

"Constance?" Harry said as she leaned to kiss him.

"Why don't I go to bed?" Her kiss like a slight hit. Waft of musk.

"Why don't you go to bed?" He moved, imperceptibly, to swat her patched-jeaned rump but checked the gesture. He couldn't do that anymore. She even had breasts now, real woman's ones. He was just getting used to it. Of all the things he liked about her, he guessed his favorite was the fact that she was never called Connie by anyone. He could see that what he admired as *bearing* might appear to some others as a trace of snobbiness—it surely did often enough to Angie—but he saluted it anyhow, for the attitude he liked to think it signaled. She seemed to be in a no-boys cycle now, but *that* had begun for her with cymbals, the year before. A *senior* had asked her, a *freshman*, to his prom! Angie and she had pillaged Boston for the dress. The kid came in a tux: a handsome, six-foot-twelve first-string lineback, a throwback to the fifties but for the shoulder-length hair. That whole evening was a bag of assorted throwbacks for them, mostly jarring.

Harry thought the boy's name had been Ray but couldn't recall his face. He'd never appeared at their door again, and in all the snapshots Angie had taken of them, poor Ray's map never showed up once. He was severed at the chin, neck, or chest every time. Because Angie had had to chase around after them, shooting on the run. Because Constance couldn't *believe* that her mother could ever be doing such a gauche thing and was splitting as fast as she could, Jackie and the paparazzo. Not that Angie or Harry could believe at first that the Senior

Prom was actually resurfacing in their lifetime or that their superhip, pacifist, activist, feminist eldest was actually gowned and going. Hooting, Jake and the younger mob had carried the chase all the way to the kid's dad's Dart at the curb. Inside, Angie had frozen in laughing mid-wind of the Instamatic. "Oh, Tro."

"Gonna cry? Mama's baby all—"

"No! Don't you see what I'm doing? What I just did? Jesus, I did my mother! Oh, poor Constance!"

"No way. You gotta have pictures of your kid's first *prom,* for crying out ... Jeez, it does sound bizarre, doesn't it? Christ, *I* sound like Robert Young!"

But Angie had stayed struck-looking. That wasn't what she'd meant. "No. Oh, wow, this is ... I promised myself, I *vowed* that I'd always *think* first. Now, bing! I went right into it. The same embarrassing—"

"Ah, if you'd analyzed, you still would've taken the pictures. You're distorting it, babe. You're overreacting to being—"

"What?"

"Well ... old. Older."

"Crap. She's *young* to be going to a prom!"

Too young, it turned out. Ray's mother had come tearing up in a VW before the smaller kids were back in the house. He'd forgotten the corsage; she was trying to catch up with them. She made it, for Constance was carrying it, a wristlet of yellow roses that clashed with her dress, when she came in less than an hour later. She didn't say, "Burst." The waves of moist heat spearing him from both sides sent Harry running to the kitchen. When Angie came out later, she told him, "The reality didn't hit her until she got there. She felt way over her head. She doesn't even know the kid. Or any of his friends. They're all four years older, they're all seniors! We should have ... well, actually I did wonder."

"But what happened?"

"She said she was sick and had him bring her home."

"She *what?*"

Angie looked surprised. "What's *that* mean?"

"Well, that poor kid! It's his goddamn prom! His last one, his big one! He laid out *bread,* for Christ's—"

"Ssh. That's not the way to look at it at all."

"Bullshit! That what she's going to be? Another *beauty* who goes around dumping on guys?" High school and college memories twisted dimly.

"That's amazing."

"What is?"

"You immediately took his side. She's your daughter, Tro. And no matter how she looks and how mature and smart and all that she is, she's still so *young!*"

"Then you'd better start getting it into her head now, that she—"

"You have no idea what she did tonight, do you?"

"Well, that Ray, or *Roy,* or whatever sure as hell does by now."

"He went back, she said. I'm sure he's fine. Constance found herself in a situation she didn't like and couldn't handle, and she *got out of it,* Tro. Years ago you or I would've stayed and suffered through it all night long. You're the one who has the *great thing* with her, and you can't give her that?"

Harry had whistled feebly. "Hoo, boy. Got me that time, didn't you?" He would remember that as the moment Constance ceased to be his baby, his first child, and became someone who had qualities and stuff inside to be regarded, whether he understood them entirely or not. Watching her glide off "to bed" this night a year later, bearer of strong attitudes, made him again remember that night of the premature prom and wonder if parent could inherit from child—that casing of a bad situation and escaping it fast was one hell of an ability. His own lack and need of it seemed to be growing more acute by the day.

He shot a glance at Angie, hoping she was legitimately reinvolved with her novel, yet wondering, if he *wasn't* itching for some kind of confrontation, why he was hanging there bookless, paperless, drinkless? "To bed." How did they know what she did up there? That was for her and Jake to know and for them to find out or not. He said, "I think I'll go up and have a joint with Constance."

"Not in *that* mood. You'll crawl under the rug." Ignoring the Constance part.

"Booze yes, grass no. How do you feel about busing?"

"All right, should I just put the damn book away and we'll have a fight?"

"God, no. Read, read. Raise that consciousness. I'm going for a walk."

"Hallelujah."

It was almost May, but it felt like March, so he went back for a jacket, then left by the rear door. He whistled for the dog. There was a moon, off and on, and he looked up. He liked to see his house's jutty roofline against a night sky: a ship moving, the widow's walk a crow's nest. He whistled again and called, "Waldo!" A collar jangle, then he was there. Harry thumped him, "Yeah, yeah, let's go, going someplace swell." Waldo was a golden retriever, named that by Harry because the dog's mother's name was Molly and in college Harry had used to go drinking down a joint in Marblehead, the Molly Waldo. Which had been a code name in whaling days: When two ships passed, one skipper would bellow through his horn, *Molly!* If the reply came back *Waldo!* it meant they were both out of Marblehead and they'd come alongside each other and have a party. Harry had thought it splendid to have a dog with such a story-laden name. Too late, he learned that the kids dug the name, too, because it was the same as the dog's in *Nanny and the Professor* on the tube. But that was all right, he was pretty sure Waldo would outlive the reruns; he had street savvy and stuck very close to home. That was odd for a retriever, but explainable: Waldo still didn't know about girl dogs. Five years old and still humping the Hoppityhop. On the sidewalk Harry looked back and saw three lights, the porch one for Jake, downstairs for Angie, upstairs for Constance. *What was she doing up there?*

Angie had said it more than once: "I don't remember its being like that for me, but when you think about it, those kids have more privacy and more run of the house than we do! They never have to be in any room they don't want to be in, and they can go off to their own rooms anytime they want and just close the door!" *And do what?* Oh, read, Harry knew. Constance's room was a library. Or listen to music. Jake had headphones. Or study, write letters, fantasize, brood, sleep. Or smoke cigarettes or joints. He and Angie were sure an occasional cigarette was smoked up there, sometimes singly, sometimes together. Constance and Jake had abruptly become underground comrades this last year. Something to with Jake's transferral of two inches from his girth to his height, an achievement tromboned by the concurrent deepening of his voice by several decibels. Plus his total enjoyment and swaggering exploitation of being in the eighth grade in an eight-grade school, the last, perhaps, of life's pure peaks. One day: "Constance, just go suck an egg, will ya?" and suddenly he was a person to her. Welcome to the Tammany Tyranny of the Teens. Harry and Angie were glad to see it. Smokes or not, it was better than fighting.

They weren't so sure about the pot. Constance told Angie that she had tried it once or twice "in the past." But that could've been just her, fishing. And how do you tell if a thirteen- or a fifteen-year-old is high on something? If the English teacher complimented Constance, if Jake's "brother" Douglas cut an exceptional fart in the gym ... they'd still be flying and grinning hours later. Dope should get everybody so stoned. Actually, Harry looked forward to the day when he could sit down and smoke or drink with them: his Future Kid Talk. He had a friend in New York who did already: turned on regularly with his oldest kids, only a little older than Harry's. But then his situation was different. For one thing, he was now the parent-in-residence. He and his wife had separated years ago, though they hadn't divorced and probably never would. ("Divorce Wendy? How can I? She's family!") She had brought them up, weekdays, for twelve years; then he

took over. The Bronx is up, the Battery's down. Whereas
Harry was plugged into the square world and saw his
obligations.

At Angie's prodding ("You've got to, Tro. The Garfield,
though. Not the ecclesiastical") he had sat them down one
night shortly after New Year's and laid it on them as straightly
as he could. Booze and Smoke I. Basically, everything is timing
and learning. Of course, you have to try, but not *everything*. Use
versus Abuse. Beer can make you fat. Grass can make you lazy.
Booze can make you crazy and defeat you. ("Consider your
mother's family" ... "I heard that!") It all costs money, and
there are better things to buy, and in the buying, alcohol is
still as illegal for you two as marijuana. Tobacco. "What can I
tell you? Don't. Your mother and I do. We shouldn't. We
started because adults said don't. But they only said it stunted
your growth, made you cough and ruined your wind. You guys
have grown up watching the Cancer Society, not Marlboro
Country, yet every other kid I see is dragging on a butt. You
tell me." A stab at: Very often, as tough as it is to pull off, the
coolest thing you can do is say no to the group. Try it, it's a
kick. "Any questions? Okay, just one more thing. Let me catch
you, and I'll break your feet."

Waldo went east onto Brattle, looked back to make sure
Harry didn't go wrong, then pranced on. He'd finessed the
grass on the illegality. That's what he meant by the "obligations" he saw for himself, and it was at times like this that he
fiercely wished he possessed whatever it took to quit the square
world entirely. He'd spoken to Constance and Jake about
liquor and cigarettes as a user. He inclined toward admitting
the same on grass, but didn't, couldn't. Because if he did, he'd
have to warn them to keep it secret, and that would be dirty
pool; they had more than enough to carry around just by
getting up alive every morning. So he'd had to talk about it as
an assumed nonuser, hence lost a lot of credibility (though not
all. Constance had caught him once, the past Thanksgiving
Day. She'd come home from a football game unexpectedly,

and there was Harry sucking on a Zig Zag in the kitchen, punk smell absorbed by roasting bird and cooling pies. He did what occurred to him first: He offered it to her. She smiled. "No, thank you, Daddy," and scrammed).

Harry noticed that Waldo ahead was nearly cantering, which made him realize his own legs were walking fast, as if heading someplace. He slowed to a stroll. Good neighborhood for night walking. Old, wide-spreading trees tenting fine old houses. It pleased him to be living here in R. Lowell-H. W. Longfellow land. They used to bike up here from Liberty Square in the fall to hurl sticks up into the chestnut trees. Residents called the police, who came, took their names and addresses (Harry's was "James Connors," a kid he hated), and told them to "get the fuck back where you belong!" Now he owned a house here. He grinned in the night, walking. Then he lit a cigarette, quickly, against the sudden panic that his stream of kid things to think about had run dry. He didn't want that to happen. If it did, the coming trouble would rush into the space. If he kept walking, and kept mulling solid things over, and kept Waldo in sight, maybe it would go away. He whistled. "Here, boy. Thatta boy. Stay close, bud."

Kids. Booze. Smoke. Telling. Knowing. That was it, really, the knowing. Knowing when and when not and how much. Ah, but things change. Chestnuts fall in their own time now and lie on the ground until they rot or get raked away. Sneakers pass them by. No swift hands select the hardest-looking, drill nail holes through their centers, slip knotted shoelaces through, then have fights with them; one must do the breaking, another must get broken ... until yo-yo time. And Harry thought: Even in the house, how fast the changes happen! Amy was ten now. When Constance was ten, eleven, he and Angie didn't have to slip to their bedroom to smoke their little tokes. The kids just didn't *know*. They never smoked as openly as folks drank martinis, but they didn't have to go hide to do it either. Then again, the covertness of their rendezvous now added zing to their occasional get-highs. So

they lost, they gained. Things did, they did seem to have
balance to them. Parents find out. Nor could he and Angie be
sure how much the kids knew or didn't. Kids overhear.

Kids, kids ... soon after they had first returned to the scene
of their early years, Harry'd seduced her one night to "go all
the way" in the car, parked by the dark Charles across from
the Metropolitan District Police station. Smoking in the front
seat, Angie'd sighed. "Hell, not even a flashlight against the
fender. Well, that's what you get for blowing your chances
years ago, Tro."

"Ho, as if I didn't try."

"Oh, I don't know, I think I could've been had."

"Now you tell me."

"I know. God, though, when I think of it. The pain was so
much worse than the fear. We just should've done it, that's
all."

"Would've been a lot more honest anyhow."

"At least. I wonder if it would've changed anything."

"Sure it would've! You've ended up with a guy who pumps
gas; I would've just stayed pumping gas from the beginning.
And left the education for *our* kids, not the half-and-half deal
we got."

She'd swished her panties into her shoulder bag. "Like hell.
If you said that then, I would've dropped you in two seconds!"

"Yeah, but what's an easy lay know about social progress?"

Waldo's tongue was flapping like a third ear as he hit full
gallop, Harry only a yard behind, running. *Running?* He
stopped and laughed, pretending to the dog that he'd done it
on purpose. "Hey, how was that, huh?" He'd dropped the
cigarette. Heaving, he lit a new one. Waldo peed on a car tire.
A kid whizzed out of the night on a bike. The dog made for
him. "Waldo! You sit! Stay! Good boy ... Sorry, pal—he's
okay though, he wouldn't have—hey, that you, Jake?"

"No. Hi, Mr. Trowbridge."

"Hey, Mike! How are you, man? Seen Jake?"

"No. Night."

"Night, Mike." Harry could hear the chain of the kid's ten-speed clatter in the dark stillness, fainter and fainter, and felt anger for his son Jake. He wished it'd been him. He would have liked to have met him. But that would've made Jake a half hour or more late, and Harry'd have had to *say* something about it, a pain for them both. It would've been unusual for Jake, too. Even the ten minutes were off his stride. The boy was eminently trustworthy. Harry and Waldo rounded the corner onto Huron together and slowly. It wasn't anger, exactly, either. It was the same strain of anguish that Angie confessed she had also been experiencing toward the kid. Harry said it first: "I'm always getting pissed off at him lately, and for no reason! I don't know. I hate it. Christ, don't tell me I'm turning into one of those old cranks, taking my own problems out on my kids every night! Start kicking the dog and cats next. And I'd much rather beat the wife."

"Try it. No, I know what you mean. It's eerie. I've caught myself doing it, too."

"Really? Why, though? Shit, he's terrific, I love him!"

"It isn't *pissed off,* exactly."

"No. It's—"

"I think it might be a bounce off the Constance thing." *That* strange, new, mutual emotion had also raised itself recently, but it had been easier to figure out: She was on her way out of their house, and the idea of it saddened them. They thought Constance was starting to sense it, too.

"How? Listen, I'm not making book on *him* getting out of eighth grade!"

"He's turning the corner, Tro. Maybe we resent him for it."

"Man, first you can't believe they'll ever be gone, you can't wait for them to take off, then all of a sudden—"

"What I can't understand is, how did *they* get so old when *I* stayed so young?"

"God, if that's not a sign of menopause."

He followed Waldo back onto their street. Clouds broke, moonlight fell on his house farther up the hill, and he thought again how much he loved that huge, five-gabled, shingled, nutzy, Victorian *frigate* of a house! Unlike the New Chaumont stuckup puke, this old hellion had never fought Harry once. Just the opposite: It had been let go badly for too many years before he and Angie bought it, and when they and the mob first stampeded into it, it felt as if it were physically hugging them out of relief and joy. When he rolled the first coat of good Williamsburg paint onto its first thirsty wall, he swore he heard it relax and heave and sigh, *"Thaank you!"* And so it had behaved ever since—*it,* at least, Harry thought, had not turned to rot and trouble in his hands. He saw that only two lights burned now: the porch bulb for himself (and maybe still for Jake; he'd murder him) and the one in their bedroom. Constance had turned in. Angie must still be reading. Maybe the book was as sexy as its publicity claimed and she'd be itching to put it down!

His thoughts and his body were back in better coordination now, yet his foot sent a stick skidding along the black sidewalk and Waldo fetched it, and Harry groaned, "Oh, no." The joke with the kids was: "Don't ever throw a grenade with Waldo around!" Harry laughed and threw the stick for him. He'd fetch until he dropped. He made Frisbee impossible. "That's *all,* now! Ah, okay." The third time he turned and spun it high into a neighbor's yard. The dog shot through their hedge. Let 'em think it's prowlers or a peeping Tom, Harry mused. Jazz up their night. He still didn't know what to do about his own. Oh, Angie baby. Even if he found her oiled and reptilian and garbed in silky music and he came so often and hard he hammered his head against the wall, he still wouldn't be able to sleep yet this night. Something was coming, he just knew it. He had a sudden flash of the night of the accident.

Of course, no whammo tryst was likely anyhow. Forget his own restless, wary sensing of the Call of the Wild. Friday evenings structured around kids-due-in were poor set and setting for anything richer than reading, tubing, or brooding. He went up his walk, across the porch, and into the front hall.

Jake's bike was there; lucky for him. He flicked off the porch light, stepped back outside, sat on the top step, and lit another Lark, wishing it were a Marlboro, regretting for the moment his private underground movement against Number Ones. He whistled, once and clear, for the dog. A beautiful, street kid, fingerless whistle. Jake had it mastered already; Dennis would soon enough, and the way he could do the new Anne Frank *eeyou* police siren! Clearly a natural. *Set and setting.* Perhaps that was something he could explain to them too, in that Famous-Future-Old-Enough-Sit-Down-Drink-or-Smoke-and-Talk he was going to have with them. Mental set, physical setting. He'd found it in a book on drugs, but it applied to sex, booze, possibly everything, for all he knew. He'd leave sex out. Let them make their own seekings and discoveries. But he'd say, "Always consider where you are. The room, the space, and things around you, right? Does it feel right? Or *off,* somehow? If it's off for whatever you're going to do, fix it first." He whistled again, twice, for the dog. Either find it or forget it, huh, Wally? He stood and stretched. The moon had gone back in. Waldo came trotting onto the front slope. Harry could see the proud eyes smiling at him as the dog dropped his find at the master's feet. Harry picked it up. "That's some stick, you bananahead." It was somebody's nine iron. A Spalding.

Wonderful, Harry thought, carrying it inside with him. Hit me with petty larceny, now! Makes you a two-time loser, Trowbridge. *You're pushing your luck, mister!* He snapped out the porch light and locked the front door. The TV room was a jut off the dining room. Jake was in there, with tail-wagging Waldo's snout in his lap, sprawled in the set's eerie blue light. Harry stopped in the doorway. "Hey."

"Hi, Pop."

"When'd you get in?"

"Little while ago. I was a little late," saving Harry the effort.

"Come on, Waldo, sack time!" In the kitchen, Waldo lapped the cats' water dish dry and curled up under Angie's desk. In the light from the single bulb over the kitchen table Harry, for the first time in over five months, brought the quart of scotch out from the cabinet and went for a glass and cubes, about to violate his future Kid Sermon on Mental Set. He did consider the setting, though, peering through the glass above the café curtains to the rear windows of his bedroom. Lights out; she'd gone to sleep. He left the liquor unopened. The hell with it, he'd go see Jake instead. And he'd have the golf club returned tomorrow; being a one-time loser was painful enough. He closed the kitchen door and joined the boy. It was strange; the kid's sheer presence seemed to displace the itching sense of . . . impatience he'd been unable to sulk, walk or talk away himself. "So—how come you were late, bud?"

"Ah, damn cop stopped us."

"Who were you with—Doug?"

"Yeah."

"What were you doing? You had your bike."

"Yeah. *Nothing.* Just standing there, hanging out near the Brattle."

"That'll do it."

"Yeah."

"Doug's not . . . ?"

"No! He's okay now, Dad, he really is. He's coming to school every day and everything." Doug was literally a two-time loser; one more theft, and it'd be reform school. His mother was now disposing of husband number three. Harry liked the kid, a handsome, lithe charmer, could be cast as the Navajo chief's son; he already had the headband. Jake had adopted him, to help "save" him, he and Angie knew, and Harry had every misgiving possible but had to like Jake the more for doing it. Jake was supine at the moment, butt on chair, legs on radiator, swigging on a Doctor Pepper.

Harry dropped into another chair. "What's the flick?"

"I missed the name. Want me to get the schedule?"

"Nah."

They watched it together for a while. Harry didn't recognize it or anyone in it; one of those shot so hoopie-skoopie that he couldn't tell if it was new or made during World War II. An armored car of sorts had just broken down in the middle of a desert, filled with the hero (not Dan Duryea, not Doug McClure) and a bunch of girls in harem gossamer. No food, no gas, no cover against the sun. After a brief cutback in some "embassy," the vehicle miraculously came tearing through the city gates, the explanation footage lost somewhere in Astoria or Burbank. Jake scoffed and said ponderously, "Did you know that certain parts of those trucks are *edible?*"

Harry broke up. The laugh was all the more delicious because Jake was the kid who *didn't* have the quick lip. Or he didn't have a fast *enough* tongue—had he not been alone with Harry, he most likely wouldn't have given the line. Like his humor, everything about Jake was inside and rarely came out, home in the house anyhow. Harry slid his glance from the tube to the boy. If this first up-and-out burst was any indication, he would tower over Harry by the time he was eighteen. He had Angie's dark blond hair and her nose; it looked broken but wasn't. The nose American women loved. It had sprung out on Jake when he was around ten, and in his weak moments Harry would curse that if only *he* had had that nose, Roy Scheider wouldn't have got *The French Connection,* and James Caan wouldn't have ... he half-kiddingly entertained the idea at such times of going out and getting it busted. Angie was always prompt to offer her services.

They had named the boy after Harry's father (unnicked: Jacob) but he more and more, especially now that the size was appearing, reminded Harry of his maternal grandfather, long-dead Tony McCrossen. St. Francis in St. Peter's bulk. If he was right about young Jake, Harry was glad to see all that goodness showing up somewhere, at last ... without the near illiteracy, of course. He could remember being younger than Jake and going with Tony Mac at night all the way from Liberty Square, over the hill to Tower Square, on foot, in the winter, then out of Prospect into the Ten Hills section of Somerville, there to climb three flights to the flat of his fellow truck driver and pal from teamster days, Jimmy Quinlan, who lived alone, a widower, and was laid up with a broken leg. Tony Mac took the oil jug off its stand by the stove, and Harry followed him down the four flights to the cellar, where he filled the jug from the fifty-gallon barrel cradled on sawhorses, carried it back up to Quinlan's kitchen, stayed for a cup of tea, then made the journey home. Harry made the trip just that once and almost fell asleep in school the next day. His grandfather did it every night for more than a month, until Quinlan was up and about. Feeling Jake was ready to spin and catch him staring, Harry looked back at the movie. He felt sure that this eldest son of his was fully capable of performing the same-caliber act of mercy. It both pleased and frightened him, vaguely, at the same time.

He started to speak, but remembered that he had already told Jake about Tony Mac's black toenails. The nails of both big toes had been stomped by team horses' hooves in the slaughterhouse yards in the thirties and had remained black and hard as lumps of coal ever since. He wondered now if the kid would think Tony Mac's idea of funny was funny. He'd unfailingly say, "If that ice cream's too cold, put it in the oven for a while!" Harry doubted it. *He'd* never thought that or any other of Tony Mac's witticisms were anything but corny, and their repetition was maddening. He'd wanted to find and kill the little kid with the speech impediment who'd come to the door one Halloween and given the old man "Twick or tweat! Twick or tweat!" to say incessantly for years after. Not to mention Willy the Penguin's "Kee Kool! Kee Kool!" from the Kool cigarette commercials shown at the Inman Theater's movies. Harry, Big Jake, and Tony Mac went there Sunday nights as religiously as they and everyone else went to mass Sunday mornings. He did tell young Jake once of Tony Mac's habit of talking out loud to the movies, Harry's most memorable example being the time the screen was showing one of Tarzan's native buddies or a Stewart Granger bearer being chased through an African field by a tiger, with Tony rooting, "Run zigzag, you dumb nigger, run zigzag!"

Harry got a break. On the tube the hero was chasing an Arab. "Run zigzag, you dumb jerk," he rooted, "run zigzag!"

Jake guffawed, then added, "*Jerk* wasn't the word, Dad, but I know, I know."

"Well, it was different then. There weren't any blacks around, so you weren't hurting anybody, you know?" Christ, he always felt so old and boring when he was trying to tell a child the truth.

"Yeah, you told me that, too. People didn't know any better then."

"Right."

"And black toenails—cheez!"

"Hey, watch it. *Jerk* toenails, please."

"*Ha!* Oh, bad, Dad, that was *bad!*" Rocking and slapping his legs.

Yeah, Harry grinned, Jake didn't volunteer many lulus, but there wasn't much he didn't get. He wished *his* kids could go to the movies with *him* so religiously, but now it was two bucks a head at least, dollar nights were only during the week, and he had to go first himself to check out even the PG beauties. Most of the R's he'd *let* them see, he'd *want* them to see (Jake and Constance, anyhow) for the wit, intelligence, story, or craft displayed, but once he'd seen a good one he rarely ever felt like going again, just so they could catch it. The whole shmear rated an X as far as Harry was concerned. At least they had the TV, ha-ha.

He tried again. "I don't know. I was thinking about Tony Mac tonight. I wish you guys could've known him."

"Yeah," Jake said dispiritedly. The kid already hated death, Harry knew, and felt largely responsible. The trouble with most of his fond or funny family reminiscences was that they nearly always had to end with the same postscript: RIP. If it weren't for Angie's side, his kids would think everybody in the world popped off young or at least before they got around to meeting them. He started again but again remembered already telling Jake about Great-aunt Lil of East Cambridge, Tony Mac's sister. So fat she never left her flat once in twenty-seven *years.* Couldn't fit through the *door.* Undertakers took her out a *window.* In a *piano* sling. Had four *daughters.* All colleen-*pretty.* All giggle-and-*squeeze* machines. Thought Harry was the Infant of *Prague.* Then the *Teen* of Prague. All worked intown *Bos*ton. All wore coats with colors of *fuschia! turquoise! burgundy! grape!* Took Kendall Square *sub*way together. Were *forever* coming upon him in the rush-hour *huddle.* To pounce and giggle and *squeeze.* In goddamn *public!* What he never told any of his kids, and was certainly not going to tell Jake now, was how the one who stayed single and at home with Lil died. Right after *Lil* did. She OD'd. On two dozen jelly *dough*nuts. From Hahn's *Bak*ery. A dia*bet*ic, you see," Harry would say if telling it. It was sheer W. C. Fields to him by now, and yet . . . there was actual madness there, he felt and feared, swimming through his genes. Like tiny little *time* pills! And oh, God, so many of his seeds had taken root already.

Harry felt desperate. He realized that he wanted very badly to keep the kid there with him, at the very time he'd normally be grumbling, "'Bout time to hit the pad there, ain't it, man?" And the kid—oh, what had he gone through this day and evening? His own world. Whatever the hell that was. In his mind, Harry hummed:

> Jake McGubgub,
> Jake McGubgub,
> How's by you?
> How's by you?
> Your sister's name is Thelma,
> Her boyfriend's name is Elmer,
> How's by . . . you?

It was a ditty that he'd made up when the boy was about four. "McGubgub" wasn't made up; it was the name of a guy who once took the side of a building in midtown Manhattan to display the message "Will somebody please give Fred McGubgub a million dollars to make a movie?" Harry wondered, if he started humming it aloud now, would Jake remember, and if he did, would he explode laughing as he and Constance used to, or would he blush with embarrassment, shame, or fear and bolt? Harry didn't risk it. He was getting maudlin now, he knew, but couldn't help it. His head spun—what could he say to the kid to engage and keep his saving presence there?

Jake said, "Oh—you got any work for me down the station tomorrow, Dad?"

Harry tensed. "Uh. ..."

"No sweat if you don't, but—"

But he needed some money, Harry knew. "No, I was just trying to remember the setup for ... yeah, I can use you."

"Great. The Red Eye?"

"No, Cyrus's opening up."

"Beautiful." Jake got up. "This flick craps, I'm going up." He was over and kissing him on the forehead before Harry could react. "Good night, Dad."

"Good night, bud. Bedbugs."

"Abyssinia. The cats in the kitchen?"

"I only saw Seth."

From the kitchen, the boy called in, "Harriet's here, too; I'll shut the door," and did. The set was okay; the blur was in Harry's eyes. Soon after Jake's footfalls cleared the back staircase, he heard rock music start; then the door closed and silence rang in his ears. Sudden machine-gun fire sprang him upright: surprise ambush in the movie. He crossed and switched it off. He'd lied to the kid; he'd have to put him just on the pumps and pretend to be doing something else himself all day. Revolting development, when you had to regret twenty bucks going into your own kid's pocket instead of your own. Less than that! Harry moved and entered the kitchen like a thief. He pulled on the light; the scotch still sat on the side counter. He got a glass and ice, cracked the quart, and poured out a couple glugs of the Cutty Sark. He preferred J & B. Just as he preferred Beefeater and Smirnoff to Gordon's, Marlboros to Larks. In the unlikely event of ever renting a car, he'd go to National. His boots were not Frye. His jeans weren't Levi's. He drove, well, he owned a Plymouth Fury III wagon.

He never went so far as to consume actual crap, but since their move, he simply couldn't stand knowing his brand was everybody's. When the state had been the only one in the nation to resist Nixon, Harry had pasted the *DON'T BLAME ME, I'M FROM MASSACHUSETTS* stickers across his station's windows and tire signs as well as on his car and truck bumpers. It was the first and only time in his adult life that he'd felt the slightest sense of connection, besides taxes, to any state. And it passed. His ties to his country and church were real but renegade in both cases. Not since the Army had he ever physically felt a part of any institution larger than his own family. It gave him thin satisfaction, but some. He considered it a personal quirk, not necessarily anything for the Future Kid Talk.

He ran tap water, resting a palm on the faucet neck to feel it get cold. The two fingers of Cutty looked syrupy. His tongue and throat anticipated the desired burn. Yes, he'd missed it. He was bored with not drinking. He had never felt much real accomplishment, because it had been so easy to quit and stay off the stuff. Ready, he passed the glass swiftly through the stream and closed the tap. He stirred it with his finger, held it up, and looked at the light through it. Very bad set: He was afraid of it and didn't really want it. But he did want it because he felt he needed it, and he wasn't afraid of anything, only afraid of what he might do or what might happen to him if he checked out again. And even Angie had said he should. He hung. Having to think about it irritated him more. The glass suddenly sang, like crystal stroked. No, it was Waldo crying in his sleep, run muscles twitching. Harry watched, grinning. Go get 'em, bud. That was how he'd sleep, too, if he went now.

Then Harry's heart jumped. The light in their bedroom had come back on! He darkened the kitchen and went upstairs, carrying the tumbler of scotch.

*   *   *

Angie wasn't reading. Her overhead Tensor was swiveled up and back, casting a fan of white against the dark-brown stuccolike wall. There was a small fireplace. He set the drink on the mantelpiece. "I thought you sacked out."

"No. It's only eleven thirty or so."

"The light was out before."

"Just while I was undressing."

"Oh."

"I'm naked."

"I know. I checked your shoulders."

"Oh, damn, I thought I kept the covers up. I wanted to surprise you."

He grinned, said: "Fabulous," kicked off his boots, and stripped until he wore only his soft gray turtleneck. "The book that erotic, is it?"

"No. It's about sex, but there's none in it. Oh—that bad, is it?"

He glanced at the drink. A cube cracked. "You're the one who said I needed one."

"Not the drink. Do you think it's just some book I'm reading?"

He shot himself in the temple with a forefinger and smiled. "Sorry."

"You ought to be. No, don't." He had begun to pull off the sweater. "Leave it on awhile. That's erotic."

"Okay. Whatever turns you on."

"My God, you're blushing. Tough Tro."

"Well."

"I guess they *can* actually grow."

"Sure. Just like your tits."

"Constant attention. The key to everything."

"You got it."

"So do you."

Harry sighed, happy. "Yeah. I guess that's something, all right. You want a sip?"

"Yeah, I could use a good slug. Umh! God, is that straight?"

"I put some water in. It is too strong? I haven't had any

yet." He walked around and lay sideways atop the quilt, head at her feet.

"Oh—your record still stands? Maybe you shouldn't then. I'll keep it. Maybe you walked the blues away, huh? You still smell like outdoors." She took another sip.

He squinted. "You're playing with fire, you know."

"Eat your heart out, sucker."

He rolled upright, walked back to the mantel and lit a cigarette.

She laughed, "Is that what cockteaser means?"

"You're doing the teasing."

"I know. I'm just trying to cheer you up."

"I know." And he did. The tease was *her* drinking *at* him. Angie was an awful drinker, genetically cursed with the Gaelic chemistry (or psychology or both; science was stumped, too) that turned alcohol to venom upon contact with blood. Many Jews and most homosexuals were similarly afflicted. Like them and unlike most Gaels, Angie realized it and maintained a healthy fear and safe distance between herself and liquor. It took her some time to learn and accept it, of course. In a life offering precious few affordable cushions against the pain, it was a heavy drag to find oneself allergic to even one of them, and Angie had had her purple periods.

When all the children were there but none was yet a person, rather a mass of unrelenting hungers, needs, and noise, she'd often peel off and dive into the soft, thick clouds, sometimes to the black bottom. Likewise at other times of severe stress: after her younger sister Francie died at twenty-three ... the year Harry feverishly pursued acting talent calls in reckless neglect of the voice-over calls that paid the mortgage and bought the food and penicillin ... times when she had done hours and hours of work on a scale of some volunteer war nurse in Hemingway, showered, then went to compete in party with men and women who had done mental work on phones and at tables all day, and talked business, or children.

After each peel-off, Angie hated herself and worried morosely. Harry didn't help. He told her, hell, she'd had every

right, it had been perfectly justifiable. But she was wiser and
onto it, for she'd known what he'd scarcely noticed: the series
of in-between times. When there was no crisis, when she wasn't
overwrought or overtired or tense but relaxed, optimistic and
happy, have one drink and blam, be looped! And know it,
even when nobody else could tell, even him. That for her was
the curse, exposed at last. And ever after that she was on equal
terms with it. A glass of wine, a beer in summer, a drink before
dinner, out. Grass helped. The only things Angie disliked
about grass were the munchies she got when high that raised
havoc with her figure keeping, and its sleeping-pill effect on
her when she was tired. (Harry tried a couple of times to
substitute grass for booze, too. To keep his weight down. The
only trouble was, as soon as he'd get a little wrecked, the one
delight in all the world he'd crave was a good, stiff drink.
Ending him often with a joint in one hand and a scotch in the
other, expounding grinningly that it was okay because it was
what *"Robert Altman!"* reportedly did "all the time! And if he
can make fantastic movies on it, I guess I can run a goddamn
gas station!" However, when he discovered that mixing the
two was wasting one or the other, his sense of thrift sent him
back to just the juice, which was friendlier to him anyhow.)

He felt childish. "Tell you what. You take a mouthful, only
don't swallow it. Let me suck it out. That way I won't be
breaking my record."

Angie laughed and stretched. "Sounds spilly. Maybe we
should practice it first, a trick like that."

"Dry run?"

"Not exactly."

He knelt beside the bed, and they practiced. "Can I take my
sweater off, now?"

"No, no, not yet. Slow, babe, all right? Hours. All night. Oh,
I almost forgot. Check under your pillow."

He rose off the floor and rolled forward over her to his own
side. "Another message from the Elf?" It was. An unlined page
from a small spiral notebook, folded in half, MOM printed
large on the front in pink over green over blue over yellow over

orange Flair, with an underlined *"Please right back"* in pencil
beneath. Inside, more penciled printing, neat:

> *Dear Mom and Dad!*
>   *I am sorry I did not answer you but I was sad I am always sad. Every*
> *little luxery I want I never get it. esspecially that bike. That is all I*
> *wished for.*
>   *Love Amy over.*

And on the back, fringed with a garden of X's, one *"I love you,"*
and another *"please right!"* Harry read aloud: *"P.S. I am putting
my tooth under my pillow -(I hope I get a doller!!) Lots of love, Amy."*
    Harry laughed. "I miss her *hops.* When did she learn to spell
hope?" He refolded it and put it in the Constance-decoupaged
cigar box on his desk with all the others. Amy had been
planting notes under their pillows since she was three. Her
eleventh birthday was coming up; that's what the bike business
was about. He picked up his jeans, going for a pocket.
    Angie said, "I did the tooth."
    "Give her her *doller?*"
    "I did not. That *would* be a *luxery.*"
    He looked at his desk. In a line with the cigar box were a
pencil holder made by Kate of paint-daubed papier-mâché
(what Sister Corita was merely imitating on her Boston Edison
gas tank down Southie, Harry thought); a curvy, maroon-
glazed pottery ashtray Dennis had "thrown himself," or at
least molded; a shellacked pine desk set from Jake holding a
pen, an American flag, and a decal declaring "Our Country.
Love it or Leave it"; and a layered-sand-and-rocks garden in a
small apothecary jar, by Constance. Harry was a packrat, and
the rooms would have been fuller of such kidcraft if Angie
hadn't been a pitcher. He wondered why he should suddenly
be feeling so sad. Amy? If she was ever as sad as she said she
always was, she hid it perfectly. Like both her sisters, Amy was
very serious about school and piano and the rest, but she was
the cheeriest and sunniest personality in the lot, and the silliest.

The pants wetter, charades junkie, and attic costumes maven (caring not about congruous dialogue—in Jake's football helmet and swathed in summer curtains: "Okay, now I'm Father Thomas, open up and let me pop in the little white munchos, now. Mm, aren't they tasty?"). The Middle Child, Amy had read *The Middle Sister* more times than *Charlotte's Web* or *Harriet the Spy*. She was liaison between the "big" kids and the "little" kids, at once the favorite and the most complained about and accused. What most beguiled Harry and Angie about Amy was her vision. She *noticed*. ("You look gray, Dad, are you sick? ... Oh, you're wearing that ring, Mom! I haven't seen it in ages ... That sweater goes nice with your eyes, Jake.") The chastest kiss on the tube would make her whoop and swoon in ecstasy.

What *really* went on between and among his children, Harry could dig only when he was high enough on grass (booze never did this) to get "down" there with them. He couldn't recall it accurately enough after, and he always hated to leave. This was truest with the younger ones, their "second family," in effect, of which Amy was now only half a member. He suspected that his apparently increasing rapport with Constance and Jake had less to do with any understanding on his part, than with the fact that they were leaving Shangri-la now, too. Joining him on the outside.

He returned to Angie's side on the bed. "Say anything about the bike?"

"No. What could I say?"

"That she'll get it."

"Some surprise it'd be then. And she ... we can't, Tro. The damn things are a hundred bucks at least now, the kind she wants, and she doesn't—"

"She rode the other one into the ground."

"You going to fire Cyrus to buy Amy a bike?"

"Oh, shit."

"Well, I don't like being the villain here, but—"

"I know."

"Oh, look who's bored."

"No, I'm not!"

"I don't mean you."

He didn't have to look to know she was right. "Money strikes again."

She reached and took it.

He laughed.

"What?"

"Nothing, just ... with your eyes closed—we could call it 'Girlchild asleep holding leg of Teddy.' Kinda cute."

She opened her eyes. "Well, I never had a Teddy."

"Aw, she—"

"And I'm waiting for leg of lamb!"

It hit him wrong. He didn't know why. She let go as he suddenly sat up and rolled off to walk the floor yet again. He was sure he heard disgust in the long breath she blew out, but he didn't hear it in, "Don't, Tro. Come on back." He moved the scotch from table to mantel, cubes now almonds of ice. He sighed with clear disgust. "Ah, shit."

"What *is* it, Tro?"

"I'm almost thirty-nine years old, and I can't buy my kid a bike."

"Come—"

"Christ, *I* got a bike. A brand-new red J. C. Higgins! With a light and a horn in one unit!"

"They only *had* you."

"*You* had a bike!"

"Oh, a ratty old thirdhand wreck of a—"

"You loved it."

"I tried to *sell* it! Stood out on the goddamn street with a *sign* on it for a whole week, every day after school! Hoping somebody in a *car* would—"

He should have been smiling or laughing now. He loved the story of Angie's bike. Instead, he heard his voice ranting, "I really had to *buy* it, didn't I? Hadda *own* it. Jesus. When any fool knows you *never* own a station, you franchise it, then you keep in debt to the bastards, the more you owe them, the safer you are! Those goddamn, f—"

"Not tonight, Harry, not again, all right?" She hoisted her pillow higher up the backboard and herself with it, pulling the quilt with her to stay covered from her chest down. She lit a cigarette and shook the match out with one angry snap. "So now we know, but before we didn't. And I still *like* owning it, I don't care. I won't regret doing what we did, and if you're going to start, do it someplace else."

"Wanna hear the latest?"

"I knew there was something. What?"

"More tires. A whole frigging truckload. Poor bastard of a driver, all the way from Pennsylvania. I nearly killed him. Cyrus made it funny afterward, the guy running back up into his cab to get away from me, but I swear to God I was going to hit him, I went so crazy. And Christ, I knew it wasn't *his* fault, it was—"

"I take it you didn't receive them."

"Are you serious? They know I never ordered any goddamn—"

"Oh, maybe it was just the computer again, they wouldn't deliberately—"

"Pig's ass they wouldn't; you know they did. Man, I'll be hearing about *this* soon enough now. They'd better send the right guy, though, I'll tell you that." Rage was still pulling; he was still on the edge. He lifted the drink. His mind felt like a shattered mirror, revolving so fast it was nearly spinning, a hundred fragmented thoughts and emotions a minute. One fragment, working to save him, showed him Angie and the loving. It was there, two steps away. He wanted it and knew he needed it. He had fled anxieties to it and hidden in it before, to awaken sane and restored. Sometimes it was the only place where they could escape even from each other, the one act able to break violent deadlocks between them that words only tightened.

He could see it all, not from his stand at the mantel, but

from his place in it. He could feel the textures, smell the smells, recall shadows of the sensations. Against the rage, its call was faint, but he tried to hold onto it, hoping the glimpsing would arouse him for it and crowd out the other, darker options. How she could arch; how he could bring her to it and take such soul pleasure from just beholding it as she peaked, wave upon wave of payoff. He was in awe of it, knowing his own would be firecrackers in comparison. He didn't feel envy of it, though; he sensed it had some connection to labor and birth. He could never experience that kind of pain, so how could he envy her those corresponding extremes of pleasure? The idea of participating in it yet again excited him; hope glimmered. He glanced. Sitting and smoking still, she seemed stiffer than before. She was looking away in thought. Maybe it was already too late; maybe he'd blown his last chance. His nerves knew he should leave all other emotions whirling in air and go to her at once, but he hesitated. Too long. She spoke: "You know, you can really depress me when you want to. God! Nothing and nobody else can shoot me down like you can. It really burns me."

"Well, I don't mean—

"Oh, shut up and drink your goddamned drink or something."

"Then I'm sorry, all right?" His anger exulted. "Where the hell else can I bring my—"

"Oh, *your* troubles. *You* again. Don't you know what a bore you are about it? What *happened* to us anyhow? Where'd we go? Jesus, it's sad. I always thought we had something really special. And we did, damn it. And now it's gone. God, what a shame. What a waste."

Her tears caught glints of light. They scared and paralyzed him as a pointed, cocked gun would.

They receded when she spoke. *"Your* problems, *your* troubles. Christ, there are times when I *don't* envy your ego, I'll tell you. You can come home here and ... oh, *Jesus,* it just pisses me off no end. What? We didn't do everything right? We didn't go all the way, and *more?* What the hell else were we supposed to do?

We should've franchised"—she whined, mimicking him—*"we should've* . . . well, we didn't, and I don't regret it for a minute. We weren't looking for any fucking *safety,* if you'll remember! I wonder if you do remember lately. Who the hell else do you know ever did anything really ballsy in their lives? Who? So now you're going to take it all back. Beautiful. Jesus, I *hit* Kate or Dennis for less than that! We should've paid the taxes and banked the rest, right? Rented something down there and kept at it, right? Just think, we'd be loaded right now instead of . . . oh, all the rational, reasonable things we should've done, tell them to me. Make me puke. And put your pants on, you look stupid. Or go to bed. I want to go to sleep." She ground her cigarette out.

He was forming some blades of words when the bedside phone rang.

"Oh, God, *no!*" She shoved her head beneath her pillow.

Brring! again. Harry got it, sure it was for him, half expecting the voice to say, "This is Lucifer, Harry. The Malicious One. It's time."

"Doc?" he said. "This you, Tommy? Hello?" Thomas, Angie's oldest brother, the priest, had been nicknamed Little Doc since he had got his PhD from Harvard two years before. Harry'd thought sure it was his voice, but it had stopped after the breathy, faltering *"H-Harry? You?"* Harry called into the static, "Hey, hello? Father Tom?"

"Hang it up!" Angie growled from her foxhole.

He listened to more static, then did.

She surfaced. "Was it him? Listen, if he calls back, I'm *asleep.* Or in the hospital! I mean it, Tro, I can't take any of them tonight, especially him."

"Whoever it was asked for me."

"Good. Just remember you have to get up in the morning, though. Don't get into one of his—"

Brring!

"Hello?"

"Harry Trowbridge?" It wasn't Tommy this time.

"Yeah?"

"Ah, this is F ... Norman Michaud? I'm a friend of Tom Duffy's? Uh, this is kind of ... oh! Here he is, he—"

"Tro?"

"Yeah, Tom, what's the matter?" He sounded as if he were dying of gunshot wounds.

"Tro? You gotta come and get me!"

"Where? Listen, what's—"

"Ah, this is Norman Michaud again. Look, he's all right. This is all a weird misunderstanding. He's pretty much under the weather, but he's okay; there's nothing to worry about. Look. He wants you to come and get him. I want you to get on and tell him that's crazy, that I'll drive him, see? He—"

"Put him back on."

"Well, I can't right this minute. Can you hold on a couple min—"

"Where are you? Where do you live?"

"No, listen."

"Where the hell is he? Just tell me!"

"Oh, br — okay, okay." He gave Harry the address and directions. Harry hung up and called Albie's number.

Rena answered and said Albie had gone to the Navy for the weekend. Tommy had just called, not two minutes ago. "But he hung right up, Tro. What's the matter? Is he all right?"

"Yeah, he's probably okay, Rena."

"Should I try to call Albie in Newport?"

"No, no, I just wanted to see if he might want to go with me."

"You're not *driving,* are you, Tro?"

Oh, God, Albie had told her. "No, no, yeah, I got the license back, didn't Albie tell you? Listen, it's all right, nothin', Rena, I'll see you." He hung up.

"Oh, God, what is it, Tro?" Angie was up out of the covers again, fear in her eyes.

"Nothing really bad. Little Doc's out in Framingham someplace and won't let this guy drive him home."

"Bombed, right?"

"Sounds it."

"What do you think you're doing?"

He'd begun to get dressed. "I'll go pick him up."

"Are you insane? That's all we need! Driving to work's risky enough, this is—!"

"Nobody'll stop me. If they do, I'll say a *priest* is—"

"Let that ass stay there and sleep it off! Let him call one of his own brothers! Where's Albie anyhow?"

"Navy. Listen, you want him calling here all night?"

He wore his Army fatigue jacket as if he were going to the station. It still, after thirteen years, bore his Seventh Army "Seven Steps to Hell" patch, his cloth first lieutenant bars, and his name tag, dated by being black lettering on white instead of the New Army's olive drab; nobody had been shooting when he was in. He backed the Plymouth onto the street and took off, heading for Mount Auburn. This Michaud's directions used the Massachusetts Pike, but Harry went the old way, out through Watertown and Newton. This late, it was just as fast, safer and free. He lit a smoke, slid in a Harry Nillsen tape, and started feeling terrific. "Gotta get up, gotta get out. ... " He wasn't concerned about Thomas; it was the going that counted, the sense of mission. The wagon felt like his tow truck, heading out on a wreck call, which itself always felt to Harry like a jeep or three-quarter ton, roaring into a 3 A.M. West German night in convoy on a monthly surprise alert. It always turned him on, as they called it now. In his time the sudden alert move-outs sometimes were the start of war games, and he wouldn't see garrison for four or six weeks. Most often they led only to eating boiled eggs and bacon sandwiches in their dark forest assembly area and being back on the Kaserne by noon. Nevertheless, his first adrenalized hour on the roads would always be electrified by the remote but real possibility that he was at last heading into the Real Thing. Coke ain't. War is, action is, trouble is. He felt the same charge now. In the service he often added zip to the experience by flouting the regulations and driving the jeep or truck himself. Now it was the driving without a license.

He had obeyed the law for more than a month after the

accident, through Christmas and into '75. First, Angie got up and drove him. The toll it took on her health and the family operations made him have Cyrus do it. This made Cyrus get a little crazy and got too expensive for Harry anyhow. Then Albie did it, until Harry's conscience couldn't take it anymore: Albie taught a good hour's drive away as it was. He couldn't ask anyone else in the family without blowing his shameful secret. He wouldn't have asked any of them anyway, but he did run down the list once, in a weak moment: *The Old Man* was out of the question; like Albie, he drove an hour to work every morning and at his age and temperament was generally considered an outlaw on the roads himself.

The Mother didn't drive.

Theresa was a nun down Dedham.

Mike tended bar nearby in Somerville but lived in Arlington and worked erratic hours. His wife, Nancy, didn't drive and had four little kids to care for anyhow.

Francie was still dead.

Annie's husband, Terry "Fast" Facey, was a possibility and might even have kept it to himself, too. But Fast was away more often than he was home, traveling for his latest computer company, and home anyhow was way the hell out past Concord in what Mike called cattle country. Forgetting that and her brood of very young kids, Annie herself would've done it in a second for Harry, he knew, and probably made a party of it while she was at it, hauling baskets of chicken and jugs of martinis. Annie'd be great for a day, but she'd never make a week, and letting her in on his fiasco would be like taking an ad in the *Globe*.

That left just *Maureen* "Mickey" and *Thomas,* the youngest and eldest, 1930 to 1950 for the out. Mickey was in New York.

The red lights in Watertown Square ring loud bells for blind pedestrians. When they turned to quiet green, Harry proceeded carefully around the circle and over the river, going for Thomas but thinking about Mickey. He and Angie had no favorites, exactly, in her family, but the "kid" was the most special to them. The times seemed to have been the cruelest to the youngest: Mickey had married, right after high school, a boy out of the North Cambridge projects. A "Jerry's Pit Kid," which seemed to say it. Up from New York, Angie had slipped her a month's worth of Pill at the wedding. Eight weeks later Mickey was at their door in New Chaumont; she'd filed for divorce: The boy had been not only a user, but a dealer. His participation in Woodstock had been to get busted on the way there, near Goshen, his goods stashed in his carburetor. Her deal with him had been: *No* kids until she got through the U of Mass, Intown. But after the honeymoon: Quit school, get a job, get off the Pill, and roll up your sleeve. Try it, you'll like it.

The Duffys at large froze in furious shock at the divorce. Mickey stayed with Harry and Angie until she was waitressing, going to Queens College, and sharing a walk-up with two other girls in Little Italy. The rent was cheap, the neighborhood squalid but safe, and they all were on food stamps. Mickey tired of school and of squeezing by after two years and took a full-time job as an assistant to a major fashion stylist. Mickey was the one who most reminded Harry of Angie: Few visible doubts about herself, no public moody blues or bitching, Mickey was a 150-watt bulb almost always on, a teeth-clicking, finger-snapping self-reliant gay flapper singing "whacko-whacko!" and "cha-cha-cha!" every third sentence, swinging the hips and cracking the jokes. As if all she'd ever had to deal with in life had been going dancing and seeing Lucille Ball shows.

Mickey became a great friend of the Trowbridges', as well as a relation. Besides Christmases, she went home to Cambridge only once, for six months, the time she was trying to decide whether or not to keep seeing this guy whose wife wouldn't give him a divorce. She went back to Manhattan and the guy. She had her own tiny two-room in the East Sixties by then— and held onto it. Harry and Angie approved of it all. The guy was trapped; Mickey loved him; he and they loved Mickey. In

their letters they missed Mickey and she missed them. Angie
was a bit worried, too: The guy finally did get his divorce, had
had it a year now, and still not a hint from Mickey about any
imminent sacramentalizing of their union. It wasn't anything
she'd mention in the mail, but when Mickey came up in July
for the father's and mother's surprise wedding anniversary
blast, he knew Angie was sure to corner her on it. "I can't see
being that monogamous if you aren't married, can you?" she'd
asked.

He'd dodged, "That's in Nicaragua, isn't it?"

Not only had his Alertjeep-truck-wagon been tuned that
week, but he'd also just washed it that afternoon, so it indeed
lunged forward at the least press of his foot, piercing the
Newton night like a knife, cornering deftly like the Batmobile,
its hood a wide, flat pool of blue brilliant with fleet overhead
lights. Only his eyes shone brighter, he was sure; no hose
would burst this night, no tire blow, no fuzz give chase, for his
was a mission of holy emergency—what? Superpriest in distress? Follow us, sir, we'll send the motorcycles ahead of you!
Harry laughed aloud, alone in the car, then stopped, realizing
he was lost. He pulled into a gas station for directions. The
place was clearly a suburban station, not a city one. It smelled
prosperous. Must be a franchiser, Harry figured, and asked,
hostilely, for help. The guy knew exactly where the address was
and explained the route clearly. Harry envied him.

Moving again restored his narrow-focused sense of urgent
purpose: No one else to go to Father Thomas' rescue this night,
he mused . . . any more than there had been anyone else to taxi
him to work. Other considerations aside, Tommy-the-eldest
should have been his best bet: Free, licensed, and, Harry felt
sure, willing to do him the favor, Thomas in fact commuted
from Weston to Boston every morning anyhow and could
easily have detoured through Cambridge and Somerville to
pick him up or drop him off. Those other considerations
couldn't, however, be slid aside: Tommy was simply off limits;
couldn't be asked, that's all. Mystical, family reasons. Because
he was what he was: the priest.

Where the hell *was* this place? Harry suddenly felt anxious; it seemed that he'd been a long time coming, although he knew it hadn't been more than twenty minutes ... but what if *real* trouble waited ahead? He'd begun to think he remembered who this Norman Michaud was; yes, he was sure of it now, and yeah, it might be a lot stickier there than he'd first thought.

Thomas. Yes, a certain, invisible protective shield bubbled the priest within the family. Unofficial, unspoken, yet real enough and resented, to varying degrees, by all the other, touchable ones. It interested Harry, but he didn't really care all that much about it, leave them to their gists and mists. Even about getting rides to work; he was, truly, just as glad things were as they were; he *enjoyed* the driving without the license. It was just like the marijuana joints riding now in his jacket pocket (he just remembered, fishing for another Lark): deliciously illegal, a furtive finger to the freeze-dried surface of America. He said aloud, "Ah, Tommy, you old fart, hold on, here I come." He could see the place ahead now; if he had taken the turnpike, he couldn't have missed it, it practically touched the elevated side railings, a ten-story new apartment house with its address, 101, on its façade in neon numerals the size of "HILTON," which it resembled. So Michaud and his bride had set up housekeeping in a motel. That was modern. Ah, but that was snide, Harry knew. He'd met this guy only once, so had no reason or right to feel cynical about him personally.

In fact, Michaud was the one who'd put Thomas into the big tizzy, just a couple years back, that had sort of amused him and Angie, albeit guiltily. It had been anything but amusing for Father Thomas: Michaud had been a classmate at the seminary, then later a fellow curate for a while during Thomas' parish-priest days. They went their separate ways but stayed friends and in touch. Michaud's vocation stumbled into the sixties and got lost, though the guy did try: first as a chaplain in Vietnam, then as a teacher-coach in a Catholic boys' prep school. The woman arrived in his life long before his release papers from Rome did. He waited and waited, then said enough, set the wedding date and put it to Thomas: you ... you're the one—papers or no papers. Tommy split right down the middle, brotherhood versus the rulebook, Christianity versus Catholicism, confiding his Passion, station by station, in person and by phone, to the Trowbridges, as the days and weeks ticked by. "Oh, can it," Angie counseled, "how can you not marry them?"

This had been toward the end of Thomas' Harvard years during which he'd been oozing renewal and ecumenicalism from every pore, rooting for the Berrigan brothers, damning the universal church's political pussyfooting and the American church's stone-hearted rightism, foreseeing the advent of the worker-priest celebrating the Eucharist in rumpus rooms and kitchens, etc. If it was bluff, Michaud in heat was calling it and Harry and Angie were eager to see the real Reverend Thomas Duffy stand up please. They were still waiting. Rome's mail came one week before D-Day. They were married in church, by Thomas. "Come on, Tommy," Angie baited him afterward, "were you going to do it or not?"

He'd never say. Just: "It doesn't matter. The *key* thing is how God works. How personally involved and instrumental He is in our lives." Pushed, he always had the final ace to play: "Ha-ha—no, see, the real question was never me anyhow. It was Norm! Would *he* have done it or not? I just don't think so."

"He rented the tux, honey, and paid the caterer!"

"Well, sure, go ahead, Patricia, make a joke out of it if you want to."

Big-toothed and swarthy, Norm at the apartment door reminded Harry of the French comic Fernandel—in violet turtleneck, H.I.S. jeans, and sandals. Behind him Harry could see Thomas in the living room, in his civvies, stretched out on the couch, dead, asleep, or otherwise unconscious. "Harry? I'm Norm Michaud, hi."

"Hi." He almost said Father. "I remember you now."

"Yeah. Years ago at St. Brendan's. Well, here's your man. Uh, this is Lillian."

The woman standing beyond the couch at the fireplace wouldn't meet Harry's glance. She flicked both her cigarette ash and "How do you do" into the sputtering Duraflame Log fire. Her bra-sized knitted sweater was solidly filled. Her rope-tied jeans ended well below her navel. Her belly was flat and muscled. Standing over Thomas' body, Harry looked again at her. Up close, she appeared as much frightened as angry and disgusted. She had almond eyes and was quite lovely, except the eyes were amateurly shadowed and now Harry noticed a flume of tiny, black pubic hairs flying up her abdomen, like so many cinder specks. Harry bent and rocked Thomas by a shoulder. "Tommy! Hey! Let's go, bud."

Michaud said softly, "I've tried almost everything."

"He's really out, all right," Harry said, not entirely believing it. He reached and depressed the tip of the priest's nose with his finger. Thomas inhaled loudly, one snot-snore, but the eyes stayed shut. He was either legitimate or knew the trick. Harry would watch what he said.

Michaud sighed. "I told him ... well, I told you too—I'd be only too glad to drive him home. It's not that far from here, and Lillian could've followed in our car. But he wasn't having any of it. Damn, this is awkward."

Except for the cluttered top of the table in their dining alcove, the scene was neat, everything in place, no horizontal glasses or spills that Harry could see. He lifted a leg and shook it. "Tommy! Wake up, Father, let's go!" Released, it fell back heavily.

"Hey, Tomo! Your brother-in-law's here!"

Lillian hissed, "Shit!" and left the room.

"Gee, Harry, I don't know, I guess we'll have to lug the ... oh, hey, can I offer you anything? Have a drink?"

Harry looked to see if he was serious—he was—then smiled. "No. Thanks anyhow, Norm."

"We do feel partly responsible for this. I guess he was just too really beat. And dinner was kind of late in coming. We both work and ... you know."

"It happens. Listen, will it be all right if I leave my car out there in your lot overnight?"

"Absolutely. As long as you ... no, know what? Tell me where, and I'll bring it to you in the morning or whenever. Lillian can follow."

"That would save me a lot of grief. Yeah, I'll let you do that—and you can blame that on himself here, too, all right? You know where Liberty Square is, in Prospect?"

"Sure."

"I'm the Shell station there." He gave him the keys.

"You got it. But hey, please *tell* him, will you, for God's sake, not to worry about this. It was nothing, nothing at all. What friends are for, tell him."

Tell Lillian, Harry thought, and started fishing into Thomas' pockets.

"No, here, Harry." Michaud produced the keys. "I got these off him way back."

"Good. Hold onto them." Harry pulled Thomas up by the arms, knelt onto the rug, let him jackknife over his shoulder and down his back, then stood and completed the fireman's carry, reaching between his load's legs to grab the dangling right hand. Michaud had begun to protest that they should both carry him, but from the look Harry spied on Lillian's face now in the hall doorway, he knew this was best ... less humiliating and sad to see, anyhow. He grunted, "Lead the way, José," and turned with his burden without looking at or speaking to the outraged woman again. Norm got all doors like a bellhop. Thomas was Harry's height and much thinner, but heavier than Harry'd figured. Yet the increasing weight and pain felt sweet in him; it was such a concrete act to be performing. Real as a wreck, more satisfyingly climactic than bacon sandwiches in a jeep. Michaud opened Father Tom's '74 Grand Prix and helped unload his old pal into it.

Thomas came to halfway up the Pike to Weston, just

coincidentally, as Harry was braking for the exit. "What are you doing? Keep going."

"You going your mother's?"

"Yeah, yeah, straight ahead."

Harry changed his signals and returned to the outside lane.

Suddenly Thomas reached across and jabbed his arm. "Hey, Albie! Thank God! You got me *out* of there, huh? Fantastic!"

"It's me, Tom."

"Tro! Oh, that's right, too. Down the Navy. Old Commander Whitehead. Well, Tro-boy, you saved my life, kiddo. Or Norm's, I don't know. Hey, I appreciate this, Tro."

"You owe me one."

"Hoo, was I bombed."

"You're still bombed, go back to sleep."

"It's Friday night, Tro!"

"It's Saturday morning, Father."

"Oh, you're pissed off. Old schizo Tro the star's pissed off at me!"

"No, I'm not."

"Then don't hand me that *Father* business. You're my brother, Tro! And I love ya!"

"Okay, Tom."

"Ah, *okay* ... what're ya doing now?"

"Going to your mother's."

"No!"

"Oh, Christ." Harry pulled over and stopped. "You want to go back to your rectory?"

"No! I don't want to go the rectory, it's Friday, and I'm going down the ... let's go, take me down Sequosset, Tro."

"*Sequosset!* You're out of your mind. I have to get up at dawn!"

"Tro. Tro, Tro, Tro. Have I ever asked you for anything? Ever?"

"Well, *yeah* ... "

"No, no, Tro—listen, fuck it. Fuck work, fuck it *all!* This one time, huh?"

"Hey, I'm the one who has to ... "

"No! Stay! I don't mean come back, I mean stay with me! Let's *do* it, Tro-boy! You and me. You and I, Tro, shit, we need it, we've never *done* it! Our whole *lives,* Tro! Maybe, maybe call Albie and Mike and Bobby and just fuckit do it! First time ever! The Old Man, too! The Duffys! All of them!"

Harry was saying things, like "I'm not a Duffy," and "No way," and, "I just can't," but he didn't know why, because he already knew he was going to do it. The swelling was back in his chest. The call had come, and it wasn't to return to garrison it was to move out, *east.* Then south, in this case, turning onto the Expressway where the highways intersected in South Boston.

Three

When Thomas saw him pass the Cambridge exit, he yelped, "Tro! You're doing it! We're gonna do it, aren't we? Oh, Trowbridge, you son of a bitch, this is great!"

And Harry grinned. "You caught me on the right night, Little Doc."

"The right night. The right night of your life, huh, Tro? Me too. Oh, Tro, you don't know, you just don't ... the right night of—" Then he flaked out again.

Harry pulled off the Expressway in Neponset, to phone Angie before it got too late. She grumbled, "Good."

"How the hell can it be good?"

"Can't be any worse, you need something! If you're going, go!" She worried about the driving, though, and it was she, more asleep than awake, who thought of the obvious.

The Pontiac was getting topped off. When he came out of the Mobil's phone, he went around and picked Thomas' billfold out of his pocket. He checked the license. Except for the "Rev." he could pass for him easily—better, in fact, being

conscious. False or not, he felt a surge of security at the
insertion of the wallet next to his own. And, lapping even more
hungrily and blindly at the promise of danger, he impulsively
trotted to the all-night package store next door. He bought
with his own American Express plastic, a quart of Johnnie
Walker Red, Thomas' brand, and four six-packs of Bud
against the unlikely event of the priest's Cape house being
short on hooch. He stopped once more, ten minutes later, just
long enough to crack the quart and take two, three short swigs
Neither his "Aaah!" nor the sound of the Bud's top popping
woke Thomas, though he did begin to mutter and growl now
Harry suddenly thought it hilarious that all beer cans said
"Schlitz!" when opened and that, God, he had been bored with
not drinking.

The priest's Pontiac needed tuning; it had a spit and a ping
and lagged a hair on quick accelerations. He'd have Thomas
bring it in. Cruising at seventy on the dark lonely road, Harry
lifted his foot off the gas, then pressed it right back down a few
times, to help the engine clean itself a bit. The jerks only made
Tommy roll his head. His mumbling continued. When Harry's
second *"Schlitz!"* sneezed, he bolted awake and upright, looked
over and slurred, "Hey Tro—what's the occasion?"

Harry cracked, "The occasion is, we got 'em." Tommy
chuckled feebly and soon slumped back down to sleep. This
time, his mumblings began to congeal into periodically de
cipherable words, like knots on a string. The clearest was
"Joyce." Harry thought he meant a woman, maybe the one in
Framingham. "Her name was Lillian, Tom." Thomas rolled
his body sideways on the seat and brought both his hands up
into his neck as if he were in bed.

"Lillian," he moaned sadly, "Lillian. Norman's Lillian. Gish
Gushgash, Norm and Lillian oh what a sitcom what a cheap
shit soap I couldn't do it I couldn't play the goddamn game
anymore doc ah Norm poor Norm beat up Norm and Norm
had nothing to do with it what sorry bastards we all are but
screw him anyhow and her Christ I thought they were going to

for awhile there kissyhuggy on the couch in front of me till I burned a goddamned demonstration for poor old Tommy see little man first we do this then we do this see how easy it is and everything they say about it is true Tommy only more but indescribable delicious mounds bars and anytime we want Tommy up the chimney Norm oh we're so happy and secure in each other you can't know Tommy so open do you love me yes I love you do you love me and oh Normie got a raise doing so well makes it almost fifteen clear now fifteen almost clear forty-two years old to know you can do it is the thing Tom to know you can go out alone and sell . . . sell—"

"Hey, Little Doc!" He wanted no more of it. He wasn't the shrink or confessor or whoever Tommy was telling. Tommy rolled back and turned his visions inward again. Harry looked from the road to the priest's closed face, greened by the dashboard lighting. He'd never seen Thomas cast as a victim of anything before. The "Little" in Little Doc meant no diminishment: When Thomas won his degree, he became the second Doctor of Philosophy in the family, the other being Father Tim Callahan, the venerable Baltimore seminary uncle, who became Big Doc the same day. Thomas' new nick capped Tom, Tommy, and "the Canon," although the latter was a behind-the-backer, coined years ago by the father—lest the blessed one got too pompous or something. Even in the green, Thomas at forty-two or so looked remarkably the same as the fine-featured lad in the ordination photos gazing from the parents' living-room mantel (as well as every mantel and shelf in the south of Ireland, visitors reported) and lying in the buffet drawers of other Duffy homes. His looks hadn't worked against his becoming Boston's "TV priest." Often deacon to Richard Cardinal Cushing himself, guest preacher at the cathedral and at Mission Church in Roxbury, featured and quoted regularly in the weekly *Pilot,* Father Thomas had gone public early on.

Publicity brings its excesses, and Thomas wasn't excepted: Some aged female *Pilot* writer once fluttered, "If John the

Evangelist, the Lord's declared favorite Apostle, had been Irish instead of a Semite, he would have had the look of our own young Father Duffy." Mike Duffy had a blowup of it hung in his bar. Albie was forever saying, "Take care of my mother, will you?" Thomas' grooming stint in Rome coincided with "Xavier Rynne's" dispatches on Vatican Two; around the Hub it was rumored that ... none of it slowed Tommy's rapid rise. By the time Madeiras broke the Irish ruling streak, replacing the Cush, Thomas had branched out into the semi-secular. His media location was less often the cathedral's altar, more his own office or some newsy civic or social event. His doctorate was in psychology; he was "way high up" in the state's social welfare programs bureaucracy. Book being made on his future was no longer restricted to the ecclesiastical order. With BC Law's Father Drinan setting the precedent, Tommy's political potential occupied breezeshooters in every tavern, rectory, and K of C lodge. He could get a table without a reservation at either Pier Four or Jimmy's Harborside.

His gullet was making sinister sounds now. Harry looked again, afraid he might be getting sick. "You okay there, Doc?"

Thomas bolted up as to an alarm and dry-washed his face in his hands. "Whooh! Tro-boy! Hey, glad to see you." He spotted the Buds. "Ah, thank you, sir!" *Schlitz!* "Where are we now?"

"We're getting there, kid."

"Faster, Kato, faster," lighting a Kent. "You know the way, right?"

"As far as the canal. I've never been to the house."

"I'll show you from the bridge. My God, we're doing it, Tro, huh? I don't believe it. This is great—and you were *invited* enough times, so don't hand me any of your shit!"

Harry had been around enough Irish booze ebullience in his life to know the switchblade edge always there between cheer and bile. But tonight he didn't care and knew, besides, that Thomas feared him more than vice versa. "Stick it, Tommy ... *But don't bring the kids,*" he did Tom's voice.

"Aw, that wasn't . . . we thought you'd like the chance to get away from them for once, that's all."

"Look, I don't care, Tom. But don't try to bullshit me, okay? You didn't want anything spilled or broken or something. Forget it."

"It wasn't me, though, Tro. The other guys just don't—"

"Hey! Come to think of it—your two pals aren't going to—?"

"No, no. No way. The house is all mine this weekend."

"Good." It was out before he thought it: "And some of us *have* been down your wonderful hideout, by the way."

"Who?"

"Aye—never mind. I'm sorry I said it."

"No, come on now—who?"

"Annie. With her whole mob, too. She slipped down some-time last fall and cased the joint for the rest of us."

"We lock it!"

"She got in. Plunked a kid through an open window."

"That *bitch!*"

"Ha! Oh, God, if she ever finds out I told you, I'm mincemeat."

"Listen, what the hell's so funny about—?"

"Well, you pissed us all off with the kid thing, Tom."

Thomas apparently had gone under again, chin on collar-bone. Harry reached and took the cigarette and beer out of his loosening fingers. He smoked the Kent. Yellow grass and scrub pine whizzed to his left, dividing the highway. He thought of pitching the can into it but was afraid a blast of night air might trigger another spell of false sobriety in Thomas. He stood the Bud on the floor beneath his legs. He had speeded up during the brief, tight talk and now eased it back down steady. He'd have to stay more in control, he realized. The last thing he had appetite for tonight was argument.

What was he after, then? A bash, he decided. An old-fashioned Saturday-night Army blowout with the boys. Boy. He took a pull on his beer and grinned. That's what it would be then, simpleminded, oafish, innocent, and therapeutic.

Because he'd make it be that way. The new Bishop Sheen or
not, Tommy had never played with the really big boys, and
Harry had; it would be his show, pratfalls and slapstick, not a
wet eye in the house.

He had just decided to risk some soft radio music when
Thomas began running at the mouth again, again the "Joyce"
in the clear. It seemed to be coming from a different level this
time, either closer to or farther from the surface, he couldn't
tell. But it was easier to follow. Little Doc's eyes were open
now, too, but only in thin slits. Unseeing slits, Harry thought.
Hearing his own name scared him. "Ah, Tro, Tro. You oughta
get into Joyce." He didn't dare speak. "That bastard's got us
all. Every one of us. In 1904, 1930, now. True then, true now.
We never change, never learn. Like caterpillars. And the guy's
got us. And it's so dumb and so boring and simple he hadda
fancy up the words. My own opinion, though it was never my
discipline. And we had to ban and Index it! Proving him right.
Responding to his bell—"

James Joyce he was muffling about! That was a surprise.
Years back Harry had been dismayed to learn that for all the
schooling given him—earned by him—brainy Thomas read
virtually nothing outside of whatever the hell it was he was
studying.

"—It's all in there, Tro. So maybe you shouldn't. So now I
know. So what. Or have begun to know. Joyce. Joyce, Joyce.
Sounds like the pulley on a guillotine, doesn't it? But so what.
What good's knowing do? He had to leave, too. And left, but
didn't leave. Couldn't leave. He couldn't leave either. His
body, that's all. To Paris, that's all. That part's easy. And wait
till poor Norm in love gets hit with this. In time, he's time's a-
cummin, like he whispers to me *he* does, when she's gone to the
kitchen. *Christ, Tro!* Rationalizing her ... *loop!* Me eating
London broil, all liver and kidneys, all I could taste was her
... insides!"

Harry bit his lip to hold his laugh in.

"Ah, see, yeah, yeah, Bloom's kidneys again, and there we

are, all there, and we cannot, none of us, ever get away from the ... ha, listen Tro—*the Godpossibled souls we nightly impossiblize!* Huh? Wow, he wasn't fooling—and not just all you poor fish out there, either ... *us,* too! Oh, yeah, I know it's no news to you, cynical bastard like you, you priest haters—you know we do, and we do, we do. Perpetual teens. No real difference. Except where it lands. I know, what's real anyhow? Imagined is real, Christ said, except ... oh, you bastards, except she probably ... holds him while he sleeps is real, oh, shit, it is, the ... T we're all nailed to, the old cockaroonie, the old dong, wang, meat, pecker, tool ... ha! Remember? Member! Prick, peenie, blade, pudding, pud, joint, dick, thing, ah, old Joyceo knew em all and more, he ... Tro? *Tro!*"

"Yeah, Tommy."

"Good. Listen. The *well-pleased pleasers.* Ho, ho. And! The ... *curled conquistadors!* Like that? That's not bad, pal. What it all comes down to. Thought getting older would cool it, but. Seems to've accumulated. Just hope you're gouging yourself there, Brando...."

The pause reeled out. Harry prayed he wasn't waiting for a reply. He looked to see if Tom had gone asleep again. No, his lips were still moving: "Nuns! Nuns buns. God bless 'em. And keep 'em. Only thing that made it not so bad. So dumb. One dumb nun. No real class, no ... didn't even know enough to *shave,* for Christ's...."

Harry laughed out loud. Poor Lillian gets it again.

"Where's my beer?" Thomas was up like a judge.

"Here."

"Do you know what I'm talking about?"

"Lillian's belly. I thought it was kind of cute."

"Screw Lillian! I mean really. I've tried to be very clear with you, Tro. It isn't easy, opening up, you know."

Harry half laughed. "If that's opening up, I'd love to hear—"

"Stuff that! Don't pull that bullshit with me, pal! I *asked* you a—"

"*Hey!* Get it straight, Father. I don't know who you think

you're with, but I don't get yelled at, dig? If it ain't going to be a party, you're going to wake up in Cambridge!"

Thomas laughed and laughed, a sly, hacking cackle. "Ah, Tro. Tough-guy Tro. Dying inside like the rest of us. I love ya, Tro. The heat's right there, isn't it? Ha ha, gotcha without even trying. *Baroom!* You need help there, my friend."

Harry lit a new cigarette. Maybe it had been too long since he had played with the really big boys.

"Peace, Tro?"

"Peace, Tommy." Well, he'd delivered the message anyhow, trap or not.

"*Yes,* it's going to be a party! Boy, do I need a party. When you get to the Sag, hook down to the Bourne, okay? We're over near the bay. Ach! Beer isn't what I need, but thanks, anyway."

Harry didn't mention the scotch in the back and speeded up.

"Hey, we're actually doing it! You're the man, Tro. Just fuck it *all,* right?"

"You're talking nice for a priest, by the way. Since when all the raunch?"

"Liberty Square, Tro! That's what I'm trying to clue you in on. Like Ireland, like the church, like all of it. You can never ever leave. You can only appear to."

"You aren't Liberty Square, Duffy."

"Well, North Cambridge, what's the difference? I was a baby near *Union* Square, though, just as bad. That's where they started out from."

"People can leave, Tom."

"That's what you think. Ha! You! Christ, you came back!"

"Like hell I did." He expected Thomas to then argue that yes, he did so, or that yes, he did so—but unconsciously. He got surprised.

"I know you didn't, Tro. I know the score there all right. And you know what? Want to know something about yourself? You're a good guy. You're a prick, of course, but really a good guy. And don't think nobody knows it."

"Tell me more."

"Ah, that's okay. We know. She always got her way, one way or another."

"Who?"

"Hey! It's okay, Tro. You're in safe hands, my boy. *One* thing, though. I still can't figure it! I might as well say it. I can see her coming home, for the family—but then nobody ever sees you people! You might as well've stayed down New York! It *is* pretty strange, Tro. It isn't right."

Harry whistled thinly.

"Knock it off, Tro, or—don't tell me you're scared of her too?"

I'm scared of everyone, Tom. You never know when their minds will go. He didn't say it. He said, "We visit as often as we can, Tom."

"Yeah? When's the last time you had Sunday dinner over?"

"We don't have Sunday dinner anywhere. Dropped the habit a hundred years ago. We go someplace or just hang out. Sometimes I open the station."

"Aah, you give me a real pain in the ass when you pull that New York line on people. You saying you don't know what I'm talking about?"

"You *were* talking about getting laid, Tom. What about it?"

"Bullshit!"

"Don't withdraw—you're opening up, remember?" He felt callous, but it seemed the only way out of it. Even the Joyce ropes had been closer to the party spirit than this. Reality again to the rescue: They were mounting the Bourne Bridge now, Buzzards Bay town burning sparse electricity to the west. "Okay, start navigating, home wrecker! To the den of iniquity and step on it, huh, Tomo?"

"Yeah! Straight ahead! Stay on twenty-eight till I tell ya! Whoo!"

The grillwork sang beneath their wheels. Harry popped some music on, real funky trucker stuff luckily, and yelled over it. "Down into Nighttown, *Deddy!* Huh? No more kidneying

around! And it's your fault, Father, I'm telling you in advance!
You made me do it! To revelry! To a blast!" Perked forward
laughing, Thomas looked nine, and the road could've been the
rodeo. "Check the back seat, Little Doc!"

"Hey! Fantastic!"

"Bite off the top, and hand it chere!"

"Yahoo!"

"Suck it in, Hercules, we have work to do!"

"To the palace!"

Thatta boy. "To perdition!"

"To the Duffys!"

Oh, brother.

The priests' place was a new, contemporary, modified A-
frame beach house sitting on the top of a round hill, at the end
of a long, seashell-lined dirt road through pine woods. Like
splinters of brown snow, dead pine needles covered the ground,
deck, roofs, everything. Thomas said that but for the height of
the close-surrounding trees, Buzzards Bay itself could be seen
from here. "Less than a mile away down there, as the crow
flies." In, he turned on the heat and the lights, inside and out.
Harry opened the sliding glass living-room doors and walked,
crunching, across the main deck. The house was pine, stained a
driftwood gray. He hyperventilated some sea salt and squeezed
the railing to make sure he was there, then went back inside.

Everything smelled new, kind of tarpaperish. It was a two-
story living room, ceiling beams exposed rawly. The inside wall
was faced with fake brick. A narrow walkway ran across it like
a shelf, with two doors off it and a spiral staircase down from
it. The chimney was a free-floating, upended funnel painted
white. The circular fireplace beneath it was a well of real brick.
Somebody had left a fire built, and Thomas was lighting it, his
Bic turned full flame and flicking away. There was a third
bedroom downstairs, Tom said, off the "galley." The barewood
floors were bright with varnish and wax. Furniture was is-
landed, on and around a thick rug, eggshell white—all black

Naugahyde slung on aluminum: two couches, two chairs. A highly polished, veneered imitation old hatch door on wrought-iron legs served as coffee table in mid-rug. A unit of shelves, with magazine lectern, hung on one wall and held a stereo system, a few books, a few pieces of gnarled driftwood. The fire caught. Thomas clapped and rubbed his hands together. "What'll it be, buddy?"

"What are you doing?"

"Rob roys!" The scotch martini.

"What the hell, why not?"

Tom made them in the kitchen. Back, he said, "Well? What do you think?"

Penthouse magazine. "It's nice. Cheers."

"Slainte. Nice! Come on, it's a gas, right?"

They sat into opposite couches and looked a little awkwardly at each other. Harry smiled and said, "Yeah, it is. Real groovy pad," swiveling his head stupidly. Thomas seemed to have reached a new fathom knot of control resembling sobriety. Harry's first slug of the Roy Rogers gave him the sharp *pang!* he'd missed for so long, but it was nowhere near as delicious as his hot swigs in the car.

Eyes as pointed as his nose, Thomas said, "Geez, you can be a cool son of a bitch, Harry T."

Uncertain of what part to play, Father, they all look so good. "Gimme a chance, will you, Tom? I don't even believe I'm *here* yet! The place is neat, it really is. I guess I was expecting something squarer, that's all. Your mother called it a 'tidy little cottage.' "

"Ha!"

"It must be great for you guys, a place to escape to."

"And anonymity, Tro. That's the . . . hey, know what hit me in the kitchen? You'll dig this. We just took off down here tonight, right? Telling *no*-body. Well, way back in high school, I did the same thing. Me and these guys Paulie Warren and Bill Monagle. Just said, Hey, let's go to Times Square for coffee, and off we went. Paulie's car. So we get halfway down in Connecticut and stop to call and tell people where we are, right? They call theirs and it's okay, but then I get my *father* on, and he's says bull*shit!* Get. Home. Now. I weep—you know—the other guys are going, how am I supposed to get home? And, Tro, you could hear him across the highway: 'Ye kin slide home on yer brainless ahse, for all I care, just get here!' Ha."

Harry laughed with him.

"The other guys go oh, shit, and we turn around and beat it back. I mean, I was scared and felt like a jerk . . . but I felt kind of proud, too, you know?"

"Because he cared, I—"

"Yeah, but because of the power! The strength, the . . . presence!"

"The fear!"

"He never hit me. Never. I think Mike was the only one he ever laid a hand on our whole life. For stealing, then lying about it."

"Then why are you all so scared of him?"

"But what *great families* then, when you think of it!"

"You really think so, Tom?" Wary of it, Harry was sipping his drink gingerly, finding it hard to let the carousing happen— and *family* had become so central to his consciousness lately that he had to add, "I'm not so sure anymore."

"Come on, you have to be kidding, they were *great* families. We're one of the last of the breed. They stayed in the cities, but people like my father and mother were *pioneers*. Going forth and multiplying. Establishing close, loyal *tribes* . . . the concrete and tenement reservations!"

Harry laughed. "Phew—block that metaphor! That the title of your thesis, Doc?"

Flinty-eyed, Thomas pointed an accusing finger. "You don't know because you don't come from one. But they *were* great! It's why society's so fucked up now—there are no more. Families like ours. Anymore. The weakest link is *weak*, now! Small and flimsy and cracked."

"Ah, I dunno," was all he said. He wanted to get off it. Thomas was such a zealot on the subject. Harry'd heard the song before, and there was no arguing with it allowed. Mike and Annie would sing it too, in their cups. Angie dubbed it the Magnificent Deception and couldn't figure what good they got out of holding onto it.

"Don't give me that youdon'tknow—you oughta know, you two are the ones with the five!"

"Well, that's another story." Harry grinned. "It does in our case, but quantity doesn't make quality, Tom."

Thomas squinted. "I don't like the way you said that."

"Now, don't go losing your sense of humor."

Tom made a Nixon smile. "Okay, okay, I get it. I'm getting too sentimental again. I know. Hitting you too close to where you live. Poor Tro. Hokay, so let's just get drunk and whatta you wanna do, sing college songs?"

Harry wondered how many times the guy had been punched out in his time. "Better than doing the Duffy hustle again, I'll tell ya."

"Whatta you mean *hustle?*"

"It's all baloney, Tommy, and it's boring. We're too old for it."

"*What's* baloney? You saying they weren't great? All those immigrant families like mine?"

"Hey, I'm not saying your mother wears Army shoes and so's your old man ... but they were big, that's all. Big and scared. And they did the most with what they had, I'll give them that, and maybe they were better at *that* than people are now, but that's all they did. And it wasn't that much. Ask them sometime, why don't you? I never hear any of this greatness shit out of your father and mother."

"Because they're *innocent,* you asshole. They don't know how great they are! That's what's so beautiful about them!"

Chafed by the obscenity, Harry did the jerk-off gesture in the air. Harry drank, Thomas drank, glaring at each other. Harry was sorry he'd come.

"Man, you just know it all, don't you, Trowbridge?"

"Oh, yeah? Then what am I doing here? I thought we were going to *do* it, Tommy? Just fuck it *all* for once, leave it all up there and out of our life, for a little R and R!" He was having a hard time keeping money off his mind.

"I've always envied you that."

"Knowing it all?"

"Being in the service, having the Army thing."

"Why didn't you go chaplain, like Michaud?"

"No, not as a priest. Before. Like Shaz Mayo."

"Oh. What do you think you missed?"

"Ah, I dunno."

"It was belonging to Uncle, that's all, having this Big Momma taking care of you, belonging to a gigantic outfit you knew was never going out of business—hell, you've got that, Father, you've always had that."

"But like Shaz Mayo, guys like that. You know. At least they got a little real life in first. Women, travel, hitting towns at night with a buncha guys ... you know. You ... ah, what am I saying, you don't know shit there, old buddy! You talk a good game and I love ya, but your ass is suckin' wind, it really is! Hey, come on! You gonna nurse that little dollop all goddamn night? Your turn. Here!" He downed his drink and passed the glass. Harry downed his, too, like a blind hope, and went to the kitchen to make more, hearing Tommy continue in shouts: "No fault of yours, though, kid. Mnot saying that! How the fuck could *you* ever know anything about family an' what's great an' what isn't, *you* weirdos! Hear me in there, Troby? *Weirdos!* Ha-ha!"

Harry was laughing too. He'd decided not to water the Robs. He'd be content now with a nice, clean, prompt conk-out and a long, deep sleep. No toot seemed likely anymore anyhow. He gave Tommy his and sat down. "That's no way to talk about the clergy, Father." He grinned.

"Ha! Here's to ya, Trobo! Slainte! You're a sickie, and I don't know about your father, I think he's just as weirdo, but my father's fuckin' *great* an I donecare whatyou say, either!"

"Buenos Aires!" Harry toasted and drank. That still had the Duffys all wiggy, he chuckled inside: the night he and his father had gone at it toe to toe finally on Mike Duffy's front porch, well after midnight in the otherwise-quiet neighborhood. The memory was refreshing. There was no way he could expect any Duffy but Angie to understand how the loud, drunken, violent scene had in truth been a magic act of reconciliation. Crude, messy, and no doubt scary to witness (no one dared try to break it up), but not really all that dangerous—no more than three punches swapped, all pulled, a bit of blood and welting on both faces, much more good than harm. After Harry's mother's sudden, too-early death, his father, a lifelong teetotaler, said to hell with it and hit the Schenley's for almost four bad-news years. Harry sympathized for only two, worried for one, then exploded the night at Mike's. Big Jake said piss off, Harry said get out, his dad said make me, and Harry said you got it. Slug, slug, and they were embracing and kissing like two weeping queers on Greenwich Avenue, for themselves, for the woman they'd both lost, for the frightful, brittle thing life seemed to have become for father and son alike.

The hoary old "Amazing how much the old man learned in such a short time!" phenomenon. For years, Big Jake and Harry's college education had something in common; Harry ruefully cursed them both for inadequacy and irrelevancy. Now he took much of it back. The inadequacy had been his own, a paucity of vision. Oh, one's thirties, he now saw, are some fierce automatic washing machine-and-drier combo, all right, leaving you with one helluva pile of ironing to do! The Jesuits, without warning, had tilted his duck's-assed head and poured Plato in through the grease. His father had labored sixty hours a week with his back and hands his whole life, bought Harry a new suit every Easter at Leopold Morse's (telling the mother Anderson-Little), and told him, "Don't worry too much," and "Don't let any outfit ever own ya," body or soul. How could he have ever faulted them? A notion of what was excellent and what wasn't still glowed somewhere in the core of his innermost mind, his only despair that of achievement ... and, when first the Army, then later his Ambition had turned to Company Stores, he'd walked and he knew deep down and damned right well that his main problem was now his inability or unwillingness to admit or decide that his grand-idea, back-to-basics, new and "simple" life had likewise turned Owner on him and of him.

For himself, Big Jake, at fifty-five, had entered a Trappist monastery as a working brother. He'd been in four years now. Harry visited him now and then but not often. It didn't feel necessary. And while watching his father smile inscrutably for what seemed like hours at a time wasn't unpleasant at all, was, in fact, oddly calming and reassuring, Harry's limbs tended to numb with pins and needles, and he'd pine to leave. Big Jake had no vow of silence; he just didn't talk much anymore. Harry went mostly now just to let Big Jake witness the growth of his grandchildren and to let them witness peace and strangeness, knowing they were somehow connected to it; he wanted badly for them to dig early that life could and maybe should be atypical.

Also, he liked to hope that visiting Big Jake Beyond the Horizon might flip the mystical switch in them, since they were not attending parochial schools and were not being made go to release-time religious instruction. He and Angie were determined that none of them would get infected with the fear and ultimately the hatred of living that churchschool would forever represent to them, yet they wanted the kids to be able to believe in the unseen, in the Other. So Harry and Angie dragged them to mass most Sundays and to Big Jake every few months, with fingers crossed. *Unbelievable!* Yeah, but that's just it! *Oh!*

Not that Big Jake had ever been an *ardent* Catholic, even when it was called that. During the war he'd been laid off by Bethlehem Steel. He and another guy opened a contracting business to tide them over till the callback, and their one job had been a month's carpentry and piping work for the

Trappists. He'd liked it there and never forgot the feeling, that's all. He also told Harry that, after their slug-out on the night porch, he'd laid out his life on the table and seen three options: *One,* he could go to sea. He had his papers and an Oceanographic ship set to take him out of Woods Hole around the world. *Two,* he could find a woman. "It don't mean I still don't miss your mother, Harry, or didn't lovea or anything, Christ, there's times still now when I . . . an' I never figured I'd ever get to where, but I dunno, if the right one was ta come along an' find me, huh?" *Three,* he'd been thinking of that monastery a lot. "Come ta me right outta thin air! Buzzed up there one Sunday, an' it was like they were waitin fa me! An' you oughta see the setup, kid, shit, if there was ever a place needin' somebody who knows a wrench from a saw! An' whatta *they* know, ya know? All it really needs is. . . ."

Harry wasn't asked, but he knew he would've recommended sea and woman both, first one, then the other. As smily as Brother Big Jake came on, Harry still had warmer visions of his father starting up again with some pretty, peppy widow who'd rub his back and go golfing and square dancing with him and love him and get him to fix clocks and build her bookshelves and things with his omnipotent hands. And Harry would wonder, Do you think of her up there, Pop, of the unfound pretty peppy widow? Do you sometimes look down from a window you're leading or puttying and over the wall to the road and think you see her fretting there beside, say, a peach Cougar boiling over and go out the gate to give her a hand that ends up on the gearshift and wheel as you gun out with her giggling and touching your sleeve with her fingers? Harry liked to think so and even hoped it'd still happen. Smiling silently or not, Big Jake wasn't a man's man in his son's eyes, that's all, nor could an order hold him warm while he slept.

Boom! Ringle! Thomas had slammed his hand down on the hatch door. The ashtray had jumped with fright, and so had Harry. "Jesus Christ—what?"

Thomas looked steam-bathed now, but was beaming. "We gotta call em!"

"Who?"

"*All*uvem!" He was up and reeling toward his briefcase on the wall unit.

Harry watched in disbelief. He gulped from his drink. He was too sober to handle this. "It's after *two*, Tommy!" he pleaded, knowing it was useless. The Canon was notorious for his middle-of-the-night bombed phone calls. From his rectory rooms, from hotels and motels in Manhattan, Florida, Puerto Rico, Maine ... wherever he was and got looped, he'd call, never before midnight. He had his week-at-a-glance book out now and was flipping, reeling back, to his addresses and numbers pages. Harry felt hypnotized. This was it, from backstage. "Tommy!" he called. "Why?"

"Why wha'?"

"Why call them? Leave them alone! They're asleep! It's one of the things that pisses them off about you—don't you know that?"

"Oh, crap, that's right, he's down Newport, lemme see ... hey, go get us a refill, huh, Tro? You don't know about this. This is family."

"I know goddamn well how it feels on the other end, you yo-yo! It's a swift pain in the ass! I'm telling you, don't do it. People have kids asleep, Tommy. They gotta get up in the morning!"

"Ssaturday."

"They think it's a death, you jerk! Maybe they're making love! You gotta think about *them*, Tom! You can't—"

"Mebbe call Patricia first."

"You ain't calling her at all, man! I'll rip that fucking phone off the wall for ya! I *mean* it, Thomas!"

"Heh, heh, naw, ol Albie's the first, ol Silver Fox, ol Comman'er Whitehead."

Harry was up and pacing, furious. How had home seemed so unbearable, what had been his nerves' problem, to have

ended him here, in this pathetic scene? Gone were the faintest
wisps of pity of compassion he might have had for this
miserable priest.

"Yes, it's important. Yeah, I'll wait."

"Hang it *up*, Tommy!"

"Hey, you gonna get us a drink or wha'? They gotta go fine
'im, son the fifth floo-hoor."

Harry clawed up the glasses and stormed the kitchen. He
dropped one tear of vermouth into the Canon's scotch—maybe
it'd mickey him out. Jesus, not even the U.S. *Navy* could stop
... his anger's fever broke. He had to laugh at that. Hello,
Navy? Gimme my brother, yeah, I'll wait. Tommy was still
waiting, smoking, legs crossed. He looked scrubbed shiny now,
rather than alcohol flushed: keenly sober. "Tro! You wanna be
on when he picks up? He'll flip his wig!"

"*No!* None of them. Not a word. I'm not even here."

"HeyAlbie! Me! Whaddayamean?"

Harry went out and pissed into the night off the edge of the
deck. In again, Tommy was dialing. He walked quickly around
behind to make sure it wasn't his number.

"Nance? Hi, it's Thomas. Mike there?"

"What'd Albie say?"

"Ah, fuckin', poor uptight ... Mikeo! Hey, how the hell—"

Mike obviously hung up on him, too. Harry said nothing,
just kept pouring the drink in and keeping his eyes on the
holes under the Canon's fingers. The next was Annie. Harry
heard her "Hi!" through the phone, which he suddenly found
in his hand. He covered the speaker and whispered, "No!"

"Gotta take a wicked leak, be right back!"

"Annie? This is Tro.... Yeah, really.... Sequosset." She
was whooping. He had to wait while she ran for her drink,
cigarettes and to shut off the TV. She'd been up anyway. Fast
was in Omaha. Harry hoped Tommy'd get back before she
did, but he didn't. Once she was convinced they were really
there ("Don't tell me he's letting you wear your shoes in the
goddamn place!") she had to know who had been called first.

He said, "You," and threw the phone to Thomas, who missed. It bounced off the hatch and onto the floor. Thomas picked it up.

"Hup! Hey'd, I hurt ya? Ha-ha, so how are ya, what? Albie! . . . Hey, Tro, she says to tell ya you're a lyin' bastard. Huh? Oh, come on, Annie, everybody always calls Albie first. Sall he's good for! Then you. Honest to God. Nah, screw Mike, I think he's working tonight anyhow . . . what, prove—hey, Tro, how can we prove we're here?"

"Tell her to come down."

"He says come down! I know . . . no, it just happened that's all. I think he finally walked out on your sister, ha . . . just throwin' 'em down, that's all, solvin' the problems of the universe. You know. Yeah, it's great. We . . . where's he this time? Omaha! Oh, God. How long! I see, well, listen, did you talk to Mum this week? Why the hell not? Listen, that little lady—"

Just swell. Frantic or not, he could be home being held warm while he slept or at least sidled up close to some warmth. Instead of wandering aimlessly around this model vacation pad listening to neurotic sibling drivel, unable to get even half a bun on. His system must have forgotten how to react to the stuff. His instincts had gone haywire on him for sure, if they'd led him here: *Escape,* he'd cried, so they gave him the *Cape,* senile bastards. He walked through his reflection in the glass doors and ascended in his balloon high enough to see the two alone Duffys blithering through forty miles of telephone wire to each other, not conversing: matching monologues of self-pity.

Creatures who'd had certain nerves pulled somehow, some-time—that seemed to say Thomas and Annie for Harry. Harry could feel more genuinely for Annie than for the Canon. He knew her better and liked her: somewhere around thirty-three now, between Angie and Mickey, close to where Francie would have been, and a beauty, all right, but not keeping it up lately, letting it lose its gloss. She bounced from rooftop to cellar emotionally, rarely settling level, and it was breaking her out in blotches. The main outlet she'd found for her spirit, for what she called "being a soldier," had been in packing up and moving whole homes from one "cattle country" suburb to another across America. This was their third time back near Boston, which she claimed to loathe. All for Fast, aptly named. Harry had advised him a hundred times to just go to New York and get it over with, the clockwork Apple, the single corporation with the many names, the only machine outside politics that was programmed to feed upon and recycle the kind of overdrive Fast was possessed by. But Facey wouldn't listen, said he hated New York, and went on scrambling inhumanly for his spread-out second-rate company, in relentless pursuit of whatever passed for winning in his head. The question wasn't whether he'd make it; it was what would be left if he did. And the fear was for Sergeant Annie and her Lonely Hearts Club Band, not for Fast.

"Huh, yeah, well," Thomas was huffing, "well, you're a Duffy, kid, what can I tell you?"

He said it like *Kennedy* or *Huguenot*. Maybe it was solace for Annie, but it still sounded like pulled nerves to Harry. Then again, it was easier for him to understand guys like Facey who, like himself, came unmisted by any *great family* fogs. Like Big Jake, Fast's father wasn't sixty yet, so couldn't assume any *patriarch* cloak, willingly or otherwise. As Harry read it, all Facey I ever accomplished was to get out of a three-decker flat in Roslindale to a single home on a plot in Newton Falls, then turn J. P. Morgan on his issue. He lent Fast money for college, at interest. So Fast was Showing Him, down to and including never being without a piece of land under him, no matter how long it made his commute, no matter how remotely beached it left Annie, outside St. Louis, Chicago, Pittsburgh, Boston. God knew Angie had *told* Annie enough times. When it still seemed changeable, when Annie still was assumed capable of acting, the long-distance (premidnight) cries and whispers got real response. "It's not his fault, it's yours," Angie used to offer.

"Hire help. Go back teaching. See a shrink even. Take a course. Do *anything*. If it's too much for you, stop having them for God's sake. And *tell* him you don't give a goddamn about growing tomatoes and having a fucking lawn. He'll meet you halfway. I know he will. Move near a goddamn city. No, not next time. Now! Sell it and move, or they'll be scraping you off the walls. Then what good will you be to your wonderful babies? I'm telling you, Annie, you're going to end up being *his* mother, too, and when little boys become men, you know what they do to their mothers. Don't what me, you ninny, they *leave* them, that's what! Oh . . . no Annie, I didn't mean I think you're dumb, because you're not, but. . . ."

Yaninanina, and the beat goes on . . . was the most perplexing thing about both Annie and the Canon—the times changed, but their stories stayed the same. It was hard to muster concern or even interest after a while when you heard it all before. Thomas might have spent the four or more years at Catholic U, for all Harvard seemed to have enlarged him. Still, Harry and Angie stayed open and worried for Annie and Fast, as futile as it felt, because they at least recognized their problems. As for the Canon, nobody seemed clear on what the hell he had to be so long-suffering about. (Except the mother, again, who didn't count, being inevitably cast as Mary to his Jesus and hence disqualified for prejudice.) As they saw it, he had only his own ass to take care of.

Observing him now through Johnnie Walker eyes, Harry thought he might have just discovered a new possibility about Thomas there. Tom was always vague about his work. When his evasions came with the you-wouldn't-understand pose and tone, blood vessels would bulge, and he'd be dismissed to hell once more. But just as often, and without a single specific, he could convey the impression that he was indeed operative in pretty major stuff, taxing, draining, and somehow painful for him. Piecing together shreds and charred slips, Harry had figured that one course of real dissatisfaction for the priest had something to do with fund raising. It was taken for granted that all priests in time developed an admiration approaching adoration for well-off businessmen and professionals. But the names and functions that the Canon would sometimes let slip rang tonier bells than self-made contractors or sloop-owning lawyers. Pacing, Harry put on his Columbo coat and cigar. If, then, Thomas' vocation had come to include mingling among the flighty mighty to glad-hand for alms ... tax-deductible no doubt ... and if previous assumptions were wrong and Thomas actually drank outside as carelessly and boorishly as he did with family.... "By the way, Tommy," he shouted from the firewell, "when are you going to take over as boss of that outfit anyhow? Wasn't that supposed to happen last year?"

The Canon paled and sputtered and harumphed. Harry laughed. He had pulled the wire between himself and Annie taut, and Thomas, spun, was flailing the air for a grip. "What's holding that up anyhow?"

"Quiet! I can't hear Annie!"

"You know what she's saying anyhow. What's with the monsignor? Thought he was going to retire or something and turn the factory over to you?"

"Cut it out, will you? Ah, Tro's bombed and givin' me a hard time."

"Having second thoughts is he, Tom? What'd you do, piss in someone's pâté? Huh? Ha! Fart in their Jacuzzi? Barf in their Jag? Come on, Tom, hang up and face your accuser!"

He covered the receiver. "Will you quit it!"

"What's that, you got a Big Giver on the line? One of the Beautiful People? Tell her to skip the middleman and write the check to Liberty Square Shell, attention me. Measly ten grand or so oughta do it. I'll settle for *one!*"

Thomas was trying to laugh too. "He's gone manic on me, what'll I do? Here, bigmouth, Annie wants to talk to you."

"Where's Pat while you're down there, you bastard! She even know you're there? Know what, Tro? Fuck you! You're just the same as all of em. Your ass anyway! You expect me to

kiss your ass, well, fuck you, you. . . ." That persona of Annie's
made him sick, and he let the phone drop screeching onto the
seat of the couch. Like Thomas, Annie still drank as if she
could.

His new drink looked so dark he was afraid Tom'd used red
vermouth. "Wha', she gone?"

"No, she's waiting for you."

He sat again. "Annie? Ho, wait! It's me ... Jesus, Tro,
what'd you say toa? Thas your las pop, I'm cuttin' you off!"

Harry had to laugh. He sipped: straight scotch. Nobody'd
have to cut him off if he finished this. Good thing he didn't
have to drive. He tried to rouse the energy to bait Tommy off
the phone again, but it seemed gone. God, if half of all that
money went to phone stock instead of bills ... Christ, he'd
blinked once, and now Thomas was dialing again. Two-one-
two ... "Why don't you try Mickey, Tom?"

"I am!"

"What happened to Annie?"

"You gotta be nicer toa, Tro. That was dangerous. She's
already frantic enough on her own without you makina
worse!"

"If she was in goddamn bed, she wouldn't run the risk. And
if you didn't call her in the first place!"

"Shit, no answer."

Thank God. "She must be at Phil's."

"Prob'ly out somewhere."

"She must be with Phil!"

"Don't say that!"

"He's a good guy."

"Fuck 'im."

Harry discovered he was angry again. "Hey, you aren't
quitting, are you? Sister Theresa exempt from this shit, is she?
Oh, we can't call a convent, huh? Go ahead, you son of a
bitch, call Theresa! Ring bells in a convent in the middle of
the night for a change! She's a Duffy! Call your own goddamn
number in your fucking rectory, and see if you answer and
how well *you* take it! Jesus!"

The Nixon smile was back and the eyes of cold madness. "You better call Patricia, Tro. So she won't think you racked up again or something."

It worked. Harry was astonished. Did they *all* know then? He buried it, unable to handle it now. "I called her already."

"When?"

"When you were still out cold drunk! If you were."

"So. Couldn't just take off clean, after all. Thought you were moreuv a man than—"

Harry sat down. "I'm berserk, not irresponsible."

"Whadda you bers—?"

"The station. I think I might be losing it, all right? But you probably know all about that, too."

"God, no, I—"

"Who told you about the car, Rena?"

"Yeah."

"Wonderful. Ah, I must've been nuts to think that wouldn't get out."

"Don't ever say, though. Albie'd killa."

"Meaning you've kept it to yourself?"

"Absolutely. Until now."

"Why the hell'd Rena tell you?

"Who knows? Be surprised who tells me what, Tro."

"I'm sure I would. I don't understand any of you bastards at all! And, Christ, Rena's not even one, she's an outsider like me! That makes it even worse."

Looking very pleased, the Canon said, "Ah, but you're quick enough to pull us down, arencha. Lemme tellya, there's a lot about the Duffys you'll *never* unnerstan', Troby."

"They're great, Thomas," he surrendered, tired, "absolutely great."

"I was in there with him the night of Francie, don't forget. You wanna witness greatness." He drank and lit a cigarette. The slightest sounds, like the crackling of the fire and the cubes, seemed amplified now. "Being the oldest, and the priest. Isn't the ride you guys think it is, you know. It's . . . very lonely. It's a special place, I know, but—"

"What about Francie, Doc?"

"Oh, Christ. I still have nightmares. I still see that ungodly jungle of machines and tubes and her so tiny, like a lemon drop. He ... just *said* it, Tro. The doctor couldn't do it, so he did it. I heard him. Just me—he didn't ask me either. Didn't even look at me. Probably didn't even know I was there. He said, 'If she's gone, she's gone, shut the works down, for the love of God shut them down.' I'll never forget it. They couldn't, so he went over and did it for them! The doctor cried, Tro. When he thanked Deddy for it. He was just a young guy."

"Jesus God." If Angie knew, she'd never told him. "That'd never happen anymore, Tom. That'd get you into court and the newspapers nowadays," he said, for lack of appropriate comment.

The Canon shrugged. "It happens, Tro. Don't kid yourself. And thank God, too. She'd be a turnip. He was right. Unusual, extraordinary means. Been in the book for ages."

"My God."

"Huh? Oh, yeah, *oh*, yeah. Ah ... I could tell you more, Tro. Priest's gotta carry a lot inside. Things you can't unload anywhere. Secret, private ... awful things."

Harry didn't speak. He was curious but didn't want to be asking, like a gossip.

"Secret, Tro?"

"Who would I tell, Tommy?"

"Patricia."

"I won't if you don't want me to."

"Well, she's probably the one who could handle it. Remember last year when my mother went in St. Elizabeth's? I was going to visit her one night. He was in with her. I couldn't help overhearing it. He was saying, 'Tell me if this is it because if it is, I got the pills all ready and I'll go with ye.' Him! The super Catholic his whole life! I couldn't go in. I went back downstairs."

"She was only having varicoses removed."

"He obviously thought it was more."

"Ah, maybe he was only being romantic."

"No way, Tro. I've been through all the ... possible interpretations. But there it is, and it's got to be faced. The truth is the truth. It still scares the shit out of me."

"Wow." This was a different kind of strange from Brother Big Jake's.

The impact of recalling the incident seemed to have jarred the Canon off his tightrope of lucidity once again. He was mumbling to his feet on the table, "I know, I know, you all think I always had it the best. The first can do no wrong and all that jazz. But who do I have? Who gives a real shit about me? Anything I do never counts as real work. If I say I'm run-down or something, everybody scoffs. Say, Go the Bahamas, why doncha! Those trips and cruises and shit ya know, the charters. They're no funfa me. They make us money, is all. I go 'cause no one else will and one of us hasta. Make sure nonea the old saints gets lost. Well, you try goin' back to an empty room every night, year after year, see how you like it. And you're always just the goddamn son to 'em, the child. Never really a man. No matter what ... *laurels* you win. An' lay at their feet. It's only wha's espected! No more—why *shouldn*you do this or that, the money put into ya. The care, the attention, the tons of prayers. I'm ... sick at Norman, but I know what he means about finally doin' somethin' on his own. Killed his mother, by the way. She dint make it a year afta he left. She was sick anyhow but. Fucking women. God, they're the worst. You have no idea, Tro. What bastards they can be to ya. Either treat you like some kinda eunuch or do everything but grab your meat. *Sly,* though. Always so sly. As if they don't know they're doin' it. In case you call 'em on it, see."

"Was it like that back in the parishes too, Thomas?" He wanted to pretend this was a discussion. If he left it emotional, all he could say would be I'm sorry for you, man—and where could that go?

"Parishes are worse. Millions of lonesome, hungry housewifies out there in blue-collar land, lemme clue ya. The ones up vacuuming at dawn and the ones still in their nighties at eleven o'clock, all the same inside."

"They put it to you, would they?"

"But mean, Tro. A cruelty in it. Like they were taking something out on you, you know? I don't mean all of 'em, acourse, but enough. Plenty! Then you'd see 'em Sundays. I swear some a them make their kids cry during mass, and they'd be with their husbands and they'd look right through ya or else give ya a dirty leer—ya feel like some kinda fool after a while, that's all. An' the guys treat ya like ya some kinda kid or fruit, too, so after a while. . . ."

"Maybe it's just up here around Boston, where there's so many of you." He had no idea what the hell he was saying; he was still hearing, *Shut the works down . . . I got the pills all ready.* Harry had always seen Martin Duffy as an independent, but this was far out! Suddenly he was bored again with Thomas and said, "I'm going to tell you something, Doc—do yourself a favor and stop thinking about yourself so much. It's from spending too much time alone with yourself, I think, and goddamn it, maybe it's tough from your end of it, but you asked for it, didn't you? *Ad sum,* if I remember correctly, and I damned well do. If you aren't so sure yourselves, why don't you keep your mouths shut? Or at least leave people a few outs here and there. You send me *The Critic,* right? Well, there's a cartoon in one that shows a bunch of priests watching the tube and one's saying, '*The Moon Is Blue!* I excommunicated a guy for seeing that back in the fifties!' So that ain't so fucking funny to me, Tommy."

"Won't hold up in court, Troby."

"The point is, it delights me to hear about your great old man throwing you all the finger. Twice! And to see you so upset by it. Maybe you birds ought to start listening to people like that for a change. You're all fucking pharisees—ye lift not a finger to ease the burden! How's that? Not bad, huh?"

Thomas's eyes welled with tears. "Oh, God, it's gotten so terrible, hasn't it?"

"You put up a helluva fight, I'll give you that." His adrenaline was stirring, and he felt absolutely boorish now, as if he'd been yapping at Dennis and Kate for slamming doors.

"It's changing, Tro, it really is."

"Oh, bullshit. Where the fuck were you on Vietnam? The Right to Life! Oh, that's bringing you all out of the woodwork, all right. Sure takes balls to make a stand on that, boy. Hey, those Catholics are revolutionaries, man. I'll tell ya—the *one* thing yez did, and that was not let all the whites switch their kids into parochial schools in Southie and Roxbury. Must've killed you. Would've put all your schools back on their feet in a month. I gotta give you that, but that's about it. And I still think you must've had another motive. Man, this is really a terrific party. I'm really glad I came. I feel better already."

"I agree, I agree ... what can I say? I do think it's good, though, for laymen and priests to meet and—"

"Ho, stop! Cease! Don't do that to me. All right, all right, you drunken Irish sod, *I'll* tell you a story about your father and mother at St. Elizabeth's. *I* go up one night, okay? Me, Angie, and Constance. And there's your father, and honest to God, I think he's throwing a fit. She's propped up, going tsk-tsk, and he's bent over double, laughing, coughing, whooping, spitting, and whacking his legs and the walls and anything that comes under his hand. Just seeing him, you had to laugh yourself, you know? Okay, here's what had happened. Were you up when the other little lady was in the other bed?"

"Yeah—from Quincy Street."

"Okay, so she'd broken a hip. Got rushed to the hospital and taken care of. But when *her* old man hears about it, he runs up to see her and she's asleep and he gets so shook up he has a *heart attack* right in the room! *Your* old man arrives just as the old geezer's being wheeled downstairs, with the old dame zipping after him down the hall in her wheelchair, crying 'You're all right, Leo!'"

Thomas was doing a fair imitation of his father laughing.

"And all Martin can get out is ... 'Now *she* kin coom visit *him!*'"

"Oh ... oh! ..."

"That's a better story than yours, Doc."

Thomas was weeping pints of boozy mirth now, teeth out for the air.

Harry thought of adding, Pills wouldn't look half as foolish, but he didn't. The old guy didn't die anyhow; it was just a mild one. And Harry hadn't taken the Francie and the pills stories so lightly: A person who wields power and control over life is one thing, but one who appears to hold the strings on death as well is something else altogether. He could see now how fear might be one intelligent response to any such legend ... and if he happened to be your father, well, he would certainly be a hard act to follow, to say the least.

The alcohol had them both shrunken down to about two feet tall, now, only inches away from sleep. Harry kept one lid raised long enough to say, "It is ironic, Doc."

"Wha is?"

He said the rest behind closed eyes. "Well, just one outsider's observations, of course, but seems the Duffy girls resent not bein' boys, the boys all resent not bein' you, and you turn out to be the most fucked-up bozo in the litter!"

"Think I'm not funny, whatta you think you are, *Laugh-In?*"

At last, in the dark, Harry got to roar.

Somewhere in there he might have heard glass smash, but otherwise the kaleidoscope turned in silence showing him:

his mother in her coffin ...

Francie in a spider's web ...

the pony toppling off the bouncing pickup and being dragged ...

the baby bird being squashed by the first set of car wheels, then carried bit by bit away by others, the mother above shrieking over even the stain ...

the four separate funeral convoys on Route 128, head-lights brighter than day ...

the baby gerbil skeletons in the cage in the kids-screaming morning, having been eaten by the father . . .

Kate's floating angelfish . . .

Jake's kitten cemetery . . .

Tony Mac eating blood pudding smuggled into Prospect City Hospital . . .

the kid biker in *Easy Rider* . . .

the kid cop biker in *Electra Glide in Blue* . . .

Bobby Darin . . .

a form rising, a human shadow figure coming uphill in mist. . . . "Ooh! Christ!" He was sitting up, holding his forehead. He'd struck it against an invisible steel beam hung over the couch. He felt a blanket over his feet and jeans and remembered catching it out of the air. His eyes cleared, and he saw a huge outline of a housefront drawn by a kid with crayon and filled in with bright, pearly gray light, no doors or windows. His watch said six forty-five.

Thomas said, "It's okay, buddy, go back to sleep." He was in his black suit and white collar, face shaved and pink, combing his hair in the mirror beside the wall unit.

Harry stared, lost.

"Roll over. I have to take the seven for the local guy down here. Catch you later."

Harry lurched to his feet, rasped, "What are you, on pills?" and staggered out onto the deck. He streamed into the chill, wet morning, then flattened his back against the outside glass, inhaled ten times, stretching his frame up and down, then collapsed his joints and hung limp, his head between his knees: old Army trick. He went in to the john, put a hot facecloth on his face, then a cold one. God, he'd forgotten how great drinking could be. . . .

Thomas was letting the Grand Prix fast-idle. "Where you going, sunshine?"

"Just don't talk." Tommy's smoke was nauseating him so he lit one of his own. . . .

The church was small, red-brick with some ivy just starting

to come green. The pointed windows looked sooted opaque
from outside, but inside they were stained glass. They filtered
reds, blues, and greens into the pearly gray. Thomas marched
smartly down the side aisle to the sacristy. Harry slumped into
a sit-kneel slouch in a rear pew. A kid in surplice, cassock, and
Keds was lighting the two candles on the table-altar. The
dozen or so old people who end their lives attending the early
daily masses throughout the world were there, scattered. Four
young nuns were there, too. He knew they were nuns by their
clothes—drab, boxy, Mary-like, fifties-collegiate—and by the
way their sister superior, in head veil and black topper, kept
her eyes scanning them from behind. A little bell jingled.
Father Thomas stepped out of his ordination photo and strode
to the table. Harry stood, a beat later than the others. He saw
now that he wasn't the only male. J. Edgar Hoover was there
in a black and green lumberjack shirt. Harry lipped the *I
Confess* from the missalette, feeling sorrow but no sins stir. The
Canon's youth, sparkle, and clear baritone amazed him but
not for long; before the *Lord, have mercy* Thomas turned faceless
and nameless. For Harry, hung-over or not, was at mass again
and temporarily safe.

Harry Trowbridge was used to being one of the few males
under fifty at an early weekday morning mass. He had been
going practically every day for the past eight or nine years. Not
even Angie knew it. In New York he had rotated among St.
Patrick's, St. Agnes' near Grand Central, the UN Chapel, St.
Bernard's on Fourteenth, St. Joe's on Sixth and Washington
Place. Now he'd hit St. Paul's in Harvard Square one morning, Holy Family in Liberty Square another, or St. Joe's in
Union, St. Peter's on Huron, St. John's in North Cambridge,
St. Paul's in Tower Square, Somerville. Enrolled in no parish,
he used all their altars at will. He was neither ashamed nor
proud of his habit and practice; it was just something he
couldn't tell anybody. Who could be expected to take it right?
"Good Catholic" had come to mean too many things he
considered wrong, distasteful, or otherwise outside his idea of

his identity. Sometimes he deliberately skipped going on a Sunday just to reinforce the lines he drew. Ethel Kennedy'd been quoted someplace as saying in effect that with her luck she'd be ninety-two before the church changed its rules against marrying a divorced person, and there she'd be. Harry had to admire the steel in that hang-on obedience, but wasn't up to it himself, and didn't regret it either. To him, "sovereign" was nothing but a coin nobody used anymore. He went because. . . .

Actually he'd quit and come back. "Show me someone with a theological problem, and I'll show you someone with a moral one!" had long been a favorite slogan sneered from Catholic pulpits. Harry'd never had reason to question it. Then, the universe shifted. And gave the sun hiccups. That sent that brief blast of X-ray beams down upon the planet Earth and exposed *all* the naked emperors and feet of clay. And Harry suddenly saw that that old saw worked just as well the other way around. His moral problem at the time was, of course, artificial contraception. Facing it led him directly to the theological problem behind it, and the minute he saw *it* with its trench coat wide open, he saw that it wasn't his problem at all but Rome's. His moral problem went away, and so soon after did Harry. But his going AWOL was only incidental, really: The church and their baptisms in it never had much directly to do with his and Angie's having five versus one or no children. They'd acted pretty much personally and secularly. He'd been an only child and thought he'd hated it. She'd been one of eight and thought she'd liked it. And in America then hopes were still up and kids were still in, as was blind belief.

He came back for two reasons. The less important was that he counted all the dumdums joining him on the outside. The jimokes who didn't know the offertory from benediction were leaving in droves, and the church as loser intrigued him anew. If she was alienating those millions of meatheads, she must be doing something right. So Harry started taking sidelong glances back at the supership of his religion, being abandoned fore and aft, port and starboard by crew and passengers alike, women and children last, every man for himself. Mayday, Mayday. The truth was, he'd begun missing her from the first moment he jumped. Leaving her let him see her better. Aboard, he'd never realized what a truly massive mother she was. With suddenly only inches of rubber between his feet and the deep, he saw how stable she was, how steady she held ... how beautiful she looked against the worldwide, thunder-clouded skies. She never called a Molly to him, though, never crackled *Come back!*, so he just kept on chugging away. He'd been a son of the Owner treated like steerage. Being skipper felt better, even if it was only of a raft.

By the time his supership was a pale ghost on the horizon he was understanding Ocean better. He knew Conrad and Hemingway, but they'd been no preparation for this. It wasn't the whipping wind or the blistering sun; not the insanely pitching mountainous waves or the maddening, depressing calms. Anything natural he could take and feel toughened by. No, Harry's other and more important reason for slipping back to the church was sheerly his own self. Out there all by himself he found himself lacking. Strange, unseen forces bumped his underside day and night. His reason told him they were only natural and screened pictures of sharks, whales, squid and reminded him of his excellent supply of repellants, weapons, medicine, food, and water. That would reassure and keep him going for more weeks, more months, yo-ho. But then—Bump ... Bump ... Bump ... until his reason would be over-whelmed by something else, screening pictures of unnatural predators so terrifying they made Hieronymus Bosch's night-mare creatures and monsters look cartoon-cute. Because his were *feelings*. Terrible, slimy, formless feelings of dread, fear, and despair, they were a magnet, and he was metal, simple as that, and their invisible pull to suck him over and out and down he found impossible to resist by himself.

He had no idea how others did it. He even envied anyone who appeared to be able to survive and stay sane and function

by his own hook. He found out he couldn't, that's all. He
needed something beyond himself, something as invisible and
at least as strong as the pull those bumping terrors exerted.
Perhaps there were people who never experienced such horrors,
who were somehow spared the magnet drag of no-hope. He
didn't know or care. He did have them, and for him the power
of positive thinking just didn't hack it. Nor did denying them,
nor did dope, booze, sex, movies, books, work, the pleasures of
children, the delights of nature, the warmth of human friendship, music, handball, theater, ballet, rotation pool, new
clothes, Transcendental Meditation, existential hedonism in
general, and ethical good works, discipline, and sacrifice in
particular, hack it either. He had to have something more to
call on, to lay it all in the lap of.

Harry didn't go straight back. Strung out, he left a recording studio one Thursday night and walked to the New York
Zendo on Sixty-seventh Street. He removed his shoes, checked
his bag, dropped his two bucks in the basket, and followed the
other Beginners upstairs, thick mocha carpeting soft beneath
his socked feet. The place had a beige, hushed air he found
familiar and delicious. If Big Jake had been in then, the
smiling, brown-robed monk at the door would have reminded
Harry of him. Upstairs: rose carpeting, beige walls, black
pillows aligned straightly on the floor, lights soothingly dim,
incense burning, the faintly pungent scent of it seemingly a
part of the surrounding silence, smelling with the sound of
whispers. It was right down Harry's alley. A mossy-voiced
young monk described and demonstrated the sitting positions:
tailor, quarter lotus, half, full. Harry managed a half and held
it for the initiatory forty minutes, hands correctly folded above
his bored donk, gaze at the forty-five-degree angle, counting his
breaths from one to ten again and again, concentrating on the
abdomen. He relished enduring the pain, hearing Gregorian
chant in his mind, absorbing the pain, feeling it relax and
strengthen him. "Kneel up straight!" some nun's voice hissed
from twenty years away and made him smile.

The sisters' signals snapped! Here wood struck wood but gently, like faraway branches cracking under snow. Harry stood with the others, bowed with and to the others and to the doorways, walked in single file with the others, counting breaths still, quietly. Later the walking didn't pass the stairs but ribboned down them and wound through the first-floor rooms before ending in the main room to join the other groups. Walking, Harry felt calmness and elation. In the rear a wide, sliding glass wall stood open. The walking room was dark. There was a small garden outside, floored with smooth stones. Lights shone down from somewhere above. One young tree grew in a corner, up cedar fencing. It was October. Leaves snowed like yellow feathers through the light, down upon the stones. Autumn cologne breezed in, feeling like dry, spicy water when walked through. He was sorry they made only two passes through it.

Assembled in the large room, they were told to sit in their most favored position. Harry knelt this time, pillow wedged between his butt and heels. The guest speaker was a young monk, a teacher at the New School, a Zenner for five years en route to Zurich for some advanced Zenning. First he led a bit of chanting. It sounded more Ubangi than Gregorian, but Harry happily hummed along. Then the guest monk gave a brief homily, something about how everyone is the Light, in addition to being various-watt bulbs. Harry couldn't help it: He thought of the Mystical Body of Christ, the Tree and all its branches, the Head and all its body parts. He felt his physical, mental, and aesthetic high begin to thin. Then came the zonker. A small Buddha squatted on a pedestal behind the guest monk. Harry'd spotted it and figured it was just to hold incense, but no. They all were now to bow to it. Harry felt stabbed by an icicle. He was a Jew, and there grinned the golden calf. Thou shalt not have strange gods before Me. There it was, still in him, intact. He felt exuberant, grateful; he almost let burst a laugh. What a relief. His spine would not waver an inch. He couldn't so much as lower his eyelids. His straight-ahead gaze met that of the young monk across the mass of down-rounded backs. Harry looked refusal at him, without malice. He was answered in kind, and it was over.

Heading for the Lexington Avenue downtown IRT, Harry looked and saw his faith afloat and alight on the horizon. Nearer and all around him he noticed what had grown into fleets of fellow castaways. He was amazed at their numbers. A skipper? He felt like a chunk of flotsam or jetsam or weed in a sargasso traffic jam of bodies floating this way then that at the whim and mercy of shifting, stupid waves. He came about and headed back. People tried to wave and point him right, but he ignored them. Missing a train, he walked out of Grand Central to the still-open basement of St. Agnes', knelt down and said, "I'm back, like it or lump it. If you're anything, you're roomy." He stayed clear of crew, command, and most remaining passengers. He answered no calls to battle stations and none to social affairs. Owner's son or not, he felt like a stowaway and behaved like one, staying in the shadows. Mass to Harry was the engine room, the sine qua non. He went to it as often as he could because when he didn't, he felt totally alone. And helpless again against terrors, which didn't care what vessel held you.

He was liking this Sequosset mass being said by the ensign with Tom Duffy's voice. The table was unembellished wood; the vestments were not brocaded finery, but plain, coarse linen; the chalice was a small, glazed pottery cup. He didn't know how plumbers or poets perceived it, but Harry saw mass as a perfect one-act play, with near-equal scenes of Old Testament and New cross-vectoring to sharp-focus Jesus, the Man-God, who lives, gets killed, then lives again, only different. All in less than a half hour, talk about compression. Even when he was just *there,* as this morning, like a knot on a log, not digging the poetry in the Psalms and Prophets, the short stories in the Gospels, barely hearing anything, up to no more than Zenning his own breathing and heartbeats in his ears, Harry still got touched by something good. He didn't find it difficult to

believe that the act being performed at the table before him
was exactly the same as the one Christ did Himself at that
Passover supper some years before. Repeated for those unable
to be there at the time because He said to do so, and He was
It. Simple as air, which can't be seen either.

Something was wrong: The priest was clearly the Canon
now, and his grip had slipped. He was having trouble finding
the right page in the large mass book propped open upon a
burlap-covered pillow. The slashing sounds of the pages being
desperately flipped grated Harry's nerves. *Come on, Tom.* The
priest finally found his place and began to read. His hands
were shaking, but not his voice. He made it to the Gospel. The
people stood. Easter was coming up, so it was St. John time,
on-scene reports of Christ's progress toward Jerusalem for the
finale: Today it was Him giving some Greeks a forecast of his
imminent death via the grain of wheat that must fall to earth
and die in order ever to produce fruit. Done, the priest looked
up, facelessly once more to Harry, and said, "Stay standing for
the Prayer of the Faithful. The response today will be 'Hear
us, O Lord.'"

A lady chipmunk with hunchback led off: "For all the poor
and starving nations!"

All chanted, "Hear us, O Lord."

A young nun: "For family life here in St. Rose's parish."

The man: "For the destruction of godless Communism!" It
was J. Edgar!

"For my cousin getting a liver operation today."

"For poor Mr. Nixon and his lovely family!" cried the lady
with the hat.

"For total amnesty!" retorted a younger, fat woman.

For a second it looked like war, but détente fell and swiftly
turned to silence. *Tommy!* The Canon, looking seasick green
now, seemed to have left. The priest statue looked made of
plaster, with agate eyes fixed forever on the book. Throats
cleared. Shoes scuffled. Hoover hacked pointedly. The silent
vigil went on. Awkwardness spread like furnace heat. Harry
didn't think he could stand it, or stand period, much longer,

but gloated a little too: Tom's paralysis felt a lot more natural than that uncanny healthiness he'd started out with. Harry seriously considered snapping his fingers or whistling or anything to jolt Thomas out of it.

Then the head nun did it; into that long, deadly vacuum she abruptly shot her barbed prayer, "For all poor creatures suffering mental disorders!"

Harry was sure he giggled his "Hear us, O Lord," but no heads turned. The Canon's eyes cleared. All sat, and two women scurried up the aisle bearing gifts of bread and wine, and the priest had no trouble getting on with the real business at hand. At communion, the celebrant held up the transubstantiated host, saying, "This is the Lamb of God who takes away the sins of the world. Happy are we who are called to His supper." After that, Harry usually flipped to the back to read what he called the Anna Christie (for *Anima Christie,* and didn't O'Neill ... ?) but this whacky morning he couldn't get past the "Blood of Christ, inebriate me" line, so, bone in throat, joined the queue to receive. The priest said, "The Body of Christ," Harry said, "Amen," took it on his tongue, walked over to the table, waited for the chipmunk lady to finish (she used the linen to wipe her own lip instead of the chalice's), then sipped some Blood, retaining its wine qualities. Back on his bench he swallowed the Wafer. It was okay to chew it now (Ha! Smashed a kid in the face for doing that back in the forties! one nun he remembered could exclaim), but Harry rarely chewed it. He liked the wholeness as It went down. Inside: "What has passed my lips as food, O Lord, may I possess in purity of heart, that what is given to me in time be my healing for eternity," by which *he* meant: *Okay, I've done what I can, now just get me through whatever's waiting to come down on me out there today.* Had he known then what *was* waiting that Saturday, he later mused, he might've gone back for seconds or thirds. Or lashed himself to the holy-water font.

While the priest was doing the dishes, Harry tried to grit his brain and force the high to happen. If it did, it would be quicker but fiercer than that from amyl nitrate. But it didn't,

again. He should've known better, but this trying to force it
had become habit to him also. The scattered few times he had
actually, physically and emotionally, felt it, the reality of his
belief, it had always smacked him unawares from out of
nowhere. No arranging of set and setting seemed to matter. It
came only when Somebody felt like zapping him with it, that
farthest out of consciousness alterings. That indescribable ele-
vating of the heart, sort of. That breath-stopping mainline hit
of pure, uncut Love and Peace and Hope for which all other
highs were merely pale substitutes and searchings, said F.
Mauriac, writing of Magdalene's fancy fuckings. When Harry
didn't get it, which was 99 percent of the time, he didn't
worry. Now that he was in from the desolate cold, he had put
on a backup man, a practical, Pascalian bastard who figured,
Hey, if it's True, then I'm in on the action. If it ain't True,
what've I lost?

Tommy came out of the sacristy's outside door in a yellow
turtleneck and white ski jacket. He threw his suitcoat, collar
and bib, and black doctor's bag into the backseat with the
empty beer cans, then drove them away from the church
without speaking. He didn't look so good and young anymore.
Harry grinned. "Mental disorders!"

"Huh? Oh, yeah."

Harry said no more, even when he noticed the road to the
house fly by. Thomas kept going until they reached Old Silver
Beach; he parked in the lot by the still-shuttered hotel, got out,
and walked down onto the sand. Harry caught up just as the
Canon had stopped, walked up into the dunes, and began
throwing up his liver and kidneys. Harry didn't know whether
to go pat his back or what, so he just lit a smoke and waited in
the path, looking the other way, at the choppy horizon and the
misty, loud-crashing surf. Thomas staggered down at last, half
flushed, half drained, coughing and wiping his mouth with a
hankie. "There. Want to run or walk?"

"Let's run," flipping the Lark away.

They jogged down to the harder wet line, then along it,

They made the end, turned, and slowed to walk back. Tommy said, "Feeling better?"

"Yeah, you? That air's fantastic."

"Hungry?"

"I was, until you started calling Ralph back there in the bushes."

"Ralph?"

"That's what Cyrus calls barfing. Calling ... *Ralph!*"

No reaction. The Canon said, "Uh, you want to go find a greasy spoon or go back to the house? We're loaded with food."

"Mox nix—your card game, Father."

"I could do without seeing anybody."

Thomas walked to the kitchen as he had to the altar. Behind, Harry spotted the bits and pieces of glass scattered across the floor. The splash mark on the fake brick above hadn't faded away yet. He went on into the "galley" and found a broom and dustpan in the small wall closet. Plugging in the percolator, Thomas said, "What's that for?"

"You, uh, must've missed the fireplace, Igor."

Harry swept. Thomas stared.

"I ... don't remember doing it."

He kept sweeping. "That, ah ... happen often?"

"Sunnyside, over, or scrambled?"

"Two over easy."

Thomas had a second pan heating under bacon when Harry emptied the glass and put the stuff back into the closet. He felt estranged. Tommy felt stiff to him. It was edgy. He laughed. "Your mother finds out you can do that you're off the gravy train, you know."

"Ha."

"You know, for all she can cook, she makes the worst eggs and bacon in the world?"

Thomas smiled thinly. "I thought I was the only one who thought that. Raw bacon and dirty whites."

"Good bread, though."

"Yeah. Oh, check the freezer, will you?"

"Got it." Harry pulled a long loaf of Pepperidge Farm white down, pried four frozen slices off with a knife and set them near the toaster. He thought of telling Tom that he'd save a pan if he finished the bacon first, but decided to keep still. He'd been ignoring it but couldn't any longer; the itchiness was back. That was another thing about his mass magic; it never interfered with the moons and tides. He clapped his hands. "Ready for the best Bloody Mary you ever had?" Already reaching a can of Sacramento down from a cabinet and searching for Tabasco and Worcestershire.

"Don't make mine too hot, Tro."

"Hey, stick with the grub. I'll have you back on your feet in no time."

"Worry about yourself."

Harry decided to take it as friendly. "Some show there this morning, kid. The priest of steel!"

"Years of practice. Down to a science. How long you want to stay, anyhow? I mean, do what you want, Tro, but the car's yours if you want it. I can get one out of St. Rose's."

He checked his reflex to start jabbing his index finger around again, and did Good-Time Charley, often taken for Mickey the Dunce: "Hate to drink and run, Duffo, so I think I'll hang in for a while. Week, maybe two. You go about your own business, though, pretend I'm not even here."

"Patricia give you your walking papers?"

"Bag and baggage! I'll show her. I don't have to take any more of that goddamn . . . ah, but I told you all about that last night." Testing, testing. "The hell with it."

"Oh, yeah, that's right, too."

No, that's wrong, pal, and a worrisome sign.

"Nothing *really* serious, though, is it, Harry?"

"There you go. Slainte!"

"Slainte!"

"Aah! Gorgeous. You don't call another man serious, Father?"

Thomas breaking eggs might have just bitten into a lemon.

"Get my hands on that son of a bitch I'll break his legs. *And* hers! An ex-priest, too. Beautiful, huh? Ah, don't put me through it again, Tom. I'll end up buying a gun."

"Toast should—"

"Done!" He'd quit it. He knew he could turn Thomas' face into a slot machine at will now, his eyes spinning cherries, if he continued. "I'll go set that table by the deck window, okay, Tom? The sun's coming in there." He sank the frozen bread.

"Yeah, good. That'll be good, Tro."

Eating, Thomas tried to probe. "God. And how long have you two been married?"

"Seventeen years! If our marriage was a person, it'd be a senior in high school. With pimples. And no plans for the future." He got a flash on his own behavior from that surprise little gem: He was still a bit in the bag, with the vodka squirting lighter fluid on the flame. It was hard keeping the grin off his mouth. He studied his busy fork to hide the nutsy glint he felt in his eyes. "Ever read a book, *The Edge of Sadness,* Tom?"

"Uh—that O'Connor?"

"Yeah."

"No. Just the Curley one. What's it about? Any good?"

"Not up to the *Hurrah,* but yeah. Alcoholic priest.

"He's dead now, isn't he?"

"The priest?"

"O'Connor."

"Angie and I are fine, Doc." He looked at his rip of toast, plowing the running yolk. "There was nothing about us last night."

"So?" without a pause.

Harry still didn't look up. "So how often do you black out the night before?"

"Just when it's serious and boring."

"Oh. You can *never* remember anything, huh?"

Thomas pushed his plate away. He'd eaten only the yolk.

He lit a Kent. "Get off me, Tro. And don't sweat me either. I had a crappy week, a crappy day, and a worse night. I mean before. Not you." He sounded most weary.

Harry squinted over the lip of his Bloody Mary and decided. "Okay, Tom. You got it. Don't show me yours, and I won't show you mine. So what do you do, usually, down here? I don't want to be in your way."

"Oh, nothing. Hang around, do some homework. I'm going to go sack out some more pretty soon, I know that."

"Splendid."

They shared the cleaning up. Thomas showed Harry to the downstairs bedroom, then meeked away up the spiral stairs. Harry kicked off his boots and sat against the headboard of the double bed to finish his drink, smoking and mulling over Father Tom Duffy, PhD. He suppressed the impulse to take the Prix and split for home; the weekend there was a known quantity, good, but repeated perhaps too many times. He still felt like a marine on liberty—from Liberty. Thomas sure wasn't some grand wit. Harry, over the past year or so, had been more and more preferring the company of his own kids to most other adults anyhow....

He jumped awake four hours later horny as a satyr and full of a strange, sudden sympathy for his near brother, the priest Tommy. If he had dreamed at all, he couldn't remember a wisp of it, shades of somebody else he knew. The john was between the bedroom and kitchen. He pissed as he had before mass: lemony and smelling like peanuts. He liked the sensation and remembered he hadn't liquor-leaked like this since before his car crash. Life's little pleasures. He stripped and showered in the step-in stall; Irish Spring soap—man, these guys were in some rut. Well, two out of three: He'd noted the miniature Calvary of signposts stuck into the lawn outside—CARROLL, HUNTINGTON, DUFFY. He wondered what the locals took them for; three families obviously couldn't fit into this cute little playhouse. Dressed, he entered the main room prepared to yell

up at the balcony, but Thomas was sitting outside on the deck
in the sun, engulfed in a blanket. He looked up and smiled
tiredly, "Hey, Trowbridge."

"Hi. How about that sun? Feels like May already, huh?"

Tommy hurled the blanket at him, getting up. Harry caught
and folded it, watching Thomas lean on the railing top to look
forlornly down into the needly brown yard. With Jake and
Constance and even sometimes Amy, Harry would find himself
dead-ended by a sudden slump or lookaway of such disheart-
ened anguish that all he could do was throw an arm around
their shoulders and squeeze. The thin priest made him feel the
same way now. He checked the impulse; Thomas might suffer
cardiac arrest: The Duffy's never touched each other; for a
male in-law to. . . . He carried the blanket inside and dropped
it onto the couch. He switched on the radio; maybe music
would cheer. News. South Vietnam still being evacuated.
People dangling and dropping from choppers and planes into
the ocean. Soldiers muscling and butting women and kids out
of the way. He clicked it off and returned outside. "When
do I get to see a piece of water anyhow? I can smell it,
but. . . ."

"Want to?"

"Damn right, think I came all the way down here for a barf
in the dunes?" He got his fatigue jacket and they walked down
to the main road. They turned onto a crumbly side road and
came to water flat and round as a pewter plate. They followed
its edge around on the clean sandy beach. The road stayed
parallel. Thomas said, "What looks like marsh over there are
cranberry bogs. That's called Coonaquissit Island up ahead,
but it's been connected for years. A lot of nice houses. On the
other side is all Buzzards Bay. Want to go back on the road
and follow it around?"

"No, this is beautiful here."

Harry began skipping stones as they went. Thomas skimmed
one. Beach ended with crunch where spit began, a long,

pointed arrowhead of land reaching well out into the inlet.
"Hey, what's this, the great scallop graveyard?"

"Millions of them, huh? Want to take some home for the
kids?"

"Good idea," Harry said and started watching for perfect
ones. They reminded him of discarded, dead gas stations. They
reached the tip of the spit. Outward from here the water
looked more like real ocean, with a brisk chop running to join
heavier whitecaps. The wind hit a lot chillier here, even when
the sun shone clear. A length of huge, barkless, bleached tree
trunk from some petrified forest lay near, like a round wall.
They sat down by it, in the sun, out of the wind. Harry sighed,
"Man, I could use a year of this. Really cleans out the
cobwebs, doesn't it?"

"I forget how great it is. I ought to come down more than I
do."

"I thought you were always—?"

"Yeah, to the house. But I mean down here."

Harry shielded his eyes and pointed to the sun. "Hmmm—
two . . . twenty."

"How can you tell?"

"I looked at my watch."

Thomas let out a real laugh.

"The kids fall for that all the time."

"How they doing anyhow?"

"Better than anybody."

Thomas started frisking his pockets. "Oh, no. You bring
cigarettes?"

"Here," throwing him the flat pack. "Take my last one, go
ahead."

"We'll share it—hey, what last one? It's empty!"

"Oh, crap."

"Let's go. I can do without anything but—"

"Hold on, now, wait a minute, I thought I—oh, ho! What
have we here!"

"What's *that?*"

"A jernt, I've got, let's see—five! Fantastic. Oh, thank you, Lord."

"Marijuana?"

"Chore. I forgot I had them." He kept one twist stick out and returned the rest to his breast pocket. He uncrimped one end a little and lit the other, sucked a lungful and passed it. "Here you go." Perfect set and setting, in his estimation. The Canon was staring at it. "That's money, Tommy. Waste not, want not."

"Why not." Thomas inhaled adeptly.

"Hey, a pro!"

"Tried it a few times at Harvard," passing it back.

"Oh, of course."

"You smoke it all the time, Tro?"

"Nah, maybe once a week," hffft!

"Where do you get it?"

"Leave papers and dollars on the table at night. In the morning—bingo." Harry's connection was Flash Gordon. He'd barreled into the station at the end of the day Friday. His Powell's dairy truck had hidden compartments and secret panels. Hence the "Honey Wagon" to those hip to Flash's undercover operations. Not counting the milk, yogurt, eggs, butter, bacon, juice and other legitimate dairy products he delivered to stores in the Congo (Roxbury), grass was his most innocent commodity. He slipped Harry the Baggie-full he'd ordered, seeds and twigs intact (cleaned cost extra), stashed within an empty cream carton, then insisted upon rolling on Harry's desk the bonus joints from his own supply. He thrived on such grand gestures. He also loved seeing Cyrus tap-dance from anxiety outside, pulling lookout duty.

By the fourth time Thomas said nothing was happening, something was. He suddenly breathed, "Oh, wow."

Harry laughed to see the sight of the Canon sitting there, unaware that he wore the beatific, fixed grin of a child at the movies. "One thing this has over booze, Tommy."

"What?"

"You never have to worry about forgetting what you did the night before."

"That right?"

"Yup. You forget what you did the minute before."

The child came apart at every bodily joint, laughing. Harry felt he ought to get them onto some clothesline of contact, and said, "Lemme try to chalk-talk you into this a little, okay? First, you shouldn't talk about *it* while you're doing *it*. It's gauche and defeats the purpose. Now—violating that basic principle—"

"Ha!"

"—you're gonna hit like an impasse or brink, Tom. And you'll see your options. You can go up, go down, go to sleep, whatever. I suggest you decide to relax and decide to go *up*. Otherwise, it's a downer."

"Or a sleeper."

"Right."

"Of course, I presume that first, one must decide. To decide!"

"Absolutely. You have to decide to decide. Otherwise."

"Okay. I'm deciding. To decide. To go up."

"Beautiful. Now, after you do that, you're gonna experience a kind of bowelchill, yeah, a *bowelchill* of . . . second thoughts. And kind of some *fear*. See, we aren't kids. This isn't primal for us, isn't . . . natural or sanctioned for us, like, say, beer drinking was."

"My God, you're right, Tro. A chill! I am. I'm feeling it."

"Good. That's either it, or you're about to poop your pants."

Little Doc had the laugh of his life.

Protest from his jaws informed Harry that now he, too, had been wearing a wide, fixed grin.

"Tro! Troby! Listen . . . oh, God, is this great. Ready?"

"Yeah, yeah!"

"Okay, Wait, now." He composed himself. "All right . . . Say, pal, does this make me a . . . a . . . *high priest?*"

Harry rolled one way, Thomas the other, roaring until their stomach muscles felt as if they were in flat, flabless, hard

hape. Sitting up again, Harry said, "That's another thing. I'm
hinking fondly right now of the guy I got this stuff from. Now,
hat's nice, right?"

"It is."

"All right. Now, when's the last time you inwardly thanked
ome *liquor-store clerk* for helping you get wrecked, huh?"

"That's terrific. But not only that, Tro! I haven't *got* like this
n drink! Since God knows when!"

"Aah! That's another. . . ."

"God, I'd love a scotcherooni!"

"Me too."

"Me too."

"What were we just saying?"

"Uh . . . oh! About the . . . um."

"Doesn't matter."

"Boy, Tro. Look at that water. The *scrotum-tightening sea.*"

"Poop!"

Thomas was away, in the water. "Can you see those buoys
loating out there? Lobster traps. Under that water . . . is life!
We simply can't see it from here, that's all. Fish, clams,
callops, lobsters, anemones, God knows."

"Ever think, Doc? Who was the very first guy? Ever. In the
uistory of the world. To come up face to face with a *lobster* . . .
ind figured out . . . you could *eat* them?"

"Very hungry man."

"You got it."

"After fire, you think, Tro? Or did he just grab it and
naybe conk it against a rock and eat it raw?"

"Good thought. Probably. Yeah, probably conk and raw."

"Phew. Not knowing if it might kill him or not."

"Very, very hungry Father, bastard."

"*I'm* a very, very hungry Father, bastard."

"Oh, that's another part of the deal. You can get ravenous if
you let it. You can turn that off."

"Like sex, then. Redirect the drive, rechannel the energies to
. . hey, can we have some more, Troby?"

"Ah, we are alike, Duff. Find something terrific and want

more, want it *all!* Our downfall, I'm sure. Here we go, kid,'
lighting a new one. "You want? I got? You got!"

"That's a great saying," hffft!

"Flash says that."

"No, the spirit, Tro. That's from the spirit."

Harry didn't notice Little Doc's eyes wandering back to the
water. The wind was shifting and ruffling the inlet's fur now.
The sun was spotting the diamonds in there, just before they
dived for the deep. Harry was still getting into thoughts of his
own.

"I want a woman," Thomas announced, quiet as a clam's
yawn.

"That may be my real trouble with my station," Harry was
telling himself aloud. "To suddenly see that what I thought
was a brave, significant act, and it *was,* when we did it, to us it
was, turns out to be ... just owning a gas station. I ate, and
I'm still hungry; it just didn't fill the hole. Even if it took off,
even if I got a chain of stations and made a mint, that's all it'd
be."

"I want a woman," hffft!

"What?"

"Jesus, what do I do with this? Here!"

Harry took it. "That's a roach, Doc. The sweetest meat.
Gotta have nails or a holder, though. Or put it out and, to
demonstrate ... swallow it. Ah."

Father Thomas was up and walking to the water's edge,
crunching loudly.

Harry watched approvingly. Wouldn't you know, the white
jacket didn't get even a little smirched from the log? Well, it
was a clean log. He looked at it and touched it. Oh, tree.
Where did you stand, shouldering the sky? Or are you bone?
What behemoth's forearm, shin, dick wert thou onct?

"*I want a wom-an!*" Toes of desert boots blackening as the
wavelets plopped over them, Thomas was stirring gulls to flight
with his bullmoosing. And cracking Harry up into shell bits of
hilarity. The Canon bellowed his desire a fourth, fifth, *I want a*

woman! and sixth time, cupped palms up for megaphone. Then he turned and walked back to the log. Harry's head was in the shelly sand. He had to climb upright and was spitting a lot.

Neatly seated once more, Thomas said, "What the hell's so funny?"

"No, no—not you, Tommy. But ... I mean, you *hadda* see it, right? *Amarcord?* The Fellini? I mean, it's the best, most lovely movie ever. ..."

"No."

"Oh, God, you must've! What you just did! I thought you were—?"

"I saw *8½* years ago. With you and Patricia, in fact, remem—"

"No, no, no. This is new. Oh, Tommy, this movie. Last January, right? It's freezing and pissing rain, and I hit the pits, right? I want to die. If I go home, I'll murder somebody. I don't know what did it. Another bill I couldn't pay, maybe. If I stay, I'll destroy Cyrus, and I love him. I don't know what I'd do, I'm bleeding. I wanna get *drunk* is what I want! But I grab a bus to Sullivan. Something saves me. I go in town. I walk the Common in the rain. I walk the streets. I go through Jordan's and Filene's both, every fucking floor. I'm so down I'm crazy, and I know it, and I can't change it."

"My God."

"How'd I get into this? Nah, forget all that. Oh, I know! I go into this movie! That's it. About five o'clock. People coming out from work, going home, and I hate every face I see. I'm full of envy, hate, poison. I wanna hit and kick. *This movie,* Father. I sit through it twice. Haven't done that since I'm twelve. It ... *lifts* all the hate out of me. This guy's not a priest, huh? *This fucking guinea guy—*"

"Of course he—"

"No, no, no, no. Cut. God, I'm stoned. Never mind all that, Tom. Erase it. No! You! Down there! I thought you were doing the dimmie up the tree for me! On purpose! You *didn't* see it?"

"*Who's* a fucking dimmie in it, Tro?"

"All right. This guy is the brother of the father of this family. Our age. And he's in a nuthouse. So they go out to visit him, on a Sunday. A *car* ride, like in the thirties or forties. Fun outing. So they pick him up, and he's in a suit, and good-looking. Really nice with the kids and everybody, and you're saying, what's wrong with him? He seems saner than anybody you've seen so far, you know? Until they go to take a leak. Him and I think the grandfather—his old father. They go over to the side of the road or something, and he takes his leak all right ... except he doesn't unzip his fly! Just goes! And gives his leg a little shake when he's done! Old gink just shakes his head, but the kids see and practically pee *their* pants laughing!"

Thomas laughed.

"Getting them their ears boxed by Mama and the whole number. Anyhow, they all end up at this great farmhouse. And, to make it short—"

"Ho!"

"—the dimmie ends up way high in the branches of this huge, great tree. With a ladder up it from the ground. You gotta see it. I mean, the bastard silhouettes it, and the ... well, they can't get him down. Oh! What he's doing up there is yelling 'I want a woman!' Over and over. You can't see him. Across the whole valley, "I want a woman!" And the sun's going down. They do everything. Pretend to leave. Yell. Threaten."

"Can't one of them—?"

"Oh, that's it. He's got a pocketful of rocks, see. And every time somebody tries to go up the ladder, *conk!* right on the noggin. And all the time: "I want a woman!" I swore you were ... so finally, they get the orderlies from the asylum to come out. But again, bonk, bonk, bonk." Harry was winding down, deflated by the priest's look. He might have been listening to *Brian's Song*. Harry had no faith in the ending now and wished he could improvise some other punch line.

"How's he finally come down, or does he?"

"Oh, yeah, it's a riot. This ... *midget nun* comes. Looks just like the old dame on the Dutch Cleanser cans. Same size as your mother, and she whips out of a car, scurries over, lifts her skirts, and climbs the ladder. Down he comes." He didn't give a shit how Tommy was taking it, he collapsed in mirth.

"That is funny," the Canon tried, not smiling.

"Ah, Tom."

"I wish I saw it. Still around, is it?"

"I thought you were doing it for me, Tom. As a bit."

"No. I want a woman, Tro. I can't help it. I mean it."

"Have you ever?"

"Never."

"Not even before you went in?"

"Before I went in, I was in college. Did *you*, in college?"

"No. Close, but no." It seemed a century ago.

"Close doesn't count."

"Fear, Thomas. It was fear."

"Little pagans sure aren't afraid now!"

"It's whacko. Church makes it too important. Kids don't make it important enough. Fucking Hugh Hefner, sucking on his pipe. The fake Rod Serling."

"I have this ... not a dream, not a fantasy, Tro. A wish. Like a daydream. I'm in bed, half asleep. The door opens a hair and this pretty woman slips in. I never see her face, but I know she's pretty. She sneaks in with me ... and it's just wonderful."

A thousand cheap shots swirled in brained Harry's head, but he kept silent.

"It really drives me bughouse, Tro."

"Lotta pretty ladies willing to sneak in there with you, too, huh, Doc?"

"How you know that?"

"You told me last night."

"Shit. I don't know anymore. If it's really them or just me."

"I just had a great idea, Tom."

"What?"

"Let's go break some vows."

The Canon giggled. "You make it sound like a coupla kids. You don't mean it, do you?"

"You want me to mean it, Tommy?"

He held his breath as if it were dope, then: "I think I do, Tro. Yeah."

"Okay, let's go."

They walked the road back instead of the beach. It seemed to take forever until they reached the house; then it seemed they had flown. The new, clearer, more detailed visual perception of their altered states filled their every step and felt like slowness. The blacktopped road up-swelled beneath them, enlarging to display its moony crateredness. The sand of the shoulders was seen to be unsolid, trillion-grained. The tall pines were landed arrows, feathered wrongly. The priest was having fun seeing. Harry was glad. He lit number three.

"Now what are you laughing about? Huh, Tro? You ... silly ... bastard!"

"You. Back there, bellowing your head off."

"Well, it felt great," hffft!

Underneath, Harry was sifting and sorting it all out: All right, the plagued priest felt like a kid to him. He knew all the stories of men taking their sons to fancy, kindly women, the original Head Start program. He thought it stuffy, presumptuous, stupid, and crass. He would never want to dominate either of his sons like that or rob them of spontaneous life. Likewise with Thomas. Besides, this was the preseason Cape. And besides that, to be honest, as well as realistic, he felt no compunction whatsoever to interfere in anybody's sexual quandaries, especially a priest's, feeling brotherly to him or not. If he'd heard a call to adventure, it was his own personal thirst he'd be seeking to quench. And he wasn't sure that was such a hot idea at all. Again, not to mention plausible, down here upon *April Buzzard's Bay!* Unless they were both to wear blacks and to go faking a census. He'd have to impose a little order here, then. "Listen, Tom, this is a bit crazed."

"Yeah, yeah, you're right, Tro, forget it. Fun's fun, but this

s too much. Yeah. And I was thinking, God, for you it's
adultery, for crying out loud! I wouldn't ever want to be
responsible in any way for someth—"

"Ha! Ho! Hold it! Take it easy, now, man. First of all, no
more words like that. Don't even think them. Those are legal
terms, and we're not discussing justice here. 'Kay? Okay. Now.
Face it, we're not swordsmen by any means either. Neither one
of us. Not technicians in this. If we were, we wouldn't be here,
right?"

"Right, right," hffft!

"So, we're gonna just relax. Starting right now. And be cool.
And realistic."

"*Logical,* Tro!"

"You got it. Now, we can stay in. If we do, we already know
what that is. We can probably cook up a fairly decent meal,
have a nice wine. . . ."

"Pop a few."

"No, no hard stuff. Stay with me, now. Experiment a little.
Experience the grass thing, okay? All the way. Just this one
night. Where's that joint anyhow?"

"I ate it."

"Okay. Hope you put it out first. So we eat, and have some
wine, and have probably a long, high talk—solve the problems
of the universe, as you say. We *know* that option, and it'll be
fine, nothing wrong with—"

"Let's go out."

"Slow down!"

"We always go out and eat Saturday nights."

"Okay. That's the other option then. My only point is this:
We let what happens happen. Probably nothing will. But if
something does, we stay *open,* Tom. Open. *Open.*"

"We can't go to Falmouth or Hyannis, though."

"No?"

"No, that's where we always go. I'll be recognized."

"Okay, I'll figure that out."

"This is fun."

"Let's make it better. Great idea. And practical. You just triggered it, Tom. Who are we? We can't be us, right?"

"Right on!" Suddenly Little Doc was the TV priest, and the astonished would-be actor got, to his delight and amazement, upstaged. "All right, Tro. It'll be smart to keep our first names, or else we'll blow it for sure. So. Tom and Harry what?"

"Dickson?"

"Absolutely. Of course. Wait—are we brothers then? Sure, why not? But *what* are we? Ought to be something intriguing. Let's stream of consciousness it. Free association. Okay?"

"Great." The group of one cooperated. "Water."

"Boat."

"We own a boat."

"A big sailboat. We own it and charter it."

"It's down Woods Hole being fixed for the season." Thanks, Big Jake.

"We're using the house while we wait."

"Leaving tomorrow!"

"Name of boat!"

"*Liberty Square!*"

"Perfect."

"Just in case."

"Yeah. Just in case."

Angie called just before they were set to leave the house to try their show on the road. Tom was superhearty on the phone to her, then abruptly crestfallen. "For you, Harry. Patricia."

Kids! Fire! What? Momentarily cold sober, Harry took it. "Hi, babe, what's the matter?"

"Nothing really. What's going on down there? The Canon sounds stoned."

"He is!" and, relieved, so was he again.

"Well, when are you coming home?"

"Tomorrow."

"Oh, you're staying the night? Must be having a wonderful time."

Uh-oh. "Well, you know. You said it was a good idea."

"At three in the morning or whatever it was I'll say anything. In fact, this is why I'm calling. Not that I like to interrupt anybody's party. I've been thinking about this all day, Tro. I *got* the car, by the way. The Saturday buses from here to Liberty are charming; you ought to try it sometime. And the more I think about it, the more furious I get. Just put this in your head now, all right? It's what I feel, so it's what I'm saying. Why should I keep it in? I'm pissed. What's this all about anyhow? Off to the Cape to lick his wounds! Aren't you the lucky one! Well, it's indulgent and unfair. Just in case you didn't know. We were going to the movies tonight, I thought. It's also weak of you, Tro. I never thought I'd ever have that to say about you, but there it is. What kind of ass, what kind of robot, or a—a *nothing* am I supposed to be around here anyhow? Answer me!"

"You're drunk, right?" said the Flying Wallenda.

Slam, click, buzz.

In midair, attempting the triple, it was all he could think of to say to end it. He hung up. He hadn't let his smile crack or fade, so didn't have to resume it. "Let's go, Tom! All ashore that's goin' ashore!"

Tom bolted out the door without a question even in his eyes.

It was to that extent that Angie was implicated in the immediate causes of what happened that late April night. She was not entirely innocent, Harry would feel able to silently claim ever after.

There were, basically, only two conditions under which Harry ever earnestly entertained the impulse to snare some other woman. One, paradoxically, was when he was overwhelmingly in love with her. This state would flow after magic hours spent in the empress' bower. He'd swagger forth, virility ringing in his ears, his consciousness so full of her that he would suddenly see her in every comely female he met . . . and feel the call to do it again, again, again. He'd seen the old plaint painted on a bistro's wall: "One woman is too much, a thousand not enough," but with him they would seem all one. Good marriage was supposed to discourage concupiscence. His did the opposite. The more sated his flesh, in fact, the hungrier and wider-ranging and longer-lasting his post-Angie desire for harems of women. Just sometimes, this happened, not all the time. Sometimes he would leave her and be oblivious to even the existence of any and all other Eve creatures. That felt nice, too. But the other, with its promiscuity-from-fidelity mystery and its domino momentum, won on Jazziness. *You made me love them*, he felt he could sing at those times, *didn't want to do it, didn't want to do it*—and never did, actually, but still, it was one helluva cocky feeling while it lasted.

Underwhelmingly in love with her was the other condition under which he itched to wander: After a particularly bitter fight or after he erupted from a too-long forced march of peace, the cross hairs would fix upon Angie, the trigger would be squeezed, and blooie—*To Hell With Her!* Trapped? Me? Ha! Watch! She think I gotta be stuck looking at that face and listening to that mouth the rest of my life she got another think coming! *Sayonara*, drag, see how far it goes with somebody else! Try it on some Guido Dumbfuck, I've had it! Who needs it! And the kids go with me. Oh, yeah? Here's a hint—The Ballad of Sterling Hayden! Look it up. Yie! It hurts, and she's the hurt, and why should I hurt like this? I'll never, ever marry again! Never! Guys are insane. It's a plot. Ho, don't I know it now! Think they've got me, do they? Think I'm nailed dead, huh? Don't think they have anything to fear from me? Heh, heh, heh. I am *not* to be unfeared, boys! You almost got me ... it looks like you got me ... but oh ... no ... you ... don't. He'd never split, huh? Got him gullivered right off the boat, without half trying, huh? Well, we'll see, we'll just see about that. My gun, Yamamoto. The Beretta. And tonight, Nadine, I think. Or perhaps Clair. With the bay scallops, and Dom Pérignon, and panda breast. *Oui*, the Chinese.

He followed Tommy toward the Grand Prix, whelmed now by nothing more than the intoxication and holiday giddiness.

The call didn't really happen. If asked, which Tommy didn't, he'd say he was at peace with her. And he was, if ignorance be peace. Hell, he was Harry Dickson, single, wayfarer at large, with the *Liberty Square* in drydock for one more night. Whether it was leave, liberty, or AWOL, he was going.

Harry wore his own jeans, but had borrowed a white turtleneck and blue crestless blazer from whoever the WASC, Huntington, was. Tommy had changed into brown knit slacks and his tweed jacket. Harry convinced him to open another button on the paisley shirt and to put the collar outside. He couldn't convince Tom that he could drive far more ably on grass than on booze, so he took the wheel again. They vaulted over the canal back to the mainland and took 6 East toward New Bedford. It was fully night now. The Quiet Clam, the Buoy Ten, the Marion Inn, Trader Ziggy's, the Ling Dynasty, Fred's—everything except the Viking Diner-Eats was dark and closed. They were famished. They'd gorged briefly on peanut butter, Granola, and beer but craved meat. Near the seaport city a Holiday Inn rose, and they turned into the mostly vacant parking lot. The moment Harry keyed the engine off, the cops hit their *eeyou!* once, their lights illuminating the whole inside of the Pontiac. Harry saw a steel hole touching his side window. Tommy gasped, "Oh, my God! What?"

The cop shouted, "Out! Slow! Hands up!"

Harry got out slowly with his hands up. There were two cops. Both looked like night watchmen. They made Harry and Tom spread against the Pontiac. "Feet further apart and two steps back!" The one on Harry extracted Tommy's wallet, nearly crumbled. "Oh, geez, Fath—" then checked himself: "Okay—name!"

"Thomas Duffy," Harry said.

"Height?"

Harry answered or guessed correctly until they came to the Canon's Social Security number. "Oh, gosh, to tell you the truth, Officer, I always get it messed up."

"Ah, that's okay, Father, you can stand off, now. They're okay, Walter! Your friend a priest, too, Father?"

"No, no, he's my brother, Officer, down from Cambridge visiting me for the weekend. I have a place over in Sequosset, do you know St. Rose's parish there?" Returning the wallet to his jeans.

The police holstered their guns and explained: They'd had a call on a blue Pontiac, like this one. Two white men had held up a liquor store in Buzzards Bay not ten minutes ago. Listening to the way the man was speaking now, Harry realized that a priest was somehow older than or senior to anyone not a priest. "I see. Well, you boys sure scared the daylights out of us, I'll tell the world. Just stepping in here for a bite of dinner, we were," he said sixtily, straight from Limerick. Tommy, across the roof, was the agate-eyed statue again.

"Well, let's go, Walter. Sorry again, Father. Have yourself a good dinner now."

"After this I think we'll be needing a bit more than grub if you—"

"I know *just* what you mean, Father! Have a couple for us, too! Ha-ha."

"We will. Good luck on your chase now, and God bless you both!"

"Thank you, Father!"

"Thank you, Father!"

Thomas was faint. Harry backslapped him heartily, laughing, and walked him toward the entrance. "How the hell'd you have *my* wallet?" Harry told him. Tom agreed he should keep it as long as he was doing the driving. Inside, the place was a morgue. The dark cocktail lounge was a mini-movie theater, four men, a bartender, and a waitress in locked eyes-left up at Mary Tyler Moore. "Have one here first, Harry?"

"Nah, they'll go *ssh!*"

They went into the dining room. It was like entering hollow, charcoal-broiled steak; everything was black and red. The air smacked of sauce Béarnaise and Galliano. Hidden speakers poured instrumentalized Burt Bacharach, too loudly. The dark, plump hostess advertised Jean Naté, led them to a booth, and pinned them down with huge menus. The younger, walleyed waitress was right over. Harry couldn't refuse Tom's blue-eyed plea. "Yes, I guess we deserve one after that. Let's see, I think I'll play it safe, tonight—a Beefeater martini, please, straight up. Olive."

"Double Rob Roy on the rocks, please. *Dry* Rob Roy, make sure."

Harry had already noted that the staff were the only females in the room, except for one travel-frazzled mother trying to get hubby to get sis and junior to split an order. The rest were scattered men, eating and drinking singly, reading papers, staring blankly, all resembling Fast Facey. Reading the menu, Harry remarked that they'd be the only ones not paying with expense account money. Tom said no, they were too; he could write it off easily. Their drinks came. Tom wanted to postpone ordering, but Harry slurped, "*Steak,* Tom, aren't you starved?" making him so. He wanted to comment on all the men dining alone: It's New Bedford, do you know where your wives are? But feared it might send the priest into the loneliness jag again. To be out of there sooner, he wolfed his sirloin and salad and said no to coffee. Tom wanted Drambuie. Harry whispered, "You'll blow the you-know!"

"We still going hummin', Harry?"

"Damn right. Whatever hummin' is, that's where we're going! Now." Estimating their chances of finding sin this night at slim and none.

From the bridge, New Bedford looked underwater. They kept going. It was hardly choosing; the roadhouse, almost in Fall River, was the only living thing they saw the whole way. They decided that if it was nothing or really sleazy, they'd try downtown next. *Then go home* went unsaid. Harry couldn't tell the martini buzz from the pot high now; it was all one happy, furry glow he was sure he'd never come out of. Tommy *was* just Tommy now, moving briskly and beaming enthusiasm. Harry couldn't have sworn that Tommy didn't do this all the time. Cars filled the front lot and wound around both sides of the place. It looked like a ranch house with the picture windows shingled over. The only sign was a green, neat neon arch over the front door: CHEZ RUBY. Inside Harry expected pool tables and loud locals or perhaps a singer and suburbanite swingers. It was neither; it seemed nothing, but a tony nothing. A small dining room to the right was closed. Open was the larger room, a quiet, almost swanky bar, all indirect lighting, many large aquarium tanks alive with tropical fish, perhaps twenty tiny tables, a mahogany-looking bar of sixteen or so stools. It was about half full. Small bunches of guys drinking and talking, small bunches of women doing the same. Five or six couples, two dancing. No set age. Andy Williams sang "Dear Heart" from a 2001 jukebox. There were many more cars outside than people visible inside. In California Harry had seen similar setups; somewhere here, probably in the basement, there was action happening. On the Coast it was poker and blackjack. Here he didn't want to know. The man intercepted them between the door and the bar, his X-ray eyes finding them acceptable. "Good evening, fellas, come right in."

He was suede from neck to ankles, wore soft black loafers and yellow aviator glasses. His chest hair under the Sterling razor blade was white, but his head hair was brown, except for the graying sideburns and for the rug or transplant garden on the top, which had an orange tint when the light hit it. Resisting fifty, his round, pleasant face was lined with acne scars. He seemed to be sweating but wasn't. There was something about him Harry liked. "I'm Charley Clote, welcome to my place." His questioning glance lingered on Harry's face.

Harry smiled. "Doing some heavy drinking, Charley."

Charley smiled back, all caps, and bobbed his head toward the lounge. "You came the right place, gents. Whatever you want. Enjoy yourselves." He didn't follow them in.

Tommy scored first and almost immediately. Harry was stunned to watch it happen. Everything was seeming dopily amusing and remarkable anyhow, but this bowled him over. She was perched on the first stool, right inside the door. Then there were two guys flanking a girl. Harry and Tom had swung up onto the fifth and sixth and ordered beers. "It's just out seeing real people, you know, Harry?" Tom suggested a couple scotches, but Harry frowned.

"Remember Dorothy Kilgallen, Tom?"

"Oow, that's right."

Harry felt a little guilt at the deception, but reasoned that anything was better than having Thomas dive again into last night's grim, sad vaudeville. It wasn't her looks that drew their attention to her at once, although she was a pretty enough lady and smartly turned out. They could see her in the mirror, fragmented by bottlenecks from her throat down, like a torn photo. Her dark-auburn hair was long on the sides and in bangs; her eyes were large and softly shadowed green; her nose was thin; her lips were thin and glossy red. She would have appeared crisply sophisticated, except she was weeping. Tinsels of tears shined down both cheeks.

She was delivering a shrieky, woesome monologue to herself and to the bartender, Whitey. Harry tried to shut her out, scanning the room in the glass, but Tommy was obviously locked on her. Whitey was sympathetic and trying to be reassuring. He kept returning to her. The longer she went on the more distress he showed. The other bar people grew increasingly embarrassed, subdued, and begrudgingly attentive, Harry included. He leaned forward and shot a look down the bar. The stemmed glass in front of her was empty, stained with dry foam. Her nervous fingers alternately choked and stroked it. She couldn't believe people could be so crummy without any reason. She had money, for God's sake, just not with her, that's all. She wasn't used to being treated like this and would never get used to it either. She *worked,* for God's sake. Whitey, again, was just as surprised as she was. He was sure something must have happened to the guy. He always seemed like a good enough Joe; Whitey never would've read him for anything like this. He must have had an emergency or something. She shouldn't take it personal. She'd begin again: She didn't care; it was humiliating. ... To Harry it sounded like two players rehearsing a scene, repeating it over and over until they got it right.

Tommy finally snagged Whitey, who sidemouthed that she'd apparently been stiffed. She was with this guy when he'd come on duty. He'd assumed they had arrived together; she wasn't a regular. Have a lot of rounds at a table. Guy splits. Whitey figures the john or the phone. Never comes back. What can you do? She waits forever, finally comes up the bar. Been there ever since. Says she doesn't have either the cash or the cards. He figures she's got it but just won't bite the bullet. "I guess I'll hafta call Clote in on it. *I'm* not about to eat it, ya know?" If he bailed out every dame got stiffed, he'd be into the Beneficial for life. "Shit, she keeps it up she'll clear the whole joint." Tommy asked how much, Whitey said fifteen, and Tommy said he'd pick it up, she'd gone through enough. "Thanks a lot, pal, you're makin a lotta people happy." They watched him move down, lift her tab from the ledge, and give her the good news. Her back straightened, her face cleared, and she picked up her glass. "Thanks, Whitey. Could I have another one of these, please?"

Harry winced; Tom's mouth fell open; Whitey scolded, "Aw, Jesus Christ, lady!"

She'd been holding her other fist clenched. She brought it up, opened it defiantly, and three singles uncurled. She spilled them fluttering onto the bar. "And put it down there, okay?" pointing toward Tommy. She slid down and left the room, taking her purse, leaving her coat. It was a Brandy Alexander.

Harry saw Whitey aiming it between him and Tommy and moved fast. "Here, we'll both slide down one." Whitey tacked and put it at the empty stool to Tom's right.

She scooped the coat on her way back and moved up next to

Tom. Her big eyes were bright brown that went well with the silky dress that clung to her legs when she walked. She didn't look unclassy. "Hi. My name is Mary Carson, and I want to thank you very much. Call me Kit."

"Hi. I'm Tom Dickson, and this is my brother, Harry."

"Hi. My God, what a ludicrous situation. Wouldn't you think they'd let me leave gracefully? I'd have come back with the stupid money. I'll pay you back, too. If you'll give me your address, I can mail it to you."

"Forget it, really. My pleasure."

"Boy, you really look like Martin Sheen, did you know that? That face!"

Tom didn't have to speak at all. In the bluish glass he looked to Harry like the Boy in a forties movie, being sung to in the face. There was another face abruptly prominent in the mirror now. It seemed to be resting on Harry's left shoulder. It was definitely staring into Harry's reflection. Kit was confessing that she had "weighed two hundred pounds right up until two years ago!" Tom said he couldn't believe it, "sure never know it now!" Harry winked at the girl in the mirror. She smiled back, blowing smoke. Kit, at twenty-eight, had fallen in love is what had happened. Head over heels and not with her husband. Sex had been out of her life for so long she got pregnant just like that, snapping her fingers. "Smart, huh?" Lucky she had a half-sister living in New York State.

Harry said, "Don't be shy, tell us about yourself, Kit."

Neither she nor Tom seemed to have heard. He looked into the mirror again to make sure he was still there. He was, and so now was the face. After the wink he may or may not have given her the come-on signal with his head. He couldn't recall. She said, "Hi."

Harry said, "Hi, what're you having?"

She said, "Vodka."

Harry told Whitey. Kit was saying she got rid of both men, too, soon after. Tom was saying life could be really tough all right. "My name's Harry, what's yours?"

"Jody." Jody wore white eye shadow with center squares of a kind of rust, the same shade as her Afro. She chewed very green gum and said, "What's so funny?"

"Nothing. You sort of remind me of Harpo Marx, that's all."

"Well, better Harpo than Groucho."

"Yeah, I always liked Harpo."

"Got a light, Harry?"

"Vagina Slims, huh?"

"Right—and you thought every smart cunt smoked Kents."

What a toughie. She was wonderful. The Schaefer bubble clock said almost eleven. That seemed very late to Harry. "We're gonna have a party, want to come?" He gave her the boat story. Jody didn't like boats. He quickly threw in the house. He'd have to see Charley Clote first, but it was groovy with her.

"I saw Charley already; what's he got to do with it?"

Jody worked for him, sort of. "You'd never know it, but Ruby's a real swinging place. It'll get going again starting next month or so."

Harry asked Whitey to get him Charley.

"No can do, Jody. He had to split for a while, be back in a couple hours."

She asked Harry, "You sure you saw him before?"

"Anything you say, Jody."

"Bet your ass," she said and slid to the floor. Kit was wondering if maybe she'd scared that first creep or something. Tommy was saying that was absurd and to put it right out of her mind.

Jody had a white Mustang and wasn't going anywhere without it. Harry thought Tommy would stay on Kit's case, but he insisted on going in the Pontiac. Kit drove her Volvo wagon, between them and Jody. Tommy was a jubilee of lust and disbelief and kept looking out the back window. "This is wild, Tro! We're doing it!"

"They're doing it, Tom. You've been picked up, man."

"The poor ... she's in the middle of very serious business here, Tro. She's been on the take end of a ton of cruelty for a long time, and I'm afraid she's buckling. Thinks it's all her fault, you know? Amazing how paths cross, isn't it?"

" 'Mazing, Tom."

"Know what she said to me? She said she's got it all arranged not to be home until tomorrow, and if she ends up home tonight after all, she'll know she's a total failure. Huh? Isn't that classic? And sad? And listen—she wanted to know if I'd think she was a slut for wanting to come live it up with us! Talk about insecurity."

"She say slut, Tom?"

"No, but you know."

Harry grinned. He felt weirdly glad to see poor Tom so weirdly boyish and hopeful.

Tom suddenly laughed. "My God, Tro, what the hell are we doing?"

"Exactly what we want, Tommy," accepting its truth as he said it: The problems, pains, booze, dope, pity were merely lubrication; they were both simply doing what they wanted, perhaps had to do.

"Hey, come on, though, Harry—they didn't pick us up!"

"Okay, Tom, we picked them up."

"And in about two seconds! I never thought it'd be so easy!"

Harry lit a cigarette and felt old. "Well, nobody else was asking them anything, right?"

Stoned Harry mused, *Ah, women, with their curly little arrows, as if we didn't know where it is!*

Jody had a bush black as an eight ball. It had been trimmed across the top, evenly, to stay below the waistband of her bikini panties, which were flesh-colored and on the floor with her pantyhose. The Afro was atop her sequinned T-shirt and Jesus jeans on the chair seat, above her Dingo boots. Her fun fur was out on the floor of the main room, inside the glass doors, where she had dropped it entering the house. Her head hair was colored elk-blond and short and turned her pixyish, so he made her put the wig back on. She was mouthy and bony and smelled spicy and was fastly affectionate with her large hands. Her arms were as warm as her legs and seemed as long. She kept her head turning slowly and steadily in its socket and held her chin down, not up. He instinctively started to go down but remembered and turned back at her navel. She wore a gold-looking love chain around her belly. Her nipples were copper dimes, up and flaring porously. The sailor felt his luck had served him fairly. He was still experiencing the sweet shock of seeing a pretty stranger's naked body suddenly revealed. He had stood gawking for a moment; she had unshyly grinned and taken his heil in a brief, funny hand-shake: "Howdy Doody!" Harry tried to be gentle; she was tighter than he'd expected, then put his hand between her head and the bedboard and drove her. Her sound was *hut, hut, hut, oh, hut* . . . either a lover or fair actress. Harry was a good actor. Jody had had grass now, too.

She'd put the lit end into her mouth and went around feeding them sexily, Kit first, then Tommy, open-beaked baby birds in the nest. When she blew it into Harry's mouth, she let her lips touch his, starting it. Not long after, she whispered, "Let's get it on, man." He liked the laugh impulse she triggered in him and let it pass for fondness. When he pushed up and took his weight into his palms, she slid her knees up onto his sweat-damp chest, and they smiled at each other. The conscientious objector in him thought: Some good is coming from this for me; rocking and melting, Jody was revealing how his heart did stir so keenly when with Angie. Here it was remaining hard, not mean or cruel but simply still, dry, untouched. It was reassuring to learn. On her stomach, it was still prowess, and at first when she was astride him it was prowess, but then he felt it change and wanted to tell her no, please don't feel impatient or challenged. She must have had long hair once; if it were still long, it would be whipping him softly on the face, left to right and back.

She rested, panting. "Every time I pee tomorrow I'll think of ra." He was glad she wasn't testy. He said they could take a smoke break. She said, "Like hell, a hard man's good to find," and fucked him the higher and harder. He thought, Fucking and making love aren't synonymous after all. He took her hips in his hands. He could take the driving back and end it, end it with only a few select thoughts, with fewer moves, but he didn't. To end it would be to acknowledge beginning it, which he hadn't done yet, really. He could foresee ending it and dreaded it. He wasn't just prolonging enjoyment. He didn't especially like letting her labor so, either; he knew she no longer expected to come again but was just being randy or generous or competitive or trying to store it up or something. No, it was a circle or ellipse, and he didn't want to be back at the beginning again. He might consent again, and what would that mean about him? But then he went ahead and ended it anyhow, jumping the gun on that "decision," too. Jody's last-word contractions and collapse surprised him.

When she jounced back from the kitchen john, she grinned, "Let's go back out and have a drink at the fire and dance or something." Jody had the heavy Boston talk. Earlier she'd called him a "real pissa!" a lot.

Harry said, "Wait a minute," and went to the toilet. He was faking, to stall for time. He didn't want to intrude on Thomas and Kit-baby, taking the longer talk route. Dickson looked back from the mirror, a friendly-seeming guy Harry didn't feel he knew well enough to speak to, though he felt no compulsion to avoid his open stare. Inside, Jody had pulled Harry's gray sweater on. It covered her fanny. He lit a cigarette and gave it to her, then one for himself. "Hungry?"

"Naw—you got any more grass, though? I don't think I caught up with you yet."

He said yeah and took his fatigue jacket off the door hook.

She grinned at the name tag, "What'd you say your last name was?"

He thought oh, shit, and said, "Dickson. Bought this in an Army and Navy," hffft!

She took the joint. "Trowbridge. That used to be our phone

exchange when I was a kid, TR-six. Then they made it all numbers," hffft!

So she was from Cambridge somewhere, hffft! He didn't pursue it. He moved her clothes and sprawled supine in the easy chair.

She said, "We ain't going outside?" and sat on the bed, her back against the headboard, crossing her ankles.

"I like it here, babe. You keep the joint for a while, okay? I'm pretty quiffed."

"You're the boss, doll."

"See what you can get on that transistor there." She stretched to the night table and found music. Watching her, he found his thing rising again.

Jody laughed. "Ho, up periscope!," hffft!

"You've got incredible legs, lady."

"Thanks."

But he was thinking, It's really all in the arms, though, isn't it? Women's arms. The female arms. Old Tough Shit Eliot had nailed it dead on, hadn't he? Speaking of Michelangelo or Michelob or anything or nothing, the women had arms that were different from men's arms. How they moved. "Come chere, woom." She crabbed to his end of the bed. "Sit here, Jody."

"You're already sitting there," hffft!

"I mean, sit here."

"Oh. Okay." She sat, removing the sweater.

It was her arms he was after. He ran his fingers along their insides and smelled them. "What is that?"

"Arrid."

"No, you jerk, the scent."

"I know! It's Charlie."

A brand he'd remember to forget, but enhancing his arms appreciation just fine at the moment. She covered his ears with her hands, and he looked up her arms at her eyes, which were taking a soft glaze. She wasn't going to be able just to sit. She got him horizontal without losing him and rode his thigh tops back and forth. His eyes crossed, and he nearly bit his tongue, and even during it he couldn't help thinking how much they must look like figures on a vase, and his laugh, sperm and a fart all shot forth at the same time. Her shudders rippled through her arms into his head. He had never before felt so detached from his body. Had a good time for itself without him, didn't it, the bad-news bastard.

This time he said it: "Hey, I'll tell you, I'd just as soon not cramp my brother's style, you know? I'll get you a drink in the kitchen, if you—"

Jody's head popped up through the neck of his sweater again. "Those two went upstairs nine hours ago, I heard 'em."

She was right. He fed the failing fire. She put on the radio, having shuffled through the records earlier. She wouldn't let him make her the drink. "I'll do it, Harry. You want?"

"Some wine, yeah, there's a jug of Almadén there someplace." She had a vodka. She curled up in the chair closest to the fire and, staring into it, looked suddenly both much younger and much tougher to him. Sparking another flash: If she were not so tough, and simply free instead of trampy, and he fell in love with her, it could never work, and it would be his fault. He would tell her she could continue to be free and then go nuts jealous and possessive the first time she took a fugitive blink. He wouldn't want to go to discotheques. He'd want her to have babies and to get smarter and classier. His gaze floated up to the closed doors off the balcony. A rush of shock bolted through him which he didn't like at all. "How's life in Fall River, Jode?"

"The pits."

"What are you doing there?"

"Tryna get out."

"How'd you get there?"

"You takin' a poll?"

"Sorry. Never mind."

Jody sighed and sipped. "I got dumped. I had this guy, older than you, and he had a wife and everything someplace

else. You know. Very big bucks all around. I lived good. Then
he got sicka me or something, I don't know."

"That's too bad. So what are you doing?"

"The best I can the fastest I can—what the fuckdaya mean,
what am I doin'? You ain't that stoned."

This shock wasn't a rush. It crept slowly over his skin like
cold ants. "Hey, wait a minute. Oh, Christ."

Her look when it slid over to Harry bore real fear, very
clearly, and the fear passed into him. The movie line "I never
paid for it in my life" uttered itself. He rejected it. Her feet
were touching the floor, and her back angled forward tautly.
"You told me you saw Clote, Harry. Jesus Christ, you *did,* dint
ya?"

"Uh, no. Not—"

"*Oh, my God!*" she whispered dismally, then rehardened:
"Cut the shit, now, I ain't kiddin'! This ain't funny, man!"

He had it all before she said it. Christ, he'd *read* it when it
was called *The Hundred Dollar Misunderstanding!* The wisp of
humor in it went out like a firefly dying.

"Jesus, he'll kill me, he'll fuckin' *kill* me! No. Maybe I can
. . . yeah, I'll tell him I set it up on my own. Yeah. I mean, like
you *got* the bread, doncha, Harry babe?"

"How much?"

"A bill."

He couldn't believe it. This was too much, in more ways
than one. He closed his eyes, to make sure this was happening
and not just himself dope-dreaming with dialogue—was she
still curled, eyeing the fire lazily? No, she was still a crossbow
aimed at him. "You don't mean a hundred, kid . . . where do
you think you are, Beverly Hills?" He said it smiling, almost
sleepily, not to hurt her feelings and to make it go away if it
could.

But she'd hardened even more and raised her voice. "It's a
bill, you turkey! It's the *night* with me! You want happy
humpies, you get happy humpies!" She sprang and moved
toward him, tiger in the grass. "Whaddaya want? You wanna

piss on me? Whip me? Got the velvet ropes in the car, baby, just say the word! Wanna get rid of crazybird up there and let a brotha jump in? Ya got it! Or her, too! I ain't no—no amateur ya got here, man! Clote ain't ... it's a *bill*, Johnny, and I ain't—"

He met her in the middle of the rug, knowing he needed to calm her. He hadn't meant to make her do this. He couldn't tell if her eyes were brimming, glistening, from pain or just fury. "Hey, hey, come down now, all right? Don't sweat it, Jody, it'll be okay." He wanted to enfold and comfort her, but she spun away from his opening arms.

"You *said* you saw Clote, goddamn it! I *need* that guy, I ... oh, fuck!"

Harry wore just his jeans. His hands ran into his pockets to hide. "Hey, Jode, come on, huh? Listen—"

"Okay!" she snapped and ran to the radio. She found rock music and began to go-go violently for him on the wood floor, tearing his sweater off again.

"Oh, Christ," he muttered, what price topless-bottomless à-go-go in Sequosset? He said, "Hey, don't—you don't have to do that." She didn't stop. She looked epileptic to him now, and idiotically he considered getting a spoon from the kitchen. "Jody! All right!" He had to go turn off the music. Then she stopped. He said, "I'll pay you, all right?" and handed her the sweater. She put it on without looking at him and walked slowly back to her chair and drink. He followed her. Half-seriously, after a wait, he grinned. "You aren't on any *cards*, I suppose?"

She was gnawing on her cuticles and had the shakes. But she laughed, taking it as his way of making it cheery again. "Sure, the machine's in my bag."

He laughed and went to retrieve his wine. He'd stay close to her now. He couldn't hope to talk her out of it from any distance. He sat on the edge of the firewell and smiled down at her. "I just thought I was picking you up, you know, babe?"

She shook her head.

"Well, I guess this makes me a hook*ee,* huh?"

She laughed a little. "Hey, watch it."

He said, "You don't look professional. Is that a compliment?"

"No."

"Oh. Yeah, but Jesus, Jody—Fall River! How was I supposed to—"

"You said you saw *Clote,* Harry."

"Can't we make believe I didn't?"

She met his gaze coolly. "No way. *I* don't need this, dig? I have my own things to do if I wanna night off."

That smarted, but he cagily kept quiet. This was going to be tricky, he thought, all too aware of the pun. At bottom he felt totally conned. Not by this girl, but by the mystique. All these years! He'd always thought it was morality and character that kept him straight; he'd never for a moment thought it wasn't *easy,* wasn't just out there all over the place for the plucking. The casual piece, the ships passing in the night, the roll, the tumble, the bang. Only the odd minority fragment *wasn't* doing it all the time, like Jews and pork. The adjusted, realistic majority *was,* all the time, unbound by medieval religious quirks. For the New Kids it was reportedly like holding hands, healthy, no big deal, only natural. Sockitome, sockitome. Christ, turns out they'd all been doing it, unpublicized, in the twenties! And in the seventeenth century. Only the jerks weren't. They were only *thinking* about it all the time and patting themselves on the soul for *Not* Doing It! Heaven, if you pushed them and they could articulate it, would be Doing It, forevermore. Hell would be Never Doing It Again because you did it on earth, Purgatory Not Doing It For While because you did it sometimes. So what the hell was this deal then? He went frolicking in the surf once—yeah, yeah, because forty was coming up and life was berserk and Tommy and all that, but what difference now did the *why* make—and blam, he was getting sucked in by the undertow! (Called *sea puss* by old salts.) #!$%¢⅔*()‡!, anyhow.

"This really burns my ass, Jody!"

"What does?"

"Goddamn *fire* I find myself sitting on top of."

She laughed and cutely made room beside her in the chair. He started to squeeze himself into it.

Thump! Bump! Shash! from upstairs.

They both looked up. Jody said, "Party's gettin' rough."

"Mm—uh, her ... Kit, she work for Clote, too?"

"Are you shittin' me?"

That was a relief, and not. Wonderful, goddamn Canon's home free, while I'm ... but then one of the muffled sounds broke clear and it was a scream.

"What the hell's that one pullin'?" Jody wondered.

Harry was up the stairs across the landing and opening the door. First he saw Thomas: naked, on the floor, wedged between the side of the bed and the wall, one knee up, the other straight out, both arms limp down his frail front, not concealing his other limpness. His face looked wet, his eyes were shut, and he had a silly, feeble grin on his mouth, mumbling incoherently. The Johnnie Walker sat next to the bedside lamp. A book flew by. Harry looked to the left. Naked, Kit was whirling frantically around that side of the sparse bedroom looking for something else to throw. One of her shoes, Harry noticed now, sat black on the pillow, seeming to be whispering into Thomas' ear. He stepped toward her. She cringed and folded her body into an even tighter crouch. "I'm not going to hurt you," he said, afraid her retreat might recoil into counterattack.

Her mouth looked smeared. Her eyes blazed but were unable to focus. Glaring, she brought one small hand up to rub two fingers unsteadily across her bottom lip. Her white abdomen bore faint, whiter rivers and tributaries; on her thighs they were blue. She had full ivory tits that swayed with her confusion. Her left, free arm came up to point at Thomas. Her voice, low, scratched like a nail on tin. "For that. For that? For *that?* I ... *for that?* You ... bastards! You ... useless! Lying! ...

I'll *kill* him, I'll . . . gimme . . ." starting to search about her again.

Harry didn't move. He said, "I'm sorry. It's all right now. Just go home, why don't you?"

She nodded, then moved down the narrow corridor between the bed and the side wall, and bent. When she came up, she was putting her bra on. She bent again and stepped into her panties. He saw her body stocking on the floor near his feet and backed up. Jody put music on again downstairs. Kit lifted the phone and flung it sidearm. Its cord jerked it back, halfway to Thomas' head. The receiver flew whackily in the air, landing back on the end table, missing the empty glass.

Harry pointed down to her mesh legs snarled crazily on the rug. "Here's your—"

They passed each other like wrestlers looking for an opening. He went and fixed the phone, then reached and fetched her shoe from Thomas' ear, bringing it to her. She sat on the foot of the bed to pull the hose up over her legs. She took the shoe and put it on. She brought her hands back to the panty stuff bunched across her groin but seemed unable to stand. She dropped her head and wept.

He dared not touch her, even gently, with his man's hands. He waited.

Empty at last, sniffling, she looked straight ahead and gasped, "Where's my other shoe? I can't—"

"I'll find it," he said and started searching.

He heard her say, "You're all right, it wasn't you, it isn't you," and turned to see that she was certainly not speaking to him.

"It's them," she whimpered, "it's them, every one of them, they're . . . the filthy motherfuckers, the . . . have no problems with whores, you bet, they're jimdandy with their cheap tramps of *secretaries!* Oh, my God, oh, God *damn* you all. A p-person, a . . . real woman . . . and oh, no, that's not what they want at all, you bet. You're Kit. You're all right, you're *right* is what, and they're wrong, they're . . ." looking up, catching him staring at her, and standing then and decisively working the pantyhose up, she screamed, "I've had babies, damn it! I've had men! Real men, and I'm not ashamed of it. I want it! I miss it and need it, and I'm *great,* and I ... can't *find* any men *man* enough anymore to ... to ... you're all such big *pukes* now! Where's my *shoe?* Can't you even find my *shoe?* Can't you do *anything?*"

He found it finally, the last palce he'd ever look, under Tommy; he must've landed on it. He ran it to her. Her arm braced against the wall, she put it on, standing, glaring hatred at him. She had her dress on now. Harry couldn't move. She stalked around him, went over to Thomas, brought her right foot back, and shot it into his balls. He lurched, vomit gushed, but he stayed out of it. She passed Harry like a bitter wind. He followed her down the stairs, past Jody in the chair, eating yogurt with her vodka now. The Kit-woman slid the closet door open savagely, pulled her coat out, and was gone.

From the deck, Harry watched her Volvo start, light and tear off down the night road through the woods. In the awful silence in her wake, his peeing sounded like hailstones.

He had already decided there was nothing in the entire Fall River-New Bedford area worth a hundred bucks. But the sight of poor Tommy smashed into a corner was changing his mind. Jody said, "Bad scene, huh?" as he passed her, hurrying upstairs. He got surprised again: Tommy was a neat log beneath the sheet, sleeping soundly. He'd left the bathroom light on and a faucet running. Harry shut both off and went softly down to Jody, his new idea burning feverishly. He knelt before her, rubbed her nubbly calf, and fixed his look on a spot between her eyes to make her think he was looking into her eyes. "I have something special I want you to do for me, okay?"

"What?"

He sang, rough, "Hey, Jode ... don't let me down ..." and she smiled sexily.

"Come on—what?"

"Okay. First, you've gotta trust me for the money. I'll send you a check tomorrow. Believe me."

"I believe you, Harry, but I can't, man. I mean, like why can't you give me a check now? I'll take a check, I will, even though Clote'll go psycho on me."

Of course, why hadn't he thought of it? He'd seen it when Tommy was making his mad calls. "Okay." He went to the priest's attaché case and opened his checkbook. Three to a page. What the hell. If the Canon squawked seriously, he'd go halves on it. "To you or the joint?"

"To me. Hart, H-A-R-T."

Writing, he laughed. "Unfuckingbelievable! The whore's all heart, Jesus."

"What was that, smartass?"

"Nothing." Thomas had been paying his bills. Harry forged the signature pretty well and wrote "Amarcord" on the stub. He gave her the check folded.

She held his wrist, tugged him down, and kissed his tonsils. "I'll make it worth it, Harr, honest."

"Let me tell you what I want. No, shut up, now. That's my brother up there, right? Well, he's a terrific guy, and he's had a bad deal. I want you to take off your sweater, put on your coat and go up. He's got this . . . *wish*, kind of. Just slip in the door, no lights, and get in with him."

"Then what's he *wish?*"

"I don't know. Nothing . . . crazy, though. He's nice."

Resigned, Jody shrugged and got up. "Hey! Where the hell *is* my coat? That bitch. . . ."

"No, no, she . . . look in the closet, kid."

"Yeah, she probably dusted and . . . holy shit! What the fuck's *this?*"

The Canon's collar and blacks. *Jesus!* Harry took a slug of vodka.

"Hey, he ain't no goddamn *priest*, is he?"

"No, no, that's—"

"Are *you?*"

"*No!* The guy that owns the house is. We—"

She opened the check. "You ... son of a bitch!"

Harry pressed both temples with one hand, smelling his palm. He couldn't tell her it wasn't his check. "Just get your coat, will you?" When he looked, Jody had shrunk her body into the same animal crouch as Kit's.

"You *scum,* Harry! Or's it *Fatha* Harry?"

"Hey, what's the big deal? You're a *pro,* right?"

"*No priests!* I got one fuckin' rule and that's fuckin' it!"

God, he thought, how deep the fingerprint goes. But she hadn't finished: "I *hate* you! I hate every priest that ever lived! I wouldn't *shit* on a priest! I'm gettin outta here." She headed for the rear bedroom. He grabbed her arm. "Tommy isn't, Jody. He's just a guy!"

"You're a *priest,* and ya buyin it for ya brotha?"

"*Yes!*"

She squinted up into his eyes and grinned and said quietly, 'You're a liar, Harry. You ain't no priest ... your wedding ring left a groove."

His stupid left hand shot up to his face, blowing his case.

"Ha-ha, gotcha," Jody said. "Don't make me, okay, Harry?"

"I'm asking you, Jody. Please."

Her eyes filled with tears. "*You,* Harry. Anything y—"

"No. Him."

She spoke to his chest. "Everybody's got a bottom line, Harry. That's mine. I hate them. It's the worst thing I could do. Don't make me, okay? Please?"

He knew her jumbled head hadn't made the check connection yet, but he said, "That check's good, Jody, even though I signed it. Believe me."

"Oh, hey, that's ... you sure?"

"Positive. Go ahead now," lifting his sweater off her from the bottom. She went limp, not helping, not resisting. He felt as if he'd pulled some vital nerve in her. She looked like his feelings, and he nearly called it off. But the wheels were rolling; his blind sense that this was crucial for Tommy now, that he no longer had any real choice in it, that he had to force the circle closed now or else everything else had been futile, overpowered all his other emotions. "Pretend he's somebody else, Jody."

"Sure," she said dryly, beaten. She got her coat and climbed the stairs like an aged dog.

Waiting, he sat in the chair, sipped her vodka, and went up in his balloon, not to see into the upstairs room but to start leveling the past twenty-four hours' events into his everyday life as fast as possible. Watched the tube Friday night with Jake, did this tonight with Uncle Thomas, ta-dum, ta-dum . . . Jody was back down. "Nothing," she said.

"Come on!"

"I knew you'd think I'm fakin' it, but I ain't. I couldn't even gettim ta wake up."

"Was *he* faking?"

"What's the difference?"

"Damn."

"I'm glad, you know."

"I know. . . . Thanks anyhow." He almost said he was sorry for making her do what she called her "worst," but he felt plumb lied out. She was behind him. She started giving him a neck rub, then sledded her hands down his chest, beneath his jeans, into his fur, nicking his shoulder skin with her teeth, her fun-furred arms warm and soft against his neck. "You can split, Jody," he sighed.

"No. I'll feel . . . guilty about the bread."

"So feel guilty. Or give it back."

"Like a little slurp-slurp?" tonguing his ear.

His flesh was all party hats, but he said, "Night's over, Jody. *Adios.*"

"Ah, come on."

"Will you go upstairs again?"

"Aw, no, please, I—"

"Then split, will you?"

She ran for her clothes in the bedroom. She left the house without speaking. He looked only at the fire's flames in front of him. Her Mustang started like Bert next door's Harley. He could hear her, diminishing, for a long time in the still night; then her sound went out like a stone landing. He lit a cigarette and threw the Dannon cup into the fire. It burned weird green flames and spit noisily.

Thomas appeared on the landing in a bathrobe, a glass of scotch in his hand. He came down and sat on the edge of the hatch table. "I still can't believe it," he said in a hospital waiting-room voice. "Saved again."

Harry finally turned his head and looked at him. So that was what saved looked like. "It cost you a hundred bucks, Father. She was a hooker."

"I don't care."

"I didn't think you would." He stood and put his sweater on. It smelled faintly of Charlie. He put on his boots and fatigue jacket. Thomas' wallet coming out felt like a curse lifting. He dropped it into the attaché case and picked up the car keys.

"Hey, where you going, Tro?"

"Home."

"Yeah, well, I'll tell you one goddamn thing, hotshot—shit like this never happens on booze!"

Harry stopped on the deck and went back inside. From the doorway he yelled, "Father!"

Saved Thomas turned.

"Bless me, Father, I committed adultery! If it offended God, I'm sorry!"

The Canon looked shot.

"Absolve me, you son of a bitch!" Thomas just stared at him. It was Harry's first confession in more than ten years. He left. He made the six o'clock mass at Arch Street, in Boston. When he made the house, Dennis and Kate were watching *Yogi Bear,* eating bowls of Sugar Crisp. He got some Rice Krispies and joined them, prying Waldo out of his chair with the toe of his boot. He said, "It's against the rules to bring food into the TV room. I've told you a thousand times!" and they laughed.

Four

Small knuckles rapped softly on the bedroom door. The digital clock flipped to 6:47. Harry was already awake. He rasped "What?" Angie stirred. Damn it, he'd warned them: This was a sleep day. They'd even gone to the Saturday evening mass the night before, loathed by all.

The glass doorknob turned; the door opened to frame their beaming youngest child, Kate, bearing the breakfast tray. Behind her, Dennis yelled, "Happy Mother's Day!"

Angie woke and sat up. "You guys! You *didn't!* Oh, look."

"*I* did it *all,*" Kate sang righteously.

"She did, Mum."

She'd got up and proceeded to mix the juice, scramble the eggs ("*Just right,* Kates—nice and wet!"), toast and butter the English muffins, cut the daffodil and forsythia sprig, fold the napkin, place the utensils, and make the stairs with the tray. Dennis had waked in time to knock and open the door. "And I *could've!*" Kate made clear.

Constance materialized, rolled up her eyes, groaned, "*Brunch* isn't at *dawn,* you turkeys," and huffed into the bathroom.

Angie, he knew, needed to pee, hated to eat before her coffee, and didn't like meals in bed, especially from a legless tray. But she was radiating pleasure and digging in. "All by yourself, Kate! What a smart girl!"

"I was so *scared,* Mum!"

"Were you careful at the stove?"

"Yeah, I stood on the bag of dog food."

Outdone, Dennis had the good grace and timing to wait for Angie to finish before bringing his gifts out from behind his back: a blister-packed Papermate ball-point and one of his Steinberg-like drawings. Kate had made a wooden jewelry box in school. Nightied Amy was in with sleep in her eyes, praise for Kate's feat, and her gifts: a small embroidered pillow and, of course, a long letter of love, praise, and thanks that had received an A, which she'd erased. Constance delivered her crocheted change purse and went back to bed. Prince Consort Harry prayed silently that no-show Jake had also, somehow, forgotten the day.

No such luck. When Angie, dressed, got halfway down the front stairs, the house's air crackled suddenly with static; then Mick Jagger came serenading her at full volume: "*Angie. . . .*" Blushing, Jake mumbled, "Got you the album. *Goat's Head Soup.* And these." Sunglasses, wing-shaped and outrageous with rhinestones. She put them on. The kids roared. Jake said, "Ha. Elton John's mother."

Bringing up the rear, Harry felt like the Heap, fresh from the swamp. To save his life, he couldn't recall *what* he'd done for her on Mother's Days past, but was sure it had never been nothing. How could he ever have forgotten? He couldn't believe he had forgotten. (He felt the same as he'd felt on the morning of Grinch Christmas, some seven years before: They'd mail-ordered *everything* from Creative Playthings, and *nothing* had been delivered in time. All tiny then, the kids had come down to a limp note from Santa and gifts of snowsuits and gloves and a fruitcake, all from Ma Duffy.) In the kitchen he made coffee and decided he'd better spill it fast: "I don't know

ow to say this, Ange, but I forgot all about it. Never gave it a
hought. Boy, I'm sorry. It's incredible. I'll get you some candy
r something later, okay?"

She said, "Don't be silly, I'm not *your* mother."

"That's right, but I always do something, don't I?"

"I don't know, do you?" The gaudy lenses hid her eyes from
im. She sat, took them off, and started reading the Sunday
lobe.

He said, "Hey, who got the papers?"

Jake said, "I did."

"Oh, way to go, bud."

"Thanks, Jake."

"That's okay, Mum."

Harry guiltily dished out food for the cats and dog. He
vasn't, but felt hung-over as hell. "You, uh, get your mother
omething?"

"Yes," she told the magazine section, "I sent her a dozen
oses."

He posed at a window, looking out. "Jesus! How did I *miss*
t? Incredible!"

Angie turned a page. "Oh, forget it." She lit a cigarette.
'But your wonderful mass was so *full* of it last night. Thought
'd throw up."

Meaning, Where had *he* been? God, after forcing them all to
;o, too. He couldn't remember why he'd decided it so impor-
ant. He disliked the Saturday-evening mass as much as they
lid. Made you get cleaned up early, made dinner late, etc. It
ust didn't seem a *time* for mass, that's all. And how They had
roclaimed that it could count for the next day only confirmed
he arbitrariness of Their rule-makings anyhow. *Stupid!* Why
ad he done it? When the real fact was that anytime he did go
o the Saturday he felt he missed it entirely. (Come to think of
t, he did recall a woman lector rather aggressively reading
ome McKueny treacle about how fulfilling it was to be a slave
o hubby and *Kinder,* but if she ever used the actual words
'Mother's Day," Harry didn't catch them.) There'd probably

even been a Bing Crosby special on the tube for Christ's sake
And he'd probably even watched it! No. It was a plot. They
were *pretending* it was Mother's Day to kid him. They'd noticed
the attention, concern, and affection campaign he'd been
waging upon her ever since the Sequosset weekend:

He'd showered her with maidenhead ferns and Tobler
chocolates for Easter. He'd overcome, cold turkey, his involuntary reflex of interrupting her, or tried to, in several conversations. He'd touched her a lot, casually, which she liked. He
thought to ask her specific questions about her studies, careful
to refrain, when he could, from offering unsolicited pieces from
his own knowledge. He undressed in the bathroom so she
wouldn't beat him to picking up his clothes and think he, like
a sixth kid, hadn't intended to deposit them in the laundry
hamper. He thought of the storm windows and replaced them
with the screens. He—but this was fancifying, too. In truth he'd
been no less attentive or alternately rude to her than normal.
He had, indeed, felt more appreciative of having her, after the
peccadillo with the Canon, but made no overt moves to show
it, because Angie detected aberrant behavior the way a seismo-
graph marks tremors a hundred miles down. He had, though,
acted as if the prodigal weekend had worked, had blown dem
blues away, bye-bye Miss American *Angst*, hello cope, just what
the doctor ordered: "You know, all those guys who go up the
Maine lodge, hunting and everything, have the right idea.
Everyone, as part of their regular life, oughta—"

"Kid, it never crossed my mind that being able to get *away*
wouldn't be terrific," she'd said.

Weird to him: in the first days back he had felt some guilt
and remorse, but mostly he'd felt kind of . . . benignly wrecked:
beaten down, humbled, and brought low, but not to any
expected pit of regret or self-loathing. Instead, he felt strangely
full of a new compassion. He felt sharply less special than the
next poor boob, and it didn't feel bad. Needing forgiving, he
supposed, he discovered in himself a sorrowfully sweet urge to
forgive everybody everything human. An impulse he'd never

known in what he'd considered his states of grace. Nor did he feel, although he'd thought he would, that he'd hurt or taken anything from Angie. He thought he *should* feel he had, but he couldn't. Funny. He even thought the unthinkable: that Angie might sometime too, or possibly already had, and it wouldn't be the end of the world for him or them. That insight felt like a release of some kind, a burden lifted. Of course, if he *found out* about it, there'd be holy bloody murder to be paid, as there would be were she to catch wind of his escapade. But short of that, now that he'd done it, it seemed less heinous, that's all. Just penises and vaginas, which sounded like species of flowers.

A trickier aftermath of Sequosset for him had been the near return of the Taste. He'd started drinking again, a couple casual balls of scotch a day for a week or so afterward, until he realized what was happening, recalled the accident, and cut it down again. Still, he found himself mightily craving a gimlet or Bloody Mary this Mother's Day noon, when it rolled around. It wasn't just Angie's fixing herself the small batch of Marys; it was her doing so in front of him without so much as a "Want one?" in his direction. Was she pissed at something or not, and if so, what about, surely not his forgetting dumb, Hallmark-enriching Mother's Day! He poured himself more coffee, whistling an innocent tune.

Otherwise, the Sunday spun itself out normally, except that all the kids stayed home. Amy perched at the baby grand and resumed her relentless attack on "The Sting," difficult enough in itself but made harder by the piano's having a cracked sounding board. All the kids took weekly lessons on the teacher-maddening old Knabe, but Amy *loved* to play the thing, crippled as it was. And Harry loved to hear it played no matter who was at the keys—and just when could he hope to replace the thing with a decent one, and just how long could they keep affording the lessons? But never mind, the tune was rippling cheerily through the house *now* and was soothing his heart. Dennis' passion was the Jake-abandoned set of drums, played to full-volume Beatles, Stones, Led Zeppelin, and Bette

Midler records. He'd wanted to today, but Harry solved the
conflict by fixing the coin toss in Amy's favor. So Dennis was
down in the cellar taking it out on yet another bird feeder.
Their yard abounded in Dennis-designed bird feeders. They
thanked God that Dennis had the liking for such physical
outlets. If he didn't, the mayhem and destruction inevitably
wreaked would boggle the mind. Skinny, high-voltage Dennis
was as upfront as Jake was inside. If he thought it, he said it.
He swallowed nothing but enormous quantities of food, junk
and quality alike, which added not an ounce of flesh to his
bony, solid frame. Some miracle of metabolism, envied by
everyone else in the family. All their kids had very light eyes,
even black-browed Amy, remarked upon by strangers less
around Boston than back in New York, but Dennis' were so
blue they approached whiteness. Harry thought they mirrored
accurately the boy's threshold for stupidity, which was virtually nonexistent.

He and Angie made a point of getting in touch with all
teachers personally, letting it be known, from the start each
year and as gently as possible, that any Trowbridge kid would
be dicked with only at great peril. They tended, one or the
other, to visit Dennis' teachers more often; he tolerated *no*
bullshit and reported all displays of it. When he was right—
namely, nine times out of ten—they took his side against the
villain, but usually with as much diplomacy and empathy as
possible, all too well aware of the kid's ability to drive you up
the wall with his zest, energy, and untiring penchant for gags,
sight and word. His laugh made whole busloads of strangers
dissolve in giggle. He told jokes and did bits, a natural mimic
and pratfall artist ... endlessly, and with an urbanity far
beyond his years. "Well, well"—he smirked on the Nahant
beach at the sight of two suitless tots in the surf—"nudie-one
and nudie-two." He was nine. According to him, Chinese
people's eyes were like that because rice was constipating and
when they did dumps, which he demonstrated, they had to
strain and go *Eeee-eeee!* (Harry confided to him that when *he*

was a kid, pregeography, he thought that working in a laundry made you look like that. Dennis didn't laugh. He said, "Yeah, I can see how you thought that.")

Jake was being made to stay in, this being Angie's last chance to fit him for his *Oliver* costume, which she was making out of one of Harry's early-sixties, narrow-lapeled suits. Dress rehearsal was that Wednesday. Constance was up in her room cramming for finals and prepping for SAT's. Kate had brownies in the oven and was on the phone telling her entire world exactly how she had made Angie's eggs. Harry heard her giving the details to some kid's father, the kid being out. Plump and glowing, Kate would one day be not President, but Chief Justice of the Supreme Court. She was the one child who had undergone marked change since infancy, and for the better. They used to tell friends that if Kate had come first, she'd have been an only child, and they weren't joking. Angie had had a terrible time both carrying and having her. Home, she was colicky. Walking the three o'clock in the morning floors with her made Harry begin to understand those *Daily News* people who threw infants against walls. There was no pleasing or appeasing her. They didn't know what they had on their hands—and was it Kate at all? Or was it themselves, had they worn so badly that they no longer could have a happy kid? One reason they'd kept having them was the joy of it, ta-da, another gurgling, grinning little *baby,* who slept soundly through the night and woke to goo and ga and roll its eyes up and around while munching on the nipple, finding Similac scrumptious, even the powder. Kate spit up food and broke out in rashes and turned violet screeching. Her widest smile was another kid's pout. It was hard not to see her orneriness as a reflection of how mean their own spirits had turned in half a decade. It depressed them. But by her third birthday the cranky cloud suddenly wasn't there anymore. She didn't lose any of her hair-splitting righteousness, she'd still go to the electric chair before compromising her rights, but some miracle of lateral development had happened apparently overnight.

Her new qualities, her humor, her derring-do, her laying-on-of-hands affectionateness, her plain-out smartness and hunger to learn and act all balanced off her ... indignation, thank God.

Kate idolized Amy as fervently as Amy worshiped Constance. As Constance had a special *thing* with Dennis, so Jake and Kate enjoyed a fond, secret connection. Harry would often ask Angie if the Duffy mob of her own youth had had similar or dissimilar relationships, but Angie's memory tended not to work that way. She knew that she and Mike had been deep, thick pals all the way through, like Dennis and Kate, but the rest was blurred for her. She vaguely recalled that Albie and Mike had fought as viciously as Jake and Dennis did, and that encouraged Harry, for the two Duffy brothers were great, close buddies now. He hoped his own sons would iron it out before adulthood, though. There was something in Jake, the Tony Mac spirit perhaps, that kept him from ever belting Dennis out once and for all. It was too late now, and Dennis, to Jake's misery, knew it. He had the viper's tongue, and Jake didn't. The most help Harry could give was to tell Jake that he *knew* his dilemma and to give Dennis the arm-and-ass belts that Jake couldn't. He foresaw without relish a showdown when Dennis had closed the size gap again, probably in their late teens. He prayed that by then it wouldn't have to happen.

Luckily, when they weren't hating each other, they got along very well, owing primarily to Dennis' recognition of his older brother's wisdom in practical matters and to Jake's innate comfort in the role of teacher. Old Man Duffy's nick for him was the Monsignor. Jake's luck was the opposite of Dennis': He always got caught. Harry delivered the mandatory "In the long run you're lucky to be unlucky. If you didn't get caught, you'd do it again and then it becomes habit and ..." but inwardly his heart sagged for the kid. Nevertheless, Harry had the inkling that the easygoing, closemouthed Jake might prove to be the most *modern* person of the lot; the sole poor reader and getter of low marks, Jake was a vessel of enormous quantities of information. Whether it was ingested nonaterally, nonverbally or not, haltingly, slowly expressed or not, ie *knew* more than Harry dared imagine. He only hoped that he fury pent up in that ever-hardening and enlarging body vould find the time and way to dissolve or be vented healthily. [ake's lifelong attraction to and for the outcasts, underdogs, ind outlaws of his world worried Angie more than Harry, who emembered clearly how boring the nice, wholesome kids were. Down Liberty Square, in his time, "You nice," meant you were *ptally* an asshole.

Harry was sprawled in the loveseat in the rain of Amy's music, pretending to be reading the New York *Times,* thinking iow great it was to have them all home at the same time and vhat in hell *was* bugging Angie anyhow? Maybe he actually hould shoot down the square or up Huron and get her some :andy. It'd be buying *them* candy, not her, though. She'd never jut more than one into the exercised, taut bod anyhow. Still, he gesture might— "I'll get it!" he yelled and ran for the jhone ringing in the front hall.

He wished he knew who he wanted it to be. Maybe Albie or Flash. It wouldn't be Mike. Mike never called; he was the one Duffy undaunted by Angie's discouragement of drop-ins, and Defore, Harry had been half hoping he'd come thundering in, ilone or with a couple of his tiny kids in tow, a sixer of Bud in nand. Just to disrupt the calm, in which Harry was beginning to sense the presence of teeth. "Hello?" It was no Duffy or any friend of theirs or the kids. It was Charley Clote.

"You know, the Chez Ruby? Down by Fall River?"

"Yeah, I know." He sat on the stairs to try to stop the shaking.

"Well, first, my congratulations to Father Duffy. Right up there with Teddy and White on the news last night, huh? It was in the paper this morning, too, you see it? Takes a great picture, don't he ... our good Father."

"Listen, get me at work tomorrow, Clote."

"Just what I was gonna say, Harry. My thoughts exactly. Let me guess—the Liberty Square Shell, up Prospect, right? We

gotta lot to talk about, Harry. I got a real heavy problem I'm
hoping you can help me work out, huh? You there, Harry
baby?"

"Tomorrow," he snarled and hung up.

Waiting, he stood at his curb and looked at Liberty Square
More irony: The old slum was making a comeback. When he
first bought the station, one of his fears was that the derelict
boarded-up, bombed-out gloom of the foiled Square predicted
similar economic disaster for himself. But Prospect was a pass-
through city, and most of his business came from suburbanites
commuting between work and home, who didn't care about or
perhaps even notice the condition of any Liberty Square en
route. In fact, the decrease of local traffic might have smoothed
out their trips and contributed to his early volume. He didn't
know what had caused the upturn, but he saw it start (at just
about the time, in '74, of his own downturn) and could see it
now in the bright awnings and window signs of new stores in
old holes, in the new Yamaha dealership where the Gorin's
had been razed, in the new school where Adams Park used to
lie, flat and dirt. The bookstore and headshop indicated the
steady advance of Harvard influences toward Brick Bottom, as
did the Head Start operation, next to Blacker's Hardware, in
what used to be the minuscule Baptist church. Holy Family's
school complex now stretched the length of Sam Hill, and the
convent had finally been painted. If only he could hold out
long enough, he thought, maybe some of the upswing would
rub off on him. The Walker waved at him from the PO's steps,
going in to steal his daily pair of eyeglasses from the Lion's box
on the counter; weird old man, Harry'd miss him ... except
he'd always thought it'd be the Walker who'd go first, found
deceased at eighty-odd, wearing lawyer gun slits, hippie Ben
Franks, or Gloria Steinem headlights, depending on what day
his number came up.

His gaze drifted fondly past the precinct and bank and new
Dunkin Donuts to Superb Appliances, the last in-home busi-

ness on the Square. Joe di Pasquale. Harry had to laugh. That
son of a bitch. Joe D. and his wife, Min, had hit the Square a
few years before Harry, moving into the last residential house
facing the thoroughfare not made into a funeral home. They
started by glassing in their front porch, setting a few TV's,
radios, and washer-driers out there, and erecting the sign. The
"porch" now covered half a block, the house dwarfed to the
rear. Their office sat between their kitchen and the showroom.
Min did the books and calls. Joe ran around, sweating in a T-
shirt, railing, constantly on the brink of a heart attack or
nervous collapse. His two front teeth weren't just bucked; they
were horizontal, like staples set to shoot from his gums. Harry
had bought the Fury wagon from him. Joe D.'s baby. His
pride and joy. Harry spent half an afternoon sitting in its then
immaculate front seat listening to Joe D. recount how he
fucked Don Bosco Vocational High out of a diploma, fucked
Northeastern out of an engineering degree, fucked the Army
out of extra leave and into missing Korean combat, fucked GE
for a couple of years, fucked the Newfie out of the house,
fucked the city on variances. Harry bought the wagon from
him anyhow, beguiled or something by anyone still so charged
with his own story. Three days later the transmission went. On
the phone, Joe D. said, "Boy, dat boils me, Tro, I mean it, dat
really *boils* me!" Cyrus said it was 50–50; maybe Joe D. knew
it, maybe he truly didn't. Harry's only means of vengeance was
never to buy anything else from the proprietor of Superb
Appliances. Money was still coming in at the time, so it was
easier to absorb being suckered. And anyhow, the shitbird had
advertised his venality outright, hadn't he? As in Sequosset, it
had been Harry's own fault, and he could never deny it.

He'd expected a cut-down Caddie, a Continental, or a Benz,
but Charley Clote arrived in a Rabbit. False hope spurted like
a bad match. Harry walked back to his office door. Cyrus
came to a bay door, saw Clote Earth-shoeing toward Harry,
and returned to Judge Brennan's Olds. Clote wore a wide-
lapeled denim suit, aviator blues to match, a paisley shirt, and

string tie. It was a transplant job, not a toupee. Despite the
sludge heavy in his chest, Harry had to grant the guy his lack
of ominousness. He walked across the station's apron as at
home as a salesman. A handshake wouldn't have surprised
Harry, but none came. "You Harry Trowbridge?"

"Yeah."

"Yeah, I remember you." He shook his head slightly,
critically and sadly, like a doctor who had told him so. Harry
went inside, let him pass, and shut the door. "Business not so
hot, Harry."

"No."

"Yeah. Times tough all over. Like the goddamn thirties or
something." Clote sat. Harry leaned against his wall shelf ledge
and folded his arms to listen, the gray metal desk between
them. "Harry. You rather us go have lunch someplace?"

"No." The man made Harry think of some lawyer, here to
say he was being sued. Clote's eyes did not burn, though, as
the IRS fink's had. Harry said, "So?"

"So okay. I ... you know, it's funny being up here? I come
from Chelsea, but had an aunt lived over here. Used to trolley
over Sundays, hundred years ago. Changed! But still the same,
like, huh? Harry, I got you and the priest with your fuckin'
pants down, what can I say?"

Harry lit a cigarette. "How about nothing?"

Clote lit a cigarette. "Aah, come on. Hang-up is, something
drops in your lap like this, you don't wanta move too fast, see.
Not like I set it up or anything. Which I never would, dig. For
me it's found money, like. But I kinda need your thinking on
this, Harry, delicate like it is. Your input. I mean okay, I can
go straight to your Father Duffy with a fuck-you, pally, here it
is and pay up, *you* worry about it, *comprende?* But I say wait a
minute, maybe—"

"You wait, Clote—just what the fuck you think you got
anyhow?"

Charley Clote sighed, said he'd thought they could skip that
part, and when Harry said bullshit, he sighed again and

explained, softly, that while he knew it was Harry with Jody (and they could talk about that separately, if worse came to worst, which he hoped it wouldn't), what he had was the check made out to Jody by the priest, but what he really had was "Mrs. Carson" all hot to press charges against the good, up-and-coming, and fairly famous Father Duffy.

"Charges of what?"

"Hey, I'm no lawyer, Harry. Abduction, assault, rape, God knows."

"She's a fucking whacko!"

"Not really, Harry. You gotta get to knowa, like I have. Deserted by her old man, works, little kids at home ... don't be so quick to judge, man."

"Oh, Christ."

"That's better, Harry. That's more like it. Hey, you got a customer—go ahead."

"My guy'll get it."

"Oh. Good. So anyhow, here's how I handicap it, and you stop me if I'm wrong. I figure, I hit the priest direct, I chance having my line break on me. I mean, I'm hip the church has millions and all that, but they one, don't pay a guy like Duffy peanuts, and two, ain't never gonna shell out hush money cause he went out dippin' his wick. I figure it's *them* that better not ever get tipped to his little, uh, Chappaquiddick, huh? I figure they do and they pull his plug and he's out in Roxbury or down South America before he can pack or say good-bye, huh? Leavin' me as hard up and just tryin' to make ends meet as you and me are right now as it is. Harry, you know gas station, you got any idea the overhead on an operation like mine? Heat bill alone, fuckin' thieves. You know it *doubled* in one year? Ain't as if I used any more, they just ... course that's fuel, too, there again, ain't it, same as you. Energy. Every-body's outta energy. Bitch, ain't it? Christ, sometimes I just don't know where any of it's headin'. Now here's what I gotta learn from you—I go to him ... your priest ... what's he do? How's he take it? Like, where's he get the bread for his share in that house? Family, I figure. Maybe a little savings, some mutuals maybe, maybe a loan he's payin' on. You gotta know upfront where the other guy stands in a situation like this, am I wrong? Otherwise, bad surprises. You can blow it very easy. Now you got it, now you got zip. Bad business procedure. No need of it, this day and age. So what can I expect, bag a cashews a week? Not worth my while, not with the merchandise I'm sittin' on. You gotta help me here, Harry. That check cashed, by the way, man, your buddy's got it back by now probably."

Harry's eyes bit.

Clote laughed, "Haw, just kiddin', just kiddin'. Just wanna make a point—it's your sig, Harry, but that ain't no out, is it? So where's he get it and how much's he good for, Harry?"

"Shit. Jesus Christ, shit." It was. It was the worst, and it was happening.

"Interesting, ain't it? Course I got partners, too, Harry, and I don't think they'd wanna handle it this way at all if I told 'em, dig? But I figure, hey, what? People ain't up against it out there? You can't give 'em a little room? What's your advice, Harry?"

Rashly, Harry spit. "I'm getting a lawyer, is my advice."

Clote chuckled. "Better get a Jew, Harry. I'll recommend a couple. Trouble with your micks is they all become prosecutors, ever notice? You're defense, Harry. I'm prosecution here. Hey, hey—do I want it ever to come to that? Slow down. Think for a minute, Harry. What do I get from ruinin' the dumb bastard?"

Harry tried to think. Thomas would go to pieces. Then he'd go to his mother. It could kill her. It could surely kill his father. How much were they good for anyhow? Some stocks, he'd heard, the houses, the land out in the Berkshires. But even if they were loaded, why a cent to scum like Clote at this point in their lives? Some end for two immigrants. Fine reward for fifty years of drudgery and thrift. Via the First Son at that. That would be the killing slug. "I need some time."

"I got all day, Harry. I'm closed Mondays."

Harry glared. He wished he could hate the creep, he wished more that he could beg, *Why can't you forgive us and let us go?* Because it would be unreasonable, he knew. He asked, "How much do you want, how much do you think you can get from us?"

Clote grinned, not maliciously. "Isn't that somethin'? You know, I had this *feelin'*. Only saw you the one time, but I hada feelin' this is where you'd come out. Wait'll little Jody hears." He overlapped his hands on the edge of the desk and talked to them. "You a movie buff, Harry, like me? Watcha lot of TV?"

Harry nodded.

"Yeah. So you're gonna get the idea to call my bluff. That's always the only way to deal with blackmail. Fess up. Pay the consequences but not me. You got that kinda marriage, Harry? Send it to the Smithsonian, if you do. I know whereof I speak, believe me. It'd be a terrible mistake on your part. In the long run I'd seem cheap as nails, and I kid you not. Stop, look and listen, Harry. Don't—"

"Save it, Clote. This piece of shit's in the red. I'm going under. I don't have next month's groceries."

Then Clote turned hard. "Fuck you, chum, I forgot my violins. Tell your priest *your* problems; we're discussing mine now. You can sell your fucking house. He can sell his. All his brothers and sisters can sell theirs. I don't give a shit. I don't have parties, turkey. I deny myself stupid pleasures. Now back off! Keep your *song sung blue* for your shvartzer out there! Okay. You straight? I said—you straight?"

"Yeah. I'm straight. You prick."

"You just raised the kitty, shmuck, wise up. You're in no position to call names. I'm getting bored, now. Too bad, started so good. Okay. Forget the movie bullshit. Take my word. I won't say I won't go up 'cause I might. I can't read the future. No tellin' how big your boy's gonna get, for instance. Course, don't tell him to slack off either. Ambition should be encouraged. All right. No fat one-shot. I'd only squander it. I'll give you another break—you want weekly or monthly?"

"Fuck, man, *how much?*"

"Oh, that's right. Yeah, this is the hard part. Wish I had a clearer set of figures on you assholes. Well, somebody's gotta make a decision. Hm. Can't starve the cow if you want milk ... two hundred a week, by the week, and don't thank me Harry, I don't read it as worth much more than that yet."

Harry heard himself retardedly ask, "Why not?"

Clote said, "The odds on your boy Duffy making big time ain't so hot right now."

Harry stayed leaning there in his muggy office, feeling freezing cold, long after Clote had gone. Cyrus passed in and out, making change, frowning, curious and worried, but saying only, "Man smell like a party member there, chief."

Harry said, "Yeah, he probably is."

Good Times, at the station, had meant for Harry about thirty-five grand a year. No horn of plenty in the Nixonian seventies for a family of seven. He'd gone below twenty last year. He'd be lucky to hit twenty this year, even if he got the breaks. He wished he could take the feeling out of his body and hold it in his hand, it was so new and exotic for him; he was nearly thirty-nine and had never been in real trouble in his life. He had never seen the inside of a police station except the night of the accident. While still picking at it, he picked up the phone, called the Powell Dairy company, and asked the garage starter to tell Flash Gordon it was absolutely necessary for him to see him today. That would take care of getting the extra money he'd need to pay Clote.

He did it almost without thinking about it, as automatically as he paid any bill he received: at once, to be worried about sometime later. The panels of Flash's dairy truck carried cocaine, hash, grass, pornographic films, other drugs of all sorts in pill, capsule, and vial form, and God knew, not Harry, what other kinds of contraband. Whatever Flash had a market for in "The Congo" of his retail milk route, black Roxbury. Harry's station had a large, dry, clean cellar. Flash had long been seeking it for storage space, a safe house. Harry'd never even have to see a thing. Just collect two, maybe three if it'd make him happier, a week. For three years Harry had said no. Flash said he was a clod, but it was about their only point of conflict and disagreement and never interfered with their friendship.

Cyrus came back in, this time with a charge card, and said, "Got money in the bank, Tro?"

The inside door to the service bays was still closed. Harry sprang away from the ledge and slammed his fist into it twice. "God*damn* it! Doesn't anybody get anything right? Money in the bank is when you fucking *talk* to yourself! Not when you just fucking *stare!*"

Cyrus left, saying, "Yeah, I know that."

The outburst startled him back into control. The black and gray tiger, Pitstop, one of the station's rat patrol, was blinking him a dirty, disturbed look from his reserved seat in the window. Harry picked him up and stroked him. Pitstop's tongue felt like No. 1 sandpaper licking his jawbone. "Wake you, pal? Tough titty. Life's rough, yeah." Pitstop purred. A recent memory flashed, and Harry grinned. One day the cat had been sleeping in a wooden box that had "69¢ lb." chalked on it and Cyrus had grumped, "Hmph! I remember when cat was only *forty* cents!"

Pitstop had been fixed. Harry had hated to do it, but the tom had been spraying all over the place. Harry thought, there was something screwy when you didn't commit the follies of youth until you were middle-aged. Maybe you should be somehow fixed when you hit thirty-five or six. Or, better, be allowed to be reckless when you were young and un-blackmailable. What was he doing now anyhow? Clote's ex-haust fumes were still blueing his station's air, practically, and he was already ensnarled in the whole viny thornbush. He knew he should block it for the time being, give himself some air and time, let the emotions subside so his head could take it on coldly. He stepped outside into the tepid, noisy city air. Cyrus was waiting for the customer to sign the slip and return the pen and unwieldy plastic clipboard. Harry once again snuffed. They could put a man on the moon and make caffein-free coffee, but nobody could improve on the cockamamy gas-station charge-card process. It was where he felt he was, too: If he'd lost anything between '65 and '75, it was his faith in his intellect's reasoning ability; the alternative nonanswers always seemed as possible and viable as any "solution" he'd arrive at, leaving him despondently dizzy, almost nauseated. Might as well wrestle the emotions as the logic; it was all briar patch he hadn't been born in. In such quandaries, he usually went running to St. Anne.

He'd found her in the Army, by accident, through Angie. Newlywed, he'd asked her what the idea was of the prayer card she'd tacked to the inside of a kitchen cabinet's door. "That's St. Joseph," she'd said. "My mother always had one. You read it and believe." For all his Catholic schooling, it was his first tipoff to the erratic highs he'd later discover in the Eucharist. St. Joseph rang no bells for him, but he soon after came across a prayer that did:

> Glorious St. Anne, filled with compassion for those
> who invoke you, with love for those who suffer,
> heavily laden with the weight of my troubles,
> I cast myself at your feet and humbly beg
> you to take this present affair which I recommend
> to you under your special protection. Vouchsafe
> to recommend it to your daughter, the Blessed
> Virgin Mary, to lay it at the throne of Jesus
> so He may bring it to a happy issue. Cease not
> to intercede for me until my request is granted.
> Above all, obtain for me the grace of one day
> beholding my God face to face, and with you
> and Mary and all the saints, praising and blessing
> Him for all eternity.

Except for the final image, which didn't sound like much fun to look forward to, something in the prayer clicked with something in him. For one thing, he found he'd memorized it

automatically on the first reading. The hit of energy and
confidence St. Anne delivered was crude and mild compared to
the heroinic rush of communion, but was more dependable,
coming through for him about eight times out of ten. A kid
spun into the station on a ten-speed, turned the airometer up
to fifty-five and began topping off his tires. That was it, Harry
thought, St. Anne was like an air pump. But he was only
thinking about the prayer, not saying it. Normally he'd start
rattling it off as naturally as whistling, but he felt too ashamed
to bring this to her, at the same time being all too well aware
that this was precisely when to call for help. He only hoped
that, as was claimed, the thought itself was enough to send the
message. Pitstop dove out of his arms and darted back inside.
Harry couldn't decide if he felt more like a criminal or a leper.

"You do?" Flash's uncharacteristically soft eyes showed real
disappointment; Harry was afraid he was going to say no.
"Yeah, I do."
Flash put his hand on Harry's shoulder and said, "Sure,
mate, you got it. I'm paying two-five to this deecey-dicey spic
now, I'll give you three, deal?"
"No. Just two. Two's fine, Flash." He didn't say thanks
because he didn't want Flash to know he was in any more than
obvious, ordinary need. And he didn't take the three because,
in the intervening afternoon of brooding, he'd rationalized that
this way he wouldn't be really involved. The money would be
passing from Flash to Clote. He'd be merely a sort of conduit,
which didn't seem so ... implicating. He didn't believe this,
but he had to find some way to live with it until he got used to
it, if he ever would.
The Coke machine on the left, with the "Out of Order" sign,
was stacked with beer for the cops and other droppers by.
Flash went to it and got a Gansett. *Schlitz!* "When, Trobie?"
"Soon as you can. Whenever you want." He knew Flash
wouldn't ask, or if he did, it would be in the most oblique,
gauzed way possible, in the middle of some other conversation

sometime later. He knew too that he could just spill it if he wanted to. It'd be safe with Flash. He was half thinking of doing so. It bothered him to let Flash think the bread was going to him, Angie, and the kids. Harry didn't want to deprive him of any feeling of good-turn-being-done, but rather, he knew it would infuriate Flash to think that money of his was going to some business-minded leech like Clote. And from that fury might come some better way out of this corner than Harry could manage by himself. He didn't have it in him at the moment, though, to go passing on any fury to anybody. Passing the money seemed bad enough.

He could hardly even remember the funky night now. He and Thomas had met twice since, so blithely that Harry'd begun to wonder if it had happened at all, outside his own dopey imagination. That too kept him from confiding in Flash, his dread of the rollicking guffaws of disbelief sure to erupt from his satyric buddy. Flash was true to his sexy wife Legs in his fashion: he had sources of what he called slag scattered all over the metropolitan area (which bore all too suddenly appropriate names, the counties Middlesex, Norfolk, Suffolk. At Suffolk University the cheers still went, "Yah, Suff ... yay, folk, yay-yay, Suffolk U!") He had a black meat-packer in a Columbus Avenue supermarket who'd suck him off in the stockroom on a moment's notice. Harry'd ridden shotgun on the Honey Wagon once, just to see a day in the life, and had seen it with his own eyes, the beginning at least, declining to accept anything from this category of Flash's boundless generosity. Flash simply didn't believe in marriage, except as a property-protecting legal device for the benefit of Legs and their twin girls, still infants. He and Legs had been together some dozen years but had only recently legalized it and then only because it had been Legs' Lithuanian mother's dying wish, amoral Flash having his sentimental side like anyone else.

All the Irish lives so closely rubbing upon them seemed so alike, so risklessly respectable and plain, that Harry and Angie needed the Gordons to keep them reminded of the worlds outside the boiled-meat walls of bitter meekness. (Her sister Annie, told on the phone that Angie was dishing out pancakes for supper, would well-meaningly say, "Oh. You give them as poor as I do." Told Angie needed periodontal work, Mrs. Duffy well-meaningly said, "At your age, just have them pulled, why don't you?" A curled stick in every meatball.) Flash, too, ostensibly seemed out of place doing what he did within the hokey Hub, but as with Harry, things had led him here. Flash was probably dangerous, but he had picked Harry as friend, and the picked don't get to unpick. Harry drew his lines with Gordon but knew the guy had, essentially, saved his Liberty Square life: He was in ocean up to here, singing and yelling for soap and his rubber ducky. He was perfectly named, for he indeed looked like a young, black-haired Buster Crabbe, except with a boxer's weights-worked body rather than a swimmer's. In summer he drove his nefarious routes bare-chested, with Clint Eastwood tan, hat, and stogie. Flash was more uncle to the Trowbridge mob than the real ones, Angie and Legs Gordon were thicker than sisters, and ... at the very least, the gear Flash scored for Harry was invariably top drawer.

Harry couldn't guess what Flash pulled down in a year. He knew he averaged at least six hundred legitimate dollars a week from Powell's. Upset by his unorthodox ways, the company severed his franchise once only to discover they needed three trucks to cover his "hazardous duty" route and begrudgingly renegotiated their agreement with him posthaste. Later they one morning assigned a "trainee" to him for a week. The first hour out Flash spotted him for a management spy. The next morning a sudden stop on Rutherford Avenue in Charlestown oddly sent a rack of steel milk crates plummeting through their end bars, batting the fink through the front window. Flash dropped him outside Mass General's Emergency entrance to fend for himself and continued on his appointed rounds. To seal the wax, Flash spent a Sunday putting the Powell traffic manager's name and address on every newspaper and magazine coupon he could find. "Ha! Huh, Trobie? That fucker'll be in the Cheese-of-the-Month Club for life! He'll have Christmas cards and shoe samples coming out his ass!" Flash carried a windup laugh bag, in addition to his revolver, but that time did the wild, fun-house cackling himself.

No six bills a week ever bought a house like the Gordons' on the coast of Marblehead. It had made one national magazine during Flash's self-designed reconstruction of it, then another one, recently, in its finished state. The articles called Legs "Liz" and quoted "Mr. Gordon, who is in the transportation business when he isn't landscaping beds for the black tulips he imported from Holland," as saying things like "I loathe square spaces. Like life, a home should be full of open ends and great expanses of light and air," sending Flash into fits of hilarity. "Fuck 'em, it'll add twenty grand at least on the price for when I sell it." There, above the sea, Harry and Angie liked to spend evenings and afternoons with Flash and Legs' crowd of acquaintances. Moneyed architects, boatyard owners, bankers, advertising people, and other stylish neighbors whom Flash made sport of—"Gatsbying them" he called it—so deftly that few ever caught it . . . thanks largely to Legs' genuine affection and care for anything that breathed, including plants.

She was a Pan Am stewardess who'd retired only the uniform and affiliation. It was impossible to even trick or push her into uttering a negative comment on anyone. One particularly pompous fop of a fool she defended thusly: "He broke wind here one day and just said, 'Pardon me,' as nonchalantly as anyone else says it when they burp. Now I'm sorry, but that is being well-mannered. Unlike *you*"—speaking to Harry—"or *Flash*, for instance!"

"Ah," Flash growled, "that's what's wrong with everybody. Nobody ever lets one really rip anymore. Or knows enough to applaud it when you do."

Harry mouth-berried coarsely.

"Nice one, Tro."

"Thank you."

Legs had acquired or been born with the knack of blind-
siding what displeased or confused her. They were fairly
certain she knew little of and asked less about Flash's off-
premises doings or means of making the money she managed
as frugally as a peasant. Which she had to. Flash liked to
claim, "Every nickel I got you can *see*," and more than half
meant it. Whether or not he truly hated money, he surely
loved things and going places He and Legs, in fact, had been
away for a month in Vail when Harry found himself down
Sequosset, and he couldn't help ruing the irony in his having
declined so many of Flash's invitations to classy, and doubt-
lessly foolproof, soirees into sin, only to finally fall so cheapshit-
tedly. How could he ever admit his folly to Flash and expect to
maintain any semblance of personal style in his friend's eyes?
For Flash did like and admire the "caper" Harry and Angie
were attempting to pull off, so opposite to his and Legs', yet in
its own way as offbeat.

The Trowbridges liked it best when they dined and hung
out alone with Flash and Legs, playing boccie and pool at the
Marblehead house, and when the Gordons, every other weekend, came to Cambridge. On Angie's turf, glamorous Legs
turned totally avuncular (as did Flash, though no less zany)
and was by now forever associated in the kids' heads with free
gum, exotic scents, individual attention on the compassionate
side, costume-and-makeup support for plays, screwdrivers without ice, and long kitchen whisper sessions with their mother, as
well as a source of folding money: Jake had worked for Legs
for two summers now, yardwork and heavy cleaning, and
Constance and Amy were her steady baby-sitters. Flash was a
hearty favorite with blood uncles Albie and Mike Duffy, not
only as Harry's best friend, but as some incarnation of their
mutually admired-at-a-distance idea of a guy "who *really*
doesn't give a sweet shit."

On the "I'd like to give the world a Coke" sticker on one of
the machines, somebody had scrawled "some" over the "a."
Flash thumbed it and said, "Hey, want to snort a little? I got

about three lines on me. Come on, it's quitting time." The
word on the street had Flash stoned on something or other all
day long, but Harry knew otherwise. In his work, he wouldn't
survive for two minutes if he weren't guerrilla alert and in
charge. After work, of course, was something else.

Harry said, "No, I'll pass," afraid a toke of anything right
now would send him so far down he'd never be seen again.

Flash sat at Harry's desk but brought out only his checkbook. He wrote a check for two hundred. "Here, Tro, we're in
business, you have to do your own Blue Cross, though, and
let's *not* be equal opportunity employers, okay? Fuck everybody."

Harry laughed. Inside he was screaming "Hey, Flash, what
can I *do* about this?" but he still couldn't let it out. It occurred
to him that he'd have to go to the bank, no, go to a different
bank, and open a new checking account from which to pay
Clote. It was getting realer and realer. The check felt clammy
in his hand.

A crazy arithmetic possessed him: Being broke and secretly
carrying Clote, he felt consumed by a thirst to spend fortunes
on Angie, to break all agreements and buy her something rare
and exquisite for their anniversary. Not in spite of his dire
straits, but weirdly, because of them. It was Angie herself who
prevented him from actually doing it; she'd been so preoccupied and dismayed by the money involved in the upcoming
anniversary bash planned for her parents that he knew any
reckless spending on his own part might send her around the
corner. The family was pooling resources to give the senior
Duffys the party and two gifts, a color TV and a month's trip
back to Ireland. She wasn't against the grand plan, nor did she
begrudge her parents a dime. It simply galled her to have to
scrape deeper than bottom for their prorated share while
having to pretend they could afford it. The least hint of a huff
toward the truth would've been taken as an insult and

poormouth by anyone concerned. If the whole idea had started with anybody but Thomas and Annie, there might have been room for at least a "Why the hell both? Who are we trying to impress?" As it was, it was far easier just to pay up and shut up. So Harry and Angie were celebrating their own anniversary alone together in La Bourgogne, a small old French place with blue ceilings near Harvard Square where not only the *vin* was *ordinaire*. They had reddish champagne cocktails. Harry clinged her glass with his and said, "Happy anniversary."

She winked, smiled and sipped, but said, "We're not supposed to say that, I thought." Actually, they were again celebrating their nonanniversary. The real one wasn't for another week by the calendar.

He said, "I don't mean *that*. I mean, this is the fourth anniversary of not celebrating the real one."

"Terrific," Angie said, "so now we can have a knock-down-drag-out brawl tonight after all because it's the anniversary of our nonanniversary! Jesus."

After their thirteenth, it was clear that their most savage, this-*is*-the-end hate-on of the year never failed to coincide with their wedding anniversary. It had happened eleven years in a row. They finally concluded that it had to be the event itself that secreted the malice in both of them. Angie said, "But why?"

"I don't know, babe, but it doesn't sound too healthy."

She pondered it. "Well, I don't hate being reminded that I've been married another year. Do you?"

He pondered it. "No. But maybe I think it's kind of dumb to have to give your marriage a birthday party."

She squinted. "I think you hit it. You said *have to*. I think that happens in me, too. Like something I don't feel like going to. Some stupid command performance, like in the Army."

After that they sort of sneaked out for dinner a week before or after the Day and exchanged no gifts. This year, trying to keep their conversation away from the kids, her parents' fiftieth, his station, her courses, and all other regular-life, anti-intimate, unromantic subjects, they both conceded that this year they probably could have celebrated the Day itself without its disintegrating into misinterpretations, putdowns, painful defenses and counterthrusts, lost appetites, cindered feelings, scraped chair legs, all-but-separate exits, and the rest. "Tides" was how Angie saw it: "I resent, and I guess I'm scared, too ... by the feeling of victim it leaves, but it does seem ... well, I have a picture of it, and it's this large wedge of water. A bay, I suppose. It's pretty, and blue, but it changes, and it's deep, and warm. Then it goes out, that's all. What's the real tides, four hours?"

"Eight."

"Well, this is about three months. From full and deep to out and gone."

"And when it's out?"

"Mud. The pits. Black ooze. Mostly from you, of course."

"Crabs, even?"

She was higher than the pun. "All of it," she said. "Eels! Rusted cans. Gluck, gunk. Glass. Fish flopping for water, for their air."

"But it always comes back."

"So far. I suppose that's what we get so desperate about. That it won't."

Harry was moving butter from dish to mouth on the end of a breadstick. He said, "That's very good."

"Meaning you don't know what I'm talking about."

"No! Meaning I think you have it incredibly right-on. Almost too ... I mean, that does leave us pretty helpless. Flopping. Christ."

"Well, maybe not. You asked me, I told you. How do you have it?"

He sipped his champagne and watched the bubbles and thought of divers and Jacques Cousteau. He started to say that he had it "bigger" but changed it to "different." Angie could be a hermit crab and duck back in faster than the hand or eye.

He said, "I think, or at least I think I think, that reality isn't neutral. That it's slanted to the down, the evil, or whatever you want to call it. And that you have to constantly work on it and improve on it with your imagination, or hopes, or fantasies, or whatever you want to call *that*. That's what I think they mean by 'you make your own world.' That if you . . . well, by itself, left to itself, I think reality will read out on the bleak side every time and suck you down."

Angie leaned forward and ignited her cigarette off the candle's flame. "But if a kid cuts a finger, it's a cut."

"Or it's a pirate's slash wound. I've heard you do that—*Ow! Who shot ya?*"

"Oh. I see."

"And the trouble comes, I think, when we stop and doubt the world we've been making that way. You know, you've got it all going cool, then all of a sudden you forget or turn chicken or something and—"

"The carriage goes back to pumpkin."

"Yeah."

The waiter came and took their orders for second drinks with a faint scowl of disapproval. Angie laughed. "You'd think their food was so great. The French are a pain in the ass, I've decided."

"Supposed to be terrific lovers, though."

"Nah. They all wear white shirts with upcurled collars and crooked dark ties. Even Belmondo."

"Maybe it's the women."

"Yeah—with all those bidets of theirs."

"All right, cynic, who are terrific lovers?"

"Why are you eating so many breadsticks?"

"Why are we knocking the poor frogs?"

"To keep from talking about money and kids and those *Onassis* anniversary presents!" She slapped the table and threw her head back in a big, silent laugh. She'd broken herself up. It was a laugh he was unable to resist even when he wished to. Her eyes were wet when she finished, and she said levelly, "Oh,

Tro, terrific lovers are any ones who are in love with each other."

Their food came with such extraordinary speed that they popped eyes at each other over the waiter's hands. When the waiter left, Harry said, "Why do all women—I know *some* men, but *all* women—raise their voices when they have something serious to say?"

"Do I?"

"Yes."

"Because it's their only way of having half a chance of being heard."

"Oh."

Angie was having escargots, Harry the house pâté. He wanted to swap halves, but she wouldn't. Zip, their salads and entrées. Angie, still relishing garlic-wet bread: "Ask Monsieur Henri if he's got a promise or what." Angie had the filet mignon. When she'd ordered it, she'd answered his glance: "Listen, we shouldn't be here at all. But as long as we are, I'm *not* going to right-side the menu!"

Harry had the ham omelet, answering hers: "I *want* it. I ate too many breadsticks." He ordered a bottle of Mouton Cadet red, right-siding the wine list. They both had coffee. Angie had the chocolate mousse.

She said, "Personally, I kind of like reality as it is. Like doing things. Even dumb things, the laundry, the meals, buying underwear, taking the subway. Eating this. All the *physical* things and necessities, I guess. Why should I pretend they're anything else? They have to get done, they occupy your mind while you're doing them, the time passes . . . oh, I know, you're going to say they *distract* your mind, but so what?"

Harry said, "I was going to say that, but I'm not sure I'm disagreeing with you. I do that at work all day long. But it ends. And your worries or problems or whatever are always still there waiting, right? So haven't you really just been escaping into that physical reality?"

"*Vive l*'escaping!"

"Nah—because you aren't *really* escaping anything, just postponing and ... giving the horrors all that time to grow and mount up!"

She exhaled a windstorm of smoke. They each shot up a cupped hand to save the bowled-over candle flame. "Getting a little bleak there for me, Tro."

"Yeah, I'm sorry. You look beautiful, by the way." Clote, he'd decided, must be something like having cancer or MS and not telling anyone about it. He tried to bear it like Jack Kennedy's bad back, like Jake Barnes' war wound, like Father Damien's numbing fingers. He tried to carry it the way Tony Mac had lugged the oil jug for Jimmy Quinlan. He'd found now that he could do it. The hard part was keeping it out of his consciousness, preventing it from permeating his system and contaminating it. Making Clote an animal and buying a hit on him was creeping up his list of options so steadily that his personal vision of himself was scarily beginning to blur.

"Thanks, Tro. I'd still head for you at a party, too."

Harry felt the blood in his face. "Thanks. That's still the greatest thing you've ever said to me."

She flicked her ash. "Be nice if we got a flood tide this time, wouldn't it?"

He grinned. "Be better if it just stayed in and never went out again."

Angie reached across and whacked the back of his hand. "Ah, come on—then what would we do for *tension*, kid? Let's pay up and split before Henry starts with the snails again."

Harry pulled out the Master Charge and began testing the wind. She whispered, "Pray your ass off it doesn't push us over the thousand. Joints like this don't call the number in, do they?" The billing process here was only slightly less cumbersome than at the station. Waiting, Angie said, "Let's not go home yet, okay?"

On the sidewalk she said, "Let's be wicked and go the Casablanca." A soft June rain was falling, turning the surfaces of the Square vinyl and drifting with it the warm, musky smell of the river. She had an umbrella but didn't put it up.

Harry said, "Everything's feeling kind of John O'Hara tonight."

She took his arm. "Oh, God, he's making me his mistress again!"

He laughed. "No, just the sometime, old friends, comforting piece."

"Sounds boring. That's not enough for this bimbo. Better jazz it up, Charley Brown."

The "Charley" stung him like a hornet: the hooker's scent, Clote's name. And such a plain old name. It was seeping too far in! There were just too many inescapable, unalterable elements of reality around him; two kids right now leaned against the Coop's dark windows, wrecked out of their gourds— *Dope! Heroin! Flash! Himself! Jake? Constance?* Oh, Jesus, how did he get into this?

Angie said, "I think the whole world's stoned all the time. Maybe they've got the right idea."

"Yeah. Depends what they're on, I guess."

"Mm. I like to see the jollies. It's the blank, empty staring that spooks me."

"Yeah. That ain't grass."

"Well. Somebody's still making tons of money anyhow."

That stung, too. Invisible hornets, following him wherever he went, like a Dick Tracy villain. Flash had reassured him that, contrary to the street word, heroin was not a part of his operation. Harry wanted to believe him. But Flash knew him so well; what else would he say, it *was?*

The place was in the cellar under the Brattle Theater. The after-movie crowd had already thinned to the usual loud mix of collegiates, swanks, and locals. Something made the Cambridge townies keep their token hand in the Casablanca, some unwillingness to give it over entirely to the college people and older BP's. Whenever Harry and Angie came here, their first conversation always was of the Boston Bamboozle, Harry's name for the phenomenon that kept the roughly eight hundred thousand permanent, ethnic citizens virtually invisible to the academic temporaries. Hence the country's befuddlement when College Town, USA, boiled over in riots over the forced busing: Who the hell *were* all those outraged, furious savages? The real homeowning residents, baby, who saw no sense in sending the black basketball star to South Boston (Hockey) High, and the white hockey star to Roxbury (B-Ball) High.

Angie got a Tequila Sunrise, Harry a Sambucca. Her Tides concept wasn't unusual for her; she was a moon person and knew it, a creature aware of the effects on her of weather, the time of day, week, night, a crystal set receiving radio messages awake and asleep. She'd stopped halfway up the stairs one Sunday afternoon, turned and run down, stating, "We have to go see Annie." They hurtled out to cattle country, without phoning, to find Annie and an empty bottle of Sominex, Fast and the kids off visiting his parents. Angie stuck her fingers down her sister's throat, poured black coffee into the vacated space, and walked her. Annie said she hadn't been *trying* anything! The sleepers had been nearly gone; she'd only popped a few, unable to relax enough to rest! And that Angie was nuts, nosy, pushy and trespassing!

In the car going home Harry said, "Think she'll make it?"

Angie said, "She'd better. Yeah, she was telling the truth—and she called me, didn't she?"

She was always after Harry to remember his dreams. This night in the Casablanca he said, "Dream!"

She brightened. "Unbelievable! Tell me!"

He felt stupid, but also relieved; he'd in fact been looking for the chance to unload it on her, unable either to ignore it or to figure its significance, if any, for himself. "Oh, put your tongue back in, it's no hot stuff. I'll tell you the weird thing about it, though—"

"Tell me the dream!"

"Wait a minute. The crazy thing is not only have I had this same dream twice in the past month"—since Sequosset, he didn't add—"but I've just realized I've had it before, like two or three times over the past ten or twelve years."

"Yummy!"

"Maybe even longer. Anyhow, okay, I'm running. I'm being chased. Kafka time. I don't know who or what's after me. And somebody's with me, but I don't know who, except that he's a guy. All right. So we're running like hell. There's a feeling of the movie where Jack Palance is carrying typhoid but doesn't know it and they have to get him—you know, a lot of sweating and hiding, all black and white and all city, not New Orleans, not here or New York, just city. I have a feeling more's happened before I like open up onto it, but the first place we're running through is a theater. You know—backstage and the line of chorus girls jumping up from the makeup tables and shrieking, but funny, and they want to help us ... and then we're out again, and we're in *disguises* now."

"What are you?"

"Oh, God, I know I shouldn't tell you this. A priest."

"Ha!"

"No *ha's!* or I'll stop!"

"Okay."

"Okay. And I don't know what the other guy's dressed as, but he's been fixed up as something, too. Then we're running up metal stairs to an outside subway station. An el, like in Everett or Queens. And the heat's right behind us. Close as hell now, and I'm scared shitless and getting tired. I pass a bum lying on a bench. Still up on this subway platform. A classic: dirt caked on his face and hands, black, with ... he's not black, the dirt's black, with red, open sores on him—vermilion red! And he stinks of shit and piss and wine. I look back and realize the guy with me, my partner, has stopped! He's gone over and sat down and taken the bum in his arms, and he's cradling him and cleaning his face and soothing him and whatever, and I say to myself: He's right. That's the right thing to do. But I'm still running like a bastard. *Adios, amigo.*

"Then, bing. Cut. I'm sitting on a chair on a platform. With other like dignitaries. A high school band's passing, drum majorettes, pompoms, a color guard, out of step and skinny and the whole bit. They eyes-left us, so I'm on the reviewing

tand. Suddenly this little kid steps up to the podium on the
front of the stand, and he's going to give a speech. About
eighth-grade age. And he's not me-young or Jake or Dennis . . .
actually he's the younger brother of, ah, never mind—anyhow,
he just starts his serious speech, when he decides the hell with
it, he's going to use the opportunity to tell jokes! He's got
routines! He's killing himself laughing at his own stuff and at
what he's pulling off and all the elders start harumphing and
getting pissed off except me! I'm breaking up. I know it's going
to blow my cover and maybe get me caught, but I'm roaring
at the kid and his material. Then I wake up."

Her Tequila Sunrise was his dream, and she was sipping it
slowly up her flat, short straw, squinting at him.

He said, "Well?"

She said, "All right, I'll tell you what I think it means. I
think it means, my darling, that your days at the station are
over. Your time's up. The deal is still working good for me, but
it isn't for you anymore, and you're going to have to do
something about it or go crazy, and you're scared, because for
the first time ever it isn't *us,* it's just you."

"Wow. What a straight man. Talk about giving somebody
an opening!"

"I've been waiting for one. I said it, and I'm glad."

He did Amy: "But how 'bout my *dream,* Ma?"

She laughed. "Listen, that one's loaded; I wouldn't go near
it. Who do you *think's* after you, the cops? The church? People
who know the terrible truth about you? Who?"

For a fleeting second of giddiness he nearly told her: a guy
named Charley Clote and a dame named Kit Carson. Maybe
Angie would immediately diagnose it and cure it: *A hand down
her throat's all that one needs!* He himself had surely had no luck
with the woman the night, two weeks after Clote's visit, that he
went to her house down in, oh, God, *Assonet,* Mass. She'd been
right there in black and white in the phone book.

He had perversely hoped to find her sodden with drink,
exulting in sweat beneath five Hell's Angels, with one kid

chained to the radiator and another covered with welts and
blacked eyes. He'd actually taken Amy's loaded Polaroid, just
in case. That wasn't the case, of course. The house was tiny
and tidy, the kids cute, the woman nervous and strident (and
psycho, he sensed, although not the court kind) but neatly
groomed and very sincere. Clote hadn't lied. She didn't care
how much Clote was milking them for, the more the merrier,
the seventy-five a week she was getting would be fine and
enough; "what with" her bookkeeper's salary from the Chevrolet dealership and all, she'd "get by nicely, thank you." So
bribing her was out, although Harry made her the offer
anyhow. Reasoning moved her not, nor did sob-storying.
Defeated, he asked her, "Why, though? I mean, you're dealing
with people's lives here, lady. You're committing a crime."

She raised her voice to say, "Nothing compared to what's
been done to me! I'd love nothing better than to see a two-
faced bastard like that priest brought low. In public, for all to
see! Why *shouldn't* you and him pay through the nose for the
swill you dumped on me?"

"He never attacked you, Mrs. Carson."

"Vuz you dere, Charley?" There it was again. "And it's *Miz,*
not *Mrs.!*"

"You can go to jail for this!"

"Now you've threatened me. I'll remember that. And I'll tell
you, I'd rather be used his way than your way any day,
dreamboat. You want more coffee?"

He said yes, and crazily considered trying to seduce her.
Rattled, he couldn't figure if that would compromise her and
defuse it or only suck him in all the deeper. He doubted
whether he could do it anyhow (his empathy for Thomas
moving from 0 to 1.5). He remembered her body being
desirable enough, but she sent off a nunlike, almost queerlike
repellent that he'd never experienced from a woman before.
He figured there wasn't enough alcohol, grass, or imagination
in the world to let him raise it for her, and to end up as
another heap of limp laundry with her couldn't help anybody.

Her presence made him see her foot shooting into cock-and-balls. When he left, he felt the sense of escape skate over his skin. He didn't even bother trying Jody.

Clote phoned to say, "Noble try, Harry. Would've done the exact same in your place. Can't take a person's word for anything nowadays. You've got to be from Missouri every time out. Your check arrived just fine, by the way"—like a kid sent on a plane, Harry thought—"and the idea struck me—listen, anytime you maybe run up against a real dry spell . . . pay my bill first, Harry, heh, heh, heh." The guy had a terrific sense of humor. Harry hung up without answering.

He and Angie closed the Casablanca. It was still raining out. They'd parked in a slot near the MTA garage and reached the car before Angie realized she'd left her bag on her chair back. He jogged back to find the doors locked. He knocked but wasn't answered, though he could hear them cleaning up inside. He went out and back down to the wide delta where Mount Auburn Street opened into the west end of the Square, slogged through the mud of the back lot, and found the rear of the theater. He opened the door and . . . fell down the stairs inside the black hole. Slick, slip, and down, down he tumbled, grappling madly. The back of his head bounced off at least eight of the thirteen cement steps. The guy who helped him up inanely said, "You got no case, mac; this ain't no entrance, ya know!"

Seeing fireworks, Harry snarled, "Fuck you *and* your fucking lawyers, just let me get my goddamn *purse!*" The jerk didn't laugh, but suffering Harry had to, and then so did Angie, in the car. "But my God, babe, you could've killed yourself! You want to go in the Mount Auburn Emergency and have them check you out?"

"God, no, at this rate they'd find goddamn Parkinson's disease! Just get me home. Slow down, now. Use your mirrors. Watch your left, watch your right, watch your firing *line* . . . commence firing! Ha! Maggie's Drawers! You bolo, I bolo, Waldo bolo! Oh, Jesus, my aching head!

"I knew it, you're delirious. I think I'll take you to McLean or Westboro State!"

The scene they found at their kitchen table made Harry forget his pain temporarily and deflated Angie's merriment: Jake sat slumped, near tears, lower than they'd ever seen him. Constance sat near him, speaking words of comfort. Harry thought at once of last summer and prayed oh, no, not again; Jake had sat waiting for them, alone that time, to confess what they'd hear officially the next day, that he'd lifted a T-shirt from a shop up Porter Square and got nailed by the owner outside. He'd explained, his voice thick with disbelief, "I was with Doug. He said, 'Take it!' And I took it, shoved it up my shirt, and just kept going. I didn't even *think*, Dad! God! I told the guy this. He's gonna call you but says he won't press charges." As usual with Jake, his confession contained its own recognition of fault, regret, and firm purpose of amendment, making any sermon by Harry or Angie redundant and unnecessary. Jake's Luck. Again.

This time it wasn't himself; it was worse: betrayal. "After all he *told* me! To my face!" His patient-friend Doug had been arrested at his home three hours before. Called by his mother, the police had found a year's worth of larceny—stereo tapes from cars, knives, money, clothes still in their wrappers—and more, and worse—two shotguns, with boxes of cartridges—and the worst, in Jake's eyes: One of the guns belonged to Sammy Donovan's father, Sammy being Doug's only other buddy besides Jake. The kid was crestfallen and inconsolable. Harry and Angie listened and did not know what to say. Harry tried: "I guess he just couldn't help it, Jake. He was an accident looking for a place to happen. You did all you could. You did more than anyone else even tried to do for him. Maybe now he'll get the kind of help he needs."

Nearly losing his fight against the hurtful tears, the big, chesty boy covered his eyes with a tented hand and rasped bitterly, "He *lied* to me! He was lying all the time! He stole from Sammy's *father*, Dad! He *knows* they're poor! All he *had* was that stupid old busted gun! I feel like killing him! Oh, geez."

Angie knelt next to his beefy left shoulder and said, simply, "Cry, Jacob."

He obeyed, and she held him until he was finished. Then he went up to bed. Then Constance did. No music came on this night.

Harry, on his back beside Angie on hers, thought of the time he'd lain, still, in a bed beside some wife-looking actress for a public service commercial (which ran, about twice, after two in the morning) about marital troubles. The slim river of white space between their bodies had been lighted and panned in a down-shot to symbolize the unbridgable abyss, nine psychic miles to the inch. He moved now until his hips, thighs, and ankles were touching Angie's. She sighed. "Poor Jake."

"Yeah."

"I suppose he was asking for it."

"Aah, fucking Douglas."

"Poor Doug, too. Really poor Doug."

"Yeah."

"How's your head?"

"You forgot your purse on purpose. You never forget your purse. Did your mother give you that bag?"

"My mother never gives me anything."

"She gives you a C-note on your birthday."

"Besides that."

"Oh. Yeah, you're right. Bridget's a bitch."

"You're still the only one who can call her that."

She didn't mean "bitch." Angie's mother was Mum, Ma Duffy, Granma, or Mrs. to all concerned except Harry (and Martin, of course). When he'd been in service school, like homing pigeons they'd make the fourteen-hour run to Boston every chance they got. One Thanksgiving, after a night at Albie's, Harry had come reeling into the Duffys' city house at about four in the morning, three sheets to the wind. The mother was up to tuck the bird into the oven and he'd sung,

"Bridgie, me *darlin'!* Lemme do that for ya, Bridget, for the sake of the good Lord." She'd been charmed and told it a bit coyishly, and after that he'd felt encouraged to be the one who could call her by her name and did.

"You're no bitch, Ange," he said, "that was perfect with Jake. That cry was good for him."

"He feels like a man already."

"Don't let it bother you. Keep hugging him."

There was a long pause, which he didn't notice, before she said, "What do you mean, don't let it bother me?"

"I don't know, nothing. Just keep on hugging. Them all. All of us."

"Who'll hug me?"

"They all will. And I will."

"Talk's cheap."

They woke and talked again, unusually, in morning light, just before getting up, him starting it. "Hi. What are you thinking about?"

She blinked and rolled on her side toward him. It was still raining out. "Just. I hope ... I hope at least one of them, sometime, stops to think and figure out how old or young we were when something happened."

It took him awhile to register it; something, maybe dreams, was still hurtling softly back and forth behind his eyes. "Oh, I know what you mean. Yeah. I remember finally realizing that. The one time my father really spanked me ... I ever tell you?"

"No."

"It was late at night. I was about eight. Well, I was nine. My mother was ironing, and she was teasing me somehow, really rankling me, and I was playing with this fat, roundish airplane that I really loved. It was made out of sawdust or something, before plastic, and I pitched the fucking thing against the wall, blasting it to smithereens, *just* as my father walked in the back door. Ten or eleven at night. He'd been working since seven in the morning. I don't know when, years later, it hit me: He was only twenty-nine!"

She was half smiling.

He sighed. "Oh, Christ, I did it again, didn't I. *Me* again."

"That's okay. That is, exactly, what I was thinking about. You always assumed he was old, but he was young."

"I'm sorry anyhow, Angie. How old was your mother?"

"Thirty-eight to forty-two."

"When she what?"

"Made me wrap the Christmas presents. I wrapped everybody's, including my own. Then, every Christmas morning, she and I had this terrific fight. Because I refused to open mine."

His head had begun to ache again. "Holy Christ," he said, "that's not like my story at all, is it. She ... mustn't have stopped to think, Ange."

"She was old enough to *know*, man."

"Jesus. Well, she, she maybe did just as many good, kind things just as ... blindly." He'd almost said *innocently*.

"Yeah," Angie said, "she must have. Do coffee and get the train rolling for me, will you? They've all got exams."

Up, his head improved. He threw on his robe, stepped into the hall, yelled, "Let's go, hit the deck!" and ducked into the bathroom while he still had the chance, thinking, Shit, even teasing's some kind of recognition.

Constance set the table. Jake fried bacon. Amy flipped pancakes. Dennis poured juice. Kate put the lunches, made the night before, out in a row along the counter, with milk money from the fruit bowl of dimes and pennies. Harry poured coffee. Buttering toast beside him, sleep-paled Angie muttered, "By the way. Financially we've only got three months anyhow. On the outside."

He didn't have to ask, "Are you sure?" He merely exhaled, like a football punctured, "Oh, my God."

Every fifteen minutes a pink couple copulating standing shot out of the Alpine Tavern's clock to the sound of a wolf whistle. Earlier, Albie had cracked, "The clods, it should go *cuckold! cuckold!*" and Harry had laughed. They were drinking beer, surrounded by loud Chelsea waterfront workers, waiting for Mike Duffy to come back. It was just six thirty, the Saturday of the anniversary party. Mike had left them only a few minutes before to drive his wagon down to the deserted-looking warehouse at the dead end of Winnissimmit Street, nearby the James S. Munro Shipyard and Drydock. Mike had exited melodramatically: "I go now, and where I go, none may follow!" He was going to collect the "discount" color TV from his "man." If all went well, they would arrive with it about an hour after the start of the party, which was being held at Harry's house, chosen for its size and central location. Albie's Rena had the senior Duffys at the Saturday evening mass at St. Peter's. Afterward she would "stop off at Pat's just for a minute" to get something, and—surprise! The TV would be a surprise, too. They had had to present the trip to Ireland openly and two months earlier, so that Bridget and Martin could make the necessary preparations. They were leaving in a week, on August 1.

Albie had just been rather surprised himself. The minute Mike was gone, Harry blurted most of the Thomas-Clote mess to him. Albie was stunned purple and ordered a shot of Old Thompson. "Jesus, Tro! You're sucking me into something, right? Hold on, now, I'll figure it, you bastard."

"I wish I was kidding."

"*Thomas?* Never. Never. Not Thomas."

"Yeah, Thomas."

"Holy Jesus in heaven."

Harry hoped Albie wouldn't dwell too long on that part of it, knowing well how deeply offended Albie could be by such rough matters. Morally, he had sensibilities delicate as Balik china. Yet Albie was the sole person Harry could tell this to. He added, "I know you had to let Rena in on the accident fandango that time, Alb, but *please,* on this one, huh?"

"You're having me. You're setting me up."

"No, I mean it, bud."

"Oh, my *God,* Tro!"

"Yeah. The Catholic boy's nightmare come true, huh?"

Albie reflexively giggled a little, dropping his head in shame and unavoidable mirth. He had the good stage actor's slightly bucked teeth. "Oh, geez. You shitbirds! You shitbirds!" He was still blushing darkly.

"What am I gonna *do*, Alb?" He hadn't included the Flash Gordon deal; Albie would've died.

"Shaz Mayo?"

"Yeah, I did call Shaz, finally. I didn't *tell* him any of it, just could he get me a fix on this Clote fucker."

"Did he?"

"I don't know yet. I just got hold of him a couple of days ago. He'll be there tonight, so I'll see."

Albie's next thought was: "I got three grand in the bank. It's yours."

"No. I love ya for that, but all that'd do is break you and only postpone things. No, I don't want money from you, Alb. I don't know what I want. Advice, I guess. Or just for you to know, because I can't dump it on anyone else." He was hating this part of it.

"We can hit Mike."

"For the Canon? Bullshit."

"Tell 'im it's something else. Well, it is, too, isn't it? It's for Herself and the Old Man."

"Yeah, it is. But since when does *Mike* have any money?"

"Just eat it, Tro, like I am. Mike does, that's all. He's fucking *rolling* in bucks. He's smart enough not to show it, that's all. We don't ask."

"Well, you bastards keep *some* secrets, anyhow. But no—I can't have somebody else pick up *this* tab. For your parents or not."

Albie downed the OT, washed it down with beer, signaled for another, and said to the glass rings near his nose, "Christ, I could fucking shoot you both in the head for this."

"Just shoot me. I'll get Thomas."

The relief Harry felt from laying the confidence on Albie

was offset equally by the regret that set in: Albie would suffer over this now. He and Albie went a long way back and deep. If Flash was his closest friend in the escape-from-square way, Albie was it in the totally square way. When he was first pursuing Angie, Albie'd been the brother in the Army, away in Korea. He came home and went through college in the same class as Harry, taking the same courses, sharing the passion for acting. The Angie connection helped, but they would have clicked without it. Albie was the one who, in freshman English, recited Edgar Allan Poe in Peter Lorre's voice, *Childe Harold* as John Wayne, and pieces of *Paradise Lost* as Mae West. For the four years, Harry and Albie spent more time in the Dramatic Society's rooms and literary magazine's offices than in class. Albie wrote sad, poignant poetry about Korean peasants and devastated landscapes, as well as tragicomic pieces from a soldier's point of view, like the one describing the GI with his drawers dropped, crouched to crap on a black winter night near his bunker: At the crucial moment, the entire sky suddenly lit up with flares, "like a night game at Fenway," and mortar rounds began bursting everywhere. "It scared the shit out of him, and also the fear. . . . He composed his hilarious obituary *(doing his duty),* dressed, and ran for his rifle, ready at last to release its safety and squeeze off rounds at other life." Harry wrote stories about sex and love, gang fights, and working for Woolworth's.

They drank beer and talked drama at the Molly Waldo and at the One Gentleman in Brighton, where old movies were projected through the din and the moving bodies to show against the wide white back wall, film dialogue mixing with real sounds, small young men talking over giant orange Steve Cochrans and Edmund O'Briens. Harry and Albie worked out a fistfight routine that only previous observers could tell was faked. Both were athletic then and foolish. They pulled it off for disruption in the cafeteria, for amusement in a Junior Show skit, and to regain an audience hissing and leaving a production of *Life with Father,* they ad-libbed it in the second act,

Father (Albie) finally and prematurely getting his knocks from his eldest son (Harry). The coarse, collegiate audience loved it. The director and other players didn't and had Harry and Albie banished to backstage chores for the rest of that season. Repentant Albie did his penance; Harry quit. But the following year he went out for *Detective Story* and made it. That was the difference between them. Albie played the lead, and Harry didn't, but didn't care either.

Albie had switched to the Naval Reserve and after graduation went to OCS, then on duty as an ensign. Harry went into the Army. They met back in Boston four years later. Harry and Angie went with Rena to watch Albie's debut. He was MC and comic for the Winchell Shoe Company's Annual Christmas Party at the Blue Marlin roadhouse on Route 1 in Saugus. Albie bombed dismally. He did an impeccable impersonation of Adlai Stevenson, for instance, which his wife, sister, and buddy (now in-law) marveled at and applauded. The rest of the packed club might have liked it, too, had any of them ever heard of Mr. Stevenson.

The band screwed Albie as well. They'd been unavailable for rehearsal, and Albie'd had to try to wing it on no more than a quick talk-through before the gig. He could do Perry Como, Dean Martin, and Tony Bennett perfectly, but only for the *first two* lines of "Fly Away with Me," "That's Amore," and "Be My Love." In each case the band went on with the whole song before starting the next, leaving Albie aground on his own voice. Harry felt sure that Albie's flawless Ed Sullivan, especially his Trigger Burke set ("Would you please stand and spray the audience for us, Trigger?") would have saved him and carried him through the night, but Albie never got to it. The rye-and-gingered, Seven-and-Sevened shoeworkers began jeering during the musical numbers, and Albie didn't take it. After failing to get the band to abort it altogether and failing also to turn it into an awful-on-purpose routine, like Jackie Vernon's trumpeter, he turned hard and still. And when none of the hecklers accepted his invite to "come up here and say that!" he tossed them all the finger atop a cross-arm, walked off the dance floor and out of the club—and out of show business.

Albie went teaching, and Harry went to New York. Harry remembered Albie's saying that the happiest day of his adult life happened the morning he walked into his high school English classroom and saw printed on the blackboard: AND NOW, THE ALBIE DUFFY SHOW! Albie loved the stuff and loved kids and kept old needs nourished by directing student productions and appearing in local community theater plays. Harry never thought to envy Albie until after he'd come back to Prospect and felt the Liberty Square station run dry under and around him. While teachers remained at low wages, they had begun receiving all sorts of recompensatory benefits, from the nine-month work year to tenure, to the vertical-horizontal, longevity-academics monkey bar of assured advancement, to paid retirement and insurance goodies and all the rest of it. When, then, the salaries themselves started to catch up with those established by industries, schools of education got very popular, and the majority of experienced teachers found themselves deprived of their "poorly paid" cloak. It didn't soften parent-teacher relations. Reports of drivers ed instructors pulling down twenty-two five weren't swallowed bonelessly by layman getting laid off. Demands for some system of performance-evaluation kept school board meetings abristle with hostility. Harry knew Albie was truly dedicated and excellent, so ribbed him only gently about what a cushy ripoff the job of public school teacher had become. Albie never defended himself or the profession. Even when they spoke seriously together and Harry would spout some version of his risk thesis ("Pay should be appropriate to the amount of balls put on the block. A guy puts his whole works out there? Lettim make a *million*. But if he keeps 'em locked away safe? Fuck 'im—minimum wage, man!") Albie would ruefully agree.

The ironic fact was that the better paid Albie had become, the less happy he grew. He was now head of the English

Department at huge Deverton High. He had two master's and some fourteen years in and was doing as okay as anyone with an 1890's brood could do in the 1970's by trying to make an honest living, and by staying in the Reserves. And he was virtually unfireable. ("Oh, don't be so sure, Tro. One of these days I'm bound to be caught with my hand up a freshman.They don't keep quiet for A's and Milky Ways anymore, you know!") Yet he was visibly showing more and deeper wrinkles of distress and frustration, quite separate from those cut by age. Asked, he'd tell Harry: He wasn't teaching enough anymore, and he missed it. He couldn't find anybody worthy of hiring, and even if he could, he couldn't fire any of the "cretins I've got, to make room for some good ones! Phony bastards, they teach one year twenty times and think they're doing the job! The kids are bored fucking senseless by everything but the videotape and movies, and these shitheads blame Vietnam and rock music! And honest to God, the young, new ones are no better than the old, dead ones. Theory, theory, theory, a kid could poop his pants and they'd never smell it!" Albie had gone to extremes before taking the administrative promotion. Desperate to keep his show alive, he'd first taken only "the geniuses, the whiz kids." Then he'd gone the other way, to "the jocks and eight balls and retards." Then he'd tried his all-blacks experiment and chuckled bleakly when he told it: "Christ, I did everything but wear a comb in my hair! Spent ten weeks just explaining *The Nigger of the Narcissus* wasn't racist! And you know where it got us? I'll tell ya! It got us a brand-new course in the curriculum the next year—*remedial Swahili!*"

Harry loved and was worried for solvent, secure alter-ego Albie, so felt all the guiltier for having to lay the Thomas thing on his shoulders the night at the Alpine in Chelsea. He hoped his blurting out of the Thomas-Clote affair wasn't the only cause of Albie's belting down the OT's and beers. He knew Albie had taken to stashing a pint under the driver's seat of his Volkswagen bus and chose to believe it was only to help him

keep peace and appearances up at home with Rena. Who wa
lovely and salt of the earth but, to Harry's way of thinkin
anyhow, rather strict and hyperdecorous. Albie did his drink
ing at Mike's and Harry's, at the Navy, and at the Deverto
Legion Hall: Children must be heard and not see anything no
strictly proper. Harry permitted himself to make no judgment
about Albie's deal with life but did think it would at leas
make pretty difficult any Future Kid Talk, if Albie wer
considering ever having one.

What Albie had apparently been considering now wa
Harry's situation. He squinted ahead toward the busy registe
and said, "How much satisfaction you getting out of it, Tro?"

"That's really funny, Alb."

"I mean it. You *like* it, right? Let's skip the paining-you
part—and I'm sure it is . . . but I know you, you bastard, you'r
doing it again, right?"

"What?"

"The more than the next guy. The more than anyone else
Gonna pull it *all* off, aren't ya? Antihero as hero. Not knockin
it, by the way. Just asking."

Harry said *Yup!* to himself, and to the bartender: "Have a
shot of Cutty and two more drafts here, pal. Another OT,
too."

"Hand it over, Tro," Albie said, "it's family."

"I'm not family?"

"Mike and I'll handle it." He'd either not heard Harry or
ignored him.

"That isn't why I told you, Alb."

"So what?"

"Oh. I get it. You're pissed at me! I got the blessed fucking
Canon into it, right?"

"Well, you got him out of it anyhow. We'll take it from
here. Where the hell've you been getting two bills a week, by
the way?"

"How's Mike flush all of a sudden?"

"Friday night bingo."

"Me too."

"Oh, Jesus!" Albie crumbled and lit a smoke from Harry's pack. "Why this? Why now?"

"Nobody's sorrier than I am."

"It sucks. It's really cheap and shitty, Tro."

"You had to be there."

"And Thomas doesn't know. Well, you're right. I guess he can't know, can he? The papers'd fucking love it, wouldn't they?"

"That's what I'm assuming."

"Can we buy somebody there?"

"Lemme clue you, Alb—start thinking that and you end up thinking murder, believe me. I've been there."

"I always thought Thomas was *stronger* than—"

"He's human."

"He's a goddamn *priest!*"

"Ah. . . ."

"I always thought you were above this kind of smut, Tro."

Harry let the Cutty sit untouched and sipped his beer. Realizing what he'd just done to Albie, he didn't need any burning shots of whiskey to snap him to. The thing was, he had already decided exactly what he was going to do. It would be hard enough to pull off by itself. Albie and Mike wanting to shoulder the payoff part would only complicate things all the more . . . or simplify them, if he wanted to look at it that way and let them do it. He escaped to the men's room. At the urinal he discovered that he'd done it again, worn Jake's skivvies instead of his own. They fitted about the same, except he couldn't work his cock out through the smaller fly flap. He went into the toilet stall, dropped his jeans and shorts and peed, feeling ridiculous. The graffiti mocked him too: A pencil had printed, "Kiss my asshole." A ball-point had replied, "Pick your spot, you're all asshole!" He wanted to be out of the stall, the john, the bar, out of Chelsea, out of it all and someplace else, fast. He returned to his barstool. Albie had quaffed his shot of Cutty. Albie looked at him, then away and said, "Where the hell's Mike all this time anyhow?"

"Maybe he got nailed."

"For what?"

"Come off it, Alb," Harry sighed gently, "we're all accessories already anyhow. Why play dumb now?"

Harry knew the right time to make his move and waited for it.

When they pulled in from Chelsea, Jake was on the front porch, sneaking a cigarette. He lumbered down to help them with the huge crate, getting under the fourth corner. Mike had had the thing gift-wrapped, a giant red ribbon taped to the top. Fast Facey held the front door open for them. The house was packed and roaring with old people, mostly, Harry noticed, women. Angie, Annie, Albie's Rena, Mike's Nance, Sister Theresa (Ragass) and Mickey up from New York were waitresses, flashes of color dashing through the mob of darkly dressed widows. Co-guest of honor Bridget was presiding from the kitchen in one of Angie's aprons, tiny, silver-haired, pigeon-breasted; doves for hands, fluttering, flying, lighting on chair backs and knife handles. Martin, the father, stood in his shirt sleeves amid the ten or so men—his surviving cronies, the Canon, Big Doc up from Baltimore, no Shaz Mayo yet, Uncle Phil, the fire chief. Hawky, wrench-handed Martin appeared to still be a large, rangy man as tall as his sons, but he no longer was; age was diminishing him, to scale. The phlegmy voice still rang strong, though, and now, at the sight of the Gift at the door, it cut across the bowling alley rumblings close around him: "Ho! So that's where yez been! Bridgie, come quick! They've bought us a coffin!" And whirling on the stopped Annie and Sister Theresa: "For Christ's sake quit mopin' there like lamps and get some glasses goin' in here; they've been workin' hard, and it's stunned them!"

They manhandled it awkwardly into the living room and
eased it down to the floor in the center of the rug. Martin
followed, leading his men. Some old ladies strained to their feet
and crabbed forward, forming a ring of wide eyes and mouths
making O's. Others stayed in their seats, crowing out, "To
your left, Minnie, let a body *see*, would you?" The mother was
let scurry through to the front rank beside Martin. Harry left
Albie and Mike to man the box, drifting back to join Angie in
the doorway. Father Thomas and Annie appeared by the Gift,
all grins of generosity. Mike said, "Well, go ahead—unwrap it,
Ma."

"Oh, no—you do it."

Mike detached the ribbon bow and passed it to her, then he
and Albie stripped off the white paper, ripped the tape down
the top, opened the flaps, tore down the corners, and pulled
the sides away, removing the slabs of styrofoam. Mike sidemouthed to the Father, "You better like it, Deddy, there's no
taking it back!" and everyone laughed. Carried away, Mike
bent to one end of the console and yelled to Albie, "Let's go—
up with it, Alb, give 'em all a good look at it!" Albie complied,
and in one heave the two of them had the great cherrywood
set held high.

"Oh, it's a *Zenith*, Margie!"

"'Tis a *color!*"

Martin boomed, amused, "Ha, now ye can talk to yer Bruins
and they'll *hear* ye, Bridgie!"

Temples bulging, Albie hissed, "Get the *legs* somebody!"

Thomas frisked through the heaps of paper and cardboard.
"My God, there aren't any!"

"Oh, Christ!" Mike groaned.

"*It's fine!*" the mother sang swiftly. "Get the coffee table
under, someone! It'll be just the porfect height. We got won to
home the same height!"

"Nah, here they are!" Fast came forward with the legs.
"They were in the foam."

"Well, gettem *on*, for. . . ." Albie's end was lowering.

Fast dropped to his knees and started looking for the screwholes. Mike huffed, "We'll never make it! *Fast*, Fast!"

"Jesus God!" Martin bellowed and grabbed a corner. Thomas moved to the other corner with Albie. "Hup!" the father commanded, and all four lifted and pressed the set up over their heads on the ends of their arms. It swayed.

"I can't look!" Angie moaned. Harry bolted through the crowd and got under it with them. Fast was spinning the legs in furiously.

"On the bias!" Martin shouted. "On the bias!"

Annie bounced on the sofa seats, Insta-Matic cubes popping merrily. "Honest to God? Talk about your Polish jokes! Fast, hold the legs still and let them spin around you!"

Fast finally got the last leg in and they lowered the shining present to the floor, stepping it off the box and papers, which Angie and Mickey scooped up and away. Guests and family cheered and clapped hands. Drinks were brought to the men. Martin winked at Harry. "Ye nearly had a houseful of tubes for a minute there," and to Angie, "Get me a ball of the real stuff this time, ye'd better. Goddamned idgits." Real stuff meant two fingers of John Jameson. That would be all he'd have for the night, and wouldn't normally have taken that much, even for an anniversary. He'd quit more than twenty years before, sometime in his fifties. Before that he'd been the inevitable heavy boozer, all right, but with a style all his own. He went on benders the same way he lived and worked: totally, but organized.

A man for whom work *was* life, the idea of vacations had no meaning. He took his times off twice a year, once in the winter, once in the summer. Summers, after the forties anyhow, they always managed to take a rental, usually at Hampton Beach, New Hampshire, a couple times down the South Shore. The father would drive them there, see they were settled, then go home and hit his own kind of beach, a one- or two-week solitary, inhouse jag, starting with shots-and-beers, peaking on the straight hard stuff, then coming out of it with plain beers. What he did on these summer binges nobody could say. They only witnessed his winter sprees. Angie recalled them as "funny and terrible ... mostly terrible." He'd sing a lot and tell them stories and go around handing out dollars left and right (followed a step behind by Herself, collecting them back). But then he would show "the black look," and there would be awful daytime silences, as he'd sit just brooding and drinking alone, and hideous nighttime sounds of bitter quarreling coming from the kitchen or their bedroom. Cannily, he'd often time his "vacations" to follow a wedding, graduation, christening, ordination, or like party event. One year, nobody could say why, he broke his rule and went drinking one midweek morning after working the night shift at the pumping station. Driving home that night, he smashed into another car and, like Harry years later, lost his license. It was Angie's senior year in high school; she'd just got her license and spent her seventeenth year driving him wherever he wanted to go. When Martin Duffy wasn't working for the city, he was working for himself, caring for the houses he owned and rented, mostly to Harvard and MIT graduate students.

Angie got to know the quickest routes to and the insides of every plumbing supply, paint, roofing, scrap metal, and used car parts outfit from Watertown to East Somerville and became a crack city driver for life. She mostly resented, partly enjoyed the enforced experience. She missed a lot of private time but gained hours of being alone with her father, something few of the others ever did. Thomas, Albie, and Mike all got to help him take out and put in hot-water boilers and to shingle roofs of three-story buildings, but to hear them recall it, it was never being with him in any soft or personal sense. Of course, even Angie had to admit that she'd always been a special child to Martin: Bridget had been carrying her when pneumonia took their first girl, Sheila, at age two. For eight months Martin walked in snow or sun to her little grave in the Mount Auburn Cemetery, four miles each way. He stopped only after Angie was born. After his accident he stopped drinking and never started again, not counting the sometime ball of the real stuff at crucial moments within major occasions. Harry had known the story before his own mimicking of it and still wasn't sure exactly why Martin hadn't just gone driving licenseless, or why he, himself, had resumed drinking so relatively soon after his own frightening accident. Because he was no more a son to Martin Duffy than Angie was?

Or maybe because he had less fear in him than the Old Man did. Or maybe just because things like going and staying on the wagon were easier when you had made it into your fifties, and pressures were less, and you perhaps had got a larger view of time and life—large enough maybe even to be able to start making out actual patterns to events, if such cycles and reassuring parabolas and all that weren't just old survivors' pipe dreams. In any case, Harry never drank like that anyhow. And even if Constance or Jake had a driver's license, he knew he'd never make a kid chauffeur his ass around for a year, whether it could pass as a personal thing or not. He'd rather risk getting nailed. And why should he be comparing himself with the Old Man anyhow, much as he admired him? Besides holding Angie special, he and Martin had only one thing in common as far as Harry was concerned, and that was being the Beginner of something, not somebody second or seventh from the top and down the line.

As he saw it, Martin's sons were, to one degree or another, stymied by their very awe of the swath their Old Man had cut from poor Cork City to the present. He hoped that neither Jake, Dennis, nor any of his own girl-persons would ever be so blocked (if he even survived, of course), but if so, it'd have to be their own problem. He sure as hell never intended a Do Like Me in either word or act and didn't think Martin ever had either. This was the main connection Harry acknowledged between himself and Mr. Duffy. And it diluted a bit the shame and dread he felt, for doing what he was going to do later.

In the meantime, it pleased him to witness the sprawling

rooms of his house teeming with Duffys, friends, and relations. Tomorrow would be time enough to worry about getting the ark of the TV set to the parents' house. Amy, Dennis, and Kate were sleeping over with Flash and Legs in Marblehead. Constance, Jake, and Albie's two oldest, Buddy and Sheila, were even now being marched by Bridget through the mandatory hot oven of introductions to the older generations. They'd soon be excused to go to the movies, then back to Albie's house for the night. Through the melee he suddenly felt Thomas watching him watching and, to avoid catching his eye, plunged forward to make his own required tour of hellos. He started with the aunts, Martin's two surviving sisters, Fran and Louise. Fran was married to fireman Phil. Louise, unmarried, lived with them. Now heartbreakingly wizened, male-voiced, and sprouting whiskers from the hormone treatments she was receiving, Fran before cancer had been always a hale, strapping, working OR nurse at Mass General, for years the family seat of medical wisdom and advice, quick to diagnose symptoms for everybody, except, it turned out, herself. Like Phil and all others, Harry behaved as if he were still seeing her original, undoomed self. She said his children were beautiful and that he had to bring them all to let her see them more often, and he promised he would.

Louise looked more like a sister of Bridget than of Martin, was petite, wore pastel toppers and smelled of lilac, was a successful dressmaker for Commonwealth Avenue stores, and was known for her rather daft ways. Upon first seeing black-crowned, coal-browed Amy, she beamed. "Won't she be so *light,* though!" Somebody earlier had remarked that he'd told Louise the party was on Friday night to be sure she'd make it Saturday. Louise hugged Harry and said she thought he'd been wonderful on *Starsky and Hutch* the other night. Farther down the couch Bridget's chum Mrs. Flynn, who had midwifed all the Duffys but Mickey, left talk of her Brendan, dead fifteen years, to tell Harry no, she *didn't* like living out in "the sticks with those two"—her daughters, one divorced thirty years before, one widowed just a year ago—"for pity's sake, you can sit at the winda for months and not see one kid go by!" No square to walk to, no church "without aching in an' out uv some *car,* always dependin' on what someone else feels like doin' for ya at the time or doesn't! Believe me, make me a free spirit and I wouldn't move again in a fit!"

Followed by another pair of sisters, Mary Hennessy and Dotty Capabianco from the Duffys' old neighborhood. Dotty was the younger at seventy-eight and called "bullying" what Mary referred to as "watching out for." They'd lived alone together for more than twenty-five years now, since Mary's Edmond hit the third rail at the Sullivan Square transit station. Mary was still a housekeeper for people on Brattle Street, not far from where she was sitting now. Dotty's stroke had made her quit practical nursing some four years before. The two put up a friendly front for Harry, but he knew they weren't speaking. Seems "after two years of watching her creep off upstairs every blessed fifteen minutes of her life until you were sick with worry for her," it was discovered that Dotty's "kidneys were as healthy as the next person's!" And what she was really doing was "sneaking smokes! Carrying snipped-in-half Kents in her hankie! Covering the stink with Air-Wick! And wouldn't it be wonderful to wake up some morning with the whole house burned to a crisp around you! That's the thanks you get. It'd serve her right."

The women. Listening, smiling, shaking liver-spotted, cool hands, catching odd sour smells among the flowery scents, Harry had to wonder, Who had the men been? Why'd they die? To hear tell, they'd been champions all, the best ever to walk God's green earth, *good to me every day of his life, God rest his soul,* oh, *how I miss him still,* hardest worker ever born, generous to a fault, the kids and me first, every time, never a thought for himself. . . . Harry couldn't help it, he had a vision of gangs of rough, cap-wearing men lining the edges of the clouds, throwing cross-arms down at all the legions of women still sitting and feeling the wet heat of tea on their tongues for lo, all these many years. He didn't resent or fear them exactly, but did have to marvel at the phenomenon of them—what did they live on? How had they raised families, as so many of them had, without their men? Could he, Albie, Mike, Fast all vanish tomorrow and not worry about their wives and children? The verdict filling his house, chatting, eating sandwiches and potato salad, fruit cake and soda bread *voraciously* from narrow laps, seemed to be in: *They'd get by, somehow.* Or did the women envy the men their deaths, too? But then, on his way, with some relief, toward Big Doc on the edge of the men, his scanning picked up the young women—Angie laughing, Annie moving, Mickey talking—then he was detoured by Mrs. Scanlon to meet a new face, her niece from New Mexico, Gerry, twenty, and in her eyes he saw her creamy breasts bared and he thought, What else but desire causes such a sweet feeling?

"Father Tim, how are you?"

"Harry! I thought you were avoiding me. Get down here, where I won't have to read your lips." The elder priest's feet barely reached the floor. He had one Peterson pipe cooling in the ashtray next to his easy chair, one freshly lighted in his teeth. A rosy, ribald elf, he was called Uncle, but it was honorary; he was somehow distantly related to both Martin and Bridget. The true bond was, he had married them. "It's not really their fiftieth, you know," he said like some dark secret.

"I know. But the family decided . . . well, you know—another five years?"

"Wise decision. You're aging well, Mr. Barrymore, you must still be liking the common labor?" his blue eyes cracking small whips.

Harry laughed. "I get outside a lot."

"About five years now? That's three more than I gave it, Harry."

"I hear you're retiring again this year, Father."

"You swine. But it *is*, it's the same story all over again—I want to, but they won't let me!" It was true; his seminary students had protested against it every year since '67. He wasn't above taking some pride in it.

"And you're going to be official host and guide for the Grand Tour, Father? I'll believe it when I see Martin get on the plane."

"Oh, he's resigned to it now. *'For her sake,'* of course. He'll be all right, as I've been telling him for years. As soon as he sees it's not all the dank poverty he imagines, he'll have a hell of a time. And to put the matter straight, my lad, I'll be *at home* there, as usual, for the whole summer. Going tomorrow from Logan, in fact. But my running-about days are long since over. A couple jaunts up to Trinity, on business, of course, is it for me in the traveling department." Then the first shoe: "They'll hardly be abandoned to their own devices, however. God forbid." Puff, puff.

"Come on. What's that mean?"

"Well, I'm not sure I'm at liberty to—"

"You want more Chivas in that glass or not?"

In the confessional whisper: "Father Thomas will be accompanying them. And Father Mayo will be accompanying him."

"Well, I'll be damned."

"Not with any luck," he said with a twinkle and put forth his empty glass.

Harry ran into Fast at the door. "Hey, Tro, hi. Listen, I want to talk to you."

"Hi, kid. I'm fetching for Big Doc, come on." Lately Harry thought Fast was always looking as if he were still in some airport or hotel lobby. It wasn't just his Johnny Carson clothes either. He and Fast were friends, but with an edge. He said, "Fast? You're looking kind of *anonymous,* you know? What's the story, you go with the CIA without telling us, or what?"

Fast gave him his dry cackle-laugh, lips squinting like his eyelids. "Not for what they're paying, pal. No—I heard Shell's opening a huge new station right near you, up the artery. That can't be helping your situation any, huh?"

Harry poured scotch. "That's the good news, right? What's the bad?"

"Oh, hey, I didn't mean. . . ."

"That's okay. In fact, between you and me as outsiders here"—he lowered his voice—"they offered me the franchise on it."

"You gotta take it, right?"

"Right . . . but I didn't. I said no."

"You're crazy. Christ, what're you going to do? Oh, you're shitting me, right?"

"Right. See you." He grinned and split. Fast was well-meaning, but so damned literal-minded Harry could rarely resist double-talking him. In this instance he did it just to avoid the sore truth. He gave Father Tim his drink and, again pretending not to see Thomas eyeing him, headed back to fix himself one; he suddenly felt real need for a belt or two. Big Mike, well on his way, was regaling the kitchen crowd with one of his Odes to Beer.

Once more Fast spotted him and came over. "I've got some news, Tro. Not for release yet, though, huh?"

Harry grinned. "Never thought *you'd* turn Duffy on me, Fast."

"Well, this isn't secret, it just isn't certain yet—I think they'll be moving us back to Oklahoma City fairly soon."

That took his breath. "You call *me* crazy. You know what your *phone bill's* gonna be from out there, man? Thought Annie hated it out there!"

"It's *up*, Tro—what am I going to do, not go?"

"Wow." He drank from the martini he'd made. "Geez, you know what you're doing, though, bud? I know her *good soldier* speech, but you sure she's really up to it? She won't go hitting the brown Hi-C again, will she?"

Fast's look betrayed his own ambivalence—something new in the guy. "It's either go or nothing, though."

"You mean out?"

"Times are tough. We're consolidating all over. Nobody's inexpendable."

"You've busted your chops for that tightassed company, Fastie! *Jesus*, man! Can't you see what a cliché pinball machine you're on? Don't you ever even read a magazine? Get the fuck out of it, kid!"

"What else is there?"

Harry let his eyes meet Fast's. "I don't know. That's the goddamn problem, isn't it?"

"What are *you* going to do, Tro?"

"I don't know, Fast," he said levelly into the younger man's suspicious gaze, meaning *I do know, but I'm afraid to say it until I start doing it because if I do, it's liable to jinx it and leave me truly not knowing what to do!* Giving him a hint perhaps of the notions behind the Duffys' penchant for secret-keeping. Besides, he knew that telling Fast couldn't in any way help the man deal with his own predicament, which, in a sense, suddenly seemed worse than Harry's own. Seeing one big company as being the same as any other, he figured Fast had choices, options, alternatives to decide among, which had to be very hard to do. Whereas Harry, having refused the franchise offer, had no choices left at all. Not counting *sink or swim.* He raised his glass to Fast. "Fuck it, let's get happy. Bartender! We'll take a case of do or die here, please!"

"Dewar's?" Fast laughed quizzically.

"Oh, Jesus, where's Albie? Later, Fasto. You should go talk to Thomas—ask him how come he gets to go with the old people to Ireland."

Sailing through the dining room, he was intercepted by Angie. "Hey, not getting too wrecked there, are you? Isn't supposed to be a wake, remember."

"I'm okay. Getting kind of too keyed up again, though, you know?"

"I know. Hang in, though, babe, all right? There'll be less

chaos when it's just family. The others are starting to go already. Go see Mickey, she'll cheer you up, she's in great shape. Have you talked to Ragass yet?"

"No. She was—"

"Well, don't then. There's nothing downer than a bagged nun."

"Are you kidding? Theresa? I did notice the companion with her this time doesn't have a mustache, but don't tell me they're allowed to—"

"It isn't too funny, really. She's very morose about something."

"Think I'll go see Mickey." He found her in the TV room, and she looked anything but cheering; she was with Sister Theresa. Seeking deliverance, he arrived as deliverer, helping Mickey's face find, in a blink, its normal sparkle.

"*There's* my lover man!" she sang, throwing arms around his neck and white-blond hair into his face and whispering, "Be funny—fast!"

Laughing, he set her down, sorry to relinquish her marvelous breasts, and stepped gently to the pretty brunette in the short head veil, white blouse, and navy blue skirt two inches higher than Mickey's. He pecked her cheek. "Hi, Sister Rags, it's great to see you again."

"Hello, Harry." Theresa smiled and held fast to his hand. He left it in her grip. Sister Theresa took after Aunt Fran, the big frame, the high cheekbones, the large teeth; she had the Duffy females' startling eyes, except hers were a different, darker blue. They were filled with water right now, exaggerating their size. She looked like a person stopped on a city sidewalk, trying to get directions without asking.

He said, "How are you, Sister, are you all right?" He could feel the tenseness of her whole body through her fingers and squeezed her hand softly to try to help relax it.

Standing close, Mickey said, "He's all laughs, isn't he, Rags?"

Theresa smiled again. "Harry's always my good friend."

She was a bit blitzed, he thought, but hardly bagged. The tenseness coming through her hand was fascinating him, like a revelation, like some previously taken-for-granted fabric being touched for the first time and being found unique, almost exotic, yet alarmingly familiar. He felt in direct contact, for the first time, with ... with a life-force of some kind, or rather some unrelaxable degree of speed at which that life-force was accelerating—it was one with his own, he realized and wondered, Was that what was driving all of them? Jesus, no wonder they were all such drinkers and smokers, breeders and phone callers, movers, laughers, and worriers. Holding her hand, Theresa reminded him of Jake; the dynamo's casing was thicker, that's all; these ones only appeared to be calm, from the outside. He said, "You've lost a lot of weight, you look fabulous. How's school?"

"Oh, it's fine."

"You still playing the guitar?"

"Oh, yes."

"What have you been reading?" As she told him—their main connection over the years had always been books; she drank and ate them—he was amused again, watching her teeth as she talked, at her semibrogue. She was born here and lived away from her parents for years with a not particularly Irish order of teaching nuns in a WASC-Jewish suburb, yet there it was. Only Mike in booze, story, or song ever tripped into anything approximating it. He found it charming in Theresa, but where did she get it? Lord, how much of the rap could heredity take anyhow?

Relieved but bored, Manhattan Mickey cut in, "Say, speaking of books, did you two see my newest? Angie said I *had* to do this for you, Tro. Somebody was asking, you know—how does a sweet, innocent, single little honey like me go unmolested in Rape City, right?" She talked and swallowed as if she were chewing gum even when she wasn't. "Go ahead—ask me! Like how do I go up my street alone at two in the morning?"

"Mickey, how—"

"Okay, I'll show ya. I have two tricks. Here's the first." She ran all the way back to the far end of the dining room and returned to them, walking like a grotesquely maimed cripple, dragging her left leg straight out behind her, a tow-haired Quasimodo with one arm crooked up under her chin.

Both Rags and Harry roared. "My God, what's the *other* one?"

"Oh, that's my best. You know how you'll see some poor clunk on a bus or subway and they're sitting there quiet and nicely dressed and then all of a sudden they'll look up, spin their head and yell *Ya! Ya dirty sonofabitchin fuckheadin fart shit bastards!* And then go back to reading the paper, right?"

Theresa was near weeping with laughter. "No! But I'll take your word for it!"

"Yeah, I have."

"Well, they do"—Mickey laughed—"and that's what I do, all the way up the street till I reach my doorman! *Ya! Ya rotten mothereffin cockadoodles shit piss!* Every four steps. The only thing I'm afraid of is some nut's liable to get turned on by it one of these nights!"

It at least had released Sister Theresa from her rigid stance; she'd let go of Harry's hand and was laughing, her body rocking loosely. Mickey winked at Harry and took the nun's empty glass from her hand. "I'm going for another round, Rags. Your's okay, Tro?"

"Fine—I got business to talk with you sometime, though."

"Angie already did. I'll get right on it, babes."

Too late, Theresa shot her hand forward. "No! Mickey! I'll get my—"

"Let her, Theresa."

Theresa sighed. "Yes. All right. That'll be much better, won't it."

"I don't know what you mean. Whatever you say, lady."

"Oh, God, Harry."

"Bad times, Sister? How old are you now anyhow, Theresa?"

"Thirty ... six?"

"Midlife crisis?"

"Maybe. Oh, I shouldn't have come. I'm sorry I did. I feel so ... left out."

"Well ... it does seem to get harder and harder to party, doesn't it. Happens to all of us, I guess. Some of us, anyhow."

"Maybe that's it, too. But you and Patricia—how are you, anyhow? Your kids are just gorgeous. I envy you your home. Constance—is she Regis bound?"

"Well, that's still down the road a ways. I don't know. We—"

"I ... oh, please don't tell, Tro. I'm in love with a man, I think. I ... he. ..."

The Canon's *I want a woman!* rang in his head. She was looking at his chest. His heart sagged. My God. Weren't any of them still all right? "Oh, wow, Theresa, is—"

"It's turrible," she whispered, barely audible, backlit against the windows, her front shadowed darkly. The sun had set; summer afterlight was fading slowly. "He's Jewish and divorced. It was a mixed marriage. I have his boy in school. He comes to see him and takes him weekends and ... for over three years now. He's a very good man, *such* a good man."

"Does he know you—"

"Yes, he knows; he started it really. Nobody has a hint, though. I'm positive of that. I just don't know what to do."

"Get out and marry him?"

"I *can't* do that! But it won't go away. It gets worse."

"Does—"

"And the boy graduates next June. And leaves."

"I—"

"Oh, don't, Tro. You don't have to say anything. Don't worry."

"Geez, Rags."

Mickey bounced back. "Here you go, Sis, and watch it, it's a bomb! Oh—you all right, hey?"

"Yeah, she's all right, Mickey."

"Uh, listen, Annie says there's some truck at the front door, says she won't leave until she sees the Sister and the ba-by! I'm up to it if you are, Rags."

"Of course." Sister Theresa put the drink down, pinched the back of Harry's hand without looking at him, and went, smiling, to do her duty with Mickey.

Harry heard Father Shaz Mayo's tenor laugh in the living room and headed for it, anxiously.

Shaz had been Thomas' seminary roommate, close friend ever since, and a Duffy in the way that Harry was, by unspoken, mutual adoption. Actually more so, in Shaz's case: When his own parents died, within a month of each other, some dozen years back, eldest Shaz became a Duffy "son" and at the same time "father" to the Mayo clan. Shaz was assistant pastor of a large parish with a school in a Boston suburb and lived in the rectory there. But he also maintained an apartment on the top floor of one Mayo three-decker in Southie. The first floor was occupied by a married brother and his family, the middle floor by a sister and hers. Next door all three floors were Mayos. Once a week Shaz held dinner and clan meet at his apartment, presiding over investments, who was or wasn't going to be lent boodle from the estate, etc. The Mayos and/or their spouses all were employed by the city, the state, the customs, the Edison, and, of course, the church. The network thus formed tended to reach its wires into various interesting corners. The TV, for instance, was a Mike Duffy-Eamon Mayo collaboration. Eamon worked for the Registry of Motor Vehicles. He could also get you diamonds.

Yes, there was at least one of them apparently still all right. A short, blond block of hard red cedarwood, yet delicately featured and slim-handed, Shaz took busloads of nuns and kids to Nantasket. Ran a parish school, K through 12. Ran release-time and CCD classes for the public school kids. Obeyed the New Law and let a parish council be organized but, really, *was* it. Gave funny, raw, bombastic sermons Sundays that re-

minded you of old-time annual mission preachers. Chased fire
engines and ambulances. Took the sacraments to nursing
homes, hospitals, and shut-ins. Ran his Southie complex.
Brought Bridget Duffy hams, shoulders, and flowers ("Don't
get wimpy, they're left over from a funeral!"). Bodyguarded
Thomas, usually, and treated him roughly ("What fund raising. Publish the list once a year, and you're home. How much
everybody gave, in black and white! They'll come across").
Now that virtually all the Vatican Council II liberal renegades
had become the establishment, Shaz had become a renegade.
He'd waited them out. At mass, Shaz wouldn't go so far as to
slip any Latin in, as a few diehards did, but he did have a way
of slipping past the sign of peace, for example. ("It embarrasses
them, and it's a crock anyhow! They just go out and bash each
other around in the parking lot after, huh?") His theology
tended to stay simple: "I tell 'em, crap, you feel guilty 'cause
you're *guilty!* Knock off whatever it is and you'll feel better in
two seconds!" On staying celibate: "Keep outta hot spots!" On
a married clergy: "Ya gotta be kidding! 'I woulda covered the
accident, but Joanne wouldn't let me!' " On homosexuality: "I
was never any good at prefixes." On abortion: "Nine outta ten
are manslaughter. But the old Prods who wrote the laws
shoulda kept their noses out of it in the first place!" On
artificial contraception: "I just do weddings, receptions, and
baptisms—no heavy cleaning, no windows." If pushed: "The
Pope's word goes. Sorry about that, huh?" On a working
clergy: "What, you think this is fun?" Or: "Who's hiring? I
know nine guys looking for jobs."

Harry entered the male circle. Shaz stepped out from
between old Martin and Thomas and threw him a handshake,
suddenly turning it into the new brothers' thumb lock, then
expanding it into the Flip Wilson slap-palms, bam-hips, hit-
elbows vaudeville routine. "How about that, huh? That's hip,
man! That's the chocolate shake, where ah comes frum! All-
right!" Then, all in the same motion, he had Harry by the
bicep and was walking him out of the group and the room.

"Be right back, guys! Got a *bone* to pick with our octane executive here, huh? Listen, you bum, you told me number six in the third, right? Well, damn it ..." and they were out, into the entrance hall.

"Any luck?"

"Well, you tell me, Tro. I'll tell you what we got, but I don't know what you want! *Charley*—right?"

"Right."

"Well, he comes up pretty clean, is all. I mean, he's on that side of the line, but nothing big or important. Runs the club, and the gyp joint on the side. Doesn't *own* it by himself, of course, but it's strictly bush-league, nobody depending on him for much, you know. Did some time in the fifties for paper-hanging but upright ever since ... local good guys like him, nobody dying to see him meet trouble ... he's widowed, plays golf, no kids, gotta brother-in-law runs a car lot somewhere close by ... and that's about all she wrote! Knock down any ducks for ya, pal?"

"No. Damn. Listen, thanks anyhow, Shaz."

"Don't ask, right?"

"Right."

"Uh ... he *might* also, well, it's pretty sure he does, but he's very careful about it, have a little stable going there, too, and some ... party catering, you know—is it anything along those lines you need to know about?"

"No, God, no."

"Glad to hear that. Well ... what? You want it pushed any farther? I mean it looks like the bottom of the barrel, but you never know, huh?"

"Christ, I don't know, Shaz. This is all just for this buddy of mine—"

"Sure."

"—and I—well, I mean, is the guy reachable? I mean, can somebody get him to do something or not do something?"

"Nobody I know, Tro. The guy sounds like he's no last of the independents, but he's way out in the bleachers where nobody gives a shit about him, huh? A nothing, just another nice guy. That bad?"

"Who knows? I'll pass it on."

"I can have Andy at least keep his ears open on him, should I?"

"Yeah, please, it couldn't hurt."

Shaz squinted and gave him a quick shot on the arm. "Hey—not messing with the dollies this stage of the game, are ya?"

"No way," Harry said straightly, wondering if Thomas had been ass enough to tell Shaz anything of the lost weekend. Just the geographic line between Sequosset and the Chez Ruby was something Shaz would connect in a blink. "Hey, thanks a lot, Shaz, I appreciate it."

"Think nothing of it, Tro. I won't."

"Good."

"And sorry about the personal question, huh?"

Harry laughed. "Which one was that? Come on, your ice cubes look lonesome." They went for the kitchen.

"'Cause you know, if it's girls you want I can get you nice, fresh young ones! They're Eskimos, but brand-new!"

Angie appeared. *"What* was that I just heard?"

Shaz hugged her. "Oh, just a punch line to an old joke you wouldn't get, so don't go blowy on us. Your better half here didn't get it either, so—"

"Say, Shaz, tell us"—Harry smirked, fixing the priest's drink—"when are you going to start packing for your trip to Ireland with Thomas?" What the hell, might as well start some trouble, it's my house.

"What?" Angie popped.

Shaz hissed, "Oh, you bastard," and covered his face with his fingers.

Near them, old Moon Mulligan sat eating at the long, wooden kitchen table. Four women sat over tea, watching and listening to him. Moon was the one who never joined the men. At all galas like this one, he paid his respects of congratulation or consolation, then marched directly to table. His wife, Nell, would soon follow, bearing silver, napkin, and a full plate, which she'd set before him, then take a seat for herself, a few feet behind him. Nell would answer cordially but encouraged no conversation. When Moon's plate was cleared, she'd up and go refill it. Moon would eat and Nan would fetch until it was time to leave—something they would have to be told. Nan was rarely seen to take anything but tea for herself. Moon was thin as a blade and dressed most nattily in pre-fifties suits, with tiepins, collar pins and vests and glistening, sharp-pointed shoes. One mystery was: Where did all that food go in him? Another was: What exactly was it that invariably drew at least two women to share the table with him? Nell's fierce, German shepherd glares over his shoulder were impossible to miss and anything but approving.

To assume it was Moon's conversation opened only another mystery, for Moon was quite mad, rattling off between chews very sincere tales of his car being riddled with machine-gun fire on their way down from Salem, of being constantly followed by foreign-looking men, of receiving unsigned letters threatening his life, and so forth. Besides, he talked through his nose. Critics said that Moon stayed so skinny because he ate *only* at other people's houses and never at his own. This was hard to prove because nobody known had ever been inside Moon and Nell's place, though both were forever saying to drop in anytime. The difficulty was, the Mulligans retired every evening of the week, when at home, at precisely six forty-five and did not get up to answer doorbells. They had no phone and no TV, or at least no visible antenna. When still very young girls just over, Bridget and Nell had been domestics in the same Beacon Hill house, was how the Duffys knew the Mulligans. Asked about them, Bridget would only allow: "Wull, it do take all kinds." About all that was known for sure, besides their customs at affairs, was that they'd been childless all their life, and that Moon, now seventy if a day, hadn't done a lick of work since he was forty-nine. He'd somehow managed to retire on three different pensions, the Coast Guard, the Salem police, and some other.

Trying to protect himself, Father Shaz Mayo now made a stab at discovering a new mystery about the Mulligans. "Hey," he whispered, "how come old Nellie just sits there shredding paper napkins into a million bits like that? Look—she's got a lap-full! Like a *gerbil*, for God's sake!"

Angie whispered back, "Because if she didn't shred them, Moon'd *eat* them! Now what's this about you going to Ireland?"

Harry put in, "I'd like to know how he gets all the broads."

Shaz said, "Yeah! What's—"

"Spill it, Shaz!"

Shaz spilled it; Angie made a fist. "Goddamn it, why doesn't anybody ever *tell* you anything?"

"Because then you'd *know*, dumbo," Harry laughed.

Suddenly Rena whisked in and up to Angie, looking ashen but controlled, as if trying to alert people without yelling Fire! "Pat, you'd better come in. It's Annie."

"Oh, no."

Shaz stayed. Harry followed, well behind, moving casually. Annie had blown and was screaming at Fast and also, for some reason, at Mike. Sister Theresa and Mickey were still at the front door seeing people off with the mother. He saw two women stop at the sounds from the living room and turn back. He bullied into the clutch. "Well, good night again now, Mrs. Dugan, Mrs. Gleason, thanks so much for coming. Watch your steps there, and straight home, no stopping off at any gin mills, you hear?" Tittering but glinting, they went on their way.

He tried to keep the Duffy women there, but Bridget caught the sounds over his blarney, "What *is* that, now—who's—" and headed in.

To the sisters he said, "I'll man the door. Go make sure whoever's in the kitchen stays there." They left him there. He couldn't hear any clear words in the sounds and didn't look in. This wasn't usual. There could be squabbles and outbursts, but never while the parents or company were still around to witness. The sounds stopped. Angie and Annie passed him and went upstairs, Annie weeping, Angie holding an arm around her bent shoulders. He shot a glance into the living room; no guests were there, after all, nor was the Old Man. Just family, looking awkward, embarrassed, confused, upset. Harry heard the downstairs toilet flush. Bridget flew by, going to waylay Martin, beating Harry to it. He turned to Rena and Nance. 'How about telling Rags and Mickey they should kick the kitchen people out?" They went. He faced the men, asking with his face. Father Thomas rolled his eyes. Father Tim was tamping a pipe, studying the fern in the fireplace. Albie was trying to stay between Mike and Fast.

Mike had the black look in the red face. "—fucker! Some kinda cockartist? She's my sister and your fuckin' *wife*, you sneaky little—"

"Sit on it, Duffy!" Fast was small but not soft.

Two dogs barking, surrounded by silence. Mike's tongue gone, the danger was that he'd start throwing punches at Facey. Albie was holding him off, talking low and soft. Harry called, "Fast!" and signaled him out.

On the porch, he lit two cigarettes, gave one to Fast, and asked gingerly, "Little ruckus?"

"Aah! Where is she? I'm getting out of this zoo."

"Let her fix her face. Thought you and Mike had made peace?"

"He's an asshole." Fast stepped off the porch. "Tell her I'm in the car."

Harry knew that regardless of what had caused the row, Annie, chronically afraid of missing something, wouldn't be willing to leave until the last light was out. Fast knew it, too. He'd go brood in his car for a while, then come back. The night air felt good. Soon the only light would be from the moon, which looked, uh-oh, full. Crossing the street to his Javelin, Fast looked small, alone, visibly slowed down. About to return inside, Harry changed his mind and walked over to him. He leaned against the car and smoked. Fast spoke through the open window. "Does it ever end, Tro?"

"What?"

"That ... self-induced schizophrenia! Their *I'm a Duffy, not a Facey or a Trowbridge* bullshit?"

"Angie doesn't do that."

"Oh. Assumed she did."

"No. Uh ... you know I usually don't ask, bud."

Facey sighed. "Aah! I ... I made the tactical error of telling her about this ... kind of affair I had a couple years ago."

"Why the hell'd you do that?"

"Have it?"

"Tell her."

"What can I say? I'm an honest person."

"When'd you tell her?"

"Today."

"Terrific timing."

"It's been bugging me for a long time."

"Feel better now?"

"Yes. Yes, I do!"

"What are you, trying to kill her?"

Lawn sprinklers and crickets made their sounds. Fast said, "Am I supposed to have a fight with you, too?"

"I hope not."

"She has to grow up."

"You have to help her. Why don't you make believe she's an assignment from your company?"

"Is that sarcasm?"

"Yeah, but not a bad idea."

"I'll think about it."

"Do that."

"She thinks their shit is ice cream, and goddamn it—"

"Ah, stick it, Fast. They *love* her, that's all. Can't you see that? Christ, you and Annie are just like Thomas. It's a problem, but it never changes, and we're all bored with it. But I'm telling you, tough guy, you'd better class up your act or you're gonna see them take her off in a straitjacket one of these days."

"I'll send you a mailgram from Oklahoma."

God, the man was a cool one, Harry had to give him that.

"I'll tell you something, Trowbridge—she *hates* Angie!"

Harry grinned. "I don't blame her." Then he saw what he was waiting for, the shadows moving at the back of his house. "You know, I take it back, Fast. I think maybe Annie's the one who knows everything, and *she'll* bury *you.*" Facey had an answer, but Harry didn't hear it.

He reached Albie's bus just as Rena was opening the driver's door. Martin and Bridget were already in. The unpleasantness was sending them home early, but not by much; their deadline was ten thirty. If it was at their house, they'd just go upstairs and the party would move to Albie's or Mike's. Tonight the excuse was leaving, the party would stay. Rena said, "Oh, there you are! I looked for you, but—"

He took the keys from her. "Thanks, Momma, be back in ten minutes."

Martin growled, "Jesus, Bridgie, it's a bloody highjackin'!"

"What is it, Tro?" Mrs. Duffy cooed, telling him she knew it was something.

"It's money," he said and backed out the driveway. He told them on the way.

In their kitchen she made tea and Martin wrote the check for the ten thousand dollars. Neither had batted an eye. Martin squinted, "Be it enough, Tro-boy? If ye have doubts, say so now and we'll make it for more."

"Listen, it's killing me to do this at all. It'll have to be enough." He'd also got three from the bank, by extending the car loan.

"Killing ye indeed." The old man smiled, lighting a Camel. "How old be ye now, man?"

"Thirty-nine next month." And he didn't have to be told: Martin hadn't even married until he was thirty-five.

"Hmph, the foolish pride don't usually stick on the bus that long. Ye should've spoke up a lot sooner, Tro. We've been wondering, ye must know."

"I'll pay it back."

"Sure you will," he said and got up, ending it. "Well, me for a farewell look at the old black and white. Guess we kin lug it up the bedroom, come to think uv it, huh, Bridge? God's luck, Tro, ye'll have our prayers for the little they're worth."

Back at the house, Angie whispered, "Thank God. But why didn't you tell me?"

"I want it between me and them. How's it going? Annie?"

"Annie's dancing. Fast went home."

"Uh-oh."

"Yeah. She can sleep on the couch, unless Thomas sobers up enough to drive her. I doubt it, though. Shaz'll probably drive him."

"Let her crash here's the safest."

"Yeah. And Thomas has been prowling all over for you, so ... oop, speak of the devil."

"God, look at 'em, the kitchen people. We *all* are! *Aren't* we! The kitchen people. Patricia, I'd like a word with Mr. T., huh?"

"Gladly."

Harry sat where Moon Mulligan had dined. Thomas sat and looked around to make sure they were alone. "Tro, I gotta tell you something. Hey, where's your drink? Get a drink. I can't tell you this unless you got a goddamn drink in your hand! Where the hell you been all night anyhow?"

Harry got a beer. It wouldn't do. He had to go back and get a toss of scotch as well and one for the Canon.

"Tro. We're still buddies, right? I mean, you ... and me. And I. We've always had something *there*, right? Something very ... *special* between us, right?"

"Right."

"What is it?"

"The night down the Cape."

Thomas straightened up and looked as if Harry had spoken in Russian; then his eyes cleared. "Nah, forget that shit. That never happened. *No!* You bastard, what I'm *sayin'* is, we're like brothers, right? Right? Or not right?"

"*Yes!* Like brothers."

"No. Unh-unh. More than brothers. Because we think alike. And we know *Joyce*, huh? Because I'm gonna tell you somethin' I wouldn't tell anya my real brothers. Or sisters or anybody. But! I mean it, you gotta *swear*, Tro! *Nobody* hears this. *Right?*"

"I swear, Thomas."

"Okay ... Shaz and I're goin to ... Ireland with em!"

"*No ... shit!*" Harry exclaimed and not sarcastically. He spoke and looked genuinely surprised, pleased, and conspiratorial. It seemed as good a time as any to start practicing his reactions, gestures, and tones. Thomas obviously believed him, and Harry felt encouraged; fragile, self-centered drunks can see through pretense like glass. Then in whaled the Mike himself, an empty beer can hourglassed in his hand. Caught close and alone with Little Doc, Harry felt vaguely disloyal and, worse, refined.

"Oh, lookit the two them! Tellin' him ya sins, Tro? How many times, boy? Were you alone or with others? Did you take any *pleasure* from it?"

"Shut your gub and sit down," Thomas ordered, and Mike obeyed, laughing and throwing his can-bearing arm around his brother's shoulders.

"Ah, Tommy, y'know? You're a pretty good old shit. You know that, Doc? Did you know that? Huh? Well, you are. A pretty good old shit. I don't care."

Harry fetched Mike a full can and popped it for him, relieved to know for sure now that Albie had kept his vow not to tell Mike a thing. If Mike had heard even the most veiled suggestion of Harry's fall, drunk or not his talk wouldn't have come within fifty feet of words like "sin." Harry was almost as fond of Mike as Angie was and just as leery as she of his Behanesque act when afloat on the suds; somewhere, inside,

Mike was always watching, wondering, recording. Harry took the crushed can out of his hand and put the full one in.

"Well? We did it for 'em, din't we? Think they liked it? Deddy had a good time, I think. What the hell. That was really nice, wasn't it?" Mike, the question man.

Thomas took the bait. "Might have been *nicer* if certain people kept their noses out of other people's business."

Mike grinned wickedly across at Harry. "That what *you* think, Mr. Dennehy?" At his tavern Mike liked to play Gleason's Joe the Bartender.

Harry did Crazy Guggenheim: *"Gee,* Joe, I din't see *nuttin'!"*

Mike removed his arm from Thomas and took a slug from the beer. "Well, why'd they go pullin that *Edge of Night* shit here? Tonight, for Christ's sake! See me and the Nance screamin in public? Violence belongs in the privacy of one's own home. Even Dickey the Dunce the bartender knows that. Come off it, Tom—what were *you* gonna do, let 'em go at it?"

"Well, it'd be better than—"

"I'm gonna waste that little prick onea these days."

"Fast's all right! He really is! It takes two to—"

"Aw, come on, Little Doc, I'm just ragging ya a little bit, now. Fuck 'em, he's gone, and she's in there doin Zorba the Greek!"

Thomas studied his drink darkly; he looked about to doze.

"Hey, we keepin you up or what, Thomas?" Mike stifled a belch. "Orm I *interruptin'* somethin'?"

Thomas' eyes were jarred alive, but his mouth could find no words.

Harry jumped in, "Hey, so how's Nance doing in the new career—she starting to bring home any money yet?" Kindergarten had revealed that one of their young children had a serious hearing problem. Getting involved in the clinics and therapy had changed stay-at-home Nance's life. Nance meeked around for years as the adorable little Kewpie-doll blonde, with apparently as much to say. Then she suddenly found herself being asked not only to join this Harvard-affiliated

roup of specialists, students, and other parents, but also to get
p in front of them in her turn and ... *talk to them!* She did it.
Vhat she called "You know, the usual," turned out to be
fficially received as "Life Experience" ... and *valued!* By
eople with degrees! The kid, tuned in, left the program;
Vance, turned on, stayed in. *"No, she ain't bringin' home any money
et, you prevert!* And don't go tryin' to get me tearahse at ya,
Troby! I was speakin' to mumblin' britches, here. You gonna
oop out on us or what, there, Father? I mean ya see us so
ften! Whyn't ya go down Ma's, see if she'll fix ya some *Postum!*
Ha! Or a little *Ovaltine,* maybe, or hey, she—"

"Why don't you want to talk about Nance, Michael?"
Thomas caseworkered deftly, sober-looking as Marcus Welby.
"You ought to be proud of her."

Which, all knew, Mike was but, perhaps for that very
eason, had decided to make major productions of being
"against it from the start!" Harry enjoyed watching Mike's
ace, squeezing reactions in their bins, selecting for this eve-
ing: "Proud my ahse! An excuse to abandon me and her
nfant children's all it is! I'm thinkin of reportin' her. A little
ducation's a dangerous thing—didn't yez ever read that? But
m I one of ya chauvinistic pigs? Not Michael P. Duffy! *Go,* I
ay. *Find* yourself!" He didn't shout the verbs; he cooed them
oftly, close to song. *"Allow* the house to become a pigsty ...
hese are only material things, my dear"—shooting Harry a
quick wink—"but the *mind,* ah!—*that's* what to keep waxed and
dusted! And the babies with pneumonia? And TB? If God
wants 'em, He'll *take* 'em! So who are *we* to—"

"She only goes a morning a week!" The Canon gaveled the table,
utraged, and looked hurt and baffled when Mike and Harry
urst out laughing. Mike whammed his priest-brother's back,
reached from his chair, and started to leave, turning back for
a moment to drop, "By the way, Tro, I came out to tell ya—
Albie ate your *Harry* record."

"He *what?*"

"Yeah. Took a huge bite out of it. I think he mighta

swallowed the Puppy Song, but he spit out Nobody Cares About the Railroads Anymore. Says he'll get you another one Monday," and, roaring, stomped back to the party.

Thomas asked, *"Harry* record?"

"Harry Nillson. Albie's always really loved it."

"Do you think he really—"

"Let's go see."

"No! Wait just a sec. I have to ask you something."

"What?"

"I feel guilty. I mean, so many of you people could use a break, a trip, you know? How will everybody take it? My going over with them?"

Harry thought of quipping, *Forget it, sex is the poor people's vacations.* And he thought of saying, *Why do I always end up seeing you as the ultimate victim of it all, Tommy?* And he also thought of saying, *Goddamn it, if you really feel so guilty, why don't you set it up for Annie and Fast?* All he did say was: "Father, don't worry about it. You'll get the usual amount of flak, but who else could go? Either they couldn't get away, or they wouldn't want to go, or they wouldn't do the old people any good if they did go. Go, bud, and have a hell of a time there, will you?"

The Canon looked no less pained, but said, "I'll try, Tro. And thanks a lot, huh? I hope you're right."

Harry stood and cocked his head toward the party. "Come on."

Thomas looked up. "Tro—you and Patricia go! I mean it! We even talked about asking you ... my mother said—"

Harry grinned. "I won't be here to go anywhere, Tom. And don't tell anybody about it yet, okay?"

To his own father, Brother Big Jake, he said, "I know there's nothing you can *do* about it, damn it! I just thought you ought to know what's happening, that's all ... and, well, maybe say a prayer or something for us, I don't know."

Big Jake grinned sleepily into the engine of the snow-blower, upon which he was performing open-heart surgery. He had it up on his long wooden workbench. He had greenish grease in his beard and sawdust on his robe. "Things sure still change fast on you out there, don't they?"

Harry sighed. "Yeah, they sure do." Men's feet in sandals crunched past the open cellar window periodically. Dust saturated the block of sunlight falling in. Harry said, "Ever see an Edward G. Robinson movie *Brother Orchid?*"

"No. Why?"

"Nothing. I always think of it when I come up here, that's all."

"Any good, was it?"

"Ah, I don't know. He was on the lam and hid out in a monastery, that's all I remember."

Big Jake grinned slyly and let it pass. He moved to the right to select a socket, making Harry back up a step and be for the moment a very young boy in the bowel-moving Liberty Square cellar, having all manual dexterity driven out of him by exposure to effortless, natural genius. As if he read his son's heart, Big Jake said softly, "Still not too hot in the praying department, Harr. There's a box for petitions, though. I can drop you in and get the guys goin' on it, that be okay?"

Harry laughed. "That'll be okay, Pop."

"Nice box, too, you should see it. Remember the little toolbox I made for you that time? Brass corners and all? It's kinda like that."

"Oh, yeah." In fact, he still had it. Young Jake and Dennis used it, both good with their hands and tools, having had only Harry to watch.

"Funny. That station was always good to old Coogan."

"Mm."

"That movie—you see it with me and Tony Mac, you think?"

"Could've. It was way back, I know that."

Big Jake was practically inside the motor now and said, "You know somethin', Harry? Your Mum and me, we always wanted you to work with your head and not your hands, and all, but inside, I was always kinda worried, even when you were gettin' the college, that you'd never get a real trade out of it. I was always afraid to say it ... cuz I wasn't sure if it was really true or not, that a man's gotta have a trade ... but in thinkin' about ya, it hit me—you did pick one up anyhow, didn't you? Maybe, I don't know, but maybe all this is just your trade callin' you back, huh, bud?"

"That may be, Dad."

"Well, you're damned lucky to have it to go to then. If you want to put it that way."

Harry said he guessed that was true, too, and left soon after. Whether his was a real trade or not, and whether it was even still there or not, much less callin' him back, he couldn't tell yet. But he did feel better. It was good to have a father somewhere, half-ass monk or not, and learn he was thinkin' about ya.

Flash looked genuinely surprised and very displeased by Harry's news. This was the second time in a month that Harry was disappointing him: He'd finally told Flash about the weekend and about Charley Clote, and on top of ribbing him, Flash had come back a few days later with: "Okay, your troubles are over; here's what we do. You, me, Albie, and Mike, we just go down there one night. No—not you. Just us, and we dress tough as shit, right? I walk up, and I take the palm of his hand, and I drop a sprinkle of horse in it, just a pinch, and I say, 'Taste it, shmuck,' and if he don't know what it is, I tell him and I tell him that we got enough of it planted in his joint, in his house, in every fucking thing he owns to put him away for life. Shut up, I ain't through. Here's the capper: We pour a pound of flour or powdered glucose in the carburetor of his car! Hey, maybe I'll let Cyrus do that, let him wear black gloves, be fucking Superfly for the night, yeah. So? Is that perfect, is it beautiful? Who loves ya, baby, who you know like the Flash, huh?"

"Nobody in the world, man, and I love it, but you have to

know I don't *want* to do that or any other deal we could figure out. I'll get out of it, but ... see, it's the priest I'm after, Flash, not Clote. Thanks anyhow, though."

Now Harry was rushing on, trying to get it over with quickly. "I tried to line up another cellar or something for you, but I couldn't find anything. You're good here for five, six weeks. Cyrus's going to run it until then. Then she shuts." He'd lost four grand on the sale to the discount self-service outfit.

"Christ. What's ... what's Cyrus going to do?"

"I got him into the new Shell. I'm sorry, Flash. Is six weeks too—"

"Nah! Not to worry! That ain't it. It's ... how can you *leave,* man?"

"Got to."

"Try *Boston!*" Flash always faced in, when he was in the station's office. Now he spun around and stood at the window, looking out at July-hot Liberty Square.

Harry was moved. "Hey, kid, what's the story? Ain't the end of the world. I'll still see you."

"Yeah—when?"

"Weekends?"

"Bullshit. Tro ... you're the only friend I ever had, Tro!"

"That's because you're a luno."

"Think I don't know that? Anybody else knew anything, I'd be in an institution! Why I don't take criticism!" He was wearing his cowboy hat and was bare to the waist. "What'll I do for *laughs,* now, Tro?"

"Go straight."

"Legs'll *rot* without you guys! You're our family, you idiot! Listen, come in with me, I need a helper, pay you a fortune! Gotta whole new deal I been thinking of adding on! I could *use* ya!"

"My God, what else is there?"

"Numbers! Why not, you know? Aw, shit, fuck, Tro!"

"Angie and the kids'll still be here."

Flash turned back in. "What's *that* mean? How the hell's *that* work?"

"I don't know. We're going to try it, though. We like it here."

"Listen, what do you want? I'll fucking buy something legit and you can run it, okay? A liquor store! Hi-fi and tapes!"

Harry laughed. "I think my, uh, merchant days are over, Flash. Appreciate the thought, though."

"Jesus, you know underneath you're more whacko than I am? At least I'm upfront about it, and you're a fucking phony! Fucking *gas* station! Who were you trying to jive, anyhow?"

"I . . . forget."

"Christ, they say *I'm* a menace to society!"

"Nothing wrong with that, is there?"

Flash laughed and lit a joint. "What are your chances down there?"

"I have no idea."

"How are you feeling?"

"Flash, I'm scared to death. I feel *old,* man."

"Yeah. Well," hffft! "Run zigzag, Tro."

"My dear, sappy boy!" Jay Wolf scolded, pacing his Sutton Place South office-apartment like a lawyer in court. "Put it right out of your mind at once! For one thing, the killers will smell it off you! Fear breeds fear, and you'll be dead before you start! Like a self-fulfilling prophecy! Harry, Harry, such a *shtumm!* I'm not merely saying Think Positive, I'm telling you, it's *true!* You're going to be hot again in two minutes! Assuming your legs are still in good shape, of course."

"Twenty-four hours a day. Anyplace, anytime, Jay."

"Well, good, but don't burn out. Pacing, remember? Pacing!"

"I'm broke! I'm worse than broke, I fucking *owe!*"

He might have said he was a dope addict, the wince of distaste Jay made—talk about infra dig! "Well, the *one* inteligent thing you did was keep up your union payments, I'll give you that." Angie's doing. "But all right, enough small talk—what time did you land at La Guardia?"

"Nine?"

"All right. You have a three o'clock audition at Benton and Bowles, hm?"

"Ah, good old Bending and Bald."

"Don't be rude, it's Frank Corre."

"Frank still there?"

"*Yes*, and so is Joe Bacal, and Paul McDonough, and Shelly Platt's *back* there! If you'd *listen* to me for a minute! Schinto's running Tinker, Joel Wayne's creative director of Grey, with Novick head of all TV! Ira Lassman! John Green! Jerry Saviola! Catherine Land, Kathy O'Grady! Les Richter's a biggie at Bates, Terry Boyle's at J. Walter. Dave Altschiller's still at Ally!" Jay threw Harry's old book at him. "Go through it yourself! Not all, but almost all your best contacts! Jack Avrett! Arty Merannus! Barbara Pesin! Lois Corey! Brian Dillon! Mitch Epstein! Zoltan Medvecki! Stu Hampel! Julie Harburger! Andy Isaacson! Joe Stone! Al Sarasohn! Gene Federico! David Leddick *is* Revlon! Jim Marks! Eric Webber and Thayer Burch are at Y&R! Jim Abel! Cynthia Weber! Joy Goldin! Jack Flynn! Bill Parrott! Read 'em and don't weep, Harry! Al Viola's back! Henry Trettin's shooting for Lee Lacey! Murray Bruce! Giraldi! Charlie Moss—well, no, he's too high at Wells now to help. He was creative director, but now he's only president. Dick Heimann's flying high! Steve Horn! Joe Sacco! Rick Baxter! Marty Stevens! Carol Hamilton! Kurt Haiman! Roy Eaton! Ruth Levine and Tom Hende! Bill McCaffrey!" He placed a plastic "cigarette" in his mouth like a rose in a vase. "I could go on all day. Oh, sure, a few left. Pieter Mayer went to Mexico. So did Bill Barrett. Joe Arleo quit to write novels. So did Jay Brothers. Fitzpatrick disappeared completely. Koenig retired. Horovitz's plays hit. Don Grady died. Beisch went to London. But what did you think, *everybody* took off when you did?"

"I guess so." Harry chuckled. "Strike New York, set up Boston."

"That's *paranoia,* I might remind you."

"You're looking great, Jay." Jay's gaiety had blossomed with his success and the years, and he wore both well.

"Shut up. You have a six o'clock appointment with George Adams. You'll need a current head sheet. He thinks Fred Ohringer's better for you, but you three can fight that out. And you're deeper in debt than you know—I put blurbs in *Backstage, Variety,* and the rest for you, starting *last* week. I don't suppose you've bothered to resume your reading yet."

"I did!" he lied. "I meant to thank you."

"Oh, bother!" Jay sissy-threw the fake up into his rare book collection and took a Rothman from the silver cup on the mantel. "No, the *intriguing* thing, Harry Trowbridge, is the *air pocket!* No *kids* came in *after* you!"

"Thank God.... But why not? You're right, I figured everybody'd be twenty-eight at the most, like we were—and I'd be automatically over the hill."

Jay took two calls at his desk, then began touring his large, grand, dark room again. "Of course, the theater is still drawing them young and wet, but not the business. I don't know. Oh, of course I do! Half were killed in Vietnam, the other half are still too hippie or too well-off, *or both,* to *need* dirty old advertising, and the other half, well, just look around you on the streets! My God, it's 1962 again! They went to business schools and bought suits! Dwell on *that,* Harry! It's 1962 again! The same gray horse has come around again, the one we all *rode* already!" He giggled with amusement. "We've all read the script before!"

"Got one for this afternoon, by the way?"

"No. Cold read."

"Against who?"

"Lewis and Marcado."

"Oh, Christ. Forget it."

"Maybe. But it's practice and reentry at the very least, and who knows? You're going to come off as fresh and new to a lot of people, dear boy—isn't that a hoot?"

Harry made his three o'clock call that first day and the photo session at six. The next day he did readings for five different agencies and at a production house was videotaped for an on-camera job. There was much new about the game that he didn't need to learn from Jay. Just watching the tube during his exile had informed him that the full-minute spot was dead, usurped by the :30, an ill enough wind in itself made worse by the content he saw, or, more often, walked out on. The standup spiel ("See this product I'm holding up? You need it. You'll like it. Buy it or we'll kill you!") had become Business' most common way of speaking to people. The "slices" (of life), being of course as inevitable and eternal as taxes, ran a close second. (With one nuance acknowledging that the times they were a-changin': now it was just as often black women in the whitefolks' dream kitchens saying, "What's wrong, Marge?"

"Oh, June, tonight's my bridge club (dinner for hubby's boss, mother-in-law's visit, etc.) and my coffee's just so yuk! (silver's so tarnished, furniture's so dull, linen's so dingy, etc.)"

"Relax, Marge, you need new Yttrium."

Demonstration.

Dissolve.

"Great bridge party (etc.), Marge ... and *terrific* coffee (etc.)!"

"Oh, thanks, Marge, but don't thank me ... thank new Yttrium!"

Announcer (voice over): "We call it new Yttrium—you'll call it terrific!")

Running a close third was really only the subtlety of using a celebrity in the standup, in place of some nobody yeoman like Harry. ("Hi, I'm Jesus of Nazareth. Y'know, it gets pretty hot and dusty out where I....") Everything else was a distant fourth and usually looked like accidents. Hardly an avid viewer, Harry could still tell that something more vital than

length had changed. Where was funny? Where was amazing?
Where was true-human? Where had dazzle gone? And fantasy,
spectacle, surprise, visual magic, verbal *gotcha?* Where was
beautiful? Either somebody had quit writing those miniature
pearls of yesterdecade, or they'd quit killing themselves trying
to get the miniature Nixons to run them. It was too bad and
kind of sad, Harry had thought from far-off Cambridge. It
even showed in the movies; with good commercials dead, and
with them the ingenuity and invention they demanded, the
movies had nothing left to learn or steal from, and so were all
looking more or less alike. Talk about un-American. But
Harry, naturally, couldn't really afford now to care about any
of this.

The surface he was operating on was sheer infantry, existential step-by-stepness. He could see cue lights in a recording
booth just as clearly for stupid words as for clever ones. Words
were words. Words were only words, no "good," no "bad." He
could speed them up, spread them out, go light or heavy, put
more or less stress or excitement wherever the hell they wanted
it, making all desired hits-to-picture while he was at it. He
could "have fun with it" till hell froze over. Words were work.
He needed all the work he could beg, borrow, or steal, so if
something was handed to him and called a word and they'd
pay him to read it the way they wanted to hear it, that was
some pretty nice word as far as he was concerned. Taste was a
luxury he wasn't sure he'd ever be able to afford again.
Luckily, he had little time in which to think about it much.

One change he had not anticipated was the one in the air of
the ad agencies' halls. They had gone quiet. Where had the
raucousness fled? The hoopla? Yeah, the people were largely
the same and, at least on the "creative" floors, still dressed
colorfully zany enough, but most seemed to stay in their offices
and walk and talk ... politely. No more raunchy jokes? No
more knock hockey, darts, or coffee-lid Frisbee? No more
singing? Where were the shouters? The wall pounders? The
pratfallers? The mask wearers? The tantrum throwers? Never

mind where were the kids? Where had gone the kids *in* these people? Jesus Christ, if this was mad Mad Ave (now predominately moved to *Third*), what must it be like in Cincinnati? Or Rochester? Or Oklahoma City? If you were bursting through your skin in Navarre, Ohio, where the hell could you run to now? What a revoltin' development *this* is, Gillis!

Harry could observe the new, sad quiet but couldn't let it affect him personally. While he, Mickey Duffy, Jay Wolf, and slews of others searched or kept their ears open for some sort of digs he could live in, Harry was crashing with Gus and Naomi Roth in New Chaumont. He found he'd lost no dread and loathing for the commuter train, but nothing else about the pre-Bolt place bothered him much. The sight of his old house didn't get a ripple out of him. He was amused, in a detached way, by the news that while Birchtree Lake was still successfully half-and-half, the entire area surrounding it had gone totally black, making "their" half of Birchtree some sort of white Berlin, *sans* wall. And he was shocked and chagrined to hear that Bert next door's kid had died of an overdose at fifteen, but all he could say was: "Maybe he should've gone south with Bert." Nor was there anything down anymore about the Roths. Harry knew this from their letters and phone calls but was still very pleased to see it, live.

Naomi had not only come home alive from zapland, but begun to flourish. She continued on in therapy, went back to school for her BS in nursing, and got a job in a Bronx methadone program, going to work in civilian clothes. Gus steadily turned out his kitchens, warehouses, and nursing homes. He and their high school girl took advanced flute lessons together Saturdays in Queens. Their older girl had gone off to college. The whole family had gone vegetarian (except Gus at lunch). For the two weeks Harry was there, he seldom arrived from the city in time for dinner, but one night he did and asked, "This eggplant kosher, Nome?"

"It's spinach, eat it."

Gus drank only Boodles gin now. ("If it's white, it's all right.

If it's brown, it's a down.") He and Harry had had a couple
and were now on wine (Chablis) with Naomi. It was a nicely
mellow evening and the only time they really talked. Naomi
was more concerned about Angie. Harry answered, "What can
I tell you? If it turns to disaster, we'll move the whole show
back down. But I think she's right: We found a good, personal
place there. Like this has always been for you guys. We've lived
there longer than anywhere else since we got married. She gets
on a bus, and she's at school or in the stores or whatever. Most
of the kids think they've always lived there. It doesn't seem it
sitting here, but close in, five, six years is a long time."

"How about you, Tro?" Gus scowled.

"Well, you know me, I could live in a tree. But, yeah, it's
sure as hell the closest thing to *my home* I've ever felt. Of course,
I've got some symbolic strings still holding there, too. I feel
that house and where it is is something I earned, you know?
Something I pulled off. I'm not going to let that go too easy.
But, listen, we're hardly doing much long-term thinking right
now, huh? It's straight day-by-day until I start seeing what
kind of bread I'm going to be averaging."

"How much you figure you need? A bundle, right?"

"Gus, I gotta do a grand a week gross. Bottom line. That's
figuring the seventy a week shuttle fare and whatever I'll be
gouged for rent when I find a place." Also figuring the two
bills a week to Clote after the station went, but he could
hardly mention that.

Naomi fanned the topic away like cigarette smoke. "Oh, you
were always a money-maker, Tro, I mean where's Angie *at?*
Where's her *identity?*" Gnomic Nome.

"Ah, Nome. Short-range, she's scared as I am. Long-range, I
think she's good. She said a good thing: Other women her age,
who didn't do what she's done, can't now. But she *can* do, now,
whatever they did do. Something like that anyhow."

That obviously satisfied Naomi, but she said, "Move back,
Tro."

"Gonna try not to. Twice a week on a plane's a hell of a lot
better for me than two hours a day on the train."

Naomi put water on to boil. "But ... well, excuse me for getting intimate, but being separated all week, Tro, aren't you depriving yourselves of, of, you know, your *center?* The stroke part?"

"That going to be for tea, Nome?"

"Yes."

"You got any white scotch, Gus?"

"And what about the *kids,* Tro?"

Gus smiled. "Oh, brown's okay for gentiles, and I got."

"I'll take, thank you." She'd hit the nerve, the main source of the downs that awaited him nights, and he wasn't about, or prepared, to answer her on it. At home, every time he got into the shower, pulled the curtain, and turned the water on, was when the bloodcurdling screams and poundings started, noises from somewhere outside the closed curtains and door, of trash cans through glass, of Constance being raped, Jake being arrested, Amy on fire, Dennis knifing off a finger, Kate under scalding water. More than once he'd actually bounded out, dripping, and yanked the door open—to house silence, of course, or to safe, normal murder. This now that he was in was some shower. Before he left, and then again on his first weekend home, he'd begun his long-planned series of Kid Talks, forced to do so by the situation, and they'd appeared to take it bravely, seemed to comprehend: Life was queer and unpredictable; one must do what one must, impervious to how it looked or what others might say; one must believe and trust; all must rally together; each must do more for the common good, etc. Upon his first Friday night return, Dennis (reportedly "just fine" all week, per daily phone calls) clutched him around the hips, broke into tears, and bawled, "It's bullshit, Dad, I missed you too *much!*"

They were too accustomed to his being around all the time, like the piano or Waldo, he and Angie rationalized privately. They spoke of their friends from Army days, the Powells, who'd stayed in. Roger was a light colonel now. He and Kathy had six kids. Roger had done two separate tours in Vietnam, thirteen months each time—how must *that* have felt? And they'd coped; they'd done it. But life seemed simpler to deal with in military terms. (But if life *was* war, why so many real wars? Another question for more leisurely, reflective times, if they were ever to return.) Trying not to rack his back seeking sleep nights was difficult work. Harry feared real fears: that Constance would feel abandoned; that Jake would assume too much fatherly responsibility and worry; that the others would miss him too much too constantly and learn bitterness and have Hope begin to dull too soon, too early. They were fears not to be dealt with rationally, and his nighttime emotions were a pushover for them. Days, like vampires, they stayed slunked away, asleep somewhere. Which at least let him function.

Jay's call found him mouthing a script to himself on a metal chair, fourth in line, at Scali, McCabe and Sloves (Scaly, Macabre and Sloven). "Great news! The feature I'm casting? No, there's no part in it for you, but the director's Pete Dohanos! Remember? Well, he knows a place! A veteran couple! I know but you don't! Anyhow, she's taking some inner-city theater thing in *Baltimore!* And he's going teaching at *Bard!* And they want to sublet for six months! Only a bill a month, Harry! They've had it since *Truman* days or something! Wonderful?"

It was a five-floor walk-up, between Sixth and Washington Square Park in the Village. A small kitchen, a small bedroom, a huge living room, all with twelve-foot ceilings. It looked, felt, and smelled like a set out of a Robert Montgomery movie: charcoal walls and white ceilings; crammed bookshelves; a brigade of British redcoats marching across the mantelpiece over the fireplace, which held imitation coal in a grate fired by gas; cracked, once-bright red leatherette easy chairs and sofa; framed early Picasso prints; a medieval map of Europe; a gateleg dining table; an inlaid-tile coffee table ... and a small color TV set that worked. Harry loved it and practically thanked it out loud. It was somebody else's place. He could use everything and own nothing. He could live in it without leaving a trace of himself. He emptied, washed, and dried the ashtrays before leaving each morning. After a while, though, he began leaving his dishes in their yellow plastic drainer instead of putting them away; he found that they provided him company, of an odd sort, more quiet than the radio or tube but somehow more personal—they were there waiting for him nights, not needing him to turn them on. And they seemed willing enough to listen to his silent soliloquies.

He had to step over and between the winos and junkies who slept on the steps, but inside St. Joseph's, mass was mass; inside, for a half hour mornings he could be anywhere in the world he wished. To forestall the vampires nights he usually walked out and around. Small Cafe Reggio was dark and loud, busy, but let him sit over espresso and Sambucca as long as he wished for seventy-five cents. The Bitter End was now the Other End, but its bar side had a poolroom in the back. He'd bring Jake there when the planned stayovers began. Most male NYU students looked like ancient, dour, bearded rabbis, but still Harry was made to feel old by them and the area. He knew that the park hosted guitar strummers, Frisbee and volleyball players, and other nonjunkie humanity during daylight hours, but he was seldom downtown before dark. He began drifting westward, past Sheridan and along West Fourth, to his and Angie's old neighborhood. It was very gay now, all the young men looking like new Marine lieutenants or Olympic swimmers. Maybe he'd send photos to the longhair-haters of Liberty Square, just to watch both barbershops go broke, too.

He reclaimed Benchley's, outside, as his usual eating place. This go-around, his favorite waitress was named Ellie. The Corner Bistro had a good bartender, Stefan, and great burgers, but he found it dark and depressing; the denizens all knew each other for years, a nod to the family of man, but the general smoke of talk rained more drunken bitterness, defeat, and self-delusion than Liberty Square's most morbid hole, Hurley's. Likewise Herdt's. The White Horse was cheerier but a draw for too many tourists voicing their disappointment in it, whatever or whoever the hell they'd come expecting to see anyway. O'Henry's was costly and aglut with expense-account out-of-towners. Everywhere dog shit rose from heels and soles, as Harry prowled. La Groceria was cold and a ripoff. Jimmy Day's was stupid with college kids. Everywhere girls and women with bold, significant eyes. But Bob and Ray were still on the radio and so was Jean Shepherd and Imus in the morning, so God wasn't just inside the derelict-thresholded church. Still, Harry learned fast to listen back to hear the click of the front door's lock as he walked the eleven steps to the first of the sixty-eight steps upstairs.

He thought of having Angie pack frozen food, so he could eat in. And some nights he made himself stay in, to stare at the box until he passed out. The trouble was, he felt divorced. He'd never again arch a mental lip at any divorced man or woman. Because he wasn't divorced, he felt wrong walking out by himself into the public nights. He went to a poetry reading at an art gallery on La Guardia Place. Donations in a fishbowl, Inglenook punch. The best poet of the night was a young girl in backpacker's clothes jabbing the ribs of San Francisco and sending bittersweet letters through the sky to her long-dead father. Her accent and attitude made Harry speak to her, and her name was Eileen Myles, from Arlington, Massachusetts! That was fine. Garbo wasn't. A small, blond, beautiful woman from Madrid asquat against a pillar in a camel's-hair-looking suit and black felt slouch hat, *she* came up to *him* with her gray eyes and glossy-lipped mouth music and invited him to a party at her place the coming Wednesday night, handing him the address printed on a napkin. He speed-walked back to the apartment, chanting the St. Anne prayer like a mantra. It took him the entire distance to ball up and throw away the napkin. The next morning his first call was to read for one of Sandy Buchsbaum's *Charlie* commercials. He didn't get the job, but the reminder of Sequosset sent an injection of ice water into his spine. That noon he called Jay to recheck his calls and bookings (it already looked certain, if these first weeks weren't a freak, that he'd be averaging his grand a week gross), and Jay relayed Angie's message to call right away. He did, to learn that Martin Duffy was dead.

They'd arrived home from Ireland that morning. The Old Man had made it through customs to just inside the Aer Lingus gate. "A heart attack," Angie said. "He asked for oxygen, but they asked if he had emphysema, and of course, he did. Mass General was closer, but he made them take him up the Sancta Maria in Cambridge. They said after that it didn't make any difference. He wouldn't have made it anyhow."

"Why the Sancta Maria?"

"The first job he ever got in this country was there. He always said he wanted to die there, but we never—"

"So he knew."

"Yeah, he knew."

"How are you?"

"I'm very good. I'm crying my ass off."

Like so many wingless, white-garbed male angels, seven priests waited on the altar: Father Thomas, Father Tim, Father Shaz, the monsignor Thomas worked for, the bishop-pastor of the Duffys' parish, and the two Fathers who co-owned Sequosset with the Canon. Harry sat on the right side of the aisle with Constance, Jake, Amy, Mike's Nance, and their two oldest, towheaded girls. He had a summer cold, and Lisa, seven, kept feeding him Kleenex. Angie was two pews ahead with her three sisters. Albie and Mike had walked the mother up the aisle, dwarfing but not supporting her; Bridget held their arms but didn't lean. Across from the family sat rows and rows of priests. Harry counted twenty-seven, excluding Norman Michaud, who sat behind the family somewhere, with his wife, Lillian. Harry wasn't surprised by the turnout of black suits; that was one thing priests did for each other: They went to one another's parents' funerals.

Behind the priests sat at least as many nuns. Like the priests,

most had also attended the wake the night before. Nuns who'd
had one or more or all of the Duffys in school. Nuns from
Sister Theresa's convent. Nuns from the Woburn nursing
home, Martin's last boiler job. Harry remembered some of the
North Cambridge nuns and tried to avoid them. He'd had
only two in all his twelve years of nuns whom he'd thought
good; neither was there. The rest, at Donelan's Funeral Home,
irritated him as nuns always did. "Do you ever see Red
Mullins?" they'd ask. "What ever happened to Paul Zic-
carelli?" And Harry would want to answer back, "Why do you
always ask just about *those* guys, Sister? They were bums,
remember? The poorest, dumbest, toughest ones whose balls
you constantly busted." And the nuns would irritate him too
by their inevitable, pea-brained once-overs; they'd look him up
and down, head to toe and back, and he could virtually hear
their crimped minds conclude, Well, he's tall and alive and
wearing a watch and shoes and everything and my Lord,
what? about forty or so now, so he must be doing just fine ...
all we did must have been right and for the good of him, then,
after all. And he'd long to weep or hit them. But their still
being alive themselves made him, this time, realize how
unancient they must have been back then, after all—even
young! This sudden, belated insight let him forgive them, at
last, their invincible ignorance, if not not their ignorant
invincibility. Too much real harm had been done. One nun-
schooled guy Harry knew confessed, at age forty-four, that he
still woke automatically in time to prevent a nocturnal
ejaculation.

Harry had to thank nuns for his grammar, elocution, and
math and maybe for some of his faith (not much, though; he
was aware that he had simply been one of the very few who
actually listened). And yeah, Ron Carey and George Carlin
had albums out trying to color their retrospectives of nuns as
funny, and maybe the records were, but the nun experience of
the forties and fifties just wasn't. Harry knew them, totally
dedicated and well-meaning or not, as the original anti-right-

to-lifers. Mortification of the Eyes, for instance, had let him find a few coins on the sidewalks but made him miss years of visions of God's world around him, girls' bodies included. And on and on. *If it felt good, it was wrong*—that caught the quick of nuns as far as Harry was concerned and explained why he and Angie never had and never could send any of their children to nuns anywhere, no matter how mediocre they found the average public school teacher.

Martin Duffy's requiem was to be one of the last services of any kind to be held in the vast upstairs main church. It had been declared unsafe, and the money to repair it had not been forthcoming from the relatively affluent but dwindling parish. Starting in the fall, there would only be the downstairs basement church. The undertaker's men rolled Martin's polished, water-dappled casket up near the table-altar and left it there. Thomas began the mass. After the stunt Tommy'd pulled back at the house the day before, Harry sucked in his breath and went tense, sensing the same happening in the other adults surrounding him. This could be a bad one. It was all in the Canon's hands now—as was his own life if he screwed it up.

The First Reading was from the Book of Wisdom, "The souls of the just are in the hand of God ..." Thomas intoning so beautifully that Harry looked to see if somebody was doing TV coverage.

Big Doc Father Tim took the Responsorial Psalm: "Though I walk in the valley of darkness, I fear no evil, for you are with me.... The Lord is my shepherd; I shall not want. In verdant pastures he..." a leaf out of the poetic, optimistic old elf's own book, him delivering it as if he'd written it, giving it bells and shadows, briar and moss. A coin hit wood and rolled. Somebody sniffed. Lisa thought it was Harry and slipped him another tissue.

The Second Reading was Shaz's, St. Paul to the Romans: "Are you not aware that we who were baptized into Christ Jesus were baptized into his death?" Former Mayor Last

Hurrah Curley to voters from the back of a truck at City Point, giving them the Hammer. The mass went back to Thomas for the Gospel, and his eulogy . . . the one he'd warned them he doubted he'd be able to get through without breaking.

All stood. The Gospel was one of Harry's favorites, Jesus bringing His friend Lazarus back from the dead after four days. Tommy delivered it well. The only embellishment he added was to look up from the book toward Angie, Theresa, Annie, and Mickey when giving the Martha and Mary sisterly dialogue. Harry's eyes drifted to the still coffin. Sunlight was hitting the beads of holy water. He thought, fondly, *So long, Mr. Duffy, you're leaving a hell of a big hole,* and wondered, Is there really, after all, any right way of doing it? As he saw it, this old man had been an urbanized peasant to the end, an immigrant who'd fled his homeland simply for the liberty to work and worship as he wanted. He'd sired and brought up nine, losing two, but without ever making any direct, sustained contact with any one of them.

His "patriarchy" was a myth. He was a Wizard of Oz fabricated by her, Bridget, the mother, and kept curtained by her to the end and beyond. He had fed, clothed, and more or less educated them, admitting publicly just his one hope, that none of them should ever know prison. Yet did any of them doubt that he'd loved them? Yeah, Harry thought, some of them doubted it. Having apparently done his maximum, though, what else, what more could he have given them? He could pick up an infant, and the baby wouldn't cry—what was it that the child sensed? Nothing scary, certainly, nothing uncaring. Maybe he could just never show it, much less say it. Maybe he thought it soft or softening to show or say it. Who knew? Did Thomas? Was he in a minute going to spring some secret on them? No, Harry knew too well how much Thomas didn't know. Nobody was holding any hope of enlightenment. What they were holding was fear, that Tommy was going to pull some Exhibition Tearjerking for his black-suited gallery of off-duty male angels.

He had actually, in front of them, asked Shaz to do it for him. Shaz said, "Unh-unh—I did it for my old man; you do it for yours."

"But he was *like* a father to you, Shaz!"

"One to a customer, Tomo. Listen, you only have to do it once, huh? Bite the bullet."

Evidently unaware that all his siblings and even Harry were getting set to crack his head open, he even asked Father Tim. The "uncle" puffed, "It's one of your main reasons for being, Thomas. As close as himself and I were, you are the son. Who am I to either bear the burden of it or to usurp the honor of it?"

Put down but not out, Thomas changed his act to soliciting everyone's help in the composing of it. The mother said only, "We figgered we had five years more." All the others, except Angie, and even Albie, declined. Confronted, they understood Thomas' problem better. It didn't win him much sympathy but did muffle their scoffing of him. Angie offered, "I know what I'd like to hear you say—say his clock quit ticking in him on the other side, but he willed the rest of him to make the trip so he could be buried here."

Thomas growled, "Where the hell'd you get an idea like that?"

She half smiled. "Graham Greene did a story on it once, the moral being that without the body the soul is a blithering idiot. Something like that."

"That's sick. Thanks for nothing."

Harry volunteered, "How about something along the lines of he died on the first vacation he ever took? Or he went out on his own time?"

"Come on, there's nothing funny about this, Tro!"

Finally, Thomas went off to write it by himself, bullet bitten. Mickey worried. "What if he really *isn't* up to it?"

Mike agreed. "Yeah, Christ, you know how weepy he can be when he's happy, what's— Should we try and get a couple belts into him before it, you think?"

Albie defended. "Don't sweat Thomas. He'll pull it off."

Annie said, "He'd better. I mean, this is what he's around for, right?"

"He knows that! Cool it."

"Well, if he knows, then what's all this crap he's pulling?"

"Maybe to make sure *we* know," Theresa said. "And it's not nothing, is it?"

If there was one truth all knew clearly about their father, it was this: In anything, he preferred a half-ass job to a perfect one that took too long. With that no doubt in mind, Sister Theresa in the morning gave Thomas perhaps the only real help he got. She said, "Make it short and sweet, Father. Nobody has to hear any more about us than they already know anyhow."

Thomas read: " '. . . and whoever is alive and believes in me will never die. Do you believe this?' 'Yes, Lord,' she replied. 'I have come to believe that you are the Messiah, the Son of God: he who is to come into the world.' " He closed the book and looked up. "This is the Gospel of the Lord."

The people chorused, "Amen," and sat down. Harry's attention had been yanked away from dead Martin's box to the missalette in his hand—had the Canon cut the story short? No, he saw that whoever had written the booklet had; they'd omitted the payoff, where Christ went into the tomb and came back out with Lazarus, His buddy, alive. He felt swindled. Why did they leave *that* out? Damn, if that wasn't where the whole blasted church was—what did they think they were gaining by leaving the action out, when that was all people really wanted or understood? He knew even Martin Duffy would have found this too half-ass a job for anybody's liking. The surprise disappointment snuffed out the last dot of hope he'd had for Tommy's pulling it off right, and as the seat creakings, foot scrapings, and coughing died down, he braced himself for the soupy, maudlin worst.

For a while that's exactly what they all got. Beginning, "Once, many years ago, there lived two small, happy children.

Girls. My sisters. Two of my parents'. . . ." Thomas gave them the death of youth as openers. Harry saw Albie's and Mike's heads drop. He saw the mother's little body shudder and seem to shrink in. He heard a thin *tch!* from either Angie or Mickey. Annie was already bawling uncontrollably. She had been closest to Francie. The device was hard to resist. To keep from listening, Harry stared at Angie's hair. Posting the dead young girls as bookends, Thomas proceeded to align the in-between stories. The hardship years of *No Irish Need Apply* and of *If You Don't Come in Sunday, Don't Come in Monday*. Harry had to think of his own lost station, his own debts, his own desperate scramblings for jobs (how many fees was he losing today?). God, Thomas, enough, enough, stop, you don't know what you're saying, it's all one, long cheap shot. Then another surprise happened in him: He raised his glance from Angie's neck to Thomas' face, fully expecting to feel anger and the urge to go gag him but, instead, felt terrific, sudden sorrow for the man.

Their odd, one-sided connection over these hard months, it seemed, had changed their relationship, at least for Harry; he felt that he had an investment of some kind in Thomas now. And that it was evaporating, failing, like his station, before his eyes. Another bad venture. Yet Thomas didn't *know* he owed him anything, so how could he really owe him anything? Harry had to admit: He couldn't, so he didn't. But Harry himself knew, goddamn it, and he felt his whole being straighten and strain; he'd *will* his poor, stunted stepchild to wake up and fly right, as they used to say. It was a concentration of energy he'd never been able to muster for the failing Liberty Square station.

Memories were not real family, Harry finally understood. The Duffys were his family. Martin had tried to let him know that from the beginning; it had taken this long for Harry to know it. If Thomas could not serve his family correctly in this, his appointed way, what on earth good could he ever be? He must be helped; he must be *made* to do it! For his own sake as well as theirs and Martin's. Practically crossing his eyes, Harry shot zap after zap of mental electricity up at the orating Canon, but doubt defeats will. His was firing as agonizingly ineffectively as a gun in a dream. He'd let it sit unused too long; it seemed to have seized. Thomas' script was taking a lighter turn now, but pro Harry knew it was only technique.

For change of pace, and lest anyone leave thinking Martin Duffy had been a total drudge, Little Doc was now telling his "slide home" anecdote, deleting the "on yer ahse!" Ah, yes, remember the humor of such men, the spirit in them, the "songs in the hearts of those soldiers of Christ among whom our father, Martin Duffy, strode so tall. Lord, let us not forget the grand times, equal, thanks to You, to the times of misery." Thomas went on then to give the impression that all their family events had rung with song, cheer, and union to the end. He made the roof climbing, the boiler lugging and the bathtubs up three flights all sound affectionate. He said, "To work is to pray," straight and solemnly, but he arched the eyebrow and lilted the voice in a way that clearly grinned: "That's what *he* thought!" and got a big wave break of moist chuckles from the crowd. He was giving them what they wanted to hear.

Harry watched, clinical appreciation trickling into his despair. Thomas, having faked the handoff, dropped back into the pocket, cocked, and drilled the ultimate heart-wrenching bullet right through them: With a choke in his voice that came and stayed, up to the immediate past now, he confided that he had had "the unforgettable honor and privilege of accompanying our father, Martin Duffy, on his first and last journey ... Home. Back, the loving son, to the land of his birth. The weight of more than fifty years of labor, sorrows, joys riding heavily upon his aged back, making him stoop, still, he ran to Erin's arms proud, strong, glad. To stoop and scoop a fistful of soil from his long-dead mother's yard. To finger the bricks of the wall of the building that had been the factory in which he had toiled as a child ... and to spit upon those bricks. And to meet—with shy laugh and gruff shake—his last surviving brother, Liam, not seen since each had fired rifles side by side against oppression in 1916. And to light a candle in the rude country church before the same statue of Mary at which he had prayed farewell so long, long ago. I wish you all could have seen that with me."

But one thing . . . one thing would stay in Thomas' heart the rest of his days. Something their father, Martin Duffy, had come upon in cottage after cottage, kitchen after kitchen, flat after flat in his brief, good-bye visit to his mother Ireland. "One same and beautiful thing. Appearing time after time in place after place to Martin Duffy on what was to be his final journey home . . . and time after time as we watched, stopping the man in his tracks. Not once did he fail to spot it. Not once did he fail to go to it and read again that one, stirring, beautiful thing. It might almost be called to serve as Martin Duffy's legacy, for it so perfectly expressed the loves and hopes and wishes he had, for his whole life, for his every son, his every daughter, and most deeply and faithfully had for his dear, loving, loyal wife, our mother." And here Father Thomas paused to gaze directly at tiny Bridget, eyes on her lap, between Albie and Mike.

By now Harry had given up trying to zap Thomas over the heads of the Duffys, praying now only that the taut tendons he noticed in most necks in front of him might mean they too were all straining to will him off it, and some might yet succeed where he, only adopted, had failed. It didn't look like it, though. Thomas now displayed a glisten in his eyes to match the choke and continued: "It was a simple thing, this wish, this love, this prayer our father, our husband, our grandfather, our father-in-law, neighbor, co-worker, and friend, Martin Duffy, had for us . . . and I will read it for you now as he read it himself so many times in Ireland, this old, Irish prayer: *May the road rise to meet you. May the wind be always at your back. May the sun shine warm upon your face, the rains fall soft upon your fields and, until we meet again, may God hold you in the palm of his hand.* Amen."

Annie whooped like soft rain turning hard. Sobs, coughs,

and sniffles were thrown up like coins from all over the packed church. Thomas' head remained bowed toward the book. No eyes of any male angel were visible. Shaz's flush could have been from his high blood pressure or embarrassment. The scufflings of people starting to stand abruptly stopped, however, and Harry looked up. Thomas was looking up and out again, and his eyes were different. He had one arm stuck out at the people, palm down, and when he spoke, the choke had gone, too. He had a perplexed but kind of amused look on his face, partly grinning. He said, "Uh ... this has taken long enough, but ... well, something strange just happened to me. I can't describe it or explain it, but I feel ... obliged to ... well, it just occurred to me that what I've just told you—most of it, anyhow—wasn't exactly true. I can't ... well, take that Irish prayer, for instance. It *was* all over the place over there, and he did stop to read it every time he spotted it ... and maybe I preferred to believe he was moved by it and in love with it, but actually—well, usually he gave it his laugh.

"As a lot of us know, he had a laugh that could send you running, and it was this particular laugh I'm talking about. He'd always wait until we were out of whoever's house it was, of course. But he'd singsong one of the prayer's lines, laugh, and ... well, to tell the truth, the last thing I remember him saying about it was, 'Ah, 'twas all right till dey started *Hallmarkin* it at us!' I just thought I'd tell you that. Listen, he did have a good time over there, but he showed a lot more impatience with them and their ways than I've led you to think. Impatience may be too nice a word for it, too. He saw everyone and everything as quickly as he could and wanted to get home. Here, I mean. His real home. He visited there the same way he'd lived all his days here, and why should we pretend any different? He wasn't a soft man. He never was, except with the smallest of children. All right. He was my father. I loved him. We all loved him as best we could. We're sorry he's dead, and we're glad to have the faith to believe that he is not gone. Amen."

The Canon went back to the altar, and the congregation stood as he resumed the mass. The rest was a lot easier now. Thomas had once more slid home on his ahse.

That November Harry Trowbridge's Massachusetts license was returned, and he went out and got a New York one as well. Eastern Airlines' "New York-Boston Shuttle" had by then become an apt title for their life. Angie came down to spend a night and return with him as often as she could, usually every other Thursday. Manhattan was bankrupt, as Liberty Square had been when he'd first taken over his station, but one thing he didn't lack was work. His fortunes seemed to go contrary to his places. A lot happened in the Duffy family after Martin's death. Observing from his distance, Harry was hard put to tell whether the strong, "great" old man had been a barrier removed, or a demonstration of the grains of wheat parable, dying in order to root and bear fruit. All the fruit wasn't sweet. Albie's seemed to be; he, Rena, and their mob moved to a small town high on the Maine coast, where they bought an old farmhouse and Albie went just teaching again. Mike's move was different.

Close upon Martin's death, the Internal Revenue Service, of course, attacked to take away from Bridget as much as it could. In his one act acknowledging his reputed, mysterious wealth, Mike stepped forward with his offer to buy two of the houses and some of the Berkshire land from her, apparently unaware that nothing could be sold until the father's estate had been settled, which took a year. Shortly after, Mike was arrested at his tavern; he'd been in the identity business. Small time, at first, fresh starts for runaway husbands and the like, but later more serious and more rewarding: Chinese immigrants. He jumped bail and vanished. Harry half expected to hear from him in New York but hadn't yet. Nance said she was "set up fine" but otherwise stayed mum. Worry permeated all spokes of the family wheel. Most had observed that Bridget's escalating war with the taxmen had its good side, in giving her something to occupy herself with and "keep her mind off," but when Mike happened, some cursed him out-right for adding to her miseries, "now, of all times!" Annie put in her bits long distance, she and Fast having moved to Oklahoma over Labor Day weekend.

Mike was missed most acutely that October, at Theresa's wedding. Albie walked her up the JP's small parlor "aisle," by himself. Only the mother and Father Thomas didn't attend. Angie went to Bridget and said they understood why she couldn't go and hoped she understood why the rest of them had to try to make it as happy a day as possible for Theresa. Bridget said she did understand. "I'll slip 'em a gift maybe, later on sometime." The Canon's position found no sympathy and put him back into the doghouse with them again.

In New York, Harry saw Mickey a lot for a while, for drinks and suppers, but then cut it way back. She began to resemble Angie too much and gave him inklings too incestuously peppered for his comfort. He took to the tube in earnest and was glued there the night of the Red Sox's sixth game against Cincinnati in the '75 Series. It was a terrible event to witness alone. When Fred Lynn seemed dead against the center-field fence ... when he got up ... when it went to the *twelfth!* ... when Boston finally lost ... such rare, passionate happenings seemed to cry for company with whom to watch and share reactions. That Christmas he was at home with them all, watching the perennial rerun of *The Homecoming,* the original for the whole *Waltons'* series in which the father, after only *one week's* absence, decides, That's it, I'm staying home for good!

The similarity was obvious all the way down to Kate; even Waldo probably got it. The room filled with a mounting silence throughout, like a throat with tears, and Harry burned to scream out, Stick it, Walton! You bastards look better fed in that Depression than anyone I've ever seen since! Quit it with your neat endings and your simple verities because they're lies and you're doing more harm than nuns in letting kids think they're true! Jake did speak: "God, I'd hate to live on a dumb farm!" Next morning Harry took particular pleasure in seeing Amy get the bike she hadn't got last July. Bikes don't grow in the ground.

He flew back that Sunday night. He had a job early that Monday morning. Tuesday Angie called to say she'd be down Thursday, even though it was New Year's and he'd be taking another long weekend home. They went to eat at the Beatrice Inn. They liked it from the old days and because it didn't accept credit cards. She lifted her margarita and clinked it against his. "Happy New Year—we're gonna be forty!"

He smiled, "Yeah," and drank, but she had something fishy swimming behind the eyes that he hadn't been able to get a fix on yet, so he was watching his moves.

She said, "The holidays are good. Break the routine."

"Yeah. Christ, it's become a schedule already, hasn't it?"

"Um. How long do you think it'll stay okay?"

"When I psyche it up, it's okay—different, but we can make it work, yagada, yagada. I can even make it a *great* thing, opening up their worlds for them, making them citizens of there *and* here ... you know. Listen, it's reality."

"I'm saving some bucks now, that help?"

"How the hell you managing that?" He knew she was good, but this was impossible. This was indeed fishy. "How much?"

She squinted, grinned, sipped margarita, and grinned some more, licking salt off her lips. "Two ... hundred ... bucks a week, shithead."

The blood rushed hot across his face. It had finally happened! It was the news he'd been waiting for. He grinned. "That's ... incredible. What are we ... giving up?"

"You know what!" she whispered.

"Albie?"

"Of course. He told Rena; she called me; I went to my mother; we both called Thomas over. I still can't believe he didn't know."

"He didn't. What—"

"He couldn't even remember the name of the place, just

where it was or where he thought it was. My mother and I drove down two Sundays ago and found it. And met your friend."

"You knew last week? *At Christmas?*"

"Yeah. Thought I'd save it."

"Oh, God, Angie, I ... I'm—"

"Really an idiot. I couldn't *believe* it! I'm *still* dizzy from it. You *ass!*"

"Believe what, exactly?"

"Oh, look who's being so fucking careful. Don't worry, no sordid details came out, and we didn't press for any. We just shut this water off."

"How?"

"Your friend Bridget did it, really. She said they could preach it from every pulpit in the city for all she cared. She told Tommy the same thing; he made his bed, and he can lie in it, no skin off her teeth."

"Thank God." There you go, Doc, something real to worry about.

"Well, she did add, 'Thank God your father's not here to see it!' I have to give you that much, I'm not sure how she would've reacted before. Compared to all the rest going down now, your little trick seemed like small potatoes."

He downed his drink and looked sincere and sorrowful, sincerely. "I was in a bad way, Ange. I—"

"Yeah, well, next time go alone."

"Should've gone with you."

"I could've told you that then."

He asked the waiter for another round and menus. He felt fantastic, now he could call Tommy and tell him to contact Flash, if he so chose. And wouldn't Flash be tickled. New margaritas came. This time he initiated the toast. "Here's, uh, looking at you, lady."

She drank and laughed. "Take a good look, because this time tomorrow you won't know me. I'm going to buy Bloomingdale's dry." Make-over time again.

"Thought you were *saving* it?"

"That starts next week. Auld lang syne, huh? And come on, knock the look off. I'll get you later for it, don't worry."

He grinned. "I'm sure you will." Then, still grinning, he added, "Christ, though—for a while there I was afraid damn Albie was *never* going to leak it!"